CW00835690

MANNY

CHAPTER 1

I tried to feign interest, but in truth, I couldn't believe her mouth kept moving. *Jeez.* She was boring me to death, and I could only pretend to be interested for so long before I snapped. This might actually be one of the worst dates I'd been on in a long time, and that was saying something considering my dating resume.

Mama always said I had a temper, so I tried to step back and analyze the situation before losing my cool. To be fair, the lady talking to me from the other side of the table was pretty. She had long, straight, naturally blonde hair, with pale skin and dark eyes. It was a unique combination and gave her a pouty model look, though her lips were thinner than I liked them. I'm certain, though, she had her pick of men from the looks she garnered when we walked in tonight.

I had asked her out due to the gorgeous exterior, but I had endured enough. *Carla was her name, right?* I think so. Carla had been going on and on about her life and work and how awesome she was. Being a very self-centered guy myself, I found this annoying. I was used to all the attention being on me, and my brothers understood that which is why

3

we all got along well. Sure, they made fun of me, but what brothers don't? The problem here was that a relationship could not have two egomaniacs, and Carla sure as hell was shaping up to be one. She would give my massive ego a run for its money, and that just would not work.

"And then I told the guy to beat it after he asked me out 'cuz those boots were doing nothing for his chances. I'm sure he worked at a Walmart or something. Then I-" She just kept rambling on about her life. She did not seem the least put out that I was not engaged. She didn't even expect an answer or any input, just a rapt audience.

For a moment, I had to admire seeing myself in another person—only this time, a woman. This date was a waste of my time which I had known would be the case before we even got here. I was currently on a date with this particular lady because my goody-two-shoes of a brother, Joey, thought I needed love in my life. What a joke. Love is and has always been for people who just decided to live together because they didn't have anything else better to do. They were those over-the-top hopeless romantics who watched The Notebook and started yearning for that mushy shit. Don't get me wrong; I love women. Sex is one of the greatest things imaginable, but commitment? Nah, I'm perfectly okay missing out on all of that crap. I don't even know why I was here. Maybe it was a moment of weakness. Yeah, that's what it was. I adore my brothers, and when they ask something of me, I'm willing to move heaven and earth to comply. That loyalty though didn't extend outside their family unit, and Joey, along with the others, needed to get on board with this ideology.

"Ugh, I can't take it anymore." I finally spoke, causing her to pause and look at me weirdly. "You are like flat champagne, hon. I can't deal with you."

I got up from my seat, dropping money for the bill on the

4

table while she stared at me in disbelief. I just felt my entire being flood with relief as I made a solid march toward the door. I liked living life by the seat of my pants, going from one night stand to a fun motorcycle ride with my brothers, without a worry of some woman trying to tie me down.

I maneuvered my way out of the restaurant and breathed a sigh of relief the moment I got outside. The cold air brushing against my face was wonderful, but I knew I still needed to clear out the nonsense I'd just gone through. So, as I do whenever I am stressed, I lit up a cigarette while walking to the side of the restaurant. The last thing I needed was the security whining at me about their rules. Inhaling its coarse contents into my lungs, I got that all-too-familiar euphoric feeling I get when I smoke. It calms my mind.

"You know that'll kill you, right?" I heard a voice say to me from the corner, and I turned to see a short-haired woman wearing a fancy dress seated on the nearby curb. I loved her look, as she was my normal type and since the date was a bust, talking her into my bed for the evening seemed a good alternative. I walked slowly over to her as I turned on all the charm and lowered myself to the curb next to her.

"I know," I replied with a slight smirk. "Calms the nerves, though, and we all have to die of something."

She smiled and looked away. "Just as long as you know." Things were awkward after she turned away from me, looking at the ground. Normally, women couldn't resist my good looks and slightly foreign-looking skin tone. This one seemed completely immune to me, though, and it hurt my feelings.

"I'm still here, you know?"

"And what am I supposed to do about that?" She bit out, and I was surprised. I wasn't used to this level of snarky retorts when I was just trying to engage with her. Is this how others felt when I did it to them? It was amusing... this lady

5

was intriguing. She didn't even glance at me when she retorted but just kept up her staring at the ground in front of her.

"Wow, you sure are feisty," I remarked.

"Trust me. You would be too if you've had the kind of day I have."

"Well—" I sat on the pavement next to her. "Why don't you tell me all about it?"

She turned and stared in shock. I wondered what was so surprising about me sitting down and wanting to listen to her issues throughout the day.

"I must warn you, though. I am known to be a douchebag, so if I laugh in moments where you expect empathy, that's on you."

She laughed for the first time. Her smile looked so mesmerizing that I found myself laughing and smiling as well. *What the heck!* I felt... weird. *What was it about this lady being happy that made me equally happy as well?*

"Good one," she commended in her slightly husky voice, which made all my nerve endings stand up and take notice.

She had me hooked, and I just needed to know more.

"What's your name?" I asked, hoping she would relent and start giving me some information. I was like a man in a desert without water for days – starving for any tidbit she would toss my direction. I should have known this could be dangerous, but my ego just let me wander right in.

"Sandi," she replied with her beautiful smile plastered on her face. "Sandi Bailey."

CHAPTER 2

What the hell was wrong with me? That question continued to run through my head as I sat in front of this timid man who kept fidgeting and talking about culinary stuff. *Why was I here? Was I that desperate for attention or love that this was my best option?*

I had been independent for a while, and I thought it was what I wanted. I was always trying to act tough and cool in front of guys as I turned them down. The problem was as I got older, I began to feel more and more alone. *What good were all my achievements as a fashion designer if no one was there to celebrate them with me?* It's not like Mom and Dad cared what I did. They barely called or even knew I was alive. Too busy in London, I guess.

"S-so… what do you do for a living?" He was so timid that I could hear myself begging him silently to talk up, square his shoulders and be a man.

Jeremiah seemed to be a nice person, but this level of shyness was not what I needed. I always loved alphas who weren't afraid to take control, and maybe that was part of the reason why I kept dating assholes. The more egocentric, self-possessed, and snarky a man – the more I fell in love.

"I am a fashion manager at Cosmon," I answered.

"Oh, yeah, th-that's… that's great," he muttered.

"Could you give me a second?" I asked. "I need to go get something outside." He nodded, and I quickly left.

I made my way through the crowd in the restaurant to the outside, spotting a nice place where I could sit and cry. I went over and lowered myself onto the pavement, burying my head in my arms. *Why was I even crying?* He hadn't been mean to me or anything. *Should the disappointment of a blind date be this painful?* I guess I was just tired… tired of waiting and searching. Maybe a successful and strong woman like me can't find a man who is even stronger and could sweep her off her feet. So many guys have dated me just for my cash or sex or me looking pretty on their arm at events. I wasn't a narcissist, but I knew. Even the one-night stands got dull after a while. I wanted something real… a true connection with a person that was intended to last.

I stayed there for a short while until smelling the disgusting smell of a lit cigarette. Ugh, *like it could get any worse.* I heard footsteps and hoped the smoker would walk past me or turn back in the direction they had come. I glanced up to see the man starting to enjoy the cig a little too much. Didn't he realize how disgusting that habit was? He didn't seem the least bit concerned about the smoke he was exposing others to, which makes me even more irritated. After a short time, I felt like he was hellbent on getting me riled up. I was already on edge, and this wasn't going to do anything to help my anger issues, as I felt ready to pick a fight to release some tension after that horrible date.

"You know that'll kill you, right?" I said after looking up to get a good look at him. He had a surprisingly nice build for a smoker. Maybe he was a casual one? The man in question turned and looked at me, shocked to see someone was there.

"I know," he replied with the kind of confidence and charm that made me immediately feel the resentment rise up. I liked confident men, even if they normally ended up being more trouble than they were worth. I smiled and promptly looked away. Gosh, he was really hot.

"Just as long as you know," I replied as nonchalantly as I could, as my insides were turning gooey just staring at the man. Need pooling in areas that my earlier date had not managed to elicit any response from.

"I'm still here, you know?" He asked with a tone that just made me itch for a fight with him.

"And what am I supposed to do about that?" I almost slapped myself on the forehead. *Why the heck did I even say that? Was I trying to drive him away because he looked like the quintessential bad boy type?*

"Wow, you sure are feisty." The man said, moving forward to lower himself next to me on the curb where I sat.

I sighed as quietly as I could. Thank God he wasn't too offended.

"Trust me. You would be too if you've had the kind of day I have."

"Well," I heard him utter before feeling the heat by my side. Turning, I saw the stranger sitting down next to me. I asked myself if this was really happening right now. "Why don't you tell me all about it?" I was still stunned at how interested he seemed to be. Normally, a man that looked that good would offer a quick ride to his place or a laundry list of reasons he was better than others of his species. They were good for one thing only and listening to her problems was not it.

"I must warn you, though. I am known to be a douchebag,

so if I laugh in moments where you expect empathy, that's on you." That actually got a laugh out of me.

"Good one." I had to give credit where credit was due.

"What's your name?"

"Sandi," I replied with a smile. "Sandi Bailey."

"I'm Manny Mendoza," he said, stretching his hand out. His dark hair was longer than mine, and I liked how he didn't style it slick with all kinds of product but instead left it ruffled. I always had a thing for guys who were rough around the edges, and he definitely fits that bill to perfection. "Nice to meet you." I accepted his handshake.

"Nice to meet you too, Manny."

"So, tell me about why you are here moping like the heroine of a tragic romance movie."

He was snappy, and I liked that. Manny's honesty and direct approach were refreshing. Working at a place where everyone is under you isn't as great as it sounds. It often makes it incredibly hard to find friends when everybody is simply trying to please you. I could make a bad joke that I knew wasn't funny, and it would arouse an unnecessary level of laughter. Little things like that got to me. Despite being the boss, I always walked on eggshells at work.

"I came here for a date," I said, and from the knowing smile he threw me, I had a feeling he already knew where this was headed.

"Ah… you too, huh?"

"Wait. You're here on a date too?" I asked, horrified that he was outside sitting with me as I moaned about my issues. Of course, he would be here with a woman! *How did I not think that?*

"Yeah," he answered. "I told her she was not my type and left."

"Rude." I couldn't imagine that being me. My level of anger would be pretty high, and I probably would have followed him outside and cut him to pieces with the sharp end of my tongue.

"Yeah, yeah… it's better to be truthful than dance around social norms' niceties and be stuck giving some poor woman the wrong idea. It would suck if she really felt things were going well, wasted a few hours with me, and then I had to make some ridiculous excuse not to take her home," he replied with a tiny shudder. "No thanks! I go with the blunt truth any day of the week."

We argued about that and some other topics for a few minutes, but I kept feeling like I forgot something… something important.

"Oh, shit!" It suddenly dawned on me what I was forgetting.

"What?" Manny looked at me with amused curiosity.

"He's still in there!" I said, getting up quickly. "My date."

Manny laughed uncontrollably, causing me to pout at him.

"You forgot your date?" he asked when he was able to control himself. "You're something, Sandi."

"Shut up. I'll be right back."

"So, you're going to do the exact same thing I did with my date after blaming me for doing it?" Manny noted.

I didn't answer him and went back inside. To both my supreme disappointment, my date was still there, seated and eating alone. Yikes. The minute he saw me, he smiled, but I was not here to resume the awkwardness with him. I had found someone far more interesting and suited to me outside.

"Oh, hey. You're back," he said with a sheepish smile that I reciprocated.

"I am so sorry," I apologized as I grabbed my coat which was hung around the chair. His look immediately changed from happiness to confusion. "Something came up, so I really have to leave." Technically, that wasn't a lie. I hated lying, which meant I'd have to find workarounds whenever I knew what I would say would offend or hurt someone.

"Huh?" Before he could respond fully, I'd waved and left. It was easier this way since I saw no future with him anyway and so just dragging the night out was unfair to him.

As I once again got outside, I walked to where Manny had been but didn't see him there. My smile immediately disappeared. Did I just stand a guy up only to get stood up by another guy? When you think about it, that's karmic.

"Hey, beautiful." His familiar voice sounded from behind me and startled me. I quickly turned around to see Manny Mendoza dangerously close to me with his pretty smirk, his crazy, long hair falling over his forehead and giving off more of that bad guy vibe. His deep brown eyes peered into me and almost enchanted my entire being—his flawlessly shaped nose... and his wet lips, which he liked to lick a lot. I went a few steps back, getting a hold of myself.

"Thought you left." I found the words tumbling from my mouth before I could properly hold them in check.

"Aww, did you miss me?" He made fun of me, causing me to scowl at him. "I'm sure you broke that guy's heart inside that restaurant."

"Shut up," I snapped, and Manny feigned being hit in the chest by my words.

"I have a proposal for you," he said with that lazy grin of his, which piqued my interest. "Since you have just had a miserable night, why don't I brighten it up a bit?"

"What do you mean?" I asked, kind of nervous. I hoped he didn't mean sex. Well, I would have loved to have sex with him since he was friggin' hot, but I was not really in the mood for that right now after the night I'd had. Plus, I liked him... like really liked him. I had a feeling that sex right now might ruin something that could be great. "You want us to fuck?" I asked in a disapproving tone. The bemusement in his face after I said that answered my question for me. That was definitely not what he had thought when he said that.

"Ugh! No, you perv," he said, making me now feel like I was the lewd one here. "But I will admit I am kinda flattered you wanna have sex with me."

"No, I did not," I quickly replied. The last thing I wanted was for him to get any ideas. "I thought you wanted to have sex with me." The whole scenario was funny, though, which was why I was smiling the whole time while defending myself.

"Just admit it." He said, arching a brow at me as he held my gaze hostage in his own.

"No!" I yelled playfully, garnering some unwanted attention. We both froze and kept quiet until they looked away... then instantly burst into laughter. "Nevertheless, what were you going to propose?"

"Who the heck uses the word 'nevertheless?" This Manny guy really loved making fun of me, huh?

"Screw you."

"I already said no, beautiful," he retorted.

My cheeks immediately turned red as I scowled at him, making him laugh. I loved his laugh; it was so natural and merciless.

"Anyways," Manny said as we began walking to God knows where. "I wanted to take you on a nice walk around the town to try and brighten your night up." *You already have, Manny.*

"I hope you're not one of those serial killers or something."

"What?!" His surprise at my suggestion made me giggle. I liked being around Manny; he made me feel like a girl, not a boss. The fact that he even wanted to help make my night better—and not by wanting to sleep with me—by taking me on a stroll was not something I was used to.

"Yeah. It's a fair question to ask," I noted. Manny thought about it for a bit and seemed to come to the conclusion that he could be misconstrued as a bad dude in this scenario.

"I guess you have a point," he admitted.

"Aha!" I said, reveling in his concession that I was right. He stared at me as I went about my overreaction of raising hands and grinning from ear to ear. He couldn't help but chuckle after seeing my theatrics.

"I even look like a bad dude," he added. "Well, my dressing is pretty formal when compared to what I normally wear."

"What do you normally wear?" I inquired curiously.

"I guess you'd have to see me somewhere other than here then," he said mischievously, leading me to roll my eyes.

"Is that your not as subtle as you think of a way of saying you wanna see me again?"

"Oh, I wanna see you again," Manny said bluntly. "I like you and your company."

I tried to hide my blush, but I was fairly sure my cheeks were burning red right then. "Let's see what you got first," I said, referring to his attempt to cheer me up.

We went to a festival kind of thing nearby that he had heard about and had an amazing time. Of course, both of us were overdressed and got a few odd looks, but we didn't care. He played some games and got me some nice gifts that were small enough to go into my purse. I didn't want any big prizes. We also watched some pretty cool card magic which fascinated me. I was a sucker for magic. We couldn't stay too long because it was already late, so to end the night, Manny and I sat on a bench, gazing at the stars.

I tried to steal a glance at him, only to find him staring at me with such captivation that it caught me off-guard.

"What?" I asked, getting a bit insecure.

"You're beautiful, beautiful," he said, looking almost like he was in a trance. "So damn beautiful." Fuck! Why did you have to make me feel so special at this moment?

His head leaned closer to mine, and I mimicked him instinctively. I loved how his hair was tousled, and I just wanted to mess it up even more. I didn't want to go home right at that moment. I wanted to stay with him on this bench. His brown eyes lingered on mine before lowering to get a view of my lips which I was biting a bit. At this moment, I was grateful for everything that led me to this very moment. The events I saw as a tragedy had become a symphony in my heart... all coming together harmoniously to sing a song leading to this point.

Then a loud honk startled us, taking Manny and me out of this beautiful minute and back into the annoying reality of society. I could see he was as disappointed as I was. I grabbed my small purse and got up.

"Thanks for tonight," I said. "It was truly wonderful."

"Yeah," Manny said in a disappointed tone. I smiled. It was flattering that a guy would be this upset at not closing lips with me. I took my business card from my purse and handed it to him.

"A deal's a deal," I said, turning around to walk away. "You've earned it."

"Good night, beautiful," Manny said as I walked away.

CHAPTER 3

"Hey, Mama," Manny said, walking into the hospital room. After the amazing night he had last night. He had hoped that he might be able to go for a long ride with his brothers to calm his nerves. It was way too early to call Sandi, or she might get the wrong impression about how interested I was.

The truth was, not another woman in my adult life had so fully captivated me as she had last night. Her ego, confidence, and snarky remarks were on par with my own. She could absolutely keep pace with me and seemed down for some great fun.

Most women that were dressed to the nines for a dinner date such as she was would not have enjoyed the dirty carnival, they spent the evening at. She wasn't bothered in the least, and she had given him quite a run for his money in several of the arcade games.

"Hey, my sweet boy," his mom said weakly from the bed. He noticed that Angela was on the chair to her right, which probably meant Joey was not far away. He leaned over to kiss his mom's cheek.

"You know I was hoping you were going to be up for some salsa dancing," he said, snapping his fingers crazily as Angela looked at him and shook her head.

"Maybe soon," his mom said as her eyes slid shut.

Angela bounced her head toward the hallway, and he followed her out of the room. They went down a little way until he found Joey sitting in a chair in a tiny nook used for hospital visitors.

"Hey, you okay?" Manny asked, worried by the sadness reflecting in his brother's eyes. "I got here as soon as the call came in."

"We went by this morning and found her on the floor, passed out," Joey said, as the breath suspended in Manny's lung.

"Oh, I'm sorry, man," he said. "I'm glad you were there. That is not good. We really probably need to ensure someone is around a lot more often. Maybe we talk with Rigo and Carlos about taking turns checking on her when she goes home. I don't think she is willing to move in with any of us, or I would recommend that."

"Yeah, we are closing on a house close and can check on her more often," Joey said as Angela slid her hand onto his shoulder.

These two were so in tuned it was amazing how his brother, who had been with Camilla – the wrong woman – had found such an amazing complementary partner. Angela is a career woman and could give me a run for my money in the confidence department. She sold real estate and was growing a highly successful firm on her own. She was also one of the sweetest souls and always willing to hang out with my family, especially his mom. I didn't have a single bad word to say about Joey's wife.

"Agreed, when Carlos, Rigo, and the girls get here, we need to discuss."

The girls were their stepsisters but honestly, when the chips were down, that never mattered. Family was family, and they did what they had to do to care for anyone that needed them – especially Mama.

"So, what are they saying is the issue with her?"

"Her heart and other organs are starting to fail. We knew this might happen, but other than making her comfortable, I don't know that we have a lot of options," Joey said as his face again turned downward.

"I just don't know what we are all going to do if something happens to her," I said, feeling the weight of sadness settling upon my heart.

Mama was the nucleus of our family. She had so many sage pieces of wisdom and a quiet strength that made everyone want to be in her presence. Her cooking, party skills, and ability to make everyone feel welcome were something no one else in the family had thus mastered. I don't know what I will do when she passes on, but I am determined to make every moment with her here count.

"I'm sorry you had to find her, Joey," I said. "I'm here now, and I will do anything needed."

"I know you will," he said with a sigh. "I just needed a moment as the adrenaline waned once we got her settled into a room. I was so scared."

"I bet," I said, feeling all the emotions he must be going through at this moment.

Joey was the best brother a man could ask for. He was loyal, the one willing to drop anything if you should call with a problem. He was also the most even-tempered of all of the four brothers.

"So, how did the date go?" He suddenly shifted the conversation on me, and I was not prepared.

"Well, she was definitely beautiful," I said, trying to go with something positive to say.

"And?" Angela asked before Joey could ask me another question.

"She would not shut up! I mean on and on about herself, the people that annoy her, and how amazing she is," I said with a huge dose of sarcasm lacing every word.

"So, a female version of you?" Joey said. "That should have been a match made in heaven."

"Right? Except she never took a breath to ask a single question of me – not one! I finally told her exactly what I thought and walked out," I said as a smile crossed my face.

"Oh, come on," Joey groused. "You walked out?"

"Yep, and there on the sidewalk, I met this stunning creature named Sandi," I said.

"Who you took home, had some crazy antics in bed with and will never see again," he said, sighing heavily.

"Nope, we went to that little carnival on the edge of town. Played arcade games, ate some bad food, and parted ways with a handshake," I said, grinning from ear to ear.

Joey and Angela sat there staring at me with huge eyes.

"And?" Joey finally asked.

"And nothing! I'm going to call her for another outing soon," I admitted.

"Whoa!" Angela said.

For a woman that hadn't known me long, she seemed to understand my game. Her shock was not misplaced with my dating history, but it did rub me a little bit the wrong way. I could hold out on the sex until a second date or maybe longer. Sure, it hadn't happened before, but there was a first time for everything.

"This woman I have to meet," Joey said.

"Nope, not giving any of you a chance to ruin this for me until I see where it is going," I replied. "I will tell you when it is time."

"I look forward to it," Joey said as a doctor entered the space, and all eyes turned to him.

The update on Mama wasn't good, and whatever good vibes had been filling the space immediately evaporated. We were facing a downhill fight for the remainder of her days, and it was going to take us all working together to manage Mama's care from this point out. We would do whatever was needed, we all vowed as the other siblings arrived to lend their support.

CHAPTER 4

I finished up the meeting and dismissed everyone with a light flick of my wrist. I was annoyed that so many of the updates on critical projects were behind schedule, and I had to get very firm with a number of the staff. That was the part of the job that I hated most and the biggest reason I had no friends at my place of business. They all feared or loathed me because of my job title, without one of them risking getting to know me personally. It wasn't very pleasant but couldn't be helped, I guess. I was going to make this company a name in our industry, which meant some tough choices.

Picking up my cell phone, which I had put on silent before the meeting, I noticed that Manny had attempted to call me. Glancing about to ensure that the doors of the conference room were all closed, I picked up the device and connected the call.

"Hey, you," I said in the sexist tone I could muster middle of the workday.

I wanted him to know what he was missing, as he had stood me up twice. We had chatted on the phone, but twice close to the time of our date, he had called off. The excuses were vague, but something about his tone each time had made her believe he truly was sorry – so she gave him a pass. That was new for her, considering most men would have been cut off at the knees and eradicated from her contacts after one missed date. There was something about Manny, though, that had her enthralled, and she didn't want to end things this early.

"Hey, back at you," he said. "Listen, I know that I have been giving you fits breaking off our dates, but I can make it this Friday evening if you are game."

"Other woman out of town or something?" I teased.

I didn't really think he would be seeing someone else behind my back, but there were moments my insecurities took hold when I didn't speak to him. It would kill me if he honestly were to disclose that he was seeing someone else, though telling him that outright was not a weakness I was willing to reveal.

"No, but she is back home resting comfortably," he said cryptically, causing me to sit back hard in my chair.

"What?" I asked, peeved. Did he really have another woman in his life? How dare he lead me on? What if he was married or one of those serial cheaters?"

"My mom just got out of the hospital," he cut into her thoughts as her heart lurched.

"Oh, I'm sorry. Why didn't you tell me when you called off on me? I would definitely not have thought so many horrible things about you," I added, trying to inject some levity into the conversation. Now that I knew the concern he was dealing with, his sad tone made sense over the last few conversations.

"I didn't know what we were dealing with, and also," he sighed, stopping from talking for a long moment, "I just don't like involving my family in my relationships as most are so brief it just isn't a good idea."

"I understand that," I said, feeling this giddy sensation deep in my belly. He sounded like this relationship meant something to him, even if we hadn't seen each other all that long. That was good and helped validate some of the similar feelings I was experiencing. "So, how is she doing?"

"Not great. She is experienced congestive heart failure on top of a litany of other health issues. It is more about making the last of her days comfortable and happy than a cure at this stage," he said.

"I'm so sorry, Manny," I said as I could feel the pain he must be going through at this moment.

"Yeah, she's the absolute best. I really hope you have a chance to meet her, as I know she will love you. She is a tough woman that loves her family madly but doesn't suffer fools easily. She is all about all of us finding our soul mates, giving her grandbabies, and living our best lives," Manny said, opening up. "I just hope she sees more of us find that before her time is up."

"Well, I hope the same thing then – and you know a good start would be actually going out on a second physical date," I offered back to him.

I wanted to know this man, spend time with him and see if this thing between us was the real thing. I obsessed over him day and night, saw him in my dreams, and honestly couldn't wait for our next conversation. All this, and it had been only five days now since we met, was scary and awe-inspiring in turn.

"I'm on it; tomorrow night at seven work?"

"Sure, where are we going?"

"That is a surprise," he said, suddenly getting quieter. "Listen, I have to go but wear comfortable shoes tomorrow, and I text me where I can pick you up." Then without another word, he hung up.

I would normally be so annoyed, but for some reason, the mystery of Manny just deepened with his odd behaviors. Tomorrow night I wrote *date 7 p.m.* in my planner sitting next to me on the table. I couldn't wait to see what he had planned, and it most certainly would be a good end to what had been a trying week.

CHAPTER 5

I took a deep breath, closed my eyes, and attempted
to calm my nerves. *Why was I acting like this or even
feeling this way?* Usually, I made fun of Joey for acting all
nervous sometimes, especially when it came to women. Now,
look at me seated in front of a diner for some nice Sunday
brunch with a girl I had grown to truly like acting like a
teenager out on his first date.

It had been two weeks since I met Sandi and shared that
first magical night with her. In the span of that time, she had
quickly become all I could think about ever since. We talked
a lot, but I didn't get to see her very often due to her work as
a fashion designer or head of fashion development; I think
was more her title. I didn't know the specifics, and honestly,
partly it was that she didn't talk about her job a lot. She was
proud of her work, but she tried almost to minimize it from
our conversations when we were together. The point is, I
couldn't pin her down. However, this only made me want her
more, as she showed the humility not to center every conversation on her own accomplishments. Add to that the absence
of not seeing her as often as I would have liked, especially

after a near-magical night, definitely increased the fascination I was exhibiting for her.

In all honesty, I had stopped by her office twice, making a little fib about a business meeting close by once. The second time is bringing her lunch that we ate together just because I had missed her. These little signs of my growing affection seemed to resonate with her but were so out of character for me – I was amazed at the hold she already had on me.

Today though, I finally had Sandi all to myself. She was free for the entire day, and I planned to make full use of the time. I don't think I'd ever thought of a girl as much as I did Sandi, and I wanted her to be my girlfriend on a steady basis. I felt like that teen jock, asking a girl to go steady. This was unchartered territory, and I was pretty nervous. The problem was how I would mess up in the future. I was not the most reliable guy—my mother would tell you that much —but for once, I actually wanted to make an effort to try. That was if she ever wanted to date me, but, c'mon, she totally dug me... I hoped.

I looked up as our gazes collided, and she walked toward me. She looked like an angel as she made eye contact and her cheeks flushed with color. I would have spotted her in a crowd as stunning a picture she made, even at such a distance from where I was seated. Her short brown hair was styled upward, giving off a badass vibe I absolutely appreciated. Sandi wore a short but simple white dress with a black belt and bag. I waved, and she smiled when she saw me. My heart started racing just from seeing her beautiful smile. *Why am I smiling? She's just a girl, Manny! Snap out of it!* I tried using anything I could to remain calm, but I only got more and more nervous and excited.

"Hey, beautiful," I said, getting to my feet to shift the chair opposite me so Sandi could have her seat.

"Hi, Manny," Sandi replied, looking impressed at my

chivalry as she sat down. "Who knew someone like you could be all gentlemanly?"

"Someone like me? I'm kinda… courteous."

She giggled. Ugh, I missed her voice. "Even you did not believe what you just said."

"Yeah, yeah. I'm courteous when I need to be," I said. "Anyway, what do you want to eat?" I called over the waiter, and we placed our orders. While we waited, we chatted about random shit. It was great, though, because talking with her was amazingly easy. We didn't just connect on a romantic or sexual level but also on this social level were just being with her and talking made me feel amazing.

"So, how's your family?" Sandi asked inquisitively.

"They're fine as always, and we are getting into the new routine of caring for Mama. We have this calendar that my sister-in-law Angela developed for all the kids to take turns staying with Mama in her house. She wants to stay where she is most comfortable, and we are making it work."

"You seem to be connected to your family, but also there is this sad tone you sometimes get when discussing them," she observed. "Why is that? Don't you get along with them?"

"Oh, I do… at least most of them. It's more that I'm the black sheep of the family, so there's always that X factor with me that some people might not like," I explained as well as I could without getting too deep with it. "Plus, you've met me. I'm not the most likable person if you know what I mean."

"For what it's worth, I like you," Sandi said with an appreciative smile.

Hearing her say that right to my face was amazing and made my ego soar. I loved the way it made me feel. I couldn't help but smile. "I like you too, beautiful." I contemplated asking her about firming up our relationship right then and there and there. Before I spoke, though, I decided to wait until brunch was over and we went to the other locations I had planned.

"You said you have three brothers, right? Carlos, Rigo? And Jooo…ey?"

"Yeah," I answered. "I'd love to say they are a pain in my ass, but it's honestly the other way around." We both laughed at my remark. "How about you? I can't believe I've never asked about your family before."

It was just now hitting me. We'd known each other for two weeks and talked online and in person. Not once did I ask. Maybe it was because I didn't want her to ask about mine. I don't know. The point is, she asked about mine, so knowing about hers too was important.

"Oh, don't be sorry. I'm glad you didn't."

"Estranged?" I asked, watching her face for clues. The tightening of her jaw and the way she glanced away told me this was a touchy subject.

"Not really… well, I guess you could say so. Yeah, I'm estranged from my parents." Apparently, Sandi was battling it out with herself.

When I heard estranged from her parents, I wondered if that was due to their behavior or something she had done. She seemed a pretty direct person, and maybe they didn't appreciate that. Whatever the case from her tone and expressions, it must be a really hard relationship.

"Nevertheless, I have two brothers also." I could never get over the reality that she used the word 'nevertheless' in actual conversation. I tried hiding my smile in check, but she noticed.

"Now, why are you smiling?"

"Oh, I just uhm… remembered something funny."

"It's because I said 'nevertheless,' isn't it?" She promptly caught on, and I burst into a fit of laughter. "Screw you, asshole."

"I… I'm s-sorry. It's… just… t-too funny!" I loved how she made me feel free and laugh that we could laugh at each other's little quirks without feeling attacked.

"Ugh! My siblings and I are not really that close, but it's not like we have any problems either." Sandi began elaborating on her family. I suddenly stopped laughing and listened attentively. "My parents, on the other hand. Sometimes I'm unsure if they even know I am alive."

"Jeez. That bad, huh?"

"Yeah," she said. "What about your parents?"

"I definitely didn't have a great run with my papa, and my Mama and I have an… interesting relationship."

"What do you mean?" Thankfully, the waiter returned with our meals.

"Let's just eat," I said, but I think she could tell I was trying to avoid the whole thing.

Just as we were about to begin our food, a guy who seemed annoyed brushed by Sandi's chair violently, making her yelp in surprise. He didn't even say sorry. I was already tense due to the talk about Mama when this idiot added to my annoyance. Sandi immediately turned to see who had bumped her so aggressively. It was evident that she was pissed but didn't want to make a scene. I, on the other hand, never minded making a scene.

"Hey!" I stood up from my chair and called the asshole, who turned around and looked at me. I knew from his face that this was a classic case of transferring aggression. The thing is, I was also trying to transfer my aggression… or my annoyance. "You know what you did."

"What are you talking about?" he asked, frowning at me viciously. Was that supposed to scare me?

"You bumped her chair on purpose, then just walked away," I pointed out, glaring at him.

"It's fine, Manny. You don't n-"

29

"No. I want him to apologize," I said to her with such conviction that she immediately kept quiet, watching how the events would unfold. "You, apologize to her... now." The tension in the air was palpable, and I could sense people looking at us in anticipation of a fight breaking out. I didn't care; I was ready for anything this asshole sent my direction.

"No," he said curtly. "Go screw yourself." He tried to walk away, but I reached out held him back from moving. The adrenalin was coursing through my veins, and I was ready for a fight to turn physical should it go that direction.

"Manny, stop!" I was not listening to anything Sandi was saying right now. That part of me that always pushes for the extreme was on full throttle. I could feel the anger build up and become a competitive need to show dominance over this guy.

"You better let me go before I beat the shit out of you," the guy warned. He puffed out his chest and tried to look the big shot, but I just cackled at him.

"And you better learn how to be a sensible person in society before I show you what true violence looks like."

Immediately after I finished saying that, he swung at me. I was used to fights with my brothers and rough, dangerous fights in my neighborhood growing up. This made it easy for me to know when someone was on edge and about to get physical. He was much faster than I thought, though, and I just managed to evade him before going for the legs and flipping him to the ground. He clamped his hands together and hammered my back while I pummelled his ribs.

Unfortunately, the security for the restaurant came and separated us. They had to really hold me back because I was already in all-out mode. When I finally calmed down, we were kicked out of the restaurant without even paying for the food. Well, we didn't get to eat either.

I knew she was angry, but right now, I was in one of my

moods. That last thing I needed Sandi to do was speak. After walking in silence for a few minutes, the last thing I wanted to happen occurred.

"What was that?" She asked angrily.

"What do you mean?" I replied with a question of my own. "That guy was a jackass."

"Are you being serious right now?" Sandi asked rhetorically. Her voice was raised a little, so I could tell she was becoming agitated. "You joined him in being a jackass. What kind of nonsense macho bullshit was that? I didn't need you to come to my rescue."

"Oh, so when I open the door or shift the chair for you, you're okay with my chivalry, but when I tell an asshole to apologize, you don't want it?" I was pissed. This was why I didn't try to be nice to women. They were simple, too hard for me to understand. *No good deed goes unpunished.* I was getting even angrier that she was getting on my case for helping her.

"What the hell has gotten into you?" Sandi continued. "You literally fought with a guy over something as trivial as that? Do you think I wasn't upset? Do you think I didn't want to berate him right there? Did I do that? No! Because it wasn't worth it! I was the one who was shoved, not you. Why do you think fighting at a public place like that over something that flimsy was okay?" Now she was the one getting animated. It was like a switch had been flipped in her head. Sandi was fuming and looked animated, but I didn't have time for this shit right now. *Screw her. Screw women. Screw everyone.*

"I'm outta here," I said, walking away from here to the other side of the street where I had parked my bike. I had originally planned to take her to a movie and then walk along the waterfront for ice cream, but now... she could screw herself.

I got onto my bike and drove off without so much as a backward glance in her direction. Sandi didn't call for me to stay with her either, not that I expected her to. We weren't seriously dating or anything after all. I drove aimlessly for hours and hours around the city, stopping by at some places to eat or just relax. I was afraid to go home but was unsure why. It stayed this way until late into the night when I found myself at a hopping party.

"Heyyy, handsome," a pretty blonde said to me when I was into my third tequila shot. She was standing beside me, and I was seated while resting and drinking on the counter. Scanning her body, I could see she was hot, more slender, and less curvaceous than Sandi. Sandi's slim waist and wide hips were perfect. She was tall and hot and feisty. *Wait. Why the heck am I thinking about that fucking babe when I am staring at some hot girl right here?*

"Hello-o!" she said, trying to get my attention. Well, I could understand her reaction since I just kept staring at her body without saying a word. "You like what you see, hon?" At my most vulnerable, the devil had brought a ripe, hot girl who was just screaming, *do me* based on her look and words.

"I sure do," I replied, getting off my seat and tossing some cash on the counter for the bartender. I took her with me to a secluded corner of the bar—or as secluded as I could get—and began kissing her violently. As I roamed my fingers up her thighs and sucked on her neck, all I wished for was that this would make me forget. I needed to forget the scent of Sandi… her beautifully cut hair… her red lips that I never got to taste. And here I was, trying to kiss a lesser set of lips when I should be going after hers. What the heck was I doing here? I could not just get into it with this girl regardless of how sexy she was, so I stopped abruptly, much to her surprise.

"What? What is it?" she inquired, but I just turned away,

cleaning my face with my palm. "Did I do something wrong?"

"No, no… I did," I said and left.

What was going on with me? All this for some girl I had never done anything sexual with. Was I really falling in love with Sandi Bailey? There had to be something I could do before it was too late for me!

CHAPTER 6

I was so mad after Manny left her that I immediately went home and realized that there was only one way to get rid of the anger seething in my soul. I changed into workout clothes and headed to the little gym around the corner. When I walked in, I glanced at the ledger and put her name down. I was looking for some release of her aggression, and this was the safest thing I could think of.

Finding my way to the back of the gym, I slipped into the hot, sticky room and filled my water bottle to the brim from the little dispenser in the corner. I would need it as this was always one of the most trying exercises for me. I glanced about and found an empty, stationary bike. This sweat workout was a favorite of mine, and today it was going to serve to feed my need for a healthy workout and trying to rid the anger ripping through my insides.

As I sat ready for the instructor to begin, I replayed the scene with Manny in the frame-by-frame slowness through my brain. I had honestly never had a man – any man – defend me in such away. Sure, the jerk that passed had done it on purpose, as they often did. This was one of those odd passive-aggressive behaviors that I believe all men carry over from kids. When they found a beautiful woman, they treated her badly to garner her attention in some odd attempt. The jerk today seemed to be doing just that as she glanced at him, and he gave her this odd sultry look in return.

Now, that was not an excuse by any means for Manny's behavior which had shocked her to the core. He had literally jumped right into the asshole's face and started an actual real goodness fight in one of her favorite restaurants. Part of her honestly was a bit flattered by the chivalry, and the other part mortified by the unacceptable behavior. The problem now was he hadn't given her a chance to process before he stomped away from her.

"Are we ready to sweat?" The overly excitable trainer said as she took up her position on the bike at the front of the class. Happy women like her made me want to walk up and punch her in the face, but unlike Manny, I kept my thoughts and fists to myself.

"We are just going to get warmed up but remember this is a hot cycling class. Should you feel faint, overheating, or any odd sensations, we do ask you excuse yourself to the main gym and air conditioning," she said excitedly. "Now, with that out of the way, let's go," she said.

I mirrored her behaviors and listened to her cheer personality bite at me as I pedaled faster and faster. I could feel the sweat start to surface out of every pore, and yet I went faster.

I didn't maintain the svelte look of someone my size capable of wearing every piece that our fashion house put out by not putting in the hard work. I was in a gym six days a week, and this was how I managed life.

I know that most women had friends, and sure, I had a few acquaintances. My prickly outlook on life, sharp tongue, and long work hours did not make me good friend material, though, so I exercised off the frustrations of my life instead. Today, I had anticipated was going to go very differently.

I had honestly thought that Manny and I would actually be having sex at this stage, or at least out at some new fun adventure. He loved so many of the same things I did and the ones I hadn't experienced I was good doing with him by my side. I had respected for us to really chat about where this relationship was headed and not end up going our separate ways before the food was served. This might end up being my worst date ever, and the worst part was, he was the man that I felt closest to – what a mess!

I pedaled and kept pace, with the cheery-eyed instructor continuing to match her pace. I was going to either get all the stress out of my body, or I was going to be darn tired and ready for a nap at the end – either outcome was better than calling Manny. I would not give him the satisfaction I decided – he was going to call me and apologize, or this was well and truly over.

I nearly fell off the bike as that thought crossed my brain. Seriously! What in the world was I thinking? The man got in a fight today and caused a public spectacle. Was there any way that I would hear him out or give him another chance? No! The answer was supposed to be no my brain screamed at me silently.

But he's the cutest, funniest, snarkiest man you have ever met. We all make mistakes, and maybe he deserves a second chance. My heart was arguing. I had no idea which organ was going to win the argument, but I needed to work so hard I couldn't give anything but my staying on this bike my concentration.

Standing up a bit, I moved even harder, focusing everything I had on the trainer upfront. I needed Manny out of my head, and I needed to no longer care what the man had to say! I was not going to see him again! He didn't deserve a second chance, and there was sure to be another better man I would meet soon enough!

I pushed through the pain and pedaled until so much sweat poured from me; I was going to leave a stain on the floor if I didn't mop it off my body. And still, I pushed harder as I worked with every ounce of my being to kill all thoughts of Manny from forming in my brain!

CHAPTER 7

*R*iding never felt the same. The usual freedom I felt while riding my motorcycle had changed. Instead of the badass feeling of excitement I was accustomed to, it had turned to something else... something darker. I could barely focus on anything, but riding my bike was particularly difficult. I couldn't focus, which made things really stressful and dangerous for someone on a bike. It all came from that goddamn girl.

I hated the fact that I felt this way about her. I hadn't told Mama about her because I didn't need any of her lectures since that was usually reserved for Joey, Carlos, or Rigo. I had told Joey at the hospital and Carlos when I was interested in her since he knew how to shut up and not go blabbing to people. He asked me three days ago about how things were, and I told him we weren't in contact anymore. He asked me without hesitation what I did to chase her away. The fact that Carlos already assumed it was my fault... damn. That's pretty telling of what my own family thinks of me. *Was I toxic? Was I the architect of my own problems?*

I had always loved to live life on the edge and go with the

flow of my beat, but … this was unforeseen. I hate to quote Mama, but she always said that it's the people who are the least empathetic or emotional that fall in love the hardest when they finally feel something deeply. Even though I hate to admit it, she might have been right. I heard a honking blaring to my right and weaved back into my lane. I barely missed a car because I was so caught up in my head. *Jeez! I have to be more careful, especially since it's night.*

I thought about pulling over and just taking a few cleansing breaths. *Come on! I wasn't that weak, was I?* I am a badass bike rider, letting the wind take me where it will and not someone who needed to take yoga breaths to align myself. *What kind of shit was this that my brain was putting out there?* I had to get it together and stop acting like this.

It had been just over a week since my fight with Sandi, and I had not called her to talk about it or apologize because I was a proud asshole. She didn't call either, though that was to be expected. Girls never apologize regardless of who is wrong, and it was one of those things that made them incompatible with me. I thought we were in the era of gender equality. To be honest, that didn't really matter in this scenario because I was the one at fault… or at least that was what Carlos told me when I explained what happened to him. *How would that emotionless prick even know who was wrong or right? Did he even have feelings at all?* I kept pondering whether or not to call her. *Would she even want to talk to me if I did?* She was pretty pissed when I left…

I knew that I messed up badly and again allowed the ego to take over when I should have read my surroundings better. I would expect after that scene that Angela was embarrassed that I would decide to throw punches in such a public space. While I am always up for any action needed to keep men like the one that bumped her in line, I should have been a bit more on my a-game while on a date. Sure, I realized in hindsight Angela was not impressed by the machoism that I was exhibiting, but honestly, I wasn't overly certain I could have contained it.

When I got into a mood such as that, and some incident sparked the flame of my wrath – it was like another personality took over my entire body. I had long gotten in trouble for my fights in school, my work, and even with my brothers. I hadn't ever gotten help for it as that seemed weak, and I was definitely not weak! This was the first time it cost me this dearly, though, so maybe it was time to fix that kink in my personality.

I shook my head, trying to refocus on the path ahead of me. I really needed to shake out of this funk, and for a moment, I even considered pulling over. Distracted driving was an absolute hazard to a motorcyclist, and I needed to stop this now before I paid the price.

I focused on work, the scenery, and even trying to think about my dear Mama. It was bothering me these days to see her as she weakened in front of our eyes. I was more determined than ever to spend time with her – quality time which meant I had to get myself into a good headspace and quit fretting over Sandi and our non-existent relationship.

Crap! There I go bringing it back to her once again. The woman was like a disease that had taken hold of my mind. I wondered if there was any way I was going to be rid of her. Then suddenly, a deer sprinted into the middle of the road. Unfortunately, that split second of not paying attention was enough to make me have to swerve heavily to avoid the animal.

The collision was ear-shattering and sent me flying off my bike into the air. I had always heard that in a moment like this, your entire life flashed before your eyes. There it was, riding with Rigo, Carlos, and Joey with the wind in our hair and teasing each other. Then Mama and so many amazing memories with her flitted through my head. Sandi and that first amazing night together. Finding out about my first raise and so many other images. In the time it took for me to go air bound after the collision, in slow motion, it seemed my entire life to this point played out in my mind's eye.

Then with a return to sanity, I hit the pavement and flipping on the sturdy asphalt over and over again. My helmet thankfully protected me as my head hit the ground and bounced off. The pain was so acute my body went into a state of shock. I felt that every part of my body was being shredded by immense pain that rendered me immobile.

Then I luckily felt the darkness reaching up to claim me as I passed out.

CHAPTER 8

I am sitting at the bar dressed to the nines again and hoping that this jerk who was already ten minutes late was going to be better than Jeremiah. It had been a chore to get dressed for this date, and I had tried on about twenty outfits. I had to physically reprimand myself that it was time to get back up on this horse and find someone new as the only way to get myself over Manny fully. I had given up expecting that Manny was going to call after a week of silence.

I had picked the phone up so many times and nearly talked myself into making the call to him instead of waiting for Manny. But then anger would take hold as the scene once again played through my mind of him slugging that man on our last date. I didn't know what I was thinking, pining after the man and desiring that he call me. I normally was easily able to move on to the next guy when someone disappointed me. I was stunned that Manny was sticking in my brain.

"Sorry, I'm late," Nate, the surgeon as I had nicknamed him, came alongside me at last.

"It's all good," she said, plastering a smile on her face,

despite the anguish her soul was in. The man was sandy blonde-haired, tall, well-employed, and handsome as the devil. And she just wished he was Manny from the moment she turned to see him standing there.

My breath caught in my chest, and for the span of a minute, I seriously thought I was going to have a panic attack. This was not good, and of course, I wanted to get to know this man. Nate did not look like someone that was going to start a bar brawl tonight. His big open smile and gentlemanly gestures as the host showed us to a table were exactly what I loved in a man. I needed to get my head on straight and quit thinking about Manny – he was gone!

He didn't want to apologize to me or be in my life, so I shouldn't give him any more of my precious time. The time that was slipping from me, and I so desperately wanted to find a man to settle down with, have that family time with that I craved. I craved someone to support me during the worst and best times and never leave my side. That was not Manny! *So why was I allowing him to be the third wheel on this date?*

"So, you are a fashion designer?" Nate said, immediately leaning into our conversation by asking about me. That was a great sign!

"I am. I know fashion is not as important as what you do, but it was a lifelong pursuit of mine. I am so fortunate to head of a growing brand that I think will be so influential in the years to come," I said, giving my normal speech, hoping that my insides calm down and get into the date.

"That is amazing," Nate said. "I enjoy my job but will be honest sometimes wish I had gone with my first love also."

"Which is?" I asked, trying to feign enthusiasm to get to know him. Honestly, I could care less. Despite all the signals that this is an amazing man, I am having to focus hard to keep my mind from wandering.

"I always wanted to be a science teacher," he said, widening his grin to showcase those pearly whites and deep dimples. This man definitely could attract any number of women with that single move. I checked in with my hormones, though, and there was nothing! *How ridiculous could I possibly be?*

"Ugh, I'm not a big kid person," I admit. Sure, I love the little rugrats, but the thought of caring for them scares me. I don't know babies and toddlers look so small, and I sometimes get so into my projects that I might lose focus and inadvertently put them in danger. I just avoided any sense of responsibility with kiddos and stayed far away. The thought of teaching entire classrooms of them – hell no!

"I get that," Nate said with a grin. "I struggle when it is a kid on my operating table, as they do come off so fragile," he said. "So, what do you do for fun?"

I had to think about that for a minute. I went to the gym, worked, and occasionally treated myself to evenings like this with total strangers. The list was depressing even to me in my head, so I definitely didn't need to verbalize it and scare him half to death.

I tried hard to come up with some brilliant response, but all I could think of was running from the building and this man. I just couldn't do it.

"I'm sorry," I said, pushing back my chair. "This is not going to be the evening I'm certain you had planned, so it seems best to leave it here," I said, turning to exit as fast as the three-inch heels on my feet could carry me.

"But," I heard Nate sputter, but I already had the exit in my sight. As I walked outside, the snap of cool air finally caused the tension to start sliding from me. I glanced at the sidewalk, considering walking over and sitting down as I sometimes did when I needed to think.

Tonight though, the thought just made me remember the

scene from the first night Manny and I met. I could see that smug look on his face clear as if he were standing right in front of me now. He had instantly lit something inside of me – and despite everything that transpired afterward, he had me hooked good.

I pulled the cellphone from my clutch and scrolled to the contacts. There was his name; it would be so easy to connect the call. For once, I could be the one to ask forgiveness even if I didn't feel it necessary. Maybe just to hear his voice again, I could –

I stopped the thought right there and stowed the phone again in my purse. If Manny wanted to hear from me, he knew how to find me. Instead of moping about like some lovesick teenager, I needed to grow up and realize he didn't want to see me. That was a fact, and I just needed to get over it. Maybe not date until I moved past this a bit, but still – I needed to let it go!

It was just a few blocks to my apartment, and the walk I decided would do me good as I headed in that direction. I was more determined than ever to erase all memory of Manny from my mind.

As I opened the door to my apartment, the phone in my purse buzzed. My hands shook as I dug into the purse, hoping that maybe it was Manny. The name on the caller ID was my brother, though, which made me smile. He would be a good one to bounce this current situation over.

"Hey," I said into the device as I put it to my ear, walking into the apartment and flopping on the couch.

"Hi, I hadn't heard from you in a while, "so I thought I would check in."

I didn't talk to my brother Damien a lot, but we did make an effort to check in at least once a month. Scanning my memory, I realized it had been closer to six weeks at this point since I had phoned.

"I'm alive and kicking," I said with a grin as I kicked my high heels onto the floor to further relax.

"So, who are you kicking these days," he asked, and I could hear the sarcasm and tease in the question.

"There is this guy, Manny," I started as he chuckled loudly, interrupting me.

"There is always a man when you are in a mood. What did he do this time to make you dump him?"

I stopped as he said that, as I realized that he wasn't all that wrong – I always dumped them before they could hurt me. Over the years, the number of reasons I had fabricated to eradicate the men in my life could fill a full-sized novel. But Manny was different, and try as I might, I just couldn't seem to be done with him.

"His name is Manny, and I think he might be more screwed up than me. I really like him, but he is so hard to talk to, hung up on his past and honestly driving me mad," I said as the silence from the other end of the line dragged on for a minute.

"Wow, this one sounds like a keeper. So let me guess, communication is the biggest issue you are having?" Damien asked, causing me to sit up straighter at that question. *How did he know that without further details from me?"*

"Maybe. How would you know that?" I asked, waiting with bated breath for his response.

"Sandi, you have never been the easiest person to talk to or get along with growing up. You tend to see the world through the lens you created, and sometimes empathy is not something you possess. Maybe she should see things from this guy's perspective. Sometimes we only see what we want to see, and maybe you can learn from him and be more open and not always have an attitude like people are going to hurt you," Damien said without taking a breath.

She felt his words to her core. She just sat there feeling

punched in the gut and sad in turns. Her brother felt as if maybe she didn't understand people or give them a chance? That was hard to hear, and yet it wasn't anger she was feeling. She was relieved as she did look at her life suddenly in a different way.

"I'm sorry, Damien," she said quietly. "I know I can be difficult and sometimes might not have heard you. You know I do love you, though, and value your insights."

"Thanks," he said softly. "I mean it in the best spirit and want you to be happy, Sandi."

They chatted a few minutes more before finally disconnecting. The heavy conversation stayed with her, though, as he went to bed that night. Tossing and turning, she ruminated on his words and how to handle Manny better should they ever have the opportunity to clear the air between them.

CHAPTER 9

I could hear the light beeping of machines and the sounds of many voices milling around. At first, I couldn't figure out where I was, but then with stunning clarity, the pictures of the accident flitted across my mind in slow motion. I was so irresponsible getting on my bike when I was that distracted and had no one to blame for the after-effects except myself.

I tried to open my eyes, but they wouldn't cooperate. Honestly, at this stage, I didn't know if they were swollen shut or my body was just so tired it wasn't cooperating. I felt a tear traveled my cheek as I worried that maybe I was one of those coma patients that could hear things but not wake up. Panic spiked my system, and I nervously tried to move. Pain shot up my arm, and I felt on the verge of passing out again.

"Hey," Carlos's voice sounded as he put a hand on my arm. He was to the right of me and then another hand on the other side.

"You need to stay calm," Joey's voice came through on the other side of me as he also touched my arm.

I tried to relax, but when I went to speak, no words

would come forth from my mouth. What the hell! *Had I done that much damage? Would I walk again? Would I get out of this bed again?*

"How is her?" I heard Rigo sounding like he was just now coming into the room.

"I think he is going to be a cautionary tale of what could happen at any minute to us," Carlos said.

"Yeah, we can't let Mama see this," Joey interjected. "She has enough stress going on and seeing him looking like he had the worst argument with the pavement – won't do her any good."

"Agreed," Rigo said. "I just came from there, and Angela was sitting with her. I didn't say anything, but you are risking her wrath if you don't tell her."

I listened to the bantering, just feeling better with them all in the room with me. I wasn't brain dead, obviously, and the pain was fierce enough to tell me I was definitely still alive – so that was something!

"You remember the last time we all tried to hide something from Mama?" Joey asked as I searched my memory banks. Carlos piped in as the memory surfaced in my mind.

"The time we all decided to show that kid Jake not to mess with us," Carlos said. "He was such a bully and kept pushing Manny around. Okay, granted, Manny has always had a bit of a chip on his shoulder, but there was no excuse to try and whoop on him."

"Agreed," Rigo said. "I still remember that kid's face looking so smug, and we thought we had the upper hand because there were four of us. Man, we got sucker-punched when all his brothers stepped out of the shadows."

"Yeah, and Mama was mad when she saw all the bruised faces the following morning," Joey snickered. "She didn't buy the excuses, but since she didn't know the truth, we thought we were in the clear."

"Until she met Jake's mom at a PTA meeting and invited them over for that dinner," Carlos said. "Most uncomfortable meal of my life, and Jake with his brothers sitting there in their Sunday best. You know Mama must have known something."

"She always did," Joey said.

"We can't hide this from her, even if she is sick," Rigo finally said. "I'm actually scared she might use her last bit of strength to whip us all with that sharp tongue of hers. She might not have agreed with spanking, but man, she can use that mouth to her advantage."

"Not always on us; remember her telling the principal off when my bike got impounded," Joey asked.

"That man looked like he was going to slink into his office and wet himself," Rigo remembered.

I sat there listening to them banter back and forth over my hospital bed. It was soothing to my soul to have all of them there, telling stories of my life. We were family through the good times – and bad such as this. With them around, life never got boring, and I always knew someone would show up for me when needed.

I could feel the lethargy taking hold of me. I don't know if they were giving me great drugs for the pain or what, but I felt heavier. The darkness was reaching up to gather me again into a deep sleep. This time it wasn't the trauma of hitting my head that was causing me to go totally unconscious.

I tried to hold on to Carlos, Manny, and Rigo's voices. Anchor me to reality, but it was simply more than my injured body could do. Slowly I sank into the sweet slumber of sleep again, with all my brothers still arguing over the merits of who and when to tell Mama about this accident.

CHAPTER 10

*I*t was pitch black outside my office when I finally got headed on my way home. I had stayed back a bit later than others on my team due to the slacking and slowness of my work. Yes, I had been slacking in my work for a week, and people in the office had begun to notice. My absentmindedness and inability to do my part of the projects on time had to be addressed, so I decided to take time after work to do them all. Now I was done, but I was exhausted. Because of a man, I was not about to continue to be the topic of conversation around the office. Why did I feel so sad just because of a man… a jerk, for that matter? *Ugh! Screw you, Manny Mendoza, for making me this way.*

Honestly, he didn't do anything but be himself, I thought. I was a bit too brash; I had come to think in the time since the incident on our date. My anger problem had reared its ugly head, but still, I knew I was right. Two fiery tempers did not make the situation right. *What the hell was his problem? He left me hanging there because I got upset at his behavior? Seriously?*

I still found it hard to understand or fathom that Manny could do that. He'd always insisted in our conversations and a handful of outings that he was a jackass, but I'd failed to really listen or see it because the guy was nice to me. I loved the balance of him being a bad boy towards others but also being respectful whenever he was dealing with me. I think every girl wants that in some way. But if he could act that way and leave me outside a restaurant after asking me to be there... all because of one fight, *what else could he do to hurt my feelings?*

I wasn't ready for that kind of heartbreak because I liked him more than anyone else, I had met in years. In fact, I think I was falling in love with him. This time apart made me realize how much I felt for Manny. *How the hell had this happened?* II thought I was stronger than this, but things of the heart are way beyond any one man or woman's control. *Did he feel the same way? Was he thinking about me too?*

"Ugh, stop torturing yourself!" I yelled at myself out loud, not caring about who might overhear me. "He doesn't care!"

If he did, he would have called because he missed me, wouldn't he? I really needed to get a grip and stop thinking about Manny. He is just like every other guy I've been interested in. I was only thankful that we hadn't gotten too serious dating; otherwise, this would have been much more painful. Not sure, honestly, how I would have handled things if it was more painful than this. The man had taken hold of every thought I had during the day and interfered with my work. He had managed to wreak havoc on the work that I never allowed anyone to detract me from.

I got home and went straight to my bedroom, not even worrying about food. My stomach was so tied in knots that anything I tried to consume would probably taste like cardboard. Slipping out of the dress I had worn, I hung it in the closet. It was expensive, and even in a funk, I wasn't going to risk ruining it by dropping it on the floor.

Slipping into a nightgown, I moved toward the bed. I was

tired, and all I wanted was to sleep. At the moment I went to turn out the side table lamp, my cellphone I had dropped on the piece of furniture buzzed. I glanced at the number, but I did not recognize it nor provide any name on the caller ID.

"Hello?" I said, picking it up.

"Good evening. Is this Sandi? Sandi Bailey?" a male voice inquired. It sounded like things were very hectic where this person was with all the noises being fed into my ear. I could hear screaming and some instructions. Was that... a hospital?

"Yes, this is she. Who are you?" I felt my heart thudding as I immediately tried to figure out why a hospital would be calling this time of night. Was one of my brothers or possibly my parents in trouble? Was it one of my coworkers? I mean, who would give me as a point of contact – I was now sitting up, keenly tuned into the conversation.

"I am Carlos Mendoza. Manny's brother."

My heart skipped a bit. *Why was Manny's brother calling? Did he ask his brother to talk to me on his behalf?* That would be a weak move, but I didn't care. I'd have taken anything at this point. I was that infatuated with him, and my pride would no longer allow me to ignore any news of the man. Or maybe his brother was taking matters into his own hands and wanted to reconcile things between us. Nah. From what I'd heard about Carlos from Manny, he was not that kind of person.

"Manny has been involved in an accident." I froze the moment he said that. "Usually, I wouldn't use his phone to get your number, but he kept calling your name. I know you two aren't together anymore or going through some stuff, but—"

I zoned all the words out, but he kept talking. Manny was... in an accident? The fact that he kept calling my name meant that he was alive, but it did not console me at all. He was in an accident, and that was all that mattered. *Was he going to die? He couldn't really die, right?* I didn't know what I would do if anything happened to him. The last exchange we'd had was a heated argument. At this moment, it was evident that I was in love with this man. Just the fact that he was hurt made me start to cry. I didn't even know when the tears started flowing through my cheeks.

"What hospital are you in?" I finally bit out, not caring how harsh I sounded. There was no way I was going to sleep tonight until I got to see Manny for myself.

Carlos informed me where they were, and I told him I would be by as quick as possible. Launching from my bed, I slipped into some jeans and pulled a t-shirt over my head as I ran for the door. I ran to my car and slipped inside without really considering what I looked like or anything else. I could barely breathe properly as I raced through the streets, grateful for the late hour as there was not a huge volume of traffic. I knew I needed to be careful on the road; the last thing anyone needed was for both Manny and me to be injured in accidents. That might even be better than living healthy in a world without him. Gosh, what was I thinking? My head was already unfocused from us seemingly breaking up, but now, I was a mess.

"You better not die. You better not die on me, Manny!" I said over and over while driving. But what if he did not want to see me? I know he'd murmured my name, but the last thing I could take was him asking me why the hell I was there if he woke up and saw me.

"Arrrghh! Shut up!" When I finally reached the hospital, I rushed through the door and to the reception desk.

"Hello, how may I—" The poor woman at the desk looked at her with wide eyes.

"I need to see Manny Mendoza, please," I said, strumming my fingers nervously on the countertop as I waited for her to provide the information I needed.

"Manny Mendoza. Hold on… let me check," she said, quickly typing on her keyboard. I knew from the look in her eye the minute she found his name. She looked up at me. "Are you a family member? Because only family can see him right now." *Shit. I had nothing.*

"Hey, she's fine. She's with me," a familiar voice said, and I turned around to see a handsome man who looked a lot like Manny. His voice had already given him away; this was Carlos. I guess the tall, dark, handsome, and dangerous genes ran through the entire family. There was no mistaking Carlos was Manny's brother, from his build, carriage, and facial features.

"Carlos, right?" I asked as I moved around the reception desk and approached him.

"Yeah. Nice to meet you," he said while we walked briskly toward the elevators.

"How is he?" I had to know what we were dealing with, as the worst scenarios had played through my head since getting the call. He hadn't gotten overly detailed when he called, and that made me wonder if he was saving the worst information for when I arrived here on the scene in person.

"He was really bad when he was first brought here, but now… he's better." The words were carefully selected, and he wouldn't meet my eyes for a moment. I sighed in relief, bending and resting my hands on my knees as I leaned against the elevator. I decided not to push for further details until I could see Manny myself.

The elevator opened, and Carlos extended his hand to allow me to walk out first. He then pointed to Manny's room, and I walked in.

"Who is this pretty lady?" a woman said, standing up from the chair next to Manny's bed.

I glanced at Manny and found tears immediately surfacing in my eyes. He looked horrible, with lots of cuts,

55

scrapes, and such on his face that was still very swollen. His arm was wrapped, but I couldn't tell if it was a cast or, again, just for bandaging more injuries like his face. I turned to the sweet lady staring at me, eagerly awaiting an introduction.

"She's a… friend of Manny, Mama."

Mama? That would make her Manny's mom. I saw another man seated nearby who I decided must be Joey, the youngest. Suddenly, I wished I had glanced in the mirror or taken just a minute longer to prepare for this visit. I must look a wreck, and they all were now staring at me with interest. I had nothing to add as I glanced back at Manny.

"I'm so sorry for what is happening. I'm sure you must be very distressed." I stood upright and walked up to her. "I'm sure he will be fine."

"He will be fine," she said with such calmness and assurance that it made me relax too. "Thanks for coming, my dear. I'm honestly surprised that Manny has someone that would drop everything and come see him like this in the middle of the night other than us."

I smiled as I realized she was partly testing me to see what I would say or maybe give away. I would bet Manny hadn't told her about me, and from the little I knew of this family, they shared almost everything. I could definitely see where Manny got the snarky repertoire and fast comebacks. This woman was sharp and alert to everything around her, even as Carlos took her arm and showed her back to the chair next to Manny. I remember Manny telling me she was sick, and I sincerely hoped this stress wasn't causing additional concerns for her also.

"Hello," the man I had determined was Joey said, rising he circled the bed to shake my hand.

"I'm Sandi. Nice to meet you," I said. We talked a bit more about the specifics of Manny's condition, and after talking to the doctor, it was clear that the accident wasn't as serious as originally feared.

I offered to stay with him for a while if they wanted to get some sleep or just get showers at this point. They had let me know that they had been at the hospital for three days with him now, and I figured they could use the break.

I was slightly taken aback when they agreed quite easily, and from the nervous look Joey and Carlos shot their mother, it was evident her comfort was the only reason they would leave Manny with me. I sat just staring at him for a number of minutes after they were gone before I rose to go to the window.

Laying my head against the cool planes of glass, I sighed. This family was exactly what I always wished for, Manny, the kind of man I would never have thought to turn me this inside out – but I was falling for him. If I thought my concentration was bad before seeing him like this was worse. I would have no peace in the world until I knew he was safely out of the hospital and back on the road to healing. Then he and I would need to address this thing between us. One way or the other, I wanted a shot at being part of his world. I had a feeling that when Manny loved someone, it was with everything he had in him. I desperately wanted to know what that felt like!

CHAPTER 11

I nearly jumped from the bed and did a little jig when the doctor let me know I was being released. Everyone went into motion, readying me to head back home, and soon we were headed downstairs to fresh air and freedom. Joey and Carlos helped me to Joey's truck and then got Mama up in the passenger side.

"Well, I gotta add that to my bucket list just for how insane it was," I mused with a chuckle. No one laughed. I could sense they were all upset. I was sure they would blame me for being unfocused while driving and were just waiting until I was better to start the lectures. Ugh, all this because of a fucking lady. Not that I was going to tell them the root cause of my accident, I would seriously never hear the end of it.

"That reminds me," Carlos said, turning to me. "Sandi came to see you while you were unconscious."

"What?!" I yelled much louder than I had intended to, causing Mama to frown and Joey to plug his ears with his fingers. "Why? How did she know?"

"I called her."

I was stunned into speechlessness for a moment. I couldn't believe that my brothers would gang up to call her, as Joey and Carlos at least knew exactly how I felt about her. Then the anger at her seeing me like that took hold, and my frustration and anger mixed for a volatile reaction.

"Who the heck asked you to call her? How the fuck did you even get her number?"

I was both annoyed and happy at the same time. I was upset at Carlos for doing that without consulting me—not that he could have, since I had been unconscious—and I was happy because she'd come. I would have thought she didn't care about me, but this indicated she had some feelings for me. Truly I was all over the place emotionally going from anger to happiness and back to confusion in the span of a minute.

"You gave me permission... when you kept calling out her name and saying please," he replied, and I felt my face turn red. "And I know your phone password," Carlos added for good measure. I had to make a mental note to change that, though in this case, I'm glad he used the knowledge in the manner that he did.

"Finally! You've found a girl you like!" Joey teased with a beaming grin. Mama remained silent, just giving me that knowing look of hers.

"Sandi and Manny sitting in a tree," Carlos said in a sing-song voice as I just glared at him to shut up.

"I don't like her that much. She's just another random chick that's been fawning over me." I tried not to make it obvious that I was interested in her because I didn't want them to think I was falling for her. I was a player, and I didn't believe in falling in love and just being with one person. I couldn't allow myself to be in a relationship because I would put myself in danger of getting hurt. "What I had was a nightmare. If she was in it, it couldn't have been a daydream, trust me."

Everyone went silent, and I glanced from Joey's eyes in the mirror to Carlos. Neither were buying it, but I didn't want to continue the conversation, so I just glanced out the window until we got to Mamas.

"I'm off," Carlos said once he dropped off Mama inside. "Don't kill yourself." That was my brother's way of showing affection. Mama shook her head in disappointment, but that wasn't new. What did catch me off-guard, however, was Joey's reaction.

"You may think being in love makes you look weak, but it doesn't." Joey patted me on the shoulder. He looked like he was tired of my attempts at always acting like I didn't care about anything.

"Joey, why don't you go and get a nice meal for your brother?"

I stared at Mama when she said that. Did she not understand that would mean she and I would be alone in the house? I had no intention of staying here, but then I realized that my bike was totaled. That and the fact they brought me to her house and not mine made me suddenly realized I was stuck here.

"Are you sure, Mama?" Even Joey knew the tense relationship between us and seemed uncertain about leaving us alone. "I will leave you then, but I won't be gone long."

"Yes, my dear." She nodded. "Off you go. Shoo! This will give us a chance to talk," she said with a chuckle.

"All right," Joey said and left. I forgot even to tell him what I wanted to eat. Moreover, there were more pressing issues at hand right now. Mama and I were in a tense situation as it had been an exceedingly long time since she and I had a serious conversation, just the two of us. She looked relaxed, so why did it feel like a hundred degrees to me? Mama always liked to make us feel uncomfortable when we did something wrong before finally berating us.

"Whatever pep talk you had saved up, could you just get it over with? I need to get some sleep. It's been a long day." I couldn't take it anymore. The tension was causing all my muscles to bunch up painfully.

"Manny, who are you?" she finally said, staring me dead in the eye.

I stared at her with a perplexed look. *What kind of question was that?* "You answered the question while asking it at the same time, Mama." I tried to be snarky, but Mama was not having any of that.

"You think pretending you don't have any feelings for that nice girl makes you a tough guy? If you don't open your heart to someone, you will always live a lonely existence. I don't wish that for you."

Was she seriously trying to get me angry? What the hell was this? I couldn't even walk away because of my legs. Shit, now I had to listen to all this? I didn't want to focus on who I was at this moment. I was smart enough to know that I didn't have a lot of redeeming qualities. That said, I didn't want to sit and discuss all of them with my mother, for goodness sake!

"Can you just leave me alone?" I asked. "It's not like you love me like you do Joey or the others."

The words were intentionally harsh as the frustration I had tried to hold in check came out. I didn't want to get into all the history in our family or my dicey past relationship woes with Mama. I simply wanted to be left alone to lick my wounds and sleep.

"What is that supposed to mean, Manny?" She asked, sitting forward in her chair, and waiting for a response. For so long, she had just avoided confrontation, as we made some effort to be civil when in the company of others. Today seemed to be the one she had chosen to clear the air. *Lord, help us all!*

"It means that it is now you wanna talk to me? Have you even said more than twenty words to me this year?" I snarled, no longer carrying to mince my words. I always went to family events for the sake of my brothers, but Mama you, and I would sit on opposite sides and just glance at each other – not really speaking. This had been going on for a long time, and I knew the root cause but not how to fix it, so avoidance is how I dealt with this and most other uncomfortable things in my world.

"Have you?" she retorted, and I frowned. *Why was this woman on my case? Why today of all days?*

"There is so much anger, hate, and bitterness in your heart that it worries me. Every time I have tried to talk to you, you flare up and run away. You've always been the hardest for me to talk to from a very young age. Why is that? Why don't you let the past be and just let us try to have a relationship free of all this anger?"

"You want me to give you a chance when you don't even allow me to ask questions about my father or even see him. Does that sound fair?"

Silence. She stared at me, a bit flustered at my question. I didn't remember my dad very well, and what little tidbits I had as memories or had been told were negative. Not having him around, even when my stepdad tried to fill the void, bothered me.

"Is this what this is about? Your deadbeat of a dad?"

"That didn't answer my question, Mama."

"Seriously? This is what you want to talk about right now?" Mama was getting annoyed. "After raising you and working overtime on several jobs just to put food on the table? After disciplining and praising all my hijos based on the situation and teaching you to be upstanding citizens in society? After everything I did for you, you're holding a grudge at me for not telling you about a man who walked away because of choices he made! A man who left you when you were just a kid!"

"I barely remember him, and you removed all the pictures and evidence of his existence. I have a right to know who Dad is or at least why he left us. I didn't even have the choice of having a relationship with him."

"I'm not going through this with you. It's upsetting to talk about the past, and maybe you will understand when you are a parent one day. Right now, I don't have the energy to get into this! Mama said, and I snapped.

"Then when? Have you ever thought that part of the reason I act this way is because I have so many unanswered questions? You never wanted to talk about him, and that makes me feel like you don't care about me as your son or my feelings. Everything is always about Joey this... Joey that! Just because I'm not Joey doesn't mean I'm not your fucking child too! What is so wrong with being me? In being like this? In living life to my own tune? Huh, Mama? Tell me why I need to be more like Joey to win your love?"

Joey opened the door. I didn't even hear his bike pull up. I guess I was so focused on being angry at my Mama that everything just took a backseat.

"It's time to go, Manny." It was obvious he'd heard our argument, and my mother just sat there with her head turned down. "I will take you home, as I don't think it is a wise idea for you to stay here after all."

"Joey," Mama said, but my brother wasn't budging.

I had once again alienated those around me. The problem was just once I wanted someone to tell me about my dad, as it bothered me more than I really told people to have no memory of the man. I wanted to understand and know why he left and had no interest in us. I wanted to know that my mother could love me as much as my brothers despite the ego, anger, and myriad other issues. But it seemed that today *again*, I would go without answers.

Joey didn't say a word as he navigated me home safely. He made sure I was settled.

"Call if you need anything," he mumbled and then was gone.

And once again, like always – I was alone!

CHAPTER 12

I attempted to focus on the work ahead. Many of the assignments I had delegated were finally completed, so I had people coming and going from my office all morning, needing decisions and feedback from me. There were a hundred emails to answer, several vendors to return calls to, and a litany of other tasks. You would think that my brain could have found enough to stay busy and leave thoughts of Manny alone. *As if!*

I don't know what kind of spell the man had over me, but I managed to multi-task, worrying about him alongside everything I did. Since the hospital, I hadn't heard from him, but he was front and center of my mind throughout the day. The not knowing how he was, had started to be this throbbing need I had to fix soon. I glanced at the cellphone but then decided this was crazy and returned to work at hand.

After two hours of distractedly trying to accomplish something work-related, I finally picked up the phone and texted Manny.

I hope you are feeling better. I was sorry to hear about your accident.

At this point, I didn't know if he was home from the hospital or not. I just wanted him to know that I was here if he wanted to talk and hopefully find out that he would be okay.

After visiting him in the hospital, I had thrown myself into work with everything I had. I realized he wasn't going to call as he was incapacitated, so I needed to focus on something else not to go completely bat shit crazy!

My phone vibrated, and I saw there I had a return message from Manny. I tried to school my heart not to expect much, but it was thudding a steady rhythm of happiness as I read the message.

I'm home and doing much better. My brothers said you visited me in the hospital. Thanks!

The sigh of relief that escaped my lips felt like I had been holding it in for weeks. I couldn't get rid of the sight of Manny in that hospital bed from my brain, and hearing he was out was amazing news.

I debated how to respond now but didn't want just to let things hang between us. I decided to be the better person in this case.

If you ever want to talk or grab a coffee, let me know.

My finger was still over the send button, not certain if I wanted to open this door again. I was getting better at dealing with Manny not being in my world. If I went out with him, even in just the capacity of a coffee date – it would unwind weeks' worth of my moping, slacking, and craziness. Did I want to go there? I focused hard on the message and finally hit send, then flipped the phone over. I knew it was strange like I wouldn't see any bad news if he texted that he didn't want to see me or something.

I went back to answering the litany of emails that were piling up in my inbox. It was a struggle not to glance at the phone every couple of seconds, and then wait for his reply made me go completely mad despite it being less than two minutes later.

I finished twelve emails, sent a couple of messages to my administrative assistant, and readied for a staff meeting tomorrow morning. The work made the time slip by when thirty whole minutes later, the phone danced on the table. I rolled my shoulders and reached for the device, flipping to see a text message had arrived. Opening it slowly, I read:

Can't get out right now, but if you want to stop by, I do have some coffee. And we probably need to clear the air.

My heart thudded painfully against the wall of my rib cage. Going to Manny's house seemed a huge gamble. On the one hand, I was free to rise and leave if he stepped out of line, but it would put me on his home ground. He would have the advantage.

Seriously? The man was injured from a bad motorcycle crash – how much of an advantage could he have? I just stared at the message, not certain that this was the right time. I realized that screaming or cussing at a man as hurt as Manny was not the right response. I wasn't certain I would keep my cool around him with everything that transpired from our last official date.

I put the phone down and just tried to do a couple of last things on the computer. I allowed my brain to mull the pros and cons of seeing Manny again, and finally, I picked up the device and texted.

I will bring some pastries if you make the coffee. Let me know when and where.

She hit send before her logical side could fully take back control of her actions. She knew this was probably one of the most foolhardy things she had ever done, but honestly, she didn't care. She needed to see Manny, and either moves forward or put this craziness behind her once and for all.

I'm available now, 2244 Tree Lane.

She glanced at the clock and knew that almost everyone else had gone home for the day. Looking at the calendar and to-do list, she had finished most of what she had on them for the day and could easily make this work. Besides, the address wasn't that far, and she could swing by the bakery on the first floor of the building to grab a few pastries. She finally just picked up the phone and texted.

Be there in thirty minutes.

Then closing of her laptop made short work of packing up for the day and heading out. Exactly thirty minutes later, pink bakery box in hand, she stood at Manny's front door feeling more nervous than ever. As she raised her hand to knock, he flung the door wide, hunched over crutches.

"Hey," she said, forcing a smile as the nerves ricocheted throughout her body.

"Come on in," he said, hopping backward to let her inside. She followed as he went through the hallway to a small dining table just outside his kitchen.

"How do you take your coffee?" He asked as if they were old friends just having a nice informal meeting.

"With cream, if you have it?" She said, glancing about his place.

I quickly determined that the sparse furnishings, leather couch, large screen television, dining table, and a few items were lying about screamed bachelor pad. The home itself had nice bones and was not overly messy, just not beautifully decorated. She wasn't that surprised as she realized that Manny probably didn't spend a lot of time here before his accident. Now, he was sort of stuck, and now he wished he had done more to make the space cheerier.

"I like the basic, empty look you have going here," she said, trying to crack the ice between them as he carefully juggled her mug to the table while using one crutch.

68

"Yeah, my home is my castle, but I haven't done much to jazz it up," he agreed.

She waited for him to bring a mug of coffee for himself. Rolling her shoulders, she reached for the pastries in an effort to keep herself busy. The tension in the space was thick enough to cut with a knife.

"I think I owe you an apology," Manny said, catching her totally off guard.

"Okay, for the scene at the restaurant?"

"That and even getting into this with you," he said with a heavy sigh. "I'm not the relationship type, and I know that. I do really like you, and honestly," he sighed, looking off into the distance for a moment.

She wished she could read what was going on in his head. The words he had uttered so far had made her hopeful with that apology, immediately followed with despair with his quick take on relationships. Seriously, it was like a bad roller coaster ride with Manny – and she just wanted her feet back on solid ground.

"I have a lot of resentment and bottled anger over my childhood," he said thoughtfully. "I didn't get a lot of answers regarding my dad, why he left, and such. I have so much aggression, anger, and bitterness that I normally direct at my mother – because I blame her for lying to me," he said simply.

"What did she lie about?"

"Well, she didn't really lie, she just never has wanted to discuss my father or what happened between them. I guess I just always questioned all the secrecy," he admitted bobbing his head slowly as he took a swig of coffee. "I want to have a healthy, honest relationship, get married, and have a family – I do. I just didn't have a fabulous example of that, and even though my stepdad was cool, and we all did our best – this anger still gnaws at me sometimes."

69

"I understand," I said.

I truly did. I hated the fact that the relationship with my family was so sour. That I didn't have that strong support network, I always dreamed I would. No one to celebrate my victories or cry to when life got too hard. It was part of the reason I was so hard, cynical, and sometimes way too harsh in my dealings with others. I couldn't really fault Manny for the same things.

"I know that the last day in that restaurant, I overreacted," Manny said, looking me deadpan in the face. "I just can't explain what happens to me when someone disrespects a woman or me – it is like waving a red flag at me. I go berserk and try to teach them a lesson. My emotions get the best of me, and I react without thinking. I need to learn to relax and just let it go."

"I understand and have some resentment issues myself," I acknowledge. "Which is why I probably overreacted myself with how I dealt with the situation."

"We are quite the pair, huh?" Manny said, holding his cup to his lips for a moment before taking a swig. "I can't stop thinking about."

My heart fluttered despite not wishing him to be injured in the accident. I felt amazing knowing I was not alone in my pining for him during our time apart. I just had this inkling, though, that he was working up to something, and from the expression on his face, I wasn't going to like it.

"Spit it out!" I said, not able to hold back any longer, as his forehead had deep worry lines crossing it now.

"You know as much as I adore you, and think given time, this could really be something," he stopped drawing in a deep breath, "we can't do this. I think we would be volatile and just hurt each other in the long run."

And there it was – the cold hard truth. The one man that made me feel more than all others on the planet didn't want me. I didn't have any valid arguments against his conclusion and even agreed that as up and down as things had been since we met, he was probably right that we would end up hurt in the end. That said, it didn't stop my heart from throbbing its displeasure at this outcome. I needed to end this positively and take a modicum of dignity back from this trying situation.

"I understand," I said as serenely as possible. "I think we finish this coffee and the amazing pastries, and part friends. What say you?"

"Friends," he said, holding out the mug as we clinked them together to seal the agreement.

I knew I would cry myself to sleep later, but for now, I would enjoy what little time I had left with Manny.

CHAPTER 13

I stood staring out the front window, getting lost inside my own head again. Wondering if I should just finally give in and call her. *Would I appear weak? Would she take the call? What would I say?* This indecision had become a constant companion, causing me no solid sleep, eating, or anything else without thoughts of Sandi interfering.

"I like this one," Carlos called out, causing me to turn in his direction.

The insurance paperwork had gone through, and I was in the bike shop today picking out a new ride. The last bike I had for years and had customized it to all my preferences over that time. I intended to start simple again and then add as I went along, breaking it in. It was a good distraction after nearly two weeks holed up at home. I was still off from work for another week on doctor's orders and going crazy being cooped up with only me as a company. I had asked for Joey's assistance on picking a bike, and Carlos came along for the experience. Rigo couldn't make it since he lived quite some distance away. Hopefully, he would consider moving closer since we used to ride together when we were younger, and I missed that time together. Besides, the group attack would help when working on pricing.

"So, you are getting right back up on a bike," Joey asked as I examined the lines and specs of the one Carlos pointed out.

"Of course. You know, if you get bucked from a horse, they say you have to get right back up in the saddle," I said, trying to keep the expression as cheery as possible. I figured I would definitely wait until I was fully recovered, and no longer plagued by thoughts of Sandi, though, to ensure no repeats of this last incident.

After our meeting, I had expected to feel better. I knew I had done the right thing bringing any possible relationship to a close with her. It appeared that neither of us seemed to be in a place where love, fidelity, and even non-emotional conversations were possible. I was an ass and would continue to do reckless things. She deserved better.

That did not mean it didn't hurt a lot. She didn't even try to plead a case or disagree about not starting their relationship back up. She seemed to accept his decision, and they had a nice chat about the weather, work, and the latest tv show she was watching. The coffee and conversation lasted an hour and a half, then she stood, gave him a light hug, and slipped from his home without a backward glance. It should have been a good thing, as it normally was when a woman left without putting up too big a fuss. Of course, his dreams were now fully fixated on Sandi, and even when awake, she was all he could concentrate on.

He knew this would pass, and all he could do now was keep working on healing and moving forward.

"Remember this?" Carlos said, holding up a helmet that was for a child.

"Oh my goodness isn't that the exact one Mama got you

when you turned sixteen," I asked him, recognizing the flowery pattern. "She said that she didn't realize it was for a girl because she thought only boys drove motorcycles. Besides, it was the cheapest one in the store."

"She was attempting to be okay with me wanting my first bike," Manny said with a chuckle. "But I would have been laughed out of the neighborhood if I had been caught with this."

"So, I remember helping you outfit it with flames and skull and crossbones that I painted," Carlos said with a light chuckle. "She was not happy."

"She didn't say that, but that little tick in her throat," Joey said, pointing at his own neck. "It would bulge out something fierce when she was trying to remain cool. That day it was the size of an orange. She said you looked like you were joining a bike gang," he chortled.

"I know," Carlos said. "But the naked woman that Manny put on his ended up being worse. She never did mention mine again. However, I don't remember her ever getting us bike gear either. And thanks to Manny, I think she is going to ask us all to wrap up in bubble wrap when we ride from this point forward."

"I didn't mean to crash my bike," I said, trying to defend myself.

"Right, but we also don't normally go out without telling anyone where we are for that reason," he said.

"Sorry, you know how it is when you just need to clear your head, and a ride is the only way that will work," I said with a small sigh. "Besides, my injuries can't have caused her as much as her favorite son Joey and the motorcycle incident when you were ten."

"Oh, my goodness," Manny turned, "I forgot about that one for a minute. We surely did shorten Mama's life with all the things we pulled. How exactly did you end up with handlebars in her shoulder like that?" He grimaced.

"I was riding over that blind man's bluff so fast, and it just flipped on me. I got pinned with the handlebar because the padded end was off – it went through my shoulder," Joey offered up.

"I remembered that hospital show, where the doctors told a guy not to remove the metal from his stomach. They said he could actually bleed out. So, I went and got that old set of cutters and went to town."

"It was so painful as he sawed through it and kept moving me back and forth," Joey said. "Though seriously mom's face, when I walked in and asked to go to the hospital calm as can be."

"I remember," Carlos said. "I thought one of us underaged fools was going to need to rush her and you to the hospital together."

"That turned out to be sixteen stitches and a good grounding," Joey shrugged. "That's nothing."

"Who do you think spent more time in trouble and grounded when we were little?" Manny asked as all eyes turned in my direction.

"Hey, I did you all a favor," I said with a smirk. "I mean, Mama was so busy with all my detentions and calls to the principals' office and minor brushes with the law, you got away with more."

"He's not wrong," Carlos said. "Remember prom night?" He asked, looking between Manny and Joey.

"I think to this day; no one knows who tagged the principals' car that night," Manny snickered.

"See, I believe we all did our fair share keeping Mama guessing what catastrophe she would be handling next," I defended after the earlier comments about my accident.

"That's fair," Joey said with a slight bob. "Hey, what about that blue one," he pointed into the corner as we all started that way.

This was my happy place. These were my people, and even when women came and went, accidents happened, and we fought with each other – we were always family at the end of the day. I was extremely fortunate, despite all my trials and tribulations, to have this group by my side always.

CHAPTER 14

I was sitting outside on the porch waiting for Joey. He was on his way to come and visit me because he wanted to talk about 'something.' That was all he would say when he called earlier when Carlos was here. Carlos asked me if I had called Sandi to thank her for coming to see me, and I finally confessed to the coffee meeting we had and how I had told her about not seeing each other as I was just a hopeless guy with too many problems. I couldn't even pinpoint why I was this way… I just was. On the bright side, my leg was much better now, and most of my wounds had healed to a reasonable extent. My body still hurt like crazy, though.

I froze mid-thought when Joey's bike pulled up to the curb down a ways from my house, and I sat up ramrod straight, ready for his talk – whatever that was going to entail. He was Mama's mini-me and the peacekeeper in the family. Meeting Angela had only made him focus more on family and happily building the next generation.

"How you been?" he asked as he clomped up onto the porch and lowered himself into a chair beside me. I wanted to give a snarky reply, but I could see that he was not in the mood. We hadn't discussed the incident with Mama in front of everyone as we went shopping this past weekend, and I wondered if that was where he was going with the visit and question.

"Better," I said, deciding to just go with the truth. The fact was, I would soon return to work, and I was feeling better physically and mentally.

He glared at me, and I could tell Joey was trying to curtail his frustration. He seemed to be waging an internal battle with himself, and I let him try to work through it for a few moments. Finally, I just couldn't take it anymore!

"Just let it out, bro. You're angry, I shouted at Mama, right?" I spit out. I hated having Joey upset at me, as he was the brother I really trusted most. That said, he was also Mama's favorite and so I could understand how conflicted he must be right now.

"I tried talking to Mama last night, but she wouldn't say a word to me," Joey started staring off into the distance. "I think I finally understood your issue with Mama. I just didn't realize how deep it went."

"Here we go. Mama 2.0," I mused aloud. "What do you have to tell me?" I tried to relax on the chair and not allow this tension to seize up all my muscles. But if he didn't start telling me something of substance soon, I might go stark raving mad.

"You blame Mama for not telling you all about dad."

My eyes shot wide open. I sat up and glared at him. "Papa left on his own accord, and you know that. Carlos has confirmed this for you, and he's the only one who remembers anything about him. You might be resentful or hold a grudge against Mama because she doesn't like talking about him, but that's not the real problem here."

"Watch your mouth, Joey," I growled as my fight mode

78

started to gear up. I didn't want to discuss this, and I definitely didn't want some crappy answers from him. I guess I did blame her, I was bitter, and it was that simple!

"Or what? What are you going to do with half a leg and numerous bruises?" Damn. This asshole was still making fun of me while giving me another lecture. "You know I'm right. The real problem is that you blame Mama, and you feel unworthy of being loved because Papa left. That is why you don't even try to become a better person for anyone else or open yourself up for love. You just assume they will won't love you in return."

"Dude, I know you want to be like Mama so bad, but—"

"That stubbornness of yours. That right there is your second main problem," he said. "Do you think being bitter or holding a grudge gets you anything? From what I saw in that hospital visit, you have a woman who cares a lot about you. Have you even told her your real feelings, or are you just gonna walk away instead of giving her a chance?" He kept hitting points that started pissing me off. Why was he so right? If I admitted he was right, I would feel like such a loser. I really should have called her and talked to her since she came to see me even with things were off between us.

"I did call her, and we had a good conversation. I agreed that we were not good for each other despite what you might think. I decided we should go our separate ways," I said, hoping that bit of information might shut him up for good.

"Figures," he huffed, shaking his head. "You made the decision and took the easy way out and got rid of her before she could hurt you." Joey insisted. "If holding a grudge is one of your instincts, then being bitter is your primary issue. You're a bitter person, and you just need to let it go. You will never be happy if you can't leave the past behind and stop making excuses for not deserving happiness and love. You kept calling for her when you were unconscious. Stop this,

Manny. I am your brother, and I love you. I had my relationship problems with Angela, but we figured it out. We made
an effort because we wanted to be with each other. So, ya I
do know when someone is trying to hide their inner feelings.
You need to do better with the women in your life."

I wanted to scream. Why was he so right? It was so
embarrassing being called out by my little brother.

"Can you just leave me alone? I don't want you to keep
talking!" My hands were on my ears now. I felt so conflicted
and confused. Why did I have to listen to this? I had buried
these thoughts deep inside and filled them up with confidence... or so I thought. "I am tired. I don't wanna—"

"She cried," Joey said, stopping me dead. "I heard her
crying in her room just before I left. In case you still think
she doesn't love you. You made our Mama cry, and I'm not
sure I can forgive you for that. You are so much more than
this sad excuse for a man you are projecting right now."

Joey got to his feet. "Stop blaming her for our father's
mistakes. We all blame others when we can't face the reality
of who we have become. Stop blaming Mama and just let it
go. Accept that what happened was the past, and we were
just kids. Only then can you move forward and be happy." He
left.

I sighed. I felt vulnerable and that I was being forced to
tear down all the walls I had built to protect myself. I was so
afraid that they would see me as vulnerable if I told someone
my true feelings. I guess I was wrong. I knew what I had
to do.

I headed for my truck and climbed inside. I could feel the
tension holding me in check as I put it into gear and headed
out. I was driving slower than normal, processing everything
Joey had mentioned. When I arrived at my destination, I sat
in the truck, staring up at the house and thinking about what
direction I wanted my life to go.

Finally, I opened the door slowly and got down with great difficulty due to my still-healing body. I was still in a lot of pain, but I had to push through it. Earlier that week I had several strangers coming up to me asking what had happened when they saw me walking with crutches.

I knocked on the door, and after a few seconds, Estrella opened the door for me. She and I weren't particularly close but not for any reason, probably other than the age difference and the chip on my shoulder I had been wearing for years.

"Hey," I said as we stood at the door awkwardly.

"Hey." She said, just staring at me with her jaw clenched.

"Is Mama around?" I just sat there feeling more dejected by the second. What if she didn't let me in? What if I had finally burned this bridge good? We sat there, considering each other in silence for what seemed an eternity. Finally, she moved aside for me to enter. Mama was seated on her favorite chair. She had paused her telenovela, which is a Spanish soap opera, to see who had entered. I'm sure she heard my truck and already knew it was me.

"Estrella, could you give us a moment?" she said, and Estrella nodded before going upstairs. I sat down and faced her, looking sheepish as I tried to find the words to apologize.

I just sat there, rubbing my hand together, trying to find the right words to say.

"You just can't do as you're told, huh?" she said. "You drove all the way here when you're supposed to be resting and taking it easy."

"I brought the truck, so it's a bit safer. Besides, the doctor should clear me tomorrow, anyway. Mama, I'm sorry," I said. "I don't know what came over me that last night when we were all here. I... shouldn't have treated you the way I did or said the stuff I did. I was a really stubborn kid to raise, and you did the best you could."

"Mijo, you just need to let it go. Your father left because he was unfaithful, and I was not going to allow this type of behavior," Mama said. It looked like she really wanted to get validation of her parenting from me based on her reaction. "I'm sorry too. Maybe I should have been more open and shared more about your father. But at that time, I was so angry at him for doing this, and I just didn't want to talk about the past because it was too hurtful. I just wanted to forget about it and let it go. Sometimes people will hurt us, and we just need to let it go. I should have listened to you and explain this, but I didn't want to rehash old wounds."

"I don't need to blame you or get to know him, Mama," I said. "You're enough, and I promise to make a bigger effort from now on, not just with you but in general." She smiled. "What about that girl? You should start with her."

"Oh, I plan to," I said with a sigh.

I couldn't deny it any longer that I was truly going to try and turn over a new leaf that would include making a choice to just open my heart to Sandi. She was the only woman that had so fully captured my imagination, heart, and mind – and she didn't seem all that appalled by my behaviors. As soon as I could muster it and not look a total idiot– she was going to find herself wooed until she just couldn't resist me any longer.

I sat there for a moment and then realized there was no time to waste like the present. Why wait and plan for a future when I could make now a reality! I jumped on my truck, not allowing another minute to pass, and off I went.

I got to her house and excitedly walked up the steps. This felt like the first day of the rest of my life. I was shaking as I knocked on her door and waited. I turned to see people walking around and the sun shining. The pain was keeping me alert, but it was more manageable than just days previous. Turning back to the door, I realized she wasn't there.

I wondered if she could possibly be at work. I took off but didn't find her there either. Finally, I pulled over, decided to do what I should have before starting this crazy trip, and called her.

"Hey! Where are you?" I yelled when she picked up. "I stopped by your home, but you weren't around."

I felt this stupid giddiness gurgling up. Just the sound of her voice did crazy things to me inside.

"Are you okay, Manny? Are you truly out driving around? Is it ok for you to do that with your injuries still healing?" She bombarded me with questions. "I'm standing right outside your house, as I just finished a run," she finally let me know."

"I'm on my way. Thank God it's not far from where I am right now. Stay where you are!" I clicked the touchscreen to disconnect the call as my brain went spinning in a million directions.

Within five minutes, I was driving up to the curb right in front of her place. On seeing me, she just stood with a slight wave looking so beautiful but totally confused about what was going on.

"Mann-"

I quickly opened the driver's side door, walked towards her, placed my arms around her, and gave her the biggest hug before she could even finish saying my name. There was passion in her lips and her warm cheeks. I pulled her close to me like I needed to devour even more of her than he already was taking. I wanted to give her as much as she wanted. I didn't care that we were in the street. We could be at my workplace for all I cared. I was going to hold onto this woman for the rest of my life.

Our lips finally parted, and our hearts were beating fast, and we were breathing as if we'd just ran a marathon.

"I've missed you so much," I said. "I'm sorry for everything and not getting in touch with you." I cupped her cheek with his palm.

"Where did this massive change of heart come from? You know if we do this, I don't want us to be fighting and breaking up again next week," she said, trying to protect her heart from another break from me like I had done previously.

"I am just a jerk, but I wanna be someone better... something more. I wanna do it for you because I love you, Sandi."

"I love you too, Manny. I know it is super soon to say that, but I think I knew something special about you the first time I saw you. I can't get you out of my head," she said in a tone that sounded like a confession.

"I'm not really good at expressing my feelings, so instead of going through a boring monologue, I'll just say that I love you and wanna love you forever." I kissed her again, and never in my life had I felt more loved.

"I think we should start fresh and see where this can go," she said, taking a step back from me and extending her hand. "Hi, I'm Sandi Bailey."

I took the hand with a giant grin on my face, "Manny Mendoza, tell me all about yourself, Sandi – I want to know everything."

"I don't know if you can handle everything," she told me, wrapping her arms around his neck.

"There's only one way to find out," I said, bringing my lips crashing down on hers.

CHAPTER 15

"*A*re you going to tell me where we are going?" I asked Manny as I held tight to him on the back of his spanking new bike. It was a beauty, but I still wasn't completely sold on riding these bikes. After all the ups and downs of these past weeks, it was our first official date, and I would have gone anywhere with this man.

He just shook his head and kept driving at my question. I like the mystery of not knowing. We had agreed to some dates each of us would plan, and he had gone first. It was the day after our big proclamation of love, and I felt on top of the world. Yesterday we had ordered in taking out, watched movies, and talked – really talked about everything for hours. It had been the best time, and I had learned so much. I was in love with this man, and everything I learned made it even sweeter.

Suddenly he slowed and then turned to a side road. This place was up in the hills outside the city, and she didn't really know what to expect. Suddenly, there was this huge outdoor ropes course and other activities laid out. I didn't even know these were up here. As Manny pulled over and helped me off the bike, I was taking everything in.

"I thought we could get in some great exercise as I know you love a good workout. Then I have a special lunch planned," he said with the biggest grin on his face.

I grabbed both his cheeks in my hands and pulled him in for a kiss. "That was why you mysteriously told me good workout shoes and clothes."

He nodded, took my hand in his, and started for the main check-in area. "I honestly didn't realize they had something like this up here."

"Yeah, it is great. You think it looks easy enough to do, but those topes are tough. Also over there," he pointed to what looked like a look-out area, "you can actually scale down the side of the hill – mountain as I like to call it," Manny teased.

"I want to try it all," I said enthusiastically.

We did the ropes course, which definitely was a balancing challenge. Then we did learn how to rock climb down the side of a good-sized hill, and finally, we did this obstacle course made out of trees, tires, and another climbing wall. After three hours or so, my body was screaming for some food from all the workouts.

"You finally ready for lunch?" Manny asked, drawing me away from the place. He stopped at this little shack area, and the kindest old lady handed him an old-fashioned picnic basket.

"I'm so hungry. I did not know how much work you were going to make me do on this date," I teased Manny as he walked me over to this overhang looking out over our city. It was so pretty.

"I figured a good appetite, fresh air, and good conversation over lunch would just make you love me even more," he said, dropping a kiss on my lips. I held him hostage, a few seconds and then backed up as he dropped to the ground with me right beside him.

"This is amazing," I said. "You know I am so grateful that we are taking these dates to grow with each other even more. I think we are just going to get stronger and stronger."

"Agreed," Manny said. "I realized that I can't continue to allow my past, and you can't allow yours to hold us back anymore. For instance, instead of being worried, I won't be a good dad because of the example I had in my own father, I am flipping that around. If I ever become a father, I will actually take everything I learned from my dad's bad example and turn it into lessons to help make me the best father possible," he said, drawing out a sandwich he handed to her.

I stared at him for a long time, and at that moment, I fell in love with him all over. I know this man is the one that I can grow with, love with, and walk through life with from this moment forward. He has so much to give, and deep down, he just wants to be loved and accepted just like everyone. He is finally learning from his mom and dad and no longer appears to simply blame them for everything that happened. They both would be so much better in the future if they continued to focus on the positive.

They sat there for hours again, chatting about kids, ambitions, and dreams for the future. Every moment seemed to be built on the last, and I knew as we finally climbed back on the bike at the end of that long day, I didn't ever want to be separated from Manny again. All the misunderstandings, time spent challenging each other, fighting these feelings, and nearly self-destructing had brought us together. Now I will fight with everything I am to keep them together, and luckily, I have a great partner in Manny to help me succeed in this relationship.

EPILOGUE

*E**ight months later*
       "Babe, we're gonna be late!" I said to Sandi while at the door. She was always like this—late as usual. *Why couldn't she be more on time?* I calmed myself down as I had been trying to do recently. It's how women were, or at least this one, and honestly, it was just one small part of a complicated package. I just had to get used to it. Besides, it was a small price to pay for getting to be with the love of my life.

She came down the stairs looking majestic as always. Every time I saw her, it felt like the first time. I could almost feel myself falling in love with this gorgeous woman all over again. Sandi wore a simple pink dress with some red designs, and she still looked otherworldly. I never thought I would be the guy to be fawning over dresses that women wore, but I am now happy that I was that guy. Goddamn. Sandi's red lipstick matched the red designs, and she had also dyed her hair red. Sandi usually fluctuated between hair colors, but now she was on red. Her beautiful brown eyes completed me every time I got lucky enough to gaze at them. I almost slapped myself on the face because I just couldn't believe that this lady was mine... and I was hers.

"What?" she inquired, looking a bit insecure.

"I love you," I blurted out in defeat, and she chuckled.

"You say that like three times every day," she noted. "You're making me feel like I'm not saying it enough."

I rushed over to her and kissed her on the lips. As always, she tasted perfect. I didn't even care that her lipstick was getting rubbed on my lips. Everything in this life was worth kissing her over and over again.

"Now you've ruined my lipstick," my love said after we had kissed. "You're lucky I have it in my purse." We walked out and got into the car, blasting Freddie Mercury while driving to our double date with Joey and Angela. This part of the journey was great. We always did this on our nights out in an attempt to put us in a good vibe, and it hadn't failed us yet.

On getting to the restaurant, we saw Joey and Angela already seated by the corner. They waved at us, and we walked over to them.

"You must always be early, huh?" I joked as Joey got up to his feet to give me a handshake that morphed into a manly hug while the girls did their thing.

"Slowpoke," Joey retorted. I then hugged Angela affectionately. She was as pretty and vibrant as ever.

"Hope you're keeping him outta trouble?"

"More like he's keeping me out of trouble," she said with a smile.

The truth was we balanced each other out with good communication, the occasional fight, and always agreeing not to go to bed mad. It was working better than I could ever have imagined, and my family was fast accepting her into the fold.

"Hey, how is your mom doing," Sandi said, glancing at

Joey. "I figured you would check on her before you came out."

My Mama was going downhill with each passing day. She had a constant stream of help with the family, though, and we kept each other informed of any changes. It was odd to me how something so heart breaking as her impending passing could have everyone come together. We all communicated well about anything with her and spent time these days really appreciating the small things like even a meal in each other's company. It was another blessing I like to keep on the list, despite my sorrow that soon Mama would no longer physically be here with us.

"You know I see tiny declines all the time," he said as Angela put her hand on his back.

"We will continue to take turns making her comfortable and letting her live the rest of her time on her terms," she said as Joey leaned over to kiss her soundly.

"I'm more than willing to help out in the schedule also," Sandi offered. "You just need to let me know."

I reached under the table and squeezed her hand. The family and I were having to come to terms with Mama's deteriorating condition. It was part of the reason I finally gave up the huge chip on my shoulder about my father. It wasn't her responsibility to make me feel better, but I could certainly make her remaining time happy. Sandi was helping in that regard also, and in the end, family was family. I leaned in to kiss the love of my life, so grateful for these past eight months and super curious to see where the future could take us.

CARLOS

CHAPTER 1

*T*he girl threw coffee in the guy's face, slapped him so hard even I flinched, and then she walked away, head held high. I had to wonder what that was all about. The man just sneered as if it didn't mean anything and pulled his cellphone out as he started walking away. The man was chatting animatedly now to someone on the electronic device as if nothing bad in the world could go on today. I would bet he was chatting up another woman already and looked as if he did not care a lick? I would have turned, crawling on hands and knees back to the beautiful, feisty brunette that had just let loose on him. Now she would be fun; I thought with a smile as I took a swig of coffee and turned to see what other craziness was happening here in the park today.

I loved sitting on the bench, drinking my coffee, and just observing people. I know that is kind of creepy to say, but it's the truth. People fascinated me because I always felt different from other people. Manny was basically a loveable asshole who had no problem picking up on women, starting conversations with strangers, and generally viewed people as playthings for the most part. Joey was the good old boy who everyone loved because he was easy to get along with. Joey tried to mediate issues, get along with everyone, and when they were in discord with the brothers, he was the peacemaker. Mama was akin to those badass females you see in action movies. She raised all her kids, survived the ass that was their father, and tried to keep her family together. Rigo – who lived elsewhere now and wasn't around much, was a neutral, all-around good guy. They were all fairly good at communicating with others, and that made me... uncomfortable. I wanted to see how people could act so freely around others since it was hard for me. Hence, my obsession with scrutinizing people.

Wait! I stopped middle of my contemplation as the man on the cellphone was suddenly approached by another woman, a redhead this time. He greeted her with a smarmy look as he bent to kiss her unabashedly in front of the crowd gathered in the crowd, and she returned it as if this creep were the love of her life. I didn't know how I knew he was a creep, but after observing so many people in my life, I just knew this was not a nice man. The woman leaned back and said something I could not hear, but the man's face blanched a white I had never seen before. Then I saw her...the brunette from earlier, walking back toward the two of them, and she had the most amazing smile on her face as she walked up to the guy. The redhead and the brunette were not going at this poor guy, and I sat with a smile spreading across my lips just watching this all go down and, as usual, thinking about how mundane my life was, but that kind of drama seemed a tad much...even to me. I realized I was staring and the threesome oddly and turned to get lost back in my own thoughts. I focused on other things swirling around us and did not fixate on that dramatic scene playing out.

I watched other lovers smile as they traveled the path in the park, hand in hand, lost in each other's eyes. Mothers drank their lattes and chatted with their friends while their kids played. I didn't have a lot of friends other than my brothers because I was told growing up that I had an expression that looked angry, and people felt I wasn't approachable. It became apparent early in life that there was a low chance of my meeting someone or getting married and having children. Thankfully, my mother never once nagged me about finding a girlfriend and seemed to accept me with this little quirk in my personality. I was twenty-nine now and not getting any younger, but to be honest, I was happy I wasn't pressured or given a bad time for not dating much. Even my brothers who regularly made fun of me stopped using the 'get a girl' angle. Even now that two of them were on the path to matrimony, no one seemed to expect or be pushing for a similar fate for me.

Now, though, they were with their girlfriends. Joey even proposed to Angela while I was present. Manny was happy with Sandi—and he was the last person any of us thought would settle down—and Rigo was... Rigo. Even Mama, after Papa left, found her happy ever after in her second husband and had a couple more kids, my stepsisters. It was my cross to bear that I would not be able to follow the others in this family tradition.

I always wondered why I was the odd one out. I had found comfort in my silence and solitude, but seeing others look so happy made me yearn to find the happiness they had one day. Maybe love? I have felt loved by my family, but I always wondered what true, romantic love would feel like. Rigo and I always believed that *true love* in the movies was overrated ... until he didn't anymore.

"That's enough thinking," I murmured to myself and got to my feet. "Time to work."

I went back to the mechanic shop that I owned, which was doing very well. This place was the single accomplishment that I had done that made me realize that while not emotionally able to connect, I was not a failure in life. I treated employees fairly, enjoyed working with customers, and ran an honest shop. Coming back in from my break, I saw Marco, my assistant, checking some engines.

"Marco," I said in my usual monotone way. Marco understood me and never made a fuss about the way I talked. He had been with me for years and seemed to interpret everything I didn't say aloud. He was the best right-hand man I could have hoped for to help me in this business.

"Oh, hey, boss. Good afternoon to you too," he said. Other guys were working on cars or taking their breaks. No one else acknowledged my presence, so I continued to my office. I noticed that Marco was traipsing right behind me, and I quickly realized he must need something from me. I entered, circled my desk, and sat down to wait for whatever he needed to discuss.

"Boss, can I come in?" Marco said, having stopped at the doorway. He was always considerate of my time and didn't like to impose.

I nodded after taking a seat at my desk. It was clear that he had something on his mind. Unlike me, Marco was very transparent and not good at hiding things, nor did he try to. Loyalty was a big thing for me, especially considering the childhood I'd had. I appreciated that about him, and it was one of the reasons I'd hired him. I like observing people's body language because you can tell a lot about a person by just paying attention to how they hold themselves. Ninety percent of what someone means is body language, and ten percent is what comes out of their mouths. If you know what to look for, you can usually tell if a person is lying.

"So, Marco," I said. "What can I help you with?"

He was seated across from me but wouldn't meet my gaze directly. "As you well know, boss, I am getting married in two months." I got an idea of where this was going. He looked at me, waiting for some acknowledgment, but I simply stared at him expectantly. I wasn't really certain what he needed and thus had no idea the reaction he was expecting.

"Well, after the wedding, Carol and I were thinking about going on a small honeymoon, and I wanted to ask you if I could take some time off."

I was shocked and surprised that he felt nervous about asking. *Did he really think I would say no?* I knew he was getting married, and two months' notice was plenty of time for me to prepare to cover his position.

"Of course," I said, not hesitating. He looked at me as if surprised that I understood. I guess he was expecting me not to approve his request. "Were you expecting a different answer?" He quickly shook his head. "Take two weeks. All I need before you leave on your honeymoon are the reports and ledgers," I told him. "I need to keep them updated, but I know you already know that."

"Yes, of course, boss." Marco beamed a wide grin. I could tell he was literally sweating, having to request time off. Damn. *Am I that difficult of a guy that my employees feel nervous asking me for something?* I thought to myself. Since I was a straight shooter, these things came rather easy, so I didn't understand why others would have difficulty asking. I was perplexed by this reaction, but it dawned on me that I was the boss, which might cause them anxiety. I never got mad, though and always tried to judge every request on its merit. Marco never took time and had plenty on the books. Besides, this was marriage, and I would never deny him time off during that important moment in his life.

"All right then," I said, pulling some papers toward me to show that the topic was closed. "Glad we figured that out. "Anything else on your mind?"

"No, not at all." He looked elated as he got quickly to his

feet. He headed for the door, but I stopped him before he got to it.

"Marco," I said as he reached the door, and he stopped, looking at me. "Congratulations. I am genuinely happy for you. I know you will be a great husband and father."

"Well, boss, I don't know about a great husband, but I definitely plan to be a great father. And I am sure you will be too someday when you meet that lucky lady," he replied with a smile.

I chuckled. "I appreciate you saying that, but I don't actually see that happening for me. You have a good one now," I said with a slight head bob as he slipped out the door.

I sat on my chair, staring at the ceiling and thinking about what Marco had said and what I could do to find that woman. I started thinking about my brothers finding their special someone, and now Marco was getting married. I would like nothing more than to find some woman capable of seeing the real me and still loving me without hesitation. I knew people usually became lonelier as they got older, and I still hoped to have children, so I knew I had to get started soon. But I wouldn't maintain a relationship if I didn't change some of my ways. I had no problem voicing my opinion in business situations, but communication and openness have always been issues in personal relationships. According to a therapist I had visited several times, I had blocked out a huge part of my childhood, but somehow, I always thought I would manage.

My phone rang, and I noticed it was Mama. I quickly coughed to make sure my voice was okay. Mama was the only one who could tell when I was trying to hide my feelings.

"Hello, Mama," I greeted, plastering a smile on my face as that was supposed to make you sound more approachable on the telephone; I had read someplace.

"What's wrong?" What the hell? Was this woman a psychic or something?

"What do you mean what's wrong?"

"Cut the crap, Carlos. You sound stressed." She barked back and me in that tone that was not easily argued with.

"How do you even know these things?"

"A mother always knows. What's the problem?" She said, and I knew she was not about to let it drop. My shoulders sagged as I knew I was going to have to fess up.

I took a deep breath and sighed. "I don't want to talk about it on the phone. Can we talk later this week when I come over?"

"Sure. I was actually calling to ask you to bring some of those vegetables you brought last time you came. They were really good. Can you bring some mangos and watermelon too?"

I smiled. "Sure, Mama. Anything for you."

"And whatever you're going through, I know you will be okay. You're my son, and you did help me raise your younger brothers. You can do anything," she assured me. "You're strong, Carlos. Never forget that."

"Thank you, Mama," I said gratefully. She always knew what to say to make me feel better. "Adios."

I hung up the phone and went back to thinking. It's not like I hadn't been involved with girls before; it was just that I'd never really gotten involved in a relationship. I knew it would end badly. Two different girls, in particular, really tried to take things further after we had one-night stands. They just ended because I wouldn't express my feelings, and they took that to mean I was insensitive and didn't care. I knew I needed to improve my communication skills and be more open if involved in a relationship. Looking at my own family, though, we didn't have the best role models, and being Latino; we didn't express our feelings. We were taught

99

just to suck it up and deal with it. So, communication was not easy to do and believing in love, and all that crap was not something we took seriously until we got older.

I heard a car pull in and decided to check it out to distract myself from these thoughts. Usually, Marco would go and check it out himself or ask one of the other workers to take care of it, but I needed to take my mind off things. I went outside and stopped short at what I saw... or, in this case, who I saw.

A woman was standing by her car with a hand on the open door. She was short and curvy as hell, with red hair that was neither long nor short. She had dark eyebrows and full pink lips. I walked over to her, noticing that she looked scared and confused as she watched Marco open the hood and check the car.

"Hello. Can I help you?" I asked as I approached, and she jumped a bit when she noticed me. She tilted her head back, and I could see by her wide eyes that she was taken aback by how large I was compared to her. She shifted back a bit. "Oh, sorry. I didn't mean to startle you," I replied, stepping back so as not to crowd her.

"Oh, y-yeah. Hi," she said.

"This is Carlos, the manager," Marco told her, pointing at me with a smile. "Carlos Mendoza."

"It's a pleasure to meet you, Carlos," she said softly, stretching her hand out for a handshake. "I'm Jennifer Foster." *Was it just me, or... was she blushing?* She was pretty as hell. Her smooth, soft skin felt amazing against the tips of my fingers as we shook hands. Mine was so much bigger than hers that it felt like I enveloped it completely.

"Marco, what do you think the problem is?" I asked, tearing my gaze away from Jennifer's face.

"The engine sounds a bit rough, so I think it probably just needs some servicing and a tune-up," Marco said, standing back and wiping his hands. "I'll also check the carburetor and change the oil. I don't think it's anything serious."

"Oh, dear, I hope not," Jennifer said, twisting her fingers together as she gazed at him nervously.

I chuckled. Many of our female customers didn't pay attention to their oil service and only thought about their cars when they started making strange noises. But they always knew when it was time to get their nails or hair done. They didn't mess with that.

"When was the last time you had an oil change?" I asked her, and she shook her head vehemently.

"Um... I don't know, maybe a few months ago. The sticker fell off the window, and I don't remember the last time. I thought I still had a few more miles to go since I hadn't seen any lights go on." She looked back at Marco. "Do you think it's the oil? How much is this gonna cost?" She sounded stressed. "The reason I ask is that I don't have much since I just started a new job, and I haven't gotten paid yet."

"Don't worry, it's on the house," I said, surprising myself. Marco glanced at me also like I might have just lost my mind, but he didn't say anything.

"Seriously?" She gushed, biting down on her bottom lip. "Seriously?"

Marco arched an eyebrow at me, looking as if he expected me to say it was a joke or something. I'm pretty sure he had never seen me give someone service for free. At best, it would be a discount, but free?

I was obviously so taken by this pretty lady and her openness and honesty that I wasn't thinking straight. But I'd made the offer, and I was going to stand by it. "Yeah, sure." I smiled at her. "It might take a while, so you sit and should relax while they fix it."

"Is there a place where I can wait?" Jennifer asked, and I directed her to the waiting room, which had a TV.

"We'll come to get you when it's done. Hopefully, it won't take too long," I said, and she ducked her head. *Why was she blushing so much?* This girl just met me. *And why was I so happy that she was blushing? Did the mere thought that Jennifer could like me make me suddenly so nervous I felt like running?* I turned, about to walk away, when she called me back.

"Uhm, hey!"

I turned and looked at her, trying to keep a neutral expression on my face. "Yeah?"

"I just wanted to say that I will pay you back. I appreciate this, and I will pay you every penny." She was still twisting her fingers together, and I could tell she was worried about affording it.

"Look, don't worry," I said, walking back to her. "It's really on the house. I don't normally do this, but for some reason, I can tell you are in a bind, and I want to help you."

"That's very sweet of you to help me out." She sniffed as if she was trying not to cry, and my heart did a weird flip.

I suddenly found myself sitting by her side. *What was going on right now?* I just waited for her to tell me what was wrong and see what else I might be able to do to make it all better.

CHAPTER 2

I was nearly tearing up at his generous offer and the kind way he was looking at me. *Why was my body so hot?* The beating of my heart increased exponentially the moment he sat beside me. I'd wanted him to sit down and talk to me, but now I didn't know what to do when he did! Glancing at him, I marveled at his thick dark hair, chiseled physique, and broad shoulders. I was sure he knew I was checking him out. *Why the hell had I not said anything?* I asked myself. Maybe he was a man of not many words, which was why he had not spoken yet.

"So, tell me, Carlos, do you have any sisters?" I blurted out so fast I almost did not hear myself speak. He looked at me with a slight grin, and my eyes could not keep from admiring his strong features and kind eyes. Wait. *Why the heck was I analyzing his body like it was a piece of art?* Well, he was sculpted like the statue of a Greek god, so...

He cleared his throat. "I am the oldest of seven. There are four boys total, and I have three step-sisters also," he responded.

I smiled. "I knew it! I figured you must have some sisters for you to be so understanding and helpful."

He returned my smile. "Yes, I do, and I would want somebody to help them if they were in a situation where they needed it."

I laughed at how sweet he was when talking about his sisters. I could tell he was a little uncomfortable with me asking him questions, but he was very polite and nice. The slight reddening around his collar, though, told me that he was bashful or may be uncomfortable. That seemed odd for someone his size and who looked like him, but I found it endearing again. Hopefully, he wouldn't realize how quirky I was.

"You're funny." I let him know, really excited that he hadn't just jumped up and fled from me already.

"More like different," he mused.

"I like different." I regretted saying that the moment the words left my mouth. *Why was I so nervous that I could not even filter what I said?*

"That's good to hear," Carlos responded, causing me to smile. "How about you?"

"Wait. Tell me more about yourself."

"I'm not a particularly interesting person. I own this shop, and sometimes I have conversations with pretty customers. The end."

"Somehow, I don't believe that." I made myself stop talking.

Carlos and I stared at each other in silence, our gaze fluctuating between each other's eyes and lips. The sexual tension in the air between us could have been cut with a knife. His eyes were light brown with tiny golden flecks... like honey. I like honey and wonder if his kiss would taste as sweet as the sugary liquid.

"You were saying...." Carlos finally spoke, taking me out of my head and the daydream I was having back to reality.

"Oh, yeah, sorry," I said, coughing once and ready to tell him more about myself. "I'm the youngest and have one brother. I am short, as you can see." We both laughed at that. "I love sports. Wrestling is my favorite."

"Really?" Carlos's whole face lit up gleefully at my proclamation. Looking at his build, I guessed it would not be a stretch to assume he loved fighting sports and other sports as well. He was very tall and athletic.

"Yeah, I'm serious!" I replied, happy that he was happy.

"Who's your favorite wrestler?"

And we embarked on an hour-long discussion centered around wrestling. We touched on favorite foods to eat at events when the last time we got to see wrestling and a million other details. I wished that the date...I mean, car appointments might never end. But then a man came into the room and gave Carlos a look before he turned to me.

"So... I guess your car is fixed and ready," Carlos said when Marco came in and handed him the keys. I had expected him to ask for my number and even took my time getting up, hoping he would get it over with. Nothing! Zip! Nada! The man was not going to do it. Well, it was after the time when we women had to bite our tongues and wait for a man...so I took the bull by the horns.

"Hey," I said as an idea came to my mind. "I should probably get your contact info in case I have any problems in the future."

Okay, not exactly asking him out, but at least now I had his information also.

"Oh, yeah, sure." He took out his wallet and handed me his card. "That's it right there. Call me if you have any problems."

"I will, and thank you so much." I hope he got the hint

that I would be calling him for service and not for my car. I had this mischievous look on my face as I stared at him.

He smiled. "Sounds good."

I made darn sure my backside, which I had been told was my best asset, moved seductively side to side as I walked away. The man was going to regret just letting me walk away, and I half hoped that he would run after me and drag me back to his place for a wild night of crazy lovemaking.

NOPE! I turned to find him give a little wave from the front window, and then he turned to go back to business, I presumed.

I got into my car and drove away. One thing was for sure: I would be calling Carlos before the day was over. I had fallen again, but I knew being careful should be my top priority right now. The last thing I needed was another broken heart, and Carlos looked to have all the right attributes to do just that.

CHAPTER 3

*R*iding my bike always made me feel relaxed and calm. I rarely got nervous, but this time, I was. Jen and I had frequently been chatting since the day her car got fixed. Honestly, it was the first time a woman had actually made an effort to call me before I tried to ring her. The fact was, like an idiot, I didn't even have her information, but she had taken mine, thankfully. That first night when she called, I had nearly passed out when I realized it was her. I found I loved talking to her and readily picked up the phone the second I saw it was her. It was the first time I didn't feel odd talking to a woman. She had such an easy way about her. I never felt awkward or like I wasn't good enough in any way. We started talking every day, and then she had dropped a bomb and said, "We should go to the fair this weekend. It will be fun, and we can go on the rides together. What do you think?"

"Yes, that would be great. When do you want to go?" I asked.

We made plans to meet at 6:00, but I, of course, was there at 5:30 because I hate it when people are late, so I am always early wherever I go just in case there is traffic and or an accident because you never know what can happen.

While riding, my mind was all over the place. I tried to think through topics I could entertain her with throughout the night and some of the social queues that my therapist had once gone over with me. So many thoughts flew through my brain until I remembered Manny telling me what happened the last time he got distracted on his bike and crashed.

Trying to put Jennifer out of my mind, I made the rest of the trip in short order. As I pulled my helmet off, I could feel my hands shaking and again had to chastise myself to take it easy silently. I was a grown man at the fair with a pretty woman…this should not make me feel like I was off to jail or something so grave.

I glanced at my watch and groaned. Sure, I was early, but maybe she also was someone that arrived ahead of schedule. Picking up my phone, I dialed her number.

"Heyyyy!" She said the moment she answered up the phone. I loved how lively and happy she always was.

"Hey, Jen," I said. "I'm at the fair. Should I-"

"Wait. You're there already?" She sounded half shocked and somewhat upset, to be honest.

"Yeah," I said, slinking back into myself. Maybe this was a tad too early.

"Wow. You're early."

"Yeah. It's a habit of mine."

"Where exactly are you right now at the fair?" Jen asked.

"Just outside the gate. Why?"

"Okay. I'll be right there." She cut the call short as I was kind of confused by that statement.

What the hell was she doing here this early? I waited for roughly two minutes before spotting her coming to the gate. She wore a pink top that accentuated her small waist and the flare of her wide hips. She had two gold bracelets on her wrists and a choker around her neck. Her red hair was alluring as always, but her blue eyes were simply enchanting. She bit on her lip as she approached me, and I felt my cock jerk in my pants. Damn, she was a firecracker...smoking hot and maybe a bit more than I was going to be able to handle. I was totally enthralled with Jen, though, because she was so quirky and fun despite being hot and sexy. I'm sure she could get any man she wanted or desired. Though at times she could be a little reserved, she always had a sweet and fun-loving spirit. I adored the different layers of this woman and how she made me feel so comfortable in my skin. I had never felt this way with a woman before, but I was definitely feeling something now. My heart kept beating faster and faster like I had run a marathon.

"Hey, handsome." I knew her voice was sexy as hell but hearing it in person was ten times better than over the phone. "Looks like we think alike in more ways than we realized."

"Why are you here so early?" I inquired with a confused smile.

"Well, I was a little nervous since this was going to be our first"—there was a pause— "time to get together." She avoided saying the word *date*. "So, I decided to arrive early because I didn't want to be one of those people. I'm kinda weird like that." She looked down on the ground and toyed with her fingers.

"Those people... yes, I know exactly what you mean," I agreed. "Anyway, now that we're here early, let's just go in and have a good time."

Jen smiled, holding my arm with both of hers, her large breasts pressing hard against it. I didn't think it was inten-tional, though. She was just a very breasty woman, and I loved that about her. "Yeah, let's do that."

We played a few games, and let's just say Jenn was not a

basketball or softball player. It was a different story with me having the brothers that I had. Being an extremely competitive family, we always had to challenge each other at everything we did. I won her a teddy bear that she said reminded her of one she had lost when they had moved as a child. I felt elated to win it for her and see her so happy, silently feeling better than I ever had with a woman for this long. About an hour later, after we had a corn dog and some fried artichoke hearts, Jen was ready to go on the roller coaster.

"Right now?" I asked. "We just ate, and uh, I... don't think it would be a good idea. We should probably wait a little bit."

She slapped my arm playfully. "It's fine. It'll be fun. Come on, let's go before the line gets longer."

"I didn't think you wanted to go on the roller coaster."

"Why? Because I'm a klutz?" she asked. I wouldn't have put it that way, but... *Yeah,* I thought to myself. Whenever I didn't know what to say, I just shrugged my shoulders. "I like to be adventurous and spontaneous," she said, biting her lip and giving me a teasing look that would send any man wild.

"Or maybe you think I'm afraid because you're afraid." She turned it around on me. To be honest, Jennifer did have a point. I was a relatively safe guy who usually resisted trying new things. I did like physical and manly stuff like biking and wrestling but not so many heights. Plus, we had just eaten, and I didn't want to get sick in front of her. I am the type of person who likes to plan and know all my options because I tend to obsess about what could go wrong, especially on a roller coaster.

"Don't be a scaredy-cat," she said, laughing as she trotted ahead of me. I found myself staring at her backside and realized I would follow her anywhere she demanded.

I would normally be unflappable in these kinds of situations. But things were pretty unclear this time. *Was I scared that she would see me being vulnerable? Was it because I had never attempted a roller coaster before?* I suspected that this was less about fear and more about uncertainty. I didn't engage in things without knowing all the variables, but I would do it this time for Jen because she had a way of getting me to do things that I probably wouldn't have otherwise.

I purchased our tickets, and we boarded the ride. I saw no sign of fear from Jennifer while we got in and buckled our seat belts. At first, I kept picturing all of the ways this could end badly, but the way she laughed and chattered finally distracted me from my nerves, and I concentrated on how being around her made me feel happy and calm.

Then Jen started rocking our car. I wanted to ask her to stop, but I couldn't let her know I was scared. What would she think of me? I tried not to show any fear even though I was screaming at the attendant to let me off inside. Part of my brain wondered if this relationship would work out if we were such different people, even though I knew it would be silly to break up with someone because they liked roller coasters.

"Ready?" Jen asked me with excitement.

She must really love these rides. "I guess so," I replied, trying to force a smile. She quickly faced forward as the car started to move. This was when my fear kicked into high gear. I began sweating, and my mind went back to running permutations on all the possible things that could go wrong. *What if a bolt loosened?* I'd watched Final Destination, so I knew how these things could go deadly wrong. I tried to calm myself down as we went higher, checking my seat belt and asking Jen not to shake the car. While trying to check her belt, my hand came into contact with Jen's. By now, we had reached the top, but I didn't want to look down because I was deadly afraid of heights. I remembered as kids when we'd painted our room a light blue color, and I didn't want to get on the ladder, so I'd insisted on painting the bottom part of the walls.

Jennifer turned to look at me after our hands wrapped around each other, and her sweet smile, that perfect upward arching of her lips, put me at ease. Peering into her blue eyes was enough to make me not care about what came next. She was here... and that's all that mattered. After a few seconds that I barely noticed, we went over the top and started down.

No matter how many times I tried, I could never explain the exhilarating feeling I had then. I had never been so close to a perfect blend of chaos and peace as I was at that very moment. We went down swiftly, with the sounds of the metal below us not doing much to ease my nerves. Virtually everyone was screaming, but I was just in awe. I could hear Jen screaming, so I turned to glance at her. The beautiful lady beside me was screaming and clutching my hand, and now she didn't look like she was enjoying the ride so much. For me, I didn't feel so good. My stomach felt like I'd left it at the top, and I was praying for this ride to the finish. The few seconds were becoming the longest minutes of my life, and I'd be lucky if I didn't throw up all over Jen. Forget the cinnamon roll I had been craving all day long. It was not happening now. Well, okay... maybe later I will change my mind.

After a minute, she stopped screaming and opened her eyes. Her free spirit was as mesmerizing as it was contagious. I couldn't stop staring at her despite the vicious wind blowing against my face and tossing my hair upwards. Jennifer's hands were raised to the sky, along with one of my hands since it was still locked with hers. She smiled so widely I thought her lips would stretch out of her cheeks. Her eyes watered from the wind, and I could see her white teeth, sharp canines, and pink tongue. How could I be upset at her for getting me on this ride? Just watching her joy was infectious. Amid all the fear and uncertainty that I'd felt on that ride, I would never have felt this joy either if it wasn't for her.

"Wow," she said after we got off the roller coaster. "That was pretty good for being my first time."

"Wait. What?" I stared at her. "That was your first time?"

"I never told you I had done this before, did I?"

"So why were you so insistent on doing it?"

"You only live once, right?" she replied with a smirk. "I had always been scared to go on it, but for some reason, it felt safer riding it with you. Not sure why. I guess I'm just con—"

I knew she was about to say something self-deprecating, so I stopped her... by kissing her. It was a tender and romantic kiss, with our lips connecting beautifully. It was almost as if her lips were made for mine. Stopping whatever she was going to say was just an excuse to lock lips with Jennifer. It was short and sweet. She bit my lip a little as I withdrew, which I found extremely sexy. My eyes opened just in time to catch hers open as well. Cerulean irises stared back at with immense affection.

"Well, that was...."

"Great," I said, echoing what we were both thinking. At that moment, I felt so happy and could see a future with a woman for the first time in my life. That alone should have scared me, but all I could think about was kissing her again and never letting her go.

CHAPTER 4

I stood still, staring at the mirror. Trying different outfits to decide which one he would like was more exhausting than I thought. I knew Carlos probably wouldn't really care what I wore, but I still wanted to impress him. It had been three days since we had kissed. He'd driven me home, and the feeling of hugging him with his large frame protecting me from the wind was amazing. I was falling for him faster than that first roller coaster ride we took together. This was a bad habit of mine, though. I was searching for love and falling so easily. I had never fallen for a man this fast, though. To be honest, I wasn't even looking for love. I had fought it, but everything about him was perfect. He was caring and loving while still retaining that alpha male presence I loved. He was quite a lot, which was difficult because I like to talk, but he was also a great listener, so it worked out.

"Another date?" A voice startled me.

Franklin, my brother, laughed when he realized he had scared me. He was a typical brother, always trying to get a reaction out of me...and succeeding more often than I liked.

Honestly, though, he was the best...though I would die before saying that out loud, as it would only fuel his crazy antics.

"What are you doing in my room?" I asked, masking all the sweeter sentiments I had toward him with the disdain in my voice.

"You should lock your door, sis," he said, sitting calmly on the bed. "If I were a burglar, it would have been too easy."

I scoffed and continued checking out my outfit in the mirror while seeing him over my shoulder. "Is Mom with you?"

"Nah. She had a recital." He shook his head. "Another date? I can barely keep up these days."

"Shut up," I retorted and stuck my tongue out at him for good measure. "This is the first guy I've seen more than once in over a year. Besides, I like him. I think we could be serious."

"That's what you said about Craig and Antonio before him." I glared at him, and he quickly shut up. "Okay. I'm sorry. Just... be careful, okay?"

"Is that a rare moment of genuine care from my brother?" I gave in a curious look, but he just glanced away, covering his own emotions by breaking eye contact.

He scowled, leading me to laugh. "Screw you," he said. "So, tell me about this guy." Usually, I would ignore him, but I wanted to talk to someone about Carlos. I wanted to scream out his name, tell all the people I met what a catch he was, and maybe break into show tunes. Yeah! I was feeling that good.

"His name is Carlos," I began. "He is tall, Hispanic, and reserved but genuinely nice. Anyway, he is a quiet guy for the most part."

"A quiet guy. That would be a first," Franklin jibed, and I

scoffed. "So that must mean you do all the talking as usual. Where did you meet him?"

I don't know what got into me, but I spilled everything to Franklin. From the first breakdown in Carlos's shop to the roller coaster ride. Of course, I left the kissing and some of the midnight conversations out but gave him the broad strokes, so he was mostly up to date.

"I must admit, I was wrong," he admitted as he got to his feet. I furrowed my brows, glaring at him with a confused face. "I mean, I was wrong in thinking that this was just another guy in your endless pursuit for love. You seem like you care about him. I hope it works out, and you don't get heartbroken."

"Thanks." I smiled. "But don't tell Mom, okay?"

"I won't...not yet," he said and headed toward the door.

"You're leaving?"

"Yep. You have a date, and I just wanted to come by and say hi." He walked toward the front door. "Wear blue. It matches your eyes."

I turned back to the pile of dresses and dug through until I found the perfect baby blue dress I had early discarded. Putting it on and glancing in the mirror...Franklin was right. Blue did compliment my eyes, and Carlos was sure to have to notice me in this one. I floated out of the house, ready for my date and to see just where this amazing trip of ours was headed.

A few hours later, I was sitting next to Carlos at a local bar. The deal was that since I picked the location of our first 'hangout,' as we both called it, Carlos would get to pick this one. He wanted to choose a place that best described him, and this was it. He was a manly man to the core. So here was I, seated with a beer in my hand, watching the wrestling match between Vasquez and Diop. A group of burly and muscular men was all around me, but I never once felt out of place. I felt so happy that he was honest enough to show me his den. He didn't think I was too girly for it or to be around men who, by the way, were very respectful.

"Oh, c'mon! Refff!!" I yelled at an uncalled-for cheap shot from Vasquez on Diop. We were rooting for different people, which made it more interesting. I was having a blast with the man I loved right by my side.

"Mehn, Carlos. Your girlfriend's a keeper!" the burly bald man who introduced himself as Gor, probably short for something, said to Carlos. I blushed after hearing that but remained facing the television.

"Oh, she's not my girlfriend." Carlos returned without missing a beat.

Maybe he thought I would not hear that, and honestly, I wish I hadn't. *What did he think we were? Did he just see me as a friend or someone he could kiss whenever he wanted? Why was I suddenly feeling a pit in my stomach?* I could barely concentrate on the match. *Why did this keep happening to me in my relationships? What the heck?*

The night continued with me being upset and unresponsive to most of any attempts at conversation from that point forward. I tried to be a bit nicer to Carlos' friends and ignore Carlos, just making quick responses to whatever he said. I guess it was my way of letting him know I was upset. If he were smart, he would pick up on it. But the night went on without him saying a word, which made me even more agitated and pissed off. *Could he not tell I was upset? Or did he just not care? Why would I want to date someone who was either clueless or insensitive?* The wrestling match ended, and Vasquez won. Amid all the cheers from the men behind me, I felt a hand squeeze mine; it was his. That was it. I quickly got up and left the bar. I was so annoyed and felt so humiliated. Quickly making my way through, I got outside, where I could finally breathe and get some fresh air. I did not even know what to say, so I just walked away.

"Are you okay?" Carlos called, following me.

"Yes. I'm fine." How could he not see I was annoyed and in pain? The man seemed not to be able to read me in any way. Either that or he didn't care, and I was just another cheap date along for a thrill, but not worth giving any real title...like a girlfriend.

"Then why are you crying?" He asked, bending down to capture my gaze, and he sincerely looked confused.

Are you kidding me? What? Was I crying? I didn't understand. The man seemed to be completely clueless. The only thing I could fathom was that women were meaningless objects to him, but that was not the vibe I ever got from him. I was so confused I just needed to get the heck out of here. I would not let another man destroy my self-esteem.

"You know what? No, I'm not fine. You're an ass!"

Carlos looked at me with shock, checking left and right to see if anyone else was standing there. "What's happening? Did I do something?" he asked.

Was he this clueless? "What am I to you, Carlos? What exactly am I?" I asked him point-blank. He seemed to consider this, which only annoyed me further. *Did I misread all this? Would he have kissed me if he didn't want anything more? What exactly were we?*

"You're... someone I care about," he said cautiously, obviously picking his words very carefully.

"What the hell does that even mean?"

"It means I like you, and... what do you want it to mean? I like you and enjoy hanging."

"Hanging out? Like hanging out with a friend or what? Do you like me as a girlfriend, Carlos?"

He was surprised by my question. Like, what was surprising about it? "Yeah..."

"Then why did you tell your friend that we weren't dating or that I wasn't your girlfriend?"

"Because we aren't. I don't know what you wanted me to say other than that." This guy... was he being serious right now? Did he have to make that distinction? "I didn't want to say the wrong thing. What if you didn't consider us dating?"

"You're joking, right?"

"I know it sounds strange because we kissed. But I haven't dated much, and I didn't know exactly how you felt, and I don't want to lose you."

"No, no, no, no, no. You do not get to play that nonsense. *I didn't know how you felt,* bullshit card. Do you want to date me? Yes, or no?"

"Yes, but—"

"But what, Carlos? I like you, and you like me. What's the problem?"

Carlos stared at me with such bewilderment and guilt that it made me sad. *Why did he look at me like that?* That wasn't love in his eyes; it was confusion.

Finally, he ran a hand over his eyes. "It's hard for me to communicate or express my feelings. I don't like talking about this stuff. You know I like you, so what's the problem? This is why I didn't know what to say because we never really talked about these things. See, this is why I didn't call you my girlfriend because talking about my feelings, and this stuff is not easy for me. I am trying to work on this, and I don't want to say something and have it come out the wrong way."

"Wrong way. Well, if you don't attempt, then you won't know. I don't have time to play games or get my heart broken again. If you don't learn to express your feelings, we can't be together because I can't read minds. If you can't say what you feel, then how will I know? I can't deal with this, and I don't think I want to," I said and walked away.

As I stormed off and began walking home, I started thinking about what he'd said. *Was I too harsh? Why did I have to act this way?* He had issues with expressing himself, and I knew that. Maybe I could've been a bit more understanding. I tend to react to my impulses and say hurtful things without considering others. Maybe that was one of my problems with past relationships, and these were red flags. He was also right about the fact that I'd assumed we were dating. We had never talked about it, but I'd thought he knew how I felt. We all know that we can't assume because we make an ass out of you and me when we assume. My boss once told me that, and it stuck with me. Maybe I had been overreacting, and he had a different definition of dating. Oh gosh, now what? What a mess I'd made.

However, I couldn't turn back now because I had already voiced my opinion, and I had to stand my ground. I was hoping he would run after and stop me from walking away and tell me he loved me. Tears ran down my face as I walked.

"Why do you have to be so mean?" I murmured to myself while walking. I needed someone to stop me because I was too hard and stubborn. I needed Carlos to catch me and say, *please don't go,* yanking my hand and begging me to stay. That was what I wished for, but the reality was Carlos was not running after me. He didn't stop me, and I also never looked back. I guess we both needed time to work on our communication skills, not just Carlos.

CHAPTER 5

I played the conversation with Jennifer over in my head again and again. I didn't comprehend everything that had happened. I was honest with her, and I didn't understand there at the end why she would flee from me. Honestly, I thought the argument led to us officially becoming boyfriend and girlfriend a second before she shut it all down so angrily.

The issue was my brain was processing everything in black and white facts, nothing more. In contrast, I had already come to realize that Jennifer felt more from words than just the simple meanings themselves. She was hot, cold, and a bit chaotic, which my much more reserved nature did not understand. I hated this part of my life. Those moments when I realized that all the walls I had constructed in my internal workings were again going to see a good relationship pass me by.

I got home and went into the house, pacing like a caged lion. This was new. Normally, I would just let things go and allow my brain to process it as information and hope that someone would finally come along to see life and reason things out as I could. There was one person that I really could use right now, and I would bet he was out with his perfect woman. That didn't matter – I had to try.

Taking my cellphone out of my back pocket, I dialed and waited. One ring. Two rings.

"Hello," Joey's voice came across the line.

"Hey," I said, and like Mama, I knew he would know something was up. "Are you at the new house or out tonight?"

"Give me ten minutes. Are you at home?" Joey said, not even trying to quantify my question. Like Mama, he seemed to be able to read my moods with just a few words.

I nodded but realized that would not translate to his ears. "Yeah, just got here."

"I'm coming," Joey said.

That was all Joey. I really sometimes wished I could learn from him and figure out how to better interact with others around me. I just didn't get all the nuances of human emotions, and to be honest, even when I did understand, I would try to filter my response back to individuals to negate any harsh feelings. I worried incessantly about saying the wrong thing, doing the wrong thing, or just being perceived as doing or saying the wrong thing. I wished that my brain would react the way others thought it should.

Honestly, I wasn't dumb; I thought as I lowered myself onto the chair outside my front door to wait. I sometimes saw things a bit too clearly, and others wanted to add dimensions to emotions, perceptions, and such that made no sense to me.

Putting my head back, I tried to get my racing brain to stop. This one was punching holes in my self-esteem, though. Jennifer was nearly perfect in every way for me. She was smoking hot, made me try new things, and I had thought everything was going along swimmingly – then she did a one-eighty. I did not understand.

True to his word Joey was there in record time. It was cool that he and Angela had closed on a house so close. I now had my brother around more often. Of course, part of my time with Mama was to cook her homemade chicken soups with fresh vegetables and slice her fresh fruits from the farmers market

"Hey," Joey said, stomping up onto the porch as he slapped my leg. "What happened?"

I inhaled and stared directly at him, "I ruined it. She was perfect, and we were having a good time. Then I said something stupid – I think and that was that."

"Okay," Joey said with a crooked smile. "Maybe let's take this one thing at a time. Who is she we are talking about?"

"Jennifer – here name is Jennifer. She came into the shop over a week ago, and she is amazing."

"And you managed to ask her out?"

"Sort of," Carlos said. "She actually got my number first after we sat and talked while her car was being fixed. Then she called, and it was amazing. She just slid into my life and has these odd little personality quirks that somehow make her be able to see me," I said, trying to put into words everything I had been feeling since Jennifer's arrival in my life.

"Okay, sounds amazing so far," Joey said, looking completely confused. "So, what happened?"

"I opened my mouth," I grumbled.

"Well, yeah, that isn't always the best thing for you," he teased me right back.

"Yeah, so tonight we were having an amazing time as we do, and someone referenced Jennifer as my girlfriend. I just corrected them and told her that she was not," I said. "Simple, truthful, and that was that, or so I thought. She got mad and asked me why I said that. Wanted to know what I thought we

123

were doing if not dating? And then asked me if I wanted to date her? When I said yes, it was like I lit a fire, and she ran away mad."

Joey had his fist curled into his mouth, trying to hold the laughter in. He was listening, but I could tell he already knew something about the situation that I must have missed.

"What?" I said, losing my patience.

"How often do you talk to her?"

"Every night," I said without hesitation.

"And was this a first date?'

"No, second." I was getting more confused at the moment.

"Do you have an intense attraction to her?"

"Yes! That is what I'm trying to tell you."

"But you openly in front of her said you were not boyfriend and girlfriend?"

"Yes," I said slowly as something dawned on me. "You think that she thought we were boyfriend and girlfriend? But you and Mama told me that just because someone is nice to you, talks to you all the time, and is a girl doesn't make them a girlfriend. You need to be sure to ask them if they want to be a girlfriend and ensure everyone is on the same page."

"Right, that was because you were stalking Amelia – and she was just nice because we paid her to tutor you through Math," Joey said.

My shoulders slumped. "Women are a hard man. I just need them to say what they want and be clear. You know that I try to take things at face value and don't like all those confusing emotions and crap!"

"Got some bad news for you, bro," Joey said, slapping me on the back. "Women are going to make you work for it. When they say no – half the time, they mean yes; if they say don't get me anything for my birthday, you will be in the doghouse if the gift isn't perfect. It is just the rules of the game. But in the end, you get a warm snuggly bedmate that can be your best friend, so it is worth it."

"I'm going to be single the rest of my life," I lamented. "Seriously, I don't like drama and confusion. It makes my head hurt, and I get in trouble with people because I'm just not good at reading the signs."

"So, tell people that," Joey said as I turned to him with a furrowed, consumed look.

"What just tell them that I interpret in black and white? I should tell Jennifer she needs to be clearer of her intentions."

"Yeah, and maybe give her the reasons you are like this," Joey said softly.

I bristled and drew back from them. "No one needs to know all that. It is hard, and I probably would cry and make a mess of things. You know I look like I should be tough as nails, and that would make me look weak."

"Carlos, that is not the case if you are with the right person. A woman that is a good partner understands the pain of your past and helps you heal for the future. You will have to tell someone, someday, or this cycle is just going to continue. Besides, I love you to pieces, and I know everything," Joey said.

I looked at him with a slight head bob. "Yeah, and I love you for always being there for me."

"I would bet that she has things in her past that would explain her reactions just as your experiences define how you communicate," Joey continued.

He definitely had a point, and without knowing a lot about Jennifer, maybe her communication to me did not make sense. Talking about these things could give me more information to understand her point of view.

"I guess that is probably true," I agreed.

"Honestly, I hate to say this, but you are making this way more complicated than it should be. You should just talk to her and be open, just like you are with me right now. Let your guard down and tell her exactly how you feel and be honest. Tell her you didn't think through the answer when you gave it tonight. You have never really had to be open, so this is very new, but now that you know how she felt hurt and her feelings, you will need to think about her feelings. It's new for you as well, but when you love someone, you will climb mountains and be open to new things," Joey said.

I sat there, totally absorbing what he said. I knew he had the best intentions for me and wanted to see me happy. His words were the truth I needed to hear, no matter how much it might prick my ego.

I sighed with a slight bob of my head, "thanks."

"Always," Joey said as we sat deep in our thoughts for a little while longer.

This was absolutely my happy place, with my family. I just wanted to include Jennifer and others in that circle of comfort, and that meant that first, I had to do some uncomfortable work on myself and have some tough conversations with her. I knew it was not going to be easy, but hopefully so worth it in the end.

CHAPTER 6

I thought for a while that my pen might actually catch on fire the fiery comments I was making about Carlos. The evening had been going so well, and then he had to go and make a stupid comment. Okay, so maybe we were not officially boyfriend and girlfriend yet, but did he have to sound so disgusted by that thought.

I continued to bleed my feelings onto the written page. This journaling was something that my counselor had told me to do before when things became overwhelming. My anger issues had landed me in counseling after the fallout of my parent's divorce, and over the years, I continued to work on myself through this outlet. I kept to that tradition of journaling to help alleviate my emotions in times of crisis, and it did seem to help so that I didn't say something to the wrong person.

A slight knock at the door made me glance up as my heart skipped a beat. I nearly screamed at Franklin, who I was certain it would turn out to be, to go away. Then I realized that my brother might actually be the only person who understood, even if he did give me a lecture about blowing another potential relationship.

"Come in," I grumbled, glancing up as Franklin opened the door a sliver

"Okay, that answers why you are home earlier than I expected," he said, taking one look at my face before walking further into the room and closing the door. "What happened?" He asked and plopped down on the corner of my bed.

"What makes you think something happened?" I asked, trying to keep my tone super upbeat. I even attempted a smile in his direction. I knew even then that he would see through the charade, but somehow I still attempted the impossible in faking a positive mood.

He rolled his eyes at me. "You are journaling, home before the walk of shame at the crack of dawn. Besides, I know that look, so which was it this time?"

"Which what?" I asked, not understanding that statement.

"You or him. Which one of you did something so horrible, you can not imagine ever seeing him again," he said, mocking words I had said to him in the past.

I slunk down into the pillows a good way and ducked my head. "I don't want to talk about it."

"You let your temper get the better of you again, didn't you," Franklin replied, tapping that nail right on the head. I didn't always like how perceptive the boy was, but unfortunately, I loved him enough that I couldn't get overly mad at him.

"I don't understand what happened," I said, shaking my head as I replayed the evening. "I was so mad because he actually corrected someone that called me his girlfriend. I realize that doesn't sound like a big thing, but it just sparked something inside me."

"Because you need someone to love you," Franklin interjected. "You know I'm always in your corner, and that is why I know you best. That said, you crave finding that love you have dreamed of for years. You don't let people close, though, for fear of being hurt, which causes this constant battle within you. Did you even tell Carlos what he did wrong?"

"I did," I said, furrowing my brow, "and he didn't seem to understand why it upset me. The man honestly seems to be one of those. I mean what I say, and I say what I mean."

"That should be a good thing. So what did he say exactly then that made you this mad?"

"He said he wanted to date and be girlfriend and boyfriend, but it was like my ears had tuned him out by then. I was so angry from his earlier comment I just couldn't – listen, hear him or act rationally," I said, slumping down again with a huge grimace.

"Okay?" Franklin said, staring at me like I had lost my mind. This was the part where he always had another perspective on something I did – and normally made me out in a bad light.

"Say it," I demanded, waiting for his insight. Despite my gruff exterior, I really did want to see where he thought I had gone wrong. Or maybe could do it differently next time.

Franklin shrugged, "Carlos was just being a guy and didn't really think about what he said; I would bet. He just corrected her maybe to honestly be truthful or in an effort to ensure you didn't get the wrong idea."

"I don't understand," I grumbled. Why would he say we weren't girlfriend and boyfriend as much as we talk, go out and enjoy hanging with each other. *That should just be assumed by now!*

"Men are pretty simple, and we think in black and white. From what you have described, I would honestly bet he meant nothing by the comment, and it was not meant as a slight to you at all. Maybe – just maybe – you are blowing things out of portion, and you need to cut him some slack."

"We talk all the time, and he should have just known how I felt. I just don't understand how he didn't," I said, still not a hundred percent on board with Franklin's thought process.

"What don't you understand? Your reaction maybe being a bit much, or the fact that he didn't chase after you?" Franklin asked point-blank, staring at me as he arched his brow in my direction.

I hated it when he did that! He said exactly what I had been thinking at that moment. How did this human that looked so innocent know exactly how my big old malfunctioning brain worked? It always defied logic to me.

"Is it so wrong to want a man to chase me finally?" I asked with a slight pout on my lips.

"No, but you do realize you are going to have to meet him halfway to hold him. One grand gesture is going to require a reciprocal one from you and then a lot of compromises. You are going to have to be vulnerable and talk about how you feel. It will be messy, chaotic, and at the end, so worth it."

"Right?" I didn't believe him. I know he had good intentions, but my experience was love was never worth it. I had done the compromise, the trying to be a good girlfriend, change the bad parts about me – all of it! All I got was cheated on, left behind, and dragged through the mud of another horrible breakup. Now I found that I tried to run when things started getting serious before they could injure me.

"Well, until you find that man worthy of fighting for, this is going to be the outcome," Franklin said. "And I will be here every night to pick you up, dust you off, and of course, share ice cream."

I perked up at that. "Did you say ice cream?"

"Yep, I picked up some Rocky Road on the way home.

Call it my brotherly intuition or something, but I thought it might be needed."

I wanted to hate him and how perceptive he was. I really like ice cream, though, so I decided to let it go and indulge for just a few minutes. Tomorrow I would figure out what in the hell I was going to do about Joey.

CHAPTER 7

$\mathcal{T}$he barbeque was in full swing, and everyone was having an amazing time. There was music, laughter, food, and of course lots of games and conversation going on. I was inside my own head, though, still contemplating what had gone down with Jennifer. I had not been able to shake free of it for over a week now. I was empty inside.

We had done our usual get-together, and even Rigo came home this time. It had been a while since I had seen my little brother. He seemed to be running late, considering he lived in Arizona, but everyone else was here. I looked around and could see Manny being Manny as usual and acting all loud and brash. But now he was with Sandi. *I guess crazy met crazy, huh?* As I watched them, they had eyes only for each other, and they just seemed to work in this amazing magnetic way. My mind was too clouded to partake in much. Even though I was a quiet person, I did enjoy these get-togethers. My family was close and the only people I could open up and enjoy myself around. For that reason, I cherished the moments I spent here.

"Penny, for your thoughts?" A voice said from behind me,

and I turned around to see Angela standing there staring at me. When I didn't say anything at first, she just lowered herself to a chair to my right.

"Hello, Angela," I said. "Where's Joey?" I had already seen her earlier in the day when I met with everyone, but we hadn't had a chance to talk much. To be honest, I hadn't had many conversations with her. I was sure she must think I was some prissy arrogant elitist who thought he was better than everyone, but it wasn't at all. I was just quiet.

"He went to get some supplies that we were supposed to get for Mama, and between the two of us still forgot."

I loved how both Angela and Sandi called her Mama. My Mama was the most caring person in the world and the human I adored above all others. To hear the respect, love, and admiration of these women joining our family through my brothers filled my heart and made me love each of them in turn.

"Ah," I said, remembering how forgetful Joey can be when it comes to stuff like that. We remained in silence for a while. It was not an uncomfortable silence, more of a peaceful one. I could hear the rumbles all around me, but after a short while, they all faded out, and it was just me and the stars. I was always envious of the stars, but I felt sad for them at the same time.

On the one hand, they had the luxury of never meeting another star, which was a good thing for both of them. Looking at the other side, though, it was incredibly sad that these stars would spend their whole lives alone, never moving in the current existence. Despite being much larger than the planet, I was on, they were just specs in the grand scheme of things. They never moved significantly anywhere, only simply existing. I related to these stars a lot more than I cared to admit most times. Now, though, I was in my feelings, letting me identify with the loneliness of the stars.

133

"You didn't answer my question, by the way." I had forgotten someone was even beside me. I turned, tuning back into my surroundings, and looked at Angela.

"Sorry?"

She tossed me a coin that I caught. "Penny, for your thoughts?"

I remembered that she had said that. I sighed, resting my head on the chair I was seated on. I didn't know if I should open up to her. I mean, she was Joey's wife and all, but she and I didn't know each other that well. On the other hand, she was a woman and might be able to provide a different perspective. My brain was on overdrive, calculating all the sides of this decision.

"I know that look," she said, and I furrowed my brows. *What did she mean?* "That was the same look I had when I was looking for reasons not to be with Joey." After a moment of silence, she went on. "A lot of times, we make up things in our minds. It could be because of our past experiences or our fear of what the future holds that limits us."

"I need to learn how to express my feelings and communicate," I blurted out without filtering it. I stared at her, worried about what her reaction might be.

"No shit. All you Mendoza brothers could use some help in that area!" I smirked at her reply. I guess that wasn't news after all. "But isn't that the point of meeting someone?"

"What do you mean?"

"When you meet someone that compliments you, together you are complete set finally. We are all broken and incomplete to some extent," she elaborated. "I thought it was my fate to remain broken. But when we find the right person, we want to be the best person we can be to make that other person happy. If both of you work hard to be better versions of yourself for that special someone, pretty soon you have a union that can't be broken for anything." She glanced at the bike that rolled in, Joey on top of it.

"He picked up my broken pieces, and we both want to be the best for each other. People need others so we can be better versions of ourselves." Angela smiled at me. "Take my advice; whoever that girl is, if you want to be a better version of yourself, then she's worth it. If you don't take this opportunity to leap, it might just break you more."

"Hmm... thanks for the pep talk," I said with a slight grin.

"I learned it from my sister and Joey. He just loves to give pep talks, huh?"

"Tell me about it," I responded, and we both laughed. I guess I could try to be better at talking and expressing myself. Angela had made a valid point, but I still had a way to go facing my demons. I could not be with Jen if I did not let go of what had been eating me up all these years.

"Have you seen Mama?" I asked Angela.

"Yeah. Just a moment ago in the kitchen."

"Thanks." I got up and went inside.

The moment she saw me, her head cocked to the side as if she was reading my face. She was the person that understood me better than any other, and I sometimes wondered how that was possible she could see my thoughts and feelings without a word. She looked weaker physically every day, which made me so sad I couldn't even think of it without tearing up. When she gave me that knowing smile, though, everything seemed right in my world.

"Estrella, handle the things Joey bought," she said, holding her hand out to take mine.

"Hey, Carlos! Have you seen Angela?" Joey shouted from the dining as he saw Mama leading me upstairs.

"Yeah. Out back where Mama likes to sit."

"Aiite! Thanks, man!" Mama led me to her room and closed the door. I was breathing so fast it felt like I had a panic attack. I'd thought the roller coaster was scary, but this was something entirely different. My biggest weakness had always been speaking, but now that I needed to do it to free myself, I was getting the largest panic attack of all.

"Breathe," Mama said, placing her palm on my chest, and I followed her instructions. "Breathe." With her help, I slowed my breathing down, finally getting control of it again until I was stable. "Now, stop being a wuss and tell me what the problem is." In a snap, she was back to hard-ass Mama. *Damn, how did she do it?*

"Mama, I found a girl and ruined it." Her eyes lit up, and she immediately jumped up like a little girl. *Where does a seventy-year-old woman get this much energy from?* I wondered.

"You found a girl?" She must have been so shocked and happy that I was talking to her about a girl that she ignored the latter part of what I said. "Tell me everything about her. What is she like? This is great news."

"You did hear the part where I ruined it, right?"

She shrugged. "Eh, that'll come later. First, I want to hear about the woman you met."

I smiled and spent the next ten minutes talking about every intricate nuance of Jennifer's being. Her quirky ways and clumsiness sometimes. Her bodacious figure as well as her big heart. Her energetic personality, a trait Mama, would love.

"You see?" Mama said when I was done. "Once you know all this, does the second part matter?"

I got what she was driving at. Guess that was why she made me remember and go through all the things I loved about Jennifer. "But Mama—" I braced myself for what I was about to get into. "I can't do that until I address what has been festering inside me all these years."

Her look and demeanor immediately changed. "What is it, mijo? Dime que pasa."

"Remember when you told Papa to leave the house? And I told you how I had seen him in bed with that other woman?" I replied. Mama nodded. "Ever since that day when he left, I wished I had not said anything."

"Oh, Mijo. You did the right thing. I wish you hadn't seen that!" she said.

"I'm sorry, Mama. If I had just kept my mouth shut about seeing Papa, we might have still been a family. I broke us up. I should have listened to Rigo when he told me to keep quiet. Otherwise, it would not end well. I just wonder how things would have been if you two were still together."

She sighed. "Carlitos, don't ever say that. You told the truth. I raised my kids to defend the truth and never back down from it, even if it is hard. I am just sorry you had to see that."

"You have been a great mother to us, and seeing you suffer, especially after Rigo left, made me feel bad. I still wished he hadn't, but I also understand why he did. I am still so sorry, Mama. I still wondered what would've happened if I had kept quiet."

Reaching up, she patted my cheek. "Mijo, I was sad not because of your Papa. I was sad because I didn't want my kids to go through pain. I should have left your Papa a long time before that." Her eyes began to tear up. I couldn't remember the last time she'd cried, but we were both now shedding tears uncontrollably.

My head was buried inside the embrace of my loving mother as I sobbed uncontrollably. Years of pent-up guilt poured from me in the deluge of tears, and I could feel something shift slightly inside. Her forgiveness over that act which I thought the worst I had ever done, seemed in small measure to free me somehow.

"I am so sorry that you have been carrying this guilt. Carlitos, I didn't know you were carrying this weight on

137

your shoulders. I should have known something was wrong. What kind of mother can't see the hurt her son is going through?" She held me tight, and we both cried like babies. "Mijo, you did nothing wrong," her voice crooned while I sobbed into her embrace. "You did the right thing, son. You told the truth, which is what I have taught all my children to do. I might have been taken aback all those years ago, but not for a second did I blame you."

"Mama, it wasn't your fault. How would you have known? You were always busy working, cooking, and taking care of us. Mama, I don't want to see you hurt or crying. I should have told you how I felt sooner, but I didn't, and I didn't want to hurt you again. I used to hear you crying at night in your room, and I used to pray to God to take away your pain and hurt."

"I didn't understand why you spoke less after he left, and when you did, it was always minimal. I don't remember you saying more than necessary. You started minding your own business even when you should have spoken out, and I just thought you were just quiet."

"Carlos, a mother's job is to know when something is wrong, and I didn't know that. I am so sorry. I am so sorry, Mijo. I wish I could take away all your pain and hurt. I hope you can forgive me for all this suffering you went through."

My heart was beating so fast, and I felt such a relief to let all this out and know I did the right thing.

"Mama, please don't blame yourself for this. I know you did everything you could for us. I was unable to guide you, and for that, I am so sorry." She replied to my monologue with a soliloquy of her own. "Your father, back then, was a man with many problems. We were going to split up one way or another. Being with someone is about commitment. He broke that commitment and did many other bad things that I tried to keep you kids out of. That being said, he and I should not have let things get so bad that you had to see."

"By you and him, you mean just him," I said, finally able to dry my eyes.

She scoffed. "Well, I could have left him earlier, before all this mess," she pointed out, but I was not having any of that.

"Mama, his actions were his choices, not your fault. You tried to tolerate it because you were in love with him." I took her hand and kissed it.

"You are right. I loved him." Even now, a bazillion years later, I could see the pain in her eyes. Papa had really done a number on her. "I'm glad I left, and I finally got brave enough not to take him back. My children were the most important thing to me, and I wanted them to respect women and didn't want them to treat women like your father."

"I know that, Mama, and we always got that message from you loud and clear," I reassured her.

"You know that was the final time – when he didn't come back after you and Rigo caught him. It was far from the first time your father had done that, and I knew it wouldn't be the last. I beat myself up for so long about why I kept taking him back, and if I had just left when I first found out all the pain, I would have saved my family."

"Oh, you did what you thought was right," I defended her.

"I thought he would change, but that wasn't going to happen. And I am so grateful that I finally was strong enough to leave because I found love again after we divorced. One good thing is I met Ernesto and had a wonderful life with him until I lost him too."

It was my turn to hug her now while she reminisced about the good times we'd all had with Ernesto. He had come into our lives after our father had left and had been a great role model that guided us down the straight and narrow path when we were threatening to spiral out of control. The man had taken a group of angry boys and did the absolute best he could, and his passing had wounded my Mama in ways she had never recovered from. Sometimes I would still see the sadness creep in when she looked at a picture around the house and didn't think anyone was watching her.

"I know your father wasn't here, but I hope Ernesto and I did a good job." This rare moment of vulnerability from Mama warmed my heart. "I truly believe that when one door closes, another one opens because God has other plans for us. We just need to have faith in him even when things are not going our way."

"I agree that the divorce was hard, and there have been lingering problems due to it. In the end, though, you and Ernesto made us a wonderful home, and I agree seeing you happy was the best reward after those tough years," I assured her, and she smiled.

"This is further proof why you should talk more and why silence can be dangerous, Carlos," Mama said, smacking me on the head. Jeez, this woman. "I am so glad we had this talk that had been festering inside you for years. You didn't do yourself any favors, either. That being said, I would love to meet the girl who made all this possible and finally pushed you to open up. Now you make sure you talk to this woman and let her know how you feel about her." It sounded more like a warning than a piece of advice.

"Thank you, Mama," I said.

She nodded, and I got up to leave the room. As I got to the door, she spoke. "The girl," she said. "You never told me her name."

"Jennifer," I answered. "Jennifer Foster. She is amazing and just seems to get me. Besides, she is fearless and likes trying new things even if they scare her. And I just can't tell you how exciting and amazing it feels to be with her. I just smile so much. I know I must look crazy when I get to spend time with her. I never know what she is going to do next."

"She sounds like a keeper," Mama said, patting my knee. "Now, it is up to you if you can make the changes and fight for her."

I knew she was right, and beyond that, I knew Jennifer was worth it. I was going to win her back and find a happy future for myself and, hopefully, my children one day. I would take the lessons learned from my own father and attempt hard never to repeat them!

CHAPTER 8

I kept checking his Facebook. Well, not his Facebook, since he barely posted anything on social media, but that of his brother, Manny. Going through their pictures from kids to adults on his social media made me realize that Carlos smiled less than all those around him as a kid. He did seem to love his family a lot, and I appreciated that. I was currently hidden in my blanket like I had been since I'd walked away from Carlos. I hadn't spoken much, even to my own family. My mom said she was coming to see me due to my phone and texts lately. I hadn't even gone to work in a while, calling in sick for the entire week. Now, this is what I had become: a girl who strolled through the family's social media of the guy she loved. A guy who had probably moved on and didn't even love her. *Why was I torturing myself like this?* It reminded me of my first all over again.

The doorbell rang, and I groaned, sinking lower into the bed covers. I knew Mom was finally here, and she might make a scene if I did not open the door quickly enough. I wondered how long it would take her to go away if I just didn't answer? I knew the answer was that it would take hours, and she would just stay out there getting madder with each passing moment.

Finally, I swung my legs over the edge of the bed and padded to the front door. My doorbell managed to ring three more times though as slow as I was moving before I flung the door open.

"Such impatience," I murmured to myself right before opening the door. "Hey, Mom—" I stopped when I saw Franklin. He smiled and waved when he saw me.

"You could say 'Hey, Franklin' too, you know?" he scolded, but I was having none of his crap. He was a traitor and had coordinated this visit, even though he knew I would hate it.

"You brought him?" I gave Mom a disapproving look.

"He is your brother, so yes, I did." Mom came in, pushing me to the side, with Franklin right behind her. He stuck out his tongue while walking past me, mocking me for Mom taking his side. I responded with the *fuck you* sign on his face. This was the regular banter between us siblings.

"Look at your home, Jenny!" As usual, Mom started to overreact, running around the house to point out all the problems. She was like this, and her constant nit-picking was part of our biggest breakdowns to date.

"It looks like you," Franklin observed. "Like shit."

"Shut up, poop face," I quipped back at him, sticking out my tongue as if I were twelve and not a grown woman of twenty-eight.

"Enough, you two." If I was completely honest, a part of me wanted to be left alone, but a part of me just wanted to cry on my mom's shoulder. I appreciated the time with Franklin, yet the caring brother I knew turned into a nasty sibling rivalry thing that sucked when mom was around.

Mom sat down and gestured for me to do the same.

"We're worried, Jenny," she began after I took a seat. Franklin had sat down before either of us because... he is Franklin. "You have been secluded from everybody, and it has become a habit—your friends, work, and family. You need to get over it. Is it another boy?"

"Why the hell would you assume it is always a boy?" I snapped at her, shocking her and even my brother. I think it was at that point that they realized it was pretty serious. I was hurting. "Am I a slut or something that you make it sound like I purposefully jump from man to man?"

"Okay... I can see that it was more serious than I anticipated." She nodded. "Franklin told me you started seeing a guy, and things went bad. I'm not calling you names, but you tend to jump into relationships and then back out again when things get hard."

"And I specifically told Franklin not to tell you." I turned my focus to my brother.

He held up his hands. "And I didn't... until you started hiding from society. So, hell yeah, I'm telling Mom if it will help you get over whatever this is." I could see the genuine worry in his eyes. He probably had not seen me like this since Jerry.

My mom put a hand on my shoulder. "He told me because he is worried about you, as am I." I sighed, resting my head on the couch. "Did you like him?"

"I loved him and really thought things were going to be so different this time." My admittance surprised them. I rarely said stuff like that, and even though I had been searching for love ever since Jerry broke my heart, I had never found it.

"Wow. I never thought I would hear that after Jerry," Mom admitted. "Well, if you love him, what's the problem?"

For the next few minutes, I explained everything to them. "I'm starting to think I overreacted," I said finally when I was finished.

Franklin nodded. "Oh, you did."

"Franklin," Mom cautioned, but knowing my brother, he was not going to stop.

"That doesn't mean he doesn't have issues he needs to deal with. Anyone who thinks they are unworthy of love probably is until they fix that mindset."

I stared at him, surprised that he could give advice that made sense. He was such a mystery. One minute he acted the part of an immature idiot, and the next, he was actually helpful and caring. Alright, I admitted silently, that was probably why I adored him so much – he was complex, chaotic, and beautifully broken, just like me.

My mom glared at him before turning back to me. "Ignoring your brother's usual annoying way of speaking, he does have a point. If you love him, you should have been patient rather than storming off. I think you were searching for a reason to leave due to fear of being hurt again like you were with Jerry."

I wiped my eyes. "I guess you're right. I just... I've never felt this way before."

"Then go fight for him. If he loves you too, he will fight for you. It is as simple as that, Jenny."

"Yep. As simple as that," Franklin said in such a dry and emotionless manner that it made both of us laugh. I was grateful to have a family that cared enough about me to pull me out when I was falling into the deep end.

"Thank you."

CHAPTER 9

"*T*hanks for driving me, Rigo," I said to my brother, who had come to visit me the day after the party at Mama's house. It was the first time I had seen him in many years since he lived in Arizona and rarely made the trip home. He sure had grown up a lot and seemed more secure in his own right somehow.

He grinned. "It's all good, besides it is the first time we have seen each other in years. I owe you an apology, but didn't you need to do it in front of everyone yesterday?"

"You don't owe me an apology, but it was kind of a madhouse, and everyone was shocked you came. Why did you, after all these years, pick this moment to start reconnecting?"

"I know that Mama is sick, and I don't wish to let her pass without us both getting things off our chests that need to be said," Rigo finished. "I know I blamed you for blabbing about Papa all those years ago, but honestly, I kind of felt guilty dropping all of that on you. I didn't want to face you or the rest of them."

"I understand," I said. "It was a horrible position to be in, and honestly, I couldn't sleep for weeks. I know you were so mad that I finally told Mama about us seeing Papa with that woman. I think that the scariest thing for me from that night was remembering your face when I told her."

"I replay that moment all the time," Rigo said with a huge sigh. "I felt guilty that I should have been the one to speak up first. I had known for more time and could have saved you and Mama so much heartache. I think a big reason I ran from this place was not wanting to face both of you day after day."

"We were kids," I said. "We loved Mama and wanted to protect her. I did nothing to hurt you, and Rigo, you didn't hurt me. Mama forgives us both and said that she had known about Papa honestly and just kept going back. She blamed herself, but that isn't fair either."

"I agree," Rigo said. "We all do what we think is right, but I'm done running. I want to start being a big part of this family once again."

"Great," I replied happily. "I am glad you are here now, though, and hope maybe we can spend more time together in the near future. I miss you, and I know Mama also does."

"She doesn't," Rigo said. "She barely said a word to me yesterday, and I feel so much guilt every time I look at her that it makes my transport back to those days as a kid. Seeing what we did and just all the emotions that came from holding the secret and even worse once it came out and the entire family imploded."

"We have to let all that go," Carlos said, shocking himself at that proclamation. "I don't know how you are doing, but I know that for me holding on to all that fear from the past has been holding me back. I met this amazing woman and walked away from her because I couldn't express myself. The reason I can't is that the one time I did, you left, Mama. I thought I broke, and my family went through hell for years."

Rigo turned and looked at me for the longest time.

"I honestly hadn't thought about how it all impacted you long-term." Rigo turned around to stare out the window. We didn't speak for several minutes, and then he asked me. "Where is this place, by the way?"

"It's the second one on the left." Rigo pulled up, and I got out of the car. I took a deep breath, gathering my thoughts. The last thing I wanted to do was not know what to say when I saw her. I had decided to come and apologize to Jen and ask if we could start over. She had been pretty pissed the last time we'd seen one another, so there were no guarantees.

"Just lay it all at her feet, man," Rigo said from inside the car. "We've gone through far worse, haven't we? You've got this, bro."

I smiled, nodding at him before walking to the door. I knocked, and the wait until the door opened must have been one of the longest moments of my life. The door opened, and I was met with an older woman.

"Hello, ma'am."

"Hello. How may I help you?"

"My name is Carlos Mendoza, and I am looking for a lady by the name of Jennifer Foster."

The moment I said my name, she gasped. The woman smacked me on the shoulder, much to my bemusement.

"Took you long enough," she said, and that statement made me understand that Jennifer had been thinking of me too. "She left and went to the coffee shop down the street. Go get her."

I flashed her a grin and a thumbs-up. As I turned in the direction, she pointed with a resounding "Yes, ma'am!"

"But if you break her heart again," the woman added as I rushed down the stairs, stopping me dead in my tracks, "you'll have me to answer to." What's with mothers being overprotective of their kids?

"I won't," I promised and jogged over to the car where Rigo was waiting.

"What's up? That's not her, is she?" He was peering over at the house.

I laughed. "No, bro. Anyway, I'll head on alone from here," I said. "Thanks for coming here with me, Rigo."

"You and me. Just like old times, ain't it?"

"You're damn right." We pumped fists, and Rigo drove away while I ran down the street to find the woman I loved. Little did I know it would be harder than I thought. The universe was probably making me suffer because she was worth it. When I reached the coffee shop, she wasn't there. I spent the next hour searching up and down the street for her. I could have called her, but I wanted to find her by myself. I enjoyed the chase of searching for her. It somehow felt right.

There she was.

Her red hair was packed into a bun, with one long strand of hair falling down the left side of her face. Her blue eyes seemed darker than usual, and she seemed to be in a reflective mood. I walked calmly to where she was seated in the coffee shop, right where she should have been an hour ago. I walked quietly toward her, taking my time to look at the woman of my dreams. A couple of wrestling DVDs were on the table, and she was looking at her phone. I was close to her when my phone pinged, but I didn't care about that right now.

"Hey, Jen," I said softly.

Her eyes lit up, and she quickly raised her head to face me. "Wh-what are you do...."

"I came to see you so I could apologize, but your mother was the one home. She told me you were at the coffee place, but I couldn't find you there."

Jen got to her feet. She staggered as she was standing up,

almost falling to the ground, but I caught her. She was safe…
in my arms. I wanted to hold her tight and never let go.

"S-so, how did you know I was here?"

"I ran everywhere until I found you," I admitted, and she
gasped. I wanted to get her to a standing position, but she
held my arm.

"I prefer it like this," Jen said, causing me to smile.

I took a deep breath, praying for the right words to come.
"I love you, Jennifer Foster. I'm sorry for the way I acted
before. I know I may be afraid of what the future holds, but
the scariest future is one without you in it."

She smiled. "Check your phone."

I was perplexed. "Huh?"

"Your phone."

I did as she said and checked my phone. It was a text from
her that read *I think we need to try a third date.*

"These were meant to be for you," she said, gesturing to
the wrestling DVDs. Now I felt bad for not bringing her a
gift. It didn't matter, though, because I planned to give her
whatever she needed for the rest of her life.

"I think I know exactly how we need to spend the rest of
the afternoon," I said. "You want to come back to my place."

"You know I'm not that kind of girl," Jennifer teased.

"I thought I could make you one of Mama's recipes, and
we could watch these DVDs," I said, trying to hold back the
smile trying to show thought on my face.

She put her hand on the crook of my elbow and followed
along as we chatted the entire distance back to my house.

CHAPTER 10

I was on top of the world and honestly felt like I could break into song at any moment. I could not recall feeling this happy in years, and there was no doubt in my head that Carlos and I could make this thing work if we both put in some effort.

We had watched all the wrestling DVDs, talked for nearly six hours, and had the best dinner on that first date back together. Since we talked each night and were trying something new, we would end each call by telling the other person a fun fact about ourselves.

I felt like I had slept better and woken, ready to take on the world each morning with a renewed zest for life. I had no idea that loving someone could make food taste better, the world appears brighter, and even help me get through tough days at work. I was settling into the new job pretty well and enjoying learning the various computer systems I was responsible for keeping updated. It was a small office that did plumbing for businesses and homes around the city. My job was to schedule the technicians, order supplies, and generally ensure that jobs were done on time and within budget.

I loved the thrill of learning something that was both challenging and new. The job was the best paying one I had heald to boot, and it allowed me to interact with people regularly. Oddly, despite an anger management problem and maybe a tough introverted nature – I was finding that working with people helped me work through many of those issues. I would imagine it was the same with Carlos.

He had owned up to the fact that communication was one of the hardest skills for him. Reading a room, knowing the right response in certain situations, and the like were things he struggled with. I am working hard to understand and even filter her reactions to things that occurred until I could think more about them.

"Hey," Adam, one of the plumbers, came up to my desk, suddenly ripping me from my daydreams of Joey. The man kind of made me nervous, as he always made a point to come to talk to me. Like every single day, and I, on the other hand, made constant comments about Carlos to ensure he knew I was taken.

"Hi, Adam. Is there something I can do for you today?"

"You bet there is," he said, leaning over my desk, brushing against me oddly. Immediately, I felt the need to back up from him and decided that I would be getting a picture of Carlos to show on the desk prominently. One look at his mass and tattoos, and that shut this man up for good.

"I ordered all the supplies you asked for," I said to Adam again, trying to bring the conversation back to the task at hand and get him away from me – quickly!

"I had these tickets to see a," he stopped when I held my hand up. I took a breath so as not to sound rude; I really wanted to keep this job.

Unfortunately, several times in eh past, when men came on too strong, I would say or do something inappropriate in the workplace. That had cost me more than one good job, and right now, I was trying my hardest to turn over a new leaf. Along with better communication fostering my relationship with Carlos, I hoped it might also help my job-hopping problem. So, with a settle of my nerves, I turned back to Adam.

"I don't date people I work with," I said gently, ensuring that I kept my voice level. "I just think it sets a bad precedent, and then if something happens can make things awkward. I appreciate you considering me, but I will have to kindly decline." I even managed to put a sweet smile on my face as I maintained eye contact.

He looked for a moment like he was about to get mad but then just bowed his head slightly. "I can respect that," he said and, turning, walked away.

I sat there in shock, watching him go. That ended much less confrontationally than I was expecting. Who would have imagined staying calm, giving me honest feelings on the matter, and not allowing emotions any place in the conversation could have that effect?

I smiled as I went back to work. Maybe this patience, communication, and working on my emotional outbursts were going to work out. I couldn't wait to talk to Carlos about this later!

CHAPTER 11

"You said you were game for anything," Jennifer said as we walked into the dark, packed dive bar.

I had a really bad feeling about this. First off, the last bar we visited, I did something stupid and didn't see her for weeks, and second, my brothers loved this place. I prayed that none of them would be around this time, or I was going to be in a world of hurt.

"Can we maybe try," I stopped cold as I noticed Angela, Joey, Manny, Rigo, and Sandi all staring back at me? My blood ran cold, and I thought for sure I might have a heart attack and crumple into a pile on the floor.

"No can do, big guy," Jennifer said, yanking me hard by my arm. She was pretty tough for such a tiny thing, and when she decided to go after something, there was no denying her.

I took a deep breath and started for a table on the other side of the bar when Joey stood and headed in our direction. I must have groaned out loud because she started up at me, "what's wrong?" She asked, following my line of sight.

"Who is that?" She whispered just as Joey came alongside us.

"Jennifer?" Joey asked with a huge smirk on his face.

"Yes," Jennifer said, glancing between Joey and me with the most dazed expression. "Do I know you?"

"I'm Joey," she said, and I heard Jennifer give a tiny chuckle as she laid her hand in Joey's. "Carlos's brother. That is amazing! It is great to meet you," she gushed.

"So, I can tell he didn't realize we would all be here tonight," Joey said, holding my gaze with that cocky smirk of his, "so what brings you here?"

"Karaoke," she said with a happy laugh.

Joey's eyes went the size of half dollars, and the shock on his face would have been hysterical if I hadn't felt on the verge of passing out.

"Wait! What?" I managed to ask. "I don't sing in public – ever – no way – not going to happen." I stuttered, feeling my heart racing, my palms got clammy, and seriously passing out seemed a real option at this moment.

"Oh, this I have to see," Joey said. "Come on over and join us; I think his other brothers should hear this."

Jennifer leaned over to me. "Are all your brothers here?"

"Oh yeah," I said, wishing that the floor might open wide and swallow me right then and there. I couldn't believe that one of the most embarrassing moments of my life would be witnessed by my brothers, their wives, and Jennifer. Yeah, for me! This would probably end up being our last night.

"Hey, everyone, I'm Jennifer," she said happily as introductions were made around the table. Everyone was having the time of their life getting to know each other as I stole a sidelong glance at Jennifer. She was grinning from ear to ear as Angela told us a story of her first meeting Joey, which I had been there for oddly enough.

Jennifer reached out under the table and took my hand. It

was a small sign that she was thinking of me, despite all the attention the others were garnering, and my heart pounded painfully in my chest.

As we ordered drinks, talked, and evening started to slip away, I loosened up. At one point, Rigo captured my eyes and gave an approving nod, which again made me feel on top of the world. I thought this might actually end up being the absolute best night of my life ever – and then Jennifer did it!

"That's my song," she said as the karaoke master on stage announced *Jesse's Girl* as the next selection. Jennifer made hoots and hollers until the man pointed at her and let her know she was up.

"We are going this," she said as my feet turned to lead, and I felt my insides lurch painfully. I honestly thought I was going to be sick.

"Hey, one brother goes down, we all go down," Joey suddenly piped up. "Care if we join in?" He asked Jennifer, who immediately thought that was a great idea.

At least mine wouldn't be the only voice anyone heard, I thought, as e all walked up to the little stage. I was sweating profusely and thought for sure the second I opened my mouth, Jennifer would run screaming from the stage. Then the lyrics started, and they were right there on the prompter in front of me.

Jennifer belted out the beginning, and everyone joined in with me. Imagine my shock as I heard myself singing along, albeit horribly – but I was singing in public. Soon Manny, Rigo, Angela, Joey, Sandi, Jennifer, and I had arms around each other and were singing with everything we had. It was amazing, and I almost felt like crying as I looked around – this was the best night ever, and I never thought I would be this brave in public.

As I glanced at Jennifer, I realized that I had fallen

completely in love with this woman. I vowed silently that I would not lose her even if I had to conquer every fear I kept deep inside. I would be the man she deserved!

CHAPTER 12

We were taking in the farmer's market on a bright Saturday morning. This was a regular occurrence for me as I enjoyed all the fresh options for Mama's soups, and she adored the fruits and vegetables fresh from the various vendors. Jennifer, it turned out, loved to cook also, and the fresher the ingredients, the better she told me. While I enjoyed the shopping, I was just here to spend time with her, which was how I spent every moment that I was not working these days and could coordinate time with her.

We were turning a corner to this vendor she wanted to check out for peppers when she elicited a cuss word – or rather an entire imaginative group of them strung together. I noticed she was staring at a young man and older lady not that far from us.

"Do you know them?" I asked. She had never told me of anyone she had a grudge within her past – except maybe Jerry and the details of that relationship she had kept short and succinct. They dated, he cheated, and she lost her cool and actually spent a night in jail before they broke things off.

That was it, and the kid she was staring at didn't seem to be old enough to be the ex.

"That is my brother Franklin and my mother," she growled. I had to laugh.

"Hmmm, this reminds me of something that happened to me recently," I found myself teasing her as I remembered the night at the karaoke bar.

"Your brothers are cool, I admit," Jennifer said, biting on her lip. "But Franklin and my mom can be tough."

I looked back at them and saw that Franklin had now seen us and was waving. It would be rude not to reciprocate, so I waved back, and Jennifer let a long sigh out as her mom and brother started toward us.

"Hi," Franklin said, holding his hand out to me, "you must be Carlos. The one that almost got away."

I snickered at the audacity of the introduction and nodded my head. "I guess I am, and you must be Franklin."

"I'm sure she describes me as vermin, the bane of her existence and other choice words," her brother quipped ack pretty quick, and it made me more at ease. I liked him instantly, and the camaraderie between them was similar to mine with my brothers.

"Hi," her mother said. "I'm Jane, Jennifer's mom."

"Hi, Carlos," he said, shaking her hand.

"Please excuse my two children," she offered back. "They love to hate each other in public but are really best of friends."

"I understand that. I have a bunch of brothers and sisters myself," I offered.

We stood and chitchatted for a long while. It was great, and from the expressions on both Jane and Franklin's faces, I did pretty good holding up my side of the conversation. We even made plans to have lunch together, and when Franklin asked about coming by the shop because he loved cars, I provided him the address. Then we continued to the shopping we left behind. I was feeling amazing about the interaction, but Jennifer was silent.

Mad I could handle, silent was bad.

I let her stew for a moment, thinking maybe she would say something. As we picked up some tomatoes, peppers, and other items, she talked to the clerks and such but not a single peep to me. I could feel the blood pressure building and worried that she would again leave me high and dry. The nerves were literally about to make me explode when she turned to me.

"I love you," she whispered.

My legs nearly gave way under me as I leaned in closer. I was pretty certain I had a stroke and was not understanding things correctly. I thought she was so mad, but now this?

"I love you," I said cautiously. "Where did that come from?"

"They both loved you, and that was the easiest introduction I've ever had to make," she said. "You are the one. I can't wait until we can do family things and have kids. I know that Franklin is going to adore your brothers, and I want our moms to meet."

"I want all that too," Carlos said, pulling her to him. He lowered his lips to hers and sealed the bargain with a kiss. This woman had so much power over him, and to be honest – he wouldn't change a thing.

CHAPTER 13

I had just finished handing out all the schedules for the day, ordered up the supplies, and answered about a hundred emails, it felt like. I glanced up to see if it was time for a break, yet I was surprised to find Carlos headed in my direction. And unless I saw things, he had coffee and a bag from my favorite café.

"Hey you," I said, grinning from ear to ear. I was so happy to see him as it had been a long forty-eight hours since our last visit. I could spend every moment with him and not miss a beat.

"You have time for a little break?" He asked.

"Actually, I was just heading for one," I said. "There is a little seating area right outside."

"Perfect," he responded, following my lead. When we sat down, he slid the coffee across the table. "I think I got it right."

"How did you know about this place?" I had to know because filing through my memories. I couldn't remember ever telling him about Angelo's Café.

"Franklin," he said, which caused my hands to pause in

the process of opening the bag. "He came by yesterday, and I might have bribed him with a right in a 1967 Chevy if he would tell me your favorite place to eat."

"You bribed my brother," I said, opening the bag as the smell of cinnamon and apple assailed my nose. "Crap! I can't even be mad because you got me the best strudel in the city."

"You know you really are the most old-fashioned perfect man," I said as I sank my teeth into the flaky, slightly sweet, perfect treat. "When we went to the fair, I knew it then. You open doors, ask me what I want, try to do all the little things, and literally have never said a single disrespectful thing to me in our entire time together."

"My Mama taught me that," Carlos admitted. "I also try to do the exact opposite of my Papa. He was definitely a flawed man that made Mama cry more than a smile. I wouldn't say I liked that. He even made me privy to his bad ways, and I had to tell my Mama this big secret when I was a kid. It broke her."

"I'm sorry about that," I said, feeling his pain coming off him in waves. Truly the man had the biggest heart of any person I had met. I couldn't believe that I doubted him or thought him horrible after that first simple misunderstanding. This was the kind of man all women wanted, and few could ever find.

"It's okay, because of him, I had a great example of everything I refused ever to be," Carlos said. "So, when I think about doing something, I always wonder if it is something Papa would have done. If the answer is yes – I do the opposite."

"I get that," I said, realizing that I probably did more than ever. "My father walked out on my mother without any notice. Said he just didn't know that kids and such were going to be so hard and left one day. He would see us sporadically when he wasn't too busy, but then he got a younger

162

wife, new family, and it became pretty evident it was just as he didn't want. That made me mad and, as you have probably guessed, informed some of my decisions. I'm always so scared of people leaving, I sometimes pre-emptively do so first."

"I guess everyone has lessons learned from their pasts," Carlos replied. "It's if we allow that to control the future that makes us a success or a failure."

He wasn't wrong. I allowed my anger to ruin jobs, relationships, and even my own mental health for the longest time. I had nothing to show but heartache for the effort. Since meeting Carlos and really starting to put in the work to make this relationship better – things were quickly changing.

My work was stabilizing and felt more fulfilling. My conversations with mom and Franklin were better every day, and best of all was Carlos. He did all the little things to make me feel special and talked to me about the other stuff that was still hard. That didn't mean that we didn't argue and have disagreements, but we vowed to come back to the table and discuss when that happened.

"Together, I truly believe we can overcome anything we put our minds to," I said with a huge sigh of relief. "We just need to give each other grace sometimes when those demons from our past rear up."

"I agree," Carlos said with a huge head bob. "And now that I know your favorite pastry place, I also know how to get into your good graces again when I do mess up. Because let's be honest, I will."

"You and I will, too," I admitted, not afraid for the first time to show my vulnerable side. I leaned across the table to capture his lips in a sweet kiss.

"Oh, and having your brother's number on speed dial might help," Carlos said, biting back a smile.

"Did you just make a joke? At my expense," I asked, trying to play mad. Unfortunately, Franklin and him becoming buddies was actually a great thing, in my opinion. My brother would end up with more amazing role models, and Franklin was a pretty upbeat guy who might do Carlos some good.

"I did, and trust me, I will use him for blackmail if it is called for," Carlos said, looking very proud of himself.

"It's all good. I've got your sister in laws numbers in my phone," I quipped back at him.

That did shut him up, and I happily sipped my coffee for a moment. When he caught my eye, though, that little dimple in his cheek told me he wasn't upset in the least. I sat back happily, feeling on top of the world.

CHAPTER 14

I was on top of the world as I got dressed. I had booked a fancy evening at a nice restaurant downtown to celebrate Jennifer and my two-month anniversary. Things were seriously looking up, and these last few weeks had flown by as if in a dream.

I looked in the mirror at the off-white dress shirt and decided I just didn't like its cut in the least. I pulled it off my body and picked up a light green option from the stack. I didn't have any understanding of why I was so nervous as this was Jennifer after all. The woman that literally I spilled my guts to about everything and never worried anymore that she might judge me. I loved her, she loved me, and we were beginning those serious talks about what the future might hold. If anyone had predicted this for me just a couple of short months ago, I would have laughed heartily in their face.

I decided that the green one would suffice, and tucking it into my dress slacks, took a final look in the mirror. It was as good as it was going to get. My hands I had scrubbed extra long tonight, as normally I had oil and crap under my nails – that was not going to do tonight. Everything was to be perfect, as I expected to ask Jennifer to come back to my place.

I understood that waiting in this day and age to sleep together was old-fashioned. It had been the right move for us as we had a lot of work on trust, communication, and such. This allowed the focus on those other important aspects without getting caught up in the physical side right away. I thought this was working amazingly well and had allowed both of us to do a lot of work on the communication side. I was actually finding myself more easily able to talk to employees, customers, and even my own mother.

As I was headed to the dining room, my cellphone rang. I smiled when I saw Mama's name on caller ID.

"Hello," I said with a huge grin putting the device to my ear.

"So, tonight is the big night. Are you going to ask a girl to go steady finally?" She teased me. I had been over visiting her the night before so the others could all go out on a double date. We had a really nice conversation about Jennifer, and Mama had asked that I bring her by this coming weekend. That was another big step for tonight. I normally just took my turn sitting with Mama on nights I didn't see Jennifer.

It gave us time to chat, but also, It was hard for me still to see Mama in this condition. I didn't want to bring all that sadness and worry into these early days of a relationship. I definitely wanted Jennifer to meet Mama, though, as I knew that both of them would benefit from the other so much. Now seemed the right time to facilitate that and make it happen.

"I'm not in high school, Mama," I said, getting back to her comment about going steady. "I think it's a bit more like a statement about being exclusive and maybe moving toward marriage."

"Wow," Mama said with shock in her voice, clear as day

even across the distance. "I never thought I would hear that word come out of your mouth."

"You know it has been my greatest hope for years," I sighed. "I never thought that someone could come along that just fit with me so perfectly. Since that first rough patch, it has been such easy sailing I'm over the moon to take this next step tonight."

"I'm so happy for you," Mama said. "Of course, when you come to babysit me on Sunday, I need details."

"We do not babysit you," I defended, loving the fact that she honestly had so much fight in her. I had a sneaking suspicion Mama was never going to be one that rolled over and accepted her fate. That kept her with us already well beyond what the doctors had predicted, and that was fine with me.

"What do you call it? Someone is always here these days. Hovering cooking and generally making sure I don't do anything but the restroom on my own."

"It's called caring," I replied, shaking my head. "You know we all love you and just want to take care of you for as long as we can."

"Harumph," she said. "Babysitting. You know if one of you could hurry up, maybe I would have a real baby to sit before I pass from this earth."

"How about we focus on marriages first, and you staying your feisty self for as long as possible?"

"I guess I can do that," she said. "Love you mijo. Call and let me know how the evening goes."

"I love you too, Mama" I said, hanging up the phone, shaking my head. I glanced around to ensure that my house was ready if Jennifer agreed to come back here. I had cleaned everything after work, put out candles, and even had fresh-cut flowers on the table. With a final look around, I picked up my keys, wallet and headed for the door.

It wasn't a long ride to Jennifer's house, and I was so

nervous I gripped the steering wheel for dear life. I strummed the steering wheel, singing aloud, trying to focus on anything else but this date. I honestly didn't know what my issue was, as I felt Jennifer was a pretty safe bet. We had been leading up to this, and not a single red flag had been thrown in weeks. We were good. Maybe it felt like a critical crossroad in my life, and this was a huge step.

I thought back to those years growing up. From the time I was in elementary school, I had always been so different, and kids had made fun of me incessantly. I fully understood the expression resting bitch face because so many called me resting angry face back in the day. No one understood me, and no one tried to be honest. My group of friends consisted of my brothers only, and after Rigo left, even those relationships were tried for a good long while.

Girls were complete unknowns for me, and dating had been a no in high school. If kids were cruel, asking someone out made me feel like I had the plague or something from the hysterical laughter that had occurred the two times I tried. Even once I was a successful small business owner, I could list probably twenty times that a woman had asked to speak to someone else when I was trying to help them.

From my sense of humor, quiet nature, and reserved approach to life, it seemed no matter how I tried to communicate, others rebuked me. Finally, though, it seemed I was on the verge of putting everything behind me. As I turned the corner to her house, my palms went sweaty, and I glanced in the rearview mirror. I thought I looked good tonight and hoped Jennifer would concur.

I rounded the final corner, and there ahead of me was Jennifer's stop. The car ahead of me stopped to let someone out, but my eyes went to Jennifer's when I suddenly froze.

There on the porch was Jennifer dressed to the nines. She looked stunning in a body-hugging blue dress and all that amazing hair in an updo. She had an odd look on her face as she turned to lock the door, and then I saw him. Another man slips from her doorway and slides a hand around her waist. She moved to hug him tightly to her, and my heart leaped into my throat – anger raging hot and fiery in my soul. I could not believe what I was seeing. When the man went in for a kiss, I was done. Squealing my tires, I went up on the curb, did a quick u-turn into the other lane, and revved my engine out of here.

I put my finger inside the collar of my dress shirt as I felt short of breath. Turning the air conditioner too high, I tried to get myself under control, but nothing was working. I was so pissed I was afraid I might crash the truck as I barrelled through town. I truly had no idea where I was headed, but it needed to be very far away from Jennifer until I could calm down.

JENNIFER 15

Getting out of the shower, I checked the time, mentally going through everything I still had to get done. I had no idea why I was this chaotic in my head right now, but I needed to stop. Focus on the tasks and try not to worry about what might happen.

I was so excited for this date tonight I hadn't been able to concentrate a lick at work today. Twice I caught myself re-reading the same email without any idea in the world what it said. I had not taken lunch, so I could leave thirty minutes early and come home to take a bath to calm myself down a bit. Now I worked through meticulously styling my hair, applying makeup, and stepping into the spectacular dress I had purchased just two days ago on a shopping trip with my mother. It was blue, form-fitting, and I was hoping to drive Carlos mad with wanting to take the thing off me with his teeth if I was lucky.

We had been waiting for this night for a couple of months we were dating now. Working on communication, outings, and getting to know each other priority over sex really applied a new level of intimacy to this relationship that I had

171

never experienced before. But I was now overly ready to move to the next step and see where this could lead in the near future. I saw moving in, marriage, and babies on the horizon and was ready for all of it with Carlos.

I couldn't remember ever feeling this confident in a decision I had made – none! I found that my temper was in check, I felt solid in my role at work, and everything seemed right with the world when Carlos was around. Even when certain things flair to life, we would immediately give each other that look that we needed to talk about. It was the time we would give the other to express without fear of repercussions whatever was on their mind. It was such a freeing experience to have that with someone. And Carlos held up his end of the bargain, being the best listener ever, and together, we found solutions to nearly everything without an argument. It was a long way from that night I walked away from him because he refused to call me his girlfriend, and since then, I had well and truly earned that title.

As I finished applying my makeup, though, the stupid doorbell interrupted, and I mucked up my eye. I immediately felt the giddiness for the night slip just a notch. As I glanced at the tiny wristwatch on my arm, I grimaced. Carlos had a habit of being early for everything we did, but this was super early even for him. I moved closer to the mirror, and now my hand was shaking with anticipation of seeing him. It took a bit of doing, but finally, I had the liner exactly how I wanted it and headed downstairs to answer the summons of the doorbell.

Standing in front of the door, I inhaled in order to center myself and then flung the door wide. I shook my sweaty palms out and tried to steady my breathing. Nausea that hit my system was fast, swift, and nearly doubled me in half. This was completely stupid! We had been out dozens of times now, and this should be just like any other night I chastised myself silently as I reached for the doorknob pulling it open.

"Jerry, what the hell are you doing here?" I asked as my voice shook from the shock of seeing my ex-boyfriend standing on my doorstep after all this time. I had expected Carlos to be greeting me with one of his lopsided grins, not this creep from my past. The man had cheated on me, made me feel like I was less than nothing, and then ghosted me. Now on the most important night of my life – he had the audacity to show up here.

"Aren't you going to ask me in?" Jerry asked with that cocky smile on his face that I detested as he slid past me. I tried to block him but wasn't fast enough though I just turned, refusing to be alone in my house with him.

"You need to go now," I demanded through gritted teeth.

"Don't you look beautiful," he sighed in that tone that at one time would have had me dropping my clothes for him. Now all I could do was ball my hands in fists at my sides and wish he would disappear. This could not be happening again just when I was happy.

Jerry was like that – a bad rash that reappeared just when you thought you were done with him. The truth was I had loved him to distraction and overlooked a lot of his woman-izer, lying, and worse traits for a long time. He had done a great job of tearing me down until I didn't believe I deserved better than what he was willing to dole out. Those days were over, and I would never risk what Carlos and I had for this piece of slime.

"The effort was not for you," I said as calmly as I could. "I need you to leave." I held my ground, holding the door wide for him. I prayed that for once, he would figure out where he was not wanted and evaporate back into the night like a bad dream.

Jerry and I had a fiery relationship back in the day. His

temper made mine look tame, and he could get me swearing, cutting, and throwing things in no time. I wasn't that person now and refused to go back there. Carlos and I had amazing communication, respect, and love for each other. I would not risk losing that for his man.

"I know you missed me," Jerry said, moving closer to me and trying to put his hands on either side of my face. I twisted away and backed up as fast as possible on my three-inch heels. Honestly, I felt ill at this point. Carlos could not find us like this, or he absolutely would get the wrong impression, and this evening – possibly our entire relationship – could be impacted.

"Jerry, I have someone very important to me coming over in a few minutes, and I need you gone," I demanded, pointing once again at the front door wide open, keeping my tone even.

"We need to talk first," Jerry said, not budging as he was leaning casually against my couch. He was the same self-assuming jerk that though the world revolved around him that he had always been, I realized. I glanced at my watch and inhaled.

"Talk fast. We don't have anything left to say to each other," I offered back to him.

I had to admit I had always wondered at what I would feel should Jerry and I cross paths again. The man had been my first major love, and his leaving had crushed me to pieces. I hadn't left my room for two weeks, lost my job, and nearly my apartment from the grief. That was then, and now I felt nothing. Carlos was more responsible, caring toward me and even helped me work on communication and open scars from my past. Jerry had aggravated all those and even created new wounds that I carried to this day. Seeing him today left me cold and oddly reinforced that what I had with Carlos was the real thing.

"I miss you, sugar lips," he said using my old nickname.

"Jerry, you cheated on me and left me during a huge scene at a restaurant with that woman. What happened to the perfect model you just had chase after?"

"She left me for a Podiatrist," he said with a tiny grimace. "Didn't matter, though she was a cold fish, and she hated how much I missed and talked about you."

"Well, that has been a long time, and I've moved on," I said, realizing that Carlos would be here any time now. The man was never late. Backing up to the door, I took hold of my purse and keys in hand. "I really have to go."

Jerry finally took a hint and started toward the door with me. He rubbed up against me suggestively as we both backed up onto the stoop, and I turned to lock my door. He then put his hand around my waist and leaned in to kiss my neck.

"I really did miss you," he said in a low husky tone.

The man was a master at seduction, and yet all I felt in this moment was abject fear that Carlos might pull up and see this. I would never choose Jerry over Carlos, but this might look wrong to someone just passing by.

"Jerry, please stop," I whispered as I looked up and could swear that the truck stuck behind a stopped car a bit up the road was Carlos. "You need to go now."

"Just one hug," Jerry said as he leaned in and tried to kiss me.

I heard the squeal of tires and horns honking as Jerry tried to kiss me. I pushed him away and looked over to where the sounds were coming from, only to see Carlos making a u-turn and then squealing away.

"Oops, was that him?" Jerry said with a little chuckle.

"Yes," I mumbled as I stood there trying to figure out what to do next.

"I guess you have time for dinner with me then," Jerry said to which I turned and glared at him.

"Not if you were the last man on earth. You couldn't hold a candle to that man," I said, pointing the direction Carlos went. "He is loyal, a great communicator, loves his family, and always puts me first. Those are all traits you know nothing about, and I bet you are here tonight because you are simply bored. I would wake up tomorrow to an empty bed and even emptier promises."

I felt much better to get that off my chest. I was free of Jerry's hold on my life, and in some ways, that was a gift. I had spent a lot of time wondering about what if. What if he was my true love, and I had missed my chance not holding him tighter. What ifs, though, just kept you anchored to the past and never moving forward. Tonight had been good for one thing in realizing Jerry was better left in the past and had no part in my future. Now I had to figure out a way to get my happily ever after back.

"Yeah, but will he chase you. I know you don't like to show weakness and chase after the men you want," Jerry taunted as the truth of that statement rang in my ears.

I bent down, slid my shoes off to hold in one hand. "No, Jerry – you just weren't the man worthy enough for me to want to chase," I said, leaving him standing with his mouth agape as I turned to start down the road.

Carlos was worth chasing, though, and this night was long from being over. I was going to hunt him down, explain what had happened back there and make things right. I refused to run from this until we could talk about it.

I dialed Carlos's number and waited for him to pick up.

"What?" He asked tersely when the call connected.

"You turn around now and let me explain," I spat out before hanging up. Then I kept walking, determined I would go all the way to his house three miles away and camp out if that is what it took.

I walked for about twenty minutes when a horn sounded

behind me, causing me to jump out of my skin. I turned, and my heart flip-flopped painfully in my chest when I saw Carlos in his truck pull to the side of the road. He put the large vehicle in park and exited, standing nervous-looking on the sidewalk.

I ran at him full speed and then jumped up into his arms. "I'm sorry, Carlos. So sorry, and I wish you had not had to see that."

"So do I," he said softly though he didn't sound mad, just more sad than anything.

"That was Jerry, my ex. I have not spoken to him or had any contact in a long time. And then, out of the clear blue tonight of all nights, he showed up unexpectedly. He walked into my apartment despite me not wanting him there."

"I understand," Carlos said, looking even sadder now.

I put a finger under his chin and drew his eyes to min. "I sent him away and told him that he meant nothing to me. Carlos, you are everything I need," I said into his neck as I hugged him close again before pulling back to look at him as something dawned on me. "You turned around?"

"I did," he said with a soft chuckle as a grin crossed his face. "I drove like a bat out of hell from your place to Joey's after I saw the two of you. But before I could get out to go talk to my brother, something just stopped me cold. I knew exactly what I needed to do and turned around back to you."

"You chased after me," I said, so happy I thought I might actually burst into tears.

"I guess I did," Carlos said. "I figured I needed to hear you out, even if it hurt. Even if you had left me for him, I had to know. But I will admit, I planned to make a good case for you to choose me."

"I love you," I whispered, holding tight to him. "I know it even more so when I was standing there with Jerry. I felt

177

absolutely nothing for him, and I had to find you and tell you."

"And I love you," Carlos whispered. "And I knew I loved you when I thought about actually going up to that Jerry fellow and telling him what I thought with my fists. That would have been a big first for me."

"Well, I'm glad we could settle this without violence," I laughed as I got a very different look in my eye. "You know what I'm thinking," I said with a huge knowing smile in his direction.

"Forget dinner?"

"Exactly," I replied, climbing up into the truck to put my head on his shoulder.

He put the vehicle into drive, and for once, I knew I was exactly where I was supposed to be, with the man I had always been waiting for.

EPILOGUE

ight months later

E   I was pacing the little room feeling like a man trapped in a prison of his own making. It was my wedding day, and I loved Jennifer with all my being. That said, we had written our own vows. *Seriously, I didn't know how this woman continued to talk me into things like this!*

"Are you ready?" Rigo asked as he walked into the room, looking dapper in the tuxedo he had on. "You look like you are about to get violently ill."

"I have been considering it all morning," I admitted.

"Hey, none of this cold feet shit," Joey said as he walked into the room with Manny and Franklin right next to him.

We were a sight in our tuxedos covering most of the tattoos and looking as if any one of us might burst from the clothing at any moment. I was grateful that they all volunteered to get gussied up in Jennifer's outfits to support me today.

"How is mom?" I asked.

We moved this wedding up from the original date next summer to accommodate her fast-failing health. The doctors were telling us we had days left if we were lucky. She had insisted that we do this at the church, though, and she had made Angela and Sandi swear along with his sisters to get her ready in style. He worried that she was too frail, but Mama did not hear any of it, and he expected to see her there fierce as every at the end of the aisle as he walked toward his happily ever after with Jennifer.

"She made it," Joey said, clearing his throat. "I think if we could get this big lug married,' he said, slapping Rigo on the back, "her life mission would be complete."

"What about the girls?" Manny asked.

"She says they are like her, and she doesn't worry about them," Joey grumbled. "I don't think any one of us look like we couldn't take care of ourselves in a fight – do you?"

"That is what mom always says about me. She is worried, but I honestly thought Jennifer was the one that would never marry," Franklin said, causing them all to chuckle.

There was a round of head shakes as they gazed at each other. And then it got silent.

"I think she just worried that if we didn't make peace before she left us," Rigo said. "She would end up being the only woman we were all devoted to. Making peace with our pasts, her, and all the crap that went down in our life is paying off dividends. She is leaving us knowing we are reconciled, happily settled, and she did good."

I had to shake my head in agreement as a tear rose up in my eye. "Please don't' make me cry before the ceremony," I said.

"Oh, I'm with you," Manny said, handing me a handkerchief from his pocket. "This new sensitive kick we are all one really needs to stop."

"I think you out of luck today," Joey interjected. "I'm already teary thinking of you are giving your vows," he said, turning to me. "I can't believe you found Jennifer, and together, you guys are going to have the best life."

"Oh, you know you all will be there for every step of it," Manny said. "None of us are getting rid of each other – is that understood?"

"Definitely," Rigo agreed.

"Of course," Joey said.

"I couldn't say it better," I offered. "And you too," I said, grabbing Franklin into the circle. "You are getting a passel of brothers out this today; how do you feel about that?"

"I'm good," Franklin said as he nodded, looking on the verge of tears.

"Then let's go get you married," Joey said as we came in close before finally breaking apart and heading for the door.

As I walked down the aisle to stand and wait for my bride, I couldn't believe how fortunate I was. I had an amazing, resilient family, a woman that loved me, and that was everything. Nothing would be perfect, but we would make it through stronger together with patience, faith, and love!

RIGO

RIGO

I CLOSED my eyes and let my hands walk all over her curvy body, not carrying a lick what her face looked like. I wouldn't even remember this woman in the morning, but right now, I was just trying to feel something – anything other than the mind-numbing emptiness that had taken up permanent residence in my heart. I wasn't a man in the real sense of the world, but a robot trying to get from one moment to the next without any human connection, just pain, ecstasy, and some alcohol to dull everything else.

I danced away my worries as I did every Friday night, with a hot lady in my arms, rocking the night away to the tune of the disco beat of "Staying Alive" by the Bee Gees. I barely knew who she was, and the same went for her, but we both liked it that way. Life is so much easier when you are not dealing with people you know or care about. I liked to live in the moment and not think about tomorrow or the ramifications of my actions when just cutting loose.

This night was important for me. I mean, every Friday was usually spent with the boys at either a club or the bar. However, this was special because it was my last Friday night hangout with my friends, as we all called it. I'd gotten hired for a new job which was located in my hometown in California. It was one of the reasons why I'd applied, to be closer and attend more of the Mendoza get-togethers. That and the fact was my mother was in terribly bad health and not expected to make it much longer. I wanted to spend time with her, mending fences before it was too late, and hang with my siblings. Now that Carlos, my older bro, had a girlfriend, I started wondering if maybe I could find a special someone.

I was still reeling from Carlos, finding someone like Jennifer to spend his life with. Honestly, watching the two of them together had made me double guess my decision to remain single lately. I'd never thought Carlos would ever find a woman since he was super quiet and struggled for a long time with communication with strangers. When I saw them together for the first time, though, it was obvious they were meant to be. That kind of love is something I envied. Carlos now had someone he cared for, and well, that got me thinking maybe I could also find love. Wait. *Why was I even thinking about all this right now when a beautiful woman was dancing right in front of me?*

"Yo, Rigo!" Jeremy yelled at me. "You seem out of it! Hope you're not getting all emotional before you go!"

I chuckled under my breath and smirked at him, trying to shrug it off as he simply would not understand nor appreciate my current train of thought. If I was being completely honest, I wasn't really close to these people. They were my so-called 'party friends,' and that's how I liked it. This was a group that I had met over the years, which was only about drinking, partying, and having a good time. We never really talked about anything of substance, nor did we keep in touch overly much during the week. None of them really knew anything about me or had even been to my place.

I didn't need people that wanted to get that close to me around day to day—or at least that's what I told myself. I'd always had to fend for myself ever since I left to go live with my Tia Lola, who did her best to help me get through tough times. Those years being estranged from my family had hardened me in some ways that I was still trying to recover from today. Things were hard, but they made me a stronger person, and I became the man I am today. I've never needed someone, nor will I ever. It was, and is, and will always be me, myself, and I that I relied on. I gave myself the same internal speech I had been reciting for years, and partly I believed it. On the other hand, the loneliness of this existence had started to wear on me, but that was a worry for another day, I told myself as I tried to refocus on the woman I held in my arms.

The boys and I danced a bit longer until we were worn out. After that, Jeremy, Dante, and I all made our way to the seating lined up along the nightclub bar. I was tired, and it wasn't because of the dancing. Sure, dancing with a hot chick who just never tires can be as exhausting as it is sexy, and it had drained me a bit. However, I was tired because I knew going back home would open a can of worms I had long since suppressed. There was a reason I felt more at ease in Arizona. I felt no need to be attached to anyone, and there was no family here to force my cooperation.

"Yo, Rigo! What's up? Having second thoughts?" Dante punched my shoulder with a wide grin. "Don't tell me you're gonna miss us!"

I laughed, trying to remain as lively as them. "Like anyone would miss your sorry ass if you died today."

They both shouted 'ooohh!' and feigned being shot in the chest. The reason I liked these guys was that they never tried to pry. I'm sure they had their own baggage or stories, and they understood the need for space and privacy. Our drinks arrived, and Jeremy raised his glass in the air.

"A toast… to this bastard." Dante laughed, and I scoffed while smiling.

"Anyway, man. We wish you the best in California. More life, parties, and women!" Jeremy said. We all roared, clanking our glasses, and gulping them down. The party went on for another couple of hours, and then I went home to my packed apartment and anticipated the trip home.

The next day, I was on the road when Carlos called.

"Yo, what's up?" I said, picking up the call and placing it on speaker so I could talk while driving.

"You here yet?" My brother said from the other side of the line. His tone made me grin, as I knew he was asking because the anticipation was just as strong for him as me regarding this homecoming. He was a good guy and probably the one other human on earth that understood exactly how I felt as we had travelled similar roads after the breakup of our parents.

"Don't tell me you are this excited to see me, brother." It hadn't been long since we were together as I had made a trip recently for a family gathering and to check in on Mama.

"Shut up, dude," Carlos grumbled.

I chuckled. It was easy talking to Carlos, which was why he was the only one I could open up to in the family. Manny was too volatile for my liking, and Joey was always trying to be in the middle of everything, like the negotiator with people's feelings. I just wanted to be left alone to wallow in my own feelings without having to share them. I'd also convinced myself that Mama probably had made me sound heartless to my siblings. My sister Estrella and I would email on Facebook now and then, but I rarely use that app these days. I wasn't much into social media. Heck, I could barely text and google directions.

"Just drive safe, that's all."

"Yeah, yeah. I'm not far away. I'll get settled in my apartment and call you later."

"Sure, man." Another reason why I liked Carlos a lot; he did not pry. He never asked for any details unless it was necessary, nor did he try and press me to hang out or spend more time with the Familia.

"How's your lady?" I asked, trying to make conversation. Usually, I wouldn't ask about these things, but I was curious. He was my closest sibling, especially after my Tia Lola, God rest her soul, passed. I was lonely and missed everyone so much. Maybe it was an age thing, but the anger of my youth was fast being overshadowed by the need for connections, family, and peace.

"She's fine. We are great, man. Speaking of..." I always hated it when people sounded like this. The hesitation meant they were going to say something I wasn't going to agree with or ask for something I was likely not in favor of.

"Here we go." I sighed.

"You don't even know what I was going to say."

"I know it's something I don't really wanna hear."

"Ugh, dumbass. It's about Manny." *Manny?*

"What about Manny? Is he okay?" I hoped nothing bad had happened to him. He was an asshole, but he was still my brother.

"No, no, no. Nothing like that... It's good news," Carlos quickly responded. "He is going to propose to his girlfriend, Sandi, and wants everyone to be there. He wanted me to invite you since you were going to be in town."

"For someone who doesn't say much, you sure didn't have a problem blabbing your mouth about me moving to California."

"Dude, shut up. Would you rather we both kept quiet and they found out later then get upset that we didn't say anything?" He was right. Why did I even say that to him? Well, I knew why. Memories from the past were flooding my mind, and they weren't all pleasant.

"Yeah, you're right, bro. Sorry. I should be able to make Manny's big event; after all, trying to mend bridges is part of the reason I'm moving back," he said with a mild annoyance sinking into resignation.

"Just drive safe and let me know when you make it, okay?"

"Sure, man." I clicked off the phone and drove to my new place in a comfortable neighborhood. The area looked nice, but I noticed a few homeless people—they were pretty much everywhere now. I reached my place and unloaded all my stuff. This place was … new. It had new carpet, appliances, and paint. I was pretty excited to have a new place, a new job, and start a new chapter in my life. I was going to be working at Toodle as a logistics manager. Toodle specializes in the shipping of goods locally and worldwide. I'd applied for the position back after meeting one of their managers in Arizona. Luckily, I was hired with great pay, a retirement account, and health benefits, I couldn't skip this opportunity. It was a great step for me, and I was extremely excited.

A great job, a new apartment, and some time to reconnect – life was looking up these days. Now, I just hoped nothing backfired too horribly on him as he was tired of being lonely, mad, and alone.

ELAINE

*T*hey just kept talking and talking and talking. As I sat in the limo with my head tilted back to face the ceiling, all I could hear was the rambling of their incessant mouths flapping. I needed them to stop!

"No! The Dior is going to be the best!" Donna said excitedly, trying to get the others to see her opinion as fact.

"What about Versace? Classic, babe!" Leslie retorted. They were all so... boring. I know that was ironic coming from someone with as dull a life as mine, but it is what it is.

"I'm sorry, are we boring you, Elaine?" Donna—always so temperamental—asked me after she heard me yawn. I glanced at her for a moment, not certain how to answer that question and not sound like a jerk.

"You don't want to know the answer to that question, Donna," I replied dryly, which always annoyed her. I never understood why people would bother asking questions if they weren't going to like your responses. Maybe I was just tired of always saying the right thing and acting the right way because of my parents. They expected me to be perfect no matter the circumstances or how I truly felt. I had become a person who just didn't care about anything or anyone— even myself—at this point. I just wasn't happy with my life.

I thought back over the last twenty years of my life and the huge list of concerns my parents had visited upon me. After interviewing some of her friends, she had to believe her parents were the most overbearing. They didn't allow me to make decisions on my own – not one. They approved everything from the clothes my personal shopper was allowed to purchase to the cellphone I carried. They treated me like a trophy that was trained into servitude from decorum classes, proper dining protocol, make-up lessons, and even how often I had my hair trimmed.

A few years ago, when I thought about going back to school, I was shot down before fully making my case. I thought it would help me expand my interests, but both her mom and dad felt it would just lead to unwanted attention, partying that got out of control and introduce me to bad influences. My life was simply a reflection of their own reputation and likes – nothing that allowed me to shine in any way. Heck, I even lived with them at my age because they worried about me picking a bad neighborhood, not having enough security, and saw no purpose to the cash outlay when they had a mansion that easily accommodated all of us.

All that would be great if it was intended for us to spend time together. Nope! They honestly barely knew I was around half the time, as absorbed in each other's lives as they were. It was tough to see how self-absorbed they were, yet the only attention I got was when I misstepped and had to be redirected. Even tonight, I was out, despite not being in the mood because all the press would be there, and my mother forced me to accept the invite.

"Donna..." Leslie tried to calm our friend down before she went nuts yet again. She always had to be the mediator.

"No. What exactly is your problem, Elaine?" This was like the hundredth time Donna was asking me this question. "You always act like you're better than us or that you just don't give a damn about anyone. Why are you like this?!"

By now, I was already back to my original position of staring at the limo ceiling. I did not blame her for being frustrated and pissed off. It must be so exhausting for someone like her to be around someone like me all the time.

"Why do you invite me?" I snapped at her finally, just tired of everything at this moment.

She huffed. "Because you're my friend, and that's what friends do. What I don't understand is what's really going on with you?"

The rational choice would be to just not invite me. I was used to being alone and was just fine with being do. My parents were always so busy with their own agenda they barely knew I was alive.

"Are you done?" I replied, trying to hide my frustration. I always asked myself the same question: *What exactly is my problem?* Growing up, I always behaved because of my father's political career and my mother being a popular fashionista and socialite. I was never allowed to voice my opinion on any topic for fear it would cause some social backlash for my parents; I was expected to act the part of my parents' perfect child.

Even when I was genuinely interested in something, my parents never took any interest or even wanted to know about it as they viewed me as just an accessory to their lives. I was attracted to some boys, but I never acted on it. My mother's words always echoed in my mind: *Your reputation is everything, and one single choice could destroy your father's career or mine.* As an only child, there was even more pressure on me to be perfect. I'd had gotten used to keeping my thoughts to myself… maybe even too comfortable with it.

"Ugh, you're just crazy!"

"Nope. You're the crazy one, remember?" I retorted, making her even more enraged. She sighed furiously and sat back in her seat with arms tight against her chest.

"Seriously, you girls need to calm down. We're here." Leslie deflected the attention to the red carpet. We got out of the limo and walked into the fashion show. As I walked and posed, giving my ultra-fake smile, I cringed inwardly, wondering why I kept putting on this act. I needed an escape from twenty years of repetition and stoic pain. The sad part, though, was that I was so used to it that I didn't have any idea what options there were.

"Heyyyy, Elaine!" Giuliana, a well-known fashion designer, called out to me when she spotted me inside. I was just getting to my seat when I heard my name, so I turned to greet her.

"Hey, Giuliana. You look gorgeous as always." I hugged her without even noticing what she had on. I had learned to say what people wanted to hear even if I didn't mean it.

She returned the compliment, and I nodded. We made small talk before the show started, but I couldn't have told you anything that either of us said. It was just the same routine over and over again, talking to people I didn't care about just to keep up appearances. At least with Donna and Leslie, I could somewhat express my feelings but not completely open up.

"Sometimes, I wonder how you do it," Donna said when I sat down. As expected, Leslie was seated between us. How was I doing this? How could I find the mental darkness and strength to pretend every day of my life? I hated thinking about my problems and the inability to be inspired by virtually anything. I wanted a release, even if it was temporary. In fact, I needed a release, or I would go mad. The fashion show went on and on. My friends cheered for each dress they liked on the runway, but I was just there... observing and doing what everyone expected. I knew I had to smile every now and then so that the pictures wouldn't make it seem like I did not want to be there. But at that moment, I just couldn't muster a smile up from the pits of my despair.

"Are you... high?" Donna asked me during the after-party. I'd had a lot of whisky and tequila, so I supposed I was a little drunk. I could not even think clearly. This was probably the first time my friends had seen me under the influence.

"What's going on, Elaine?" Leslie asked, looking worried.

"I... I'm t-tirrreed." I shook my head, trying to clear it. "I can't do it anymore... I can't k-keep... keep pretending." This was why I loved alcohol; it numbed my feelings, and I could just speak my mind. I usually only drank at home since my parents were always so busy they never even noticed, and I wouldn't risk offending any of my friends in public. Only Mary, our housekeeper, knew about it.

"Are you crying? You?" Donna was shocked, but not as shocked as I was. I hadn't even realized tears were coursing down my cheeks. "Quick, Les. We have to get her to the restroom before one of the cameras catches her in this state."

Leslie helped me walk while Donna tried shielding me as much as she could. As we walked, I thought of how inconsiderate I had always been toward these two girls. Donna was feisty and could handle it, but the real person I felt bad for was Leslie. The way I dismissed her sensitive talks and need for friends. She opened up a lot, and that always made me uncomfortable, so I rarely answered her.

We reached the restroom, and, thankfully, nobody was there. They locked the door and brought me to one of the sinks, washing my face for me.

"I'm sorry... I'm so sorry," I repeatedly said to both of them.

"This is what happens when you bottle up things inside,"

Donna said but was shushed by Leslie. It was the truth, though. They both took makeup out of their purses and redid my face quickly, talking about normal things so my emotions could calm down. After a few minutes, I assured them I would be okay, and they reluctantly left to give me privacy. I was still pretty tipsy, but at least I felt like I was more in control of myself. Still, there were too many people in here. I had to get some air. I took my bag and wandered off while Leslie and Donna were mingling with the other guests.

"Mom and Dad are gonna kill me," I murmured to myself as I left the building and walked away. I was just walking aimlessly, shit-faced, and completely depressed. I didn't want to go on like this day after day and knew there had to be something out there that might make me feel again. I wanted to be able to talk openly, express myself and connect with people that sparked something inside of me rather than live this life that had been designed around me.

"Why are you torturing yourself?" I asked myself while looking up at the stars. "Why... if you died now... who would even care?" I heard a loud horn and whipped around to see a car coming to a squealing stop in front of me. I had wandered into the middle of the road while looking at the darkened sky. My immediate fear quickly morphed into satisfaction. I was okay with dying here, and I had accepted that no one would care. What had I done in my life? Nothing. I might as well bite the dust in one of the most mundane ways possible, right? I closed my eyes and waited for the end.

But it never came. Opening my eyes, I saw that the car had managed to stop just as it was about to hit me. The driver jumped out of his car and came racing around to the front. He was a dashing raven-haired guy with slight stubble from what I could tell and a face that told of the terror his nearly hitting me invoked in him.

"What the hell were you thinking?!" he shouted.

I just turned with the biggest smile toward him and laughed. No, seriously, I laughed. The man was screaming at me like the lunatic I had been acting, and it was glorious!

RIGO

*D*arn it. I should have gotten groceries immediately after driving into town, but instead, I spent time unpacking and setting my apartment. Now I was weary from so much activity, hungry, and looking for a place to eat in a part of town I hadn't been in quite some time. I had called Carlos, but he was busy, so... yeah. Here I was, driving late at night in an area where everything was overpriced as hell, chastising myself for the stupidity of my actions.

"Those bastard elitist restaurants," I grumbled as I passed some of them. I did not want a Burger King cheap burger right now because I wasn't craving that, but everything else looked super-pricey. I kept driving to see if something looked good. I was so caught up staring at the stores in this new town that I almost didn't notice a young lady standing in the middle of the street, her head tilted up to the sky. I slammed on the brakes and the horn at the same time, praying that I wasn't about to kill some strange woman on my first night in town.

I managed to stop just in the nick of time. What was most shocking was the way she just stood there, staring at me like she actually wanted to die. *What the hell was she trying to do, get herself run over? Was this how crazy people in California were? Just walking in front of cars looking for someone they can blame their deaths on?* I bolted out of my car, hands clenching and unclenching. I was hellbent on giving her a piece of my mind.

"What the hell were you thinking?!" I yelled before I noticed how unbelievably gorgeous she was. I couldn't shout at her like that—Wait. This was all her fault, so why the hell was I berating myself for giving her a hard time?

She blinked at me, swaying slightly, and then she laughed. I stared at her and thought maybe she was escaped from one of those fancy "health spas" and not in her right mind. Before I could figure out what to do, she did calm herself and spoke coherently, which was even more confusing, to be honest.

"Sorry, I just wasn't thinking straight. I just wanted to go in peace quickly." She was drunk and completely out of her mind, it would seem. Her hair and makeup were impeccable, looking like she'd just had it done, and when you add the expensive dress, this was obviously one of the rich Cali girls I kept hearing about from my brothers and friends. I wanted no part in this, especially being new in this area. Who knew what kind of weirdness was going on?

I tried to turn to get back into my car, but somehow her gravitational pull would not let me go. I swear to God, this was not normal as I found my feet turning of their own volition back in her direction, realizing she was still standing in the middle of the street staring at me, confused. I couldn't just walk away from her, even though I knew she was trouble. Regardless of what I thought about her, what remained evident was the fact that this girl was drunk and obviously not in her right mind. I didn't even know where she'd come from. Looking up the block, I saw some bright lights, paparazzi, and limos at a club just up the way. *Was she from there?* It was probably some celebrity party. *All I had to do was drive her back there, right?* Then she would walk out of my life, and I could make my escape with a clean conscience. Win-win for all involved.

"Are you okay?" I asked, walking over to her. This one was fascinating to behold; I have to say. She had dirty blond hair that curled down to her waist. Her eyes were big and a cerulean blue that was so striking it mesmerized me. Even her pink lips and rosy cheeks were magnificent, like a painted doll that just made you want to examine her more closely.

"Do I look okay?" She retorted aggressively, surprising me from the tone that did not match her dainty appearance. I guess she was having a rough time. All I needed to do was take her to a safe space and then get the hell out of here and go back home.

"Okay. So, where are you coming from? The party over there?" I asked, pointing to the large building about two blocks from our current location.

Instead of answering, she put her hands on her hips and glared at me. "Why didn't you run me over?"

What the hell? Was this woman serious? Did she really want to die? It was shocking that a girl this pretty and rich did not want to live. She looked like someone that had the world at her feet. I knew people in higher economic standing killed themselves at a higher rate than the poor, but seeing it for myself was… real and disturbing at the same time. Honestly, as I saw and heard the fire inside of her, I didn't really believe she wanted to die, but definitely, there was something heavy on her mind. Glancing about, I realized she had me hook, line, and sinker. I needed to know more and reassure myself she wasn't going to do herself any harm.

"Are you crazy?" I blurted out, surprising her and myself. Ugh, I just couldn't help it, huh? I'm no therapist, but I'd assume that was not something you should say to a person with suicidal tendencies.

"No, but I'm drunk, so I'd probably say stupid things right about now," she replied. "Don't you want to move your car out of the road?"

Oh, shit! I had forgotten about that, I realized, turning around to see several people giving me the finger and waving at my vehicle. I wouldn't want someone to hit it after I'd had one close call.

"I can drive you back to your party. That's where you're coming from, right?" I tried one more time to get her to see reason.

She rolled her eyes. "I don't want to go back there. That's why I left." Ugh, this was getting more complicated. Part of my brain told me to get away from this quickly before I found myself being accused of something. For some reason, I trusted her, though, and I did not know why.

"Fine," I said, sighing. "What's your name, and where can I take you? Home?"

"Elaine, and no, not home. I just… I want you to take me somewhere else."

Oh, boy. I sighed, thinking of how I'd gotten into this mess and the easiest way to extricate myself. The sad look in those stunning eyes, though, as she contemplated me, overruled my better sense.

"I'm Rigo. Get in," I said, thumbing my finger toward the passenger side of the car. I was definitely going to regret this later, but it seemed the best option to get her out of the roadway.

She plunked herself down next to me as I put the car in drive, and we drove past the fancy party. She ducked her head to hide her face so the paparazzi wouldn't notice her. I chuckled, thinking that a minute ago, she hadn't cared about anything, much less the press.

"Why are you laughing, asshole?" She asked without any hesitation, which for some reason, just made me chuckle.

"You're very lippy, aren't you?"

"Yeah, so? And you haven't answered my question."

"You do realize that you are in a car with a stranger who is driving you to a place you don't even know," I noted, and she smiled. Damn, what a beautiful smile, I thought, wondering what that perfect pout would taste like. "What if I was a kidnapper or a serial killer?"

"That could actually be funnier than anything that has happened to me in a long time," she said, not missing a beat. The woman was on fire, and I honestly had no idea how to handle everything she was tossing out at me.

"What happened to make you such a cynic?"

She was drunk, and I knew that meant she would be more apt to tell the full truth. "Because I am tired of living this life where everyone else tells me what to do, wear, and say, duuuhhh!" Her reply broke my heart. It was sad that a girl this pretty and rich, with so much obviously going for her, wished to die. I wanted to help, but I didn't know how. "We're all just meaningless specks hovering in a minute section of the cosmos," she went on in a hopeless tone. "Nobody cares about anybody... especially someone like me."

"I know I just met you, but... I care," I said, and I was surprised to find that I really meant it. She scoffed.

"You like everyone just sees a rich girl and assume that I have everything I could ever want in life," she spat back, looking even more miserable if that was humanly possible. "My parents are wealthy, and trust me, that has never been cause for happiness. My parents work so hard to maintain their bright shiny status that sometimes I think they even forget I'm their child. They have a duty to engage with me, know what I like and dislike. Maybe they should spend quality time with me or hear me when I tell them something is not my cup of tea."

"That all seems reasonable," I said, taking in everything she was saying. It was honestly putting a lot of things into perspective for me. "You know I have a family that is super involved in everything I do – or at least they tried to be. We were not rich when I was growing up by any means, but we had each other and all these amazing times together. Then one stupid secret, and I ran away, my Mama quit trying to know me and everything went to shit! So, I get it. We all have things that suck in our lives, but it is how we choose to address those moments and rise above it that defines us as people."

She just stared at me with the most perplexed face for a long time. "So, how would you prove that you care for me, as you say you do even after this short an acquaintance?" She questioned, surprising me.

"Here, I'll show you that I care," I insisted. "I was out here driving around looking for a nice place to eat that was not overpriced. Let's drive around and find a food truck with some real food that's not overpriced."

"I don't eat at food trucks."

"I know, I can tell from your jewelry," I replied. "What, do you think it'll kill you?"

She snorted. "You think you're gonna save a lost girl so you can feel better about yourself. Sorry, but—"

"Well, at least you can say you had some real food before you died," I pointed out, and she stared at me for a minute before she finally started to chuckle. "Okay, let's do it – I mean, how bad can it truly be?"

I quirked an eyebrow in her direction, "I hope you have a strong constitution," I teased.

ELAINE

*W*hy was I spilling all my feelings to this stranger? Somewhere in the recesses of my mind, this confused me, but the alcohol hadn't fully worn off yet. Something about this man had actually reached inside and twisted up my guts, and I wanted him to like me. No, not me, the socialite that everyone thought had the perfect life but the real me!

Rigo was handsome, seemed to care even though his gruff exterior said he didn't want to, and was sincere. He didn't sugar coat anything and pretty much spouted whatever was on his mind. His muscles were large, his physique fantastic, and he had a face that made a woman go warm and gooey in places she didn't talk about in public. He had straight dark hair, and his brown eyes had a magnetic pull to them. His dark upper lip and red lower lip were rare among men but made him stand out more. They were beautiful. Every part of his looks was amazing, but that wasn't what I really cared about, though, as it was all window dressing only.

On our way to the food truck, he kept talking. I suspected that he was either nervous or trying to distract me. Usually, I wouldn't care, but now... hearing him talk, I realized it was because I was used to talking about shallow things with the people I hung out with. We lived in a bubble of riches and had no idea how the real world was. I was so clueless. Rigo was from Arizona, and he talked about the places he had been and the places he'd seen on his way here. I was fascinated hearing someone with experiences completely different from mine blabber on as it tried to keep my attention fixed on something other than my morose mood. Someone who wasn't talking about clothes, reputation, fashion, or celebrities. Just a good ol' chat.

I felt my phone vibrate and picked up the cellphone to check who it was. OMG! I'd forgotten to call Donna or Leslie.

"Hey, Leslie. Sor-" I said as I connected the call and put the device to my ear.

"What the hell is wrong with you?! Where are you?!" Leslie shouted. It was clear she was worried out of her mind about me, and I instantly regretted my actions.

"Sorry. I'm on my way home. I'll see you girls tomorrow. Thanks for taking care of me," I said, trying to sound upbeat and ease her worry.

"Are you sure you're okay?" She replied, not seeming to believe me that all was well.

"Yes. Tell Donna thank you from me."

"All right. Talk to you tomorrow."

"Bye," I said and ended the call.

"Your friends really care about you," Rigo observed. I knew where this was heading. He would use that as a way to make me feel guilty for wanting to die.

"Don't," I said gruffly, trying to stop his train of thought right then and there.

"Huh?" He asked, turning to me with the oddest of

expressions. "I was just pointing out the obvious," he said, crooking a tiny grin at her.

"Don't turn this into a sad story about how I would be doing them wrong by ending my own life. I know that, but honestly, have you ever wondered why in the world you are here and what you are supposed to be doing with this life?"

"Yes, I do have moments quite often wondering about my plight in life. I actually moved her to try and work on some old habits that I haven't been able to get over," he said without missing a beat. "You need to understand that committing something permanent to deal with your issues is not the way to go, and you need to honestly buck up and try other options. Don't play nice with all your friends if you aren't happy, and start talking to them like you feel okay doing with me."

Wow, I had never been given such brutal honesty in my life before. I was almost happy to hear it, even though I was angry as hell. How could he say that to me? Well, maybe because he had a different lifestyle than mine. He probably had a family that cared about him.

"But, I have to say it would really be a sad world without you in it," he said. "I have this pretty good gut feeling telling me that you could be a ton of fun to hang with if you really let all these resentments of yours go."

Well, *that* wasn't what I'd expected. "Corny," I noted, and he groaned, thinking he'd screwed up. "But sweet," I added.

We finally found a food truck and ordered our food. He ordered some carne asada al pastor tacos. What happened after that was one of the best nights of my life, and the food was delicious. Rigo talked about his ambition and goals in life since I didn't have any of my own. He had many, so I was able to see the world through his eyes in a different light than ever before. I learned about sports, and we discussed our musical tastes. It was a riveting evening with a handsome man I would never forget till the day I died. I prayed he would not ask about my parents because I did not want to go there.

"It's pretty late... I should take you home," Rigo finally said as he cleaned up our mess. I wouldn't say I liked the feeling of him waiting on me and actually taking the stack to throw it away, surprising both of us.

I didn't want the night to end, but I knew it had to as he appeared to have a job, new home, and family he would need to get back to – though not sure which of those were on the agenda this late at night. I found that I was more worried about tomorrow, the day after, and possibly hearing from him again. .We had a great time jamming to oldies and singing at the top of our lungs on our way back.

"You know..." Rigo began, and I turned to face him. "I could use your number."

"Is that so?" I played along, trying to hide my smile. "What would you use my number for?"

"Well, in case you ever want to get some real food and hang out. I'm pretty good at finding food trucks, you know?"

"I have my friends," I countered, though it was half-hearted at best, something made me want to see him fight for me in some small way.

"Yeah, right. And yet, here you are with a stranger taking you home."

"Fair point, Rigo...." I said in a manner that told him I did not know his last name.

"Mendoza," he supplied. "Rigo Mendoza. What about yours?"

I hesitated a bit because of my father, but he was new to Cali, so he probably didn't know anyway.

"Corvier. Elaine Corvier."

"I could have sworn I've heard that name somewhere

before." Thankfully, he couldn't remember, so I was off the hook for now. He was extremely sweet and really nice.

I made Rigo drop me off before we got to my driveway, as I didn't want to put him off with the size of my parent's mansion. He could tell from the neighborhood that this area was exclusive and priced outside his range, but it wasn't necessary to rub that in. Most of the houses had grandiose gates, with security cameras everywhere. Now, all that was left was to say goodbye. I glanced at him and leaned in, giving him a peck on the cheek.

"Thank you for saving my life tonight," I said, smiling shyly. *Why was I acting like such a mushy girl?* The same girls I made fun of in all those goofy romance movies Leslie made me watch over and over. What was it about this guy that lit a fire of affection inside me?

"Thank you too. For joining me, so I didn't have to eat alone." I stretched out my hand and was surprised he knew what I wanted. I had expected him to ask me what I was doing, but instead, he gave me his phone. Smartass. I input my number and handed it back to him.

"Call me when you miss me," I said, leaving the car.

"Will do," Rigo assured me, and I waved goodbye. I hadn't walked ten feet from his car when my phone rang. I smirked and answered it.

"Miss you already," he said in his baritone voice through the phone. I smiled and turned around, seeing him smile back at me.

Rigo drove away, and I walked the rest of the way alone. The lavish Corvier Estate. The guards were shocked to see me, mainly because I did not come back in a limo or any sort of vehicle, for that matter.

"Is everything okay, Miss Elaine?" One of them asked, and I knew that it was their job to know all aspects of my calendar and whereabouts. This showing up without an entourage or protection in tow could cause issues for everyone if it made it to my parent's ears.

I nodded. "Yes, everything is much better now." The man immediately went quiet as he opened the gate for me.

I made my way up the ridiculously long walkway and then up to my room. Apparently, my mother was around today but was already asleep, thankfully. I fell asleep within moments and woke with a genuine smile on my face for the first time in my life.

The next morning, I woke up to see both my parents were surprisingly around. They were as composed as ever around one another, engaging in talk about business. I came down the stairs and stood there, looking at them for roughly five minutes before they even noticed me. All the feelings of dissatisfaction that had dissipated from me the night before came right back up, rising to the surface. I walked to the table and sat down with a thud and a sigh, trying to get some reaction from my parents.

"Honey, how was your night? Are you okay?" Mom said, and her smile just pissed me off. But for some reason, I couldn't say anything. I was so mad but could not utter a word. Raised as a kid to always be on my best behavior, I was good at pretending that I was numb. What was wrong with me? These questions muddled my brain. I began to remember why I'd thought of ending my life. Even though I had always felt empty and hollow, I had never wanted to kill myself until last night, and now I was feeling it again. This was a problem, and I knew those feelings bottled up inside would need to be released if I were to be free and liberated.

"Ah, leave her alone," my father replied, smiling as well. "You know how shy she gets."

A tear spilled out from my left eye, but neither of them noticed. They were both laughing at the fact that I was shy. Was I just a toy to my parents? I could not keep living like this. I had bottled up too much, which meant I had to release before I could feel alive again. That feeling last night... was that what it felt like to be alive? I wanted that... I needed it. I didn't want to live my life in a lie and pretend to be someone who didn't feel worthless and lonely.

"I tried to kill myself last night."

Their heads whipped around to me in unison. The shock on their faces caused me to smile. That was the most reaction or emotion I had seen from them in all my life. They talked about fashion and politics with more excitement than they did about me... that is if they even talked about me at all.

"What did you just say?" Dad asked.

"Yeah, you heard me right. I was so fed up with both of you treating me like a mannequin with no emotions having no interests of my own, and only speaking of your careers that I thought death was the only choice."

They stared at me as realization began to dawn on them.

"But I can't keep living like this." I went on. "I feel numb and dead inside because neither of you has ever taken time to show me any affection, care, or love."

"But, honey, I just asked you how you were doing," Mom interjected, looking sincerely confused by my statement.

"The fact that you think parenting is all about the latest fashion is so painful for me because it makes me feel like that's all you care about." I broke down, crying. Enough was enough. Maybe dying was simply better.

"Elaine, I... we... I don't know what to say except that we are sorry that you felt this way," Dad said. I couldn't believe how they were reacting as I was spilling out my feelings. I realized that they seemed to focus on me, but didn't rise, come toward me or try to console me in any manner. *What kind of parents were they?* "I think we should have you visit a therapist," he added.

To be honest, that was a good idea, but I had a better one.

"I don't think I am the only one that needs a therapist," I said. "I think this is a family issue, and we need a family therapist."

They looked at each other. I had a feeling they were going to object, but they looked at each other and nodded slowly. My mom quickly added, "I know of a great family therapist that can help us."

"Yes, darling," Dad said. "I guess... we have problems too. Maybe we weren't active enough parents—not because we don't love you but because we just didn't know to be good parents. I hope you understand that we do not see you as a mannequin."

"Elaine, you are our only daughter, and we love you. We did the best we could because that's all we knew," Mom added in.

I couldn't believe what they were saying, but a part of me thought, *well, finally now they can understand what I have been going through*. At least they agreed that this was a family issue that needed to be handled immediately. Maybe it was the beginning of change for all of us.

RIGO

I stretched the following morning and found myself grinning as I sat up in bed. I glanced around as I quickly remembered where I was, in my new place. When I had returned from his crazy adventure with Elaine, I had fallen into the deepest, most refreshing sleep I had experienced in an exceptionally long time. I stretched and reached for my phone, foolishly hoping that I might have some communication from Elaine.

Zippo!

I debated sending her a cute message to let her know I was thinking of her but immediately thought better of the move. It would seem a bit desperate this fast after our night out. I moved my legs over the edge of the bed, and with another stretch of my arms toward the ceiling, rose.

BING BONG!

My doorbell sounded, which meant one of two things. Being my only family member who knew I was here already, Carlos or a neighbor I hadn't met. I realized I probably should have informed Manny and Joey that I was back in town. I wondered sometimes why I hadn't considered moving sooner to my family. Reconnecting with my Mama and all of them was the biggest reason for my relocation. I just wanted to be well-rested and ready before I took them on.

As I looked through the peek hole on the door, I confirmed it was Carlos at the door. Glancing side to side, I realized he was alone, so I opened the door.

He glanced at my near-naked state, with just boxers on my lower half. Before he shook his head from side to side, the look he gave me said everything I needed to know.

"I did check that Jennifer was not with you," he said simply. "I don't need your girlfriend getting all hot and bothered by me."

Carlos slugged my shoulder, "not funny. I don't think you could keep up with her and probably need to start with a woman that is a little bit more your speed."

"What does that mean?' Rigo retorted as he moved to retrieve the coffee maker from the box he had placed in the kitchen area last night. Filling the water and starting it to heat, he finally turned to Carlos, "I'm waiting."

"Hey, you know I'm not one of many words," Carlos said. "Me finding a woman that can tolerate me is amazing but finding one that will put up with you...that might take a miracle."

"Hey, now!" I complained at him feeling a tad bit hurt.

"I don't mean anything by it," Carlos said. "You know that you have a bit of trust issues and tend to be touchy about all things Mama, Papa, or such matters."

"I know," I agreed, knowing he was not wrong.

"I never did get to have a moment of clarity with father before he passed," I said, thinking about how I felt finding he had passed.

My feelings for my father that had cheated all those years ago on his mother were complicated. I had been the one with breaking the news to Mama about the affair and breaking the family in two. He had never spoken to Papa again, even as he lay on his deathbed. He tried to reconcile with Mama, but now with her failing health, it was even more critical than ever that he managed to make that happen. He didn't want to have regrets when his Mama passed, that he would need to carry the remainder of his life.

"I am grateful for you are coming back," Carlos said. "I know you said it was the job, but I know getting to make amends with Mama is important for both. Also," he sighed. "Joey has something he wants to talk to us about and said it needs to be in person."

"Oh no," I said with a slight rolling of my eyes. "What is he trying to fix now?"

"I don't know, but it sounded serious actually," Carlos said with a shrug. "I told him we would get to it later this week or after the get-together with all the family. Give you time to work up to all the family in one place, including Carmen, Juanita, and Estrella."

"Oh, shoot me now," I grumbled, though only half-heartedly.

As I age, I find that many of the feelings I had toward family faded and mellowed. I wanted to have someone to love in my life and possibly children. That meant coming to terms with the past, and in all actuality, starting to rebuild my relationships with my existing family. That was not a small task in the least, and definitely not one that I was looking forward to over the coming weeks and months.

"So, did you come over to just warn me about Joey, or do you have ulterior motives?"

"I thought we might take out the bikes," Carlos said.

"Really? Yeah, I could get on board with that for sure," I said excitedly. "You still have mine in storage down at the shop? I know I haven't had it out the last couple of trips."

"I've taken it on a spin or two as we discussed," Carlos said.

"Thanks," I said, glancing into the boxes at my feet and coming up with two mugs. Pouring coffee into them, I extended one to Carlos, who took it up quickly.

"Give me ten minutes to be ready," I said, hiking it to the bedroom without hearing agreement from him. Riding would definitely clear my head of the trip here, last night, and the unease at those first few meetings with my family that would be coming up.

ELAINE

$\mathcal{I}$ was not looking forward to this first therapist session and honestly was taken aback at how quickly it came to fruition. Obviously, my rantings this morning had made an impact on my parents as they had come upstairs as a unit less than three hours later, with an appointment for this afternoon. I was actually impressed they seemed to hear me and respond.

Now, here I sat across from a woman that looked to be about forty with the most serious expression. Dr. Linda Nilton made notes in her pad, giving me time to examine her from head to foot. She had shoulder-length, curly hair, green eyes, and a nice but not overly done face. The pale tan slacks, silk shirt, and lack of a ton of jewelry were efficient and understated.

"So, tell me why you are here?" She said to me, not missing a beat and going straight to the main issue. She also had this way of staring at me, as if she could see to my inner thoughts. I was odd and disturbing.

"I'm feeling lost, confused, and oddly like my life has no purpose or meaning. I actually don't understand what I'm supposed to do but be a mouthpiece for everything my parents expect of me," I said, not sugar coating my words in the least.

"Okay," she said, making a few notes. "Tell me, what do you want to do with your life if you could do anything?"

I stared at her for the longest time. "I don't know the answer to that because I'm not really allowed to try anything at which I might fail, embarrass my family, or get hurt. No sports, art was messy, dancing was too difficult, and I would be any good. They always had excuses. I was taught decorum, proper dinner protocol, making a stunning selfie from the right side, and never pushing back on paparazzi. It turns out that none of those skills can translate into a real job or even a calling to give back to those less fortunate. Nothing. I mean, can someone truly get up every day of their life, get dolled up, and just get out for people to stare at?"

"They could," Dr. Nilton said with a slight chuckle. "It does not sound like that is you, though."

"Definitely not," I sighed. "I want to feel, laugh, cry and scream without worrying about who might see, judge, or put it in the paper. I just want to be free. I still live with my parents because the world is scary, and their house is so large that it is the only sensible thing to do. I go to the events I'm invited to, and they approve. I still have friends that run in the same social circle and have been vetted by security and my parents. Seriously, I'm surprised they let me go to the bathroom without having it checked for hazards first."

"It would be hard to tell them what you want if you don't know yourself," Dr. Nilton said. "I think we have a firm handle on everything you don't want and which is causing discord. So, what say you to having us focus the session on what you would like and how we might get you there."

"I really could use some help on that for sure," I said

honestly, feeling better in the short time spent talking with the doctor than in all the years with my parents.

"Tell me; you don't have siblings, correct?"

"No," I sighed. "I think they wanted more, but it was too hard on my mom. I always thought if they had others to split time with, maybe this wouldn't have been the outcome."

"Maybe. If not siblings, who would you consider the closest friends you have?"

"I have two friends, Donna and Leslie, that have been with me through everything for years," she said. "I just can't explain it lately, though; they seem happy with the parties, fashion shows, and vacations. Always just chatting about things that I find ridiculous."

The session went on and on. Dr. Nilton asked questions and wouldn't go forward until I gave a response. It was actually amazing how many moments of ah-ha I had sitting there in her office. Somehow she knew exactly what questions I needed to get me thinking about things clearer.

We ended with her giving me an assignment of trying at least two new activities; they could be big or small before our next meeting. She also wanted one of them to be done without my friends Donna and Leslie. Either with another friend or on my own.

I left her office, and instead of feeling out of control and upset, I felt like I had a direction to go. She seriously didn't belittle my feelings or minimize my concerns because of my parent's status. Everyone normally thought that being the child of uber-rich parents somehow meant you had nothing to worry about.

Dr. Nilton, though, gave her a hearing ear and then some actionable items that I could tackle. She thought I could follow through on something that was not fashion, fun, or makeup-related – that was amazing. I left the office feeling lighter and found myself pulling the cellphone from my purse and putting the device to my ear. I knew exactly the person I needed to talk to about trying something new. Rigo had not been off my mind for a waking moment today, and I was excited to see what we can come up with to do.

"Okay, now that we have that settle," the good doctor said, "are you ready to transition into a meeting with your parents?"

I sighed, actually having forgotten that I was going to be doing this back-to-back session today. I was still feeling positive from how this one-on-one had gone, so I immediately nodded my head. This could be good; sharing my feelings had felt amazing, and I could finally see some hope on the horizon.

Dr. Nilton rose and went to the door, ushering my parents in. They didn't even make eye contact as they took the couch that was next to the chair I was sitting in. The entire feel of the room felt suddenly like a wet blanket had been thrown over everything. I sat up tall and tried to breathe lighter as Dr. Nilton sat back down.

"I would like to start," my father said, causing all eyes to turn in that direction. "We are here to be supportive of Elaine and help her get better. Of course, we cannot have outbursts about her wishing harm to herself, so anything that we need to do in order to better her state of mind," he took my mother's hand, as she sniffled into an embroidered handkerchief, "we will do."

"Awesome," Dr. Nilton said, "because I think that it would be good for both of you to discuss things that you feel, would like to see changed, and maybe we can come up with some little activities week to week to start rebuilding this relationship."

"I mean, isn't fixing her what we pay you for, and you tell us what she needs," my father said.

I couldn't take it, I piped up, "maybe what I need is more

time and attention from the two of you. To get you both to truly hear my needs, what I want and what I wish we could be as a family."

"You have everything you could want and need," my father retorted. "I think you just don't understand how amazing your life is, and like many teenagers, are simply confused. Hormones and things can be tricky."

"I'm twenty-five, father," I replied. "And this isn't hormonal. I don't want to just be an accessory to your life, but rather I want to have a life of my own."

"Great sharing," Dr. Nilton said. "Elaine, let's get really specific and dig into that."

I stared at her for a moment and knew this stranger really had heard me. Maybe with her help, we could make my parents see things more clearly, I thought. I was willing to do anything to get better and maybe move to a better place in life.

"I'm game if they are," I said, turning to see what response we might get from my parents.

After looking at each other, they gave a terse nod which was all the encouragement I needed.

RIGO

I pulled up to the curb and put the vehicle in park. Drawing a deep cleansing breath, I tried to settle myself and prepare for what was to come. I had to remind myself this was the first step toward a more robust relationship with my family, and I had to get over the tough moments. It was like ripping off a band-aid; the pain would hopefully pass quickly and lead to healing.

Walking up the sidewalk, I reached the front door and slipped inside. I felt awkward being here at the house. Carmen came to hug me with a beaming smile. It had been nearly a year since I had seen her last, and even then, it had been in passing.

"Hi, Rigo, long time no see." She was always so happy and full of energy. She never made me feel anything but wanted, though I sometimes had some unnecessary anger toward her. She and my other two half-sisters resulted from my Mama's second marriage and had been born after I was exiled from the family. It was not Carmen nor the other's fault, and I knew that any emotions I had on the subject were misplaced in being directed toward her. I decided to just try my best to let sleeping dogs lie and have a nice day.

"Hey, Carmen. It's nice to see you," I greeted her back. "Look at you!" I smiled as wide as I could, "you look beautiful."

"Thanks!" She said, lapping up the compliments. "I've been going to the gym on the regular. I'm hoping we can really connect now that you are going to be living closer and hopefully spending more time here with Mama."

"I am excited also," he said, trying to keep things civil and upbeat. "I'm sure we will see each other a lot more often in the future. I hope we can get hang out more often so I can get to know you better."

If I could not make friends with the most wholesome female in our family, what hope did I have of being on good terms with everyone?

Carmen smiled. "I'd really like that."

"Cool," I said, and she opened her arms and gave me a tight hug. I was caught off guard, but I accepted it, chuckling, and squeezing her back. She was a hugger, and I was not used to that, but it was all good as I knew it wouldn't kill me, for goodness sake.

"Come on in," she said, holding the door wide. I was not sure if I was ready, but I was here to mend my relationship with my family as best I could since I would live closer to them. I had found a place far enough away so I wouldn't be expected to visit the house every time they had a get-together. "Stop being a wuss. I want you to spend some time with us." *Us?* I raised my head and saw where Estrella and Juanita were seated.

It looked like everyone was gathered for a normal get-together. But in reality, it was a celebration where Manny was going to propose to Sandi, the woman of his dreams. Speaking of affection, I hadn't called Elaine today. I'd told her earlier in the day that I would call her before coming here, but stress had made me forget. I was so stressed out about this get-together that I'd forgotten to call the most important person in my life right now. *I'll call her later*, I thought, making myself a mental note to do just that after I left this shindig.

"So?" Carmen asked.

"Sure. You have my undivided attention for the next thirty minutes." She grinned and led me to them.

"Hello," I said while sitting down, sounding like a new kid at a middle school.

"Hi," Juanita replied even more timidly than I felt.

"So you're here." Estrella was a bit rusty, with an attitude kind of like Manny's. It seemed like she hadn't changed much and maybe even worsened.

"Ah, I see you are still as huffy as ever," I remarked with a weak smile.

"And I see you have finally stopped running away from your family." Ouch. Carmen tugged on her shirt, but she shrugged her away. I thought about everything I could say, but I reminded myself I needed to be on my best behavior. It was Estrella; she was always a pain. One of those in every family just loves to argue and knows exactly what to say to get your blood boiling.

"And I guess from that tone, you still don't have a boyfriend," I said with a sardonic twist of my lips.

Carmen and Juanita gasped, but I noticed Carmen was struggling to hide her smile. Honestly, I hadn't meant it as mean as it sounded, but rather just a jab to get Estrella off my case.

She was apparently shocked at my reply, Estrella pretended not to have heard my comment.

"Not by choice. I just haven't met the right one yet!" she said to me with a direct challenging gaze.

"Excuse me?"

"I wanted to see if you had changed after all these years or if you were just putting up an act to appease us," she explained. "Your reply gave me the answer I needed." She got to her feet and walked up to me. Being the semi-tomboy she is, I almost raised my hands in self-defence while antici-pating a punch or some sort of attack from her. To my surprise, however, Estrella hugged me tightly. And this wasn't just some light hug or whatever. She really meant it; I could feel it from the depth of her hug.

"Glad to have you home," my sister murmured into my ear. "We've missed you, especially Mama."

"Estrella," I heard an all too familiar voice say. Estrella stopped hugging me, and we both turned toward where Mama was entering the room. I quickly looked away as the tears threatened my eyes at her frail frame.

"Rigo, I see you still know your way," she said with a weak smile in my direction. Not surprised that she would say that to me.

"Okay, Mama," Estrella said, going back to her seat. I still refused to look at her. What was I going to say? After all these years, she was still upset with me for leaving and only talked to me on the phone when it was absolutely necessary.

"Ven con migo."

I knew she was referring to me. Mama started walking away. My sisters gave me a look of *you better follow her,* but I did not even need that. I knew my mother well, and she would not be disobeyed. I followed her outside, and she got seated, gesturing at the chair next to her. I reluctantly sat down, and neither of us said a word. The sky was incredibly dark tonight, with barely a star in sight and minimal moon showing.

"Ernesto always liked this field." I finally spoke, using Ernesto to try and start up a conversation. He had been a good man who had tried to mend the fractured relationship between Mama and me. The problem, though, was that both my mom and I were very stubborn people. Add that to the fact that I was incredibly young and felt I didn't want to choose between my parents. I'd decided to move in with my Tia Lola. My Mama took it as if I had abandoned her and the family. This was why she made it difficult for us to reconcile.

"Yeah, he was a great man," she agreed. An awkward silence continued, and I began to wonder why I was even here or what I was doing right now.

"Rigo," Mama said, turning to face me. I turned to her too, expecting the usual. "I'm sorry." I was certain I had a stroke and hadn't heard her correctly. Her tone was sincere, though, as my eyes grew to the size of a half-dollar. I was surprised, to say the least.

"I'm sorry. What did you say?" It had to have been a mistake. *What did I just hear?*

"I am so sorry for all the pain I have caused you, mijo," she admitted as she gave a light cough. "When Carlos told me what your father had done with that woman, I was heart-broken and had enough after years of mistreatment at his hands. I was angry, and I needed someone to blame... to direct my anger at and my pain. When I found out that you knew but didn't tell me, I turned on you... my son. You never said a word, and when you decided to leave and move in with your Tia Lola, I was still trying to cope and heal, and the thought of you leaving made me bitter and angry. I was your mother, after all, and I felt betrayed. When my sister visited and you left with her, it was... a lot to take, and my heart was broken to pieces. But over the years, I came to realize you did not choose sides. You made the sacrifice to leave because you didn't want to feel pressure to take sides, and you would be better off."

I was feeling a wave of emotions that I could not fully

225

process at this moment, but the overwhelming one was a relief. For so many years, I'd felt so bad about leaving and keeping such a pivotal secret from my Mama. When I went away, I thought that meant I was faulty and that they were better off without me. If I could leave my own Mama—a mother who'd raised six other kids—and my family, then the problem had to be with me. That meant I could leave anybody. People could not and should not trust me because I was not loyal.

Heck, this mentality made staying with my Tia Lola exceedingly difficult. She tried her best, but I was a ridiculously hard child to manage with all the rage and anger consuming me being away from the family that I adored. All my life, I kept telling myself I did not need people, that they were a nuisance. The truth, however, was that I was afraid. I was afraid that I would break more people's hearts. It is part of the reason why I had not asked Elaine out. Even a rich and pretty girl like her had her own problems—like a lack of passion. The only time I felt happiness from her was when she was with me. She might even be suicidal. What if I messed up and destroyed her trust? Her parents could come after my family or me. Worst of all, though, I would destroy a girl I was already falling for.

"Over the years, I did not even really try to mend the relationship between you and me. I left you out to dry and acted like you weren't even my kid because I was pained that you left. Ernesto was annoyed when I told him you were going to stay with Lola. He wanted me to drive down and get you right away," she admitted hanging her head forward with shame.

"Why didn't you?" I asked, totally blown away by that revelation. Ernesto had always been a good guy when I was around, but he definitely didn't try to be overly involved in the drama that lingered years after Mama's divorce.

"It was not my choice but yours, and she was more than happy to take you. I know Ernesto wanted you to stay and thought we could rebuild and put the family back together. I probably should have followed his lead, but I felt you were old enough to make your choice. I should have never created an environment that made you think that you had to leave your siblings and me. The pain was so great that I could not even look at you the day you left. Instead of battling through it like a mother should and understanding you were just a kid... I took it out all on you. Even when you got older, I did not try to mend things. I thought you chose his side over mine... wanting to protect him and abandon me. I should have stopped and considered how painful it must be for a kid to witness something like that. Sometimes as parents, we can learn from our children. We are not always right, even as adults. I never failed any of my kids... except you. I was a bad mother to you, Rigo, and I can only hope you find it in your heart to forgive me." By the time she was done, Mama was wiping tears from her eyes.

"Well, I am not innocent myself," I replied, deciding to match her honesty with some of my own. "I should have told you when it happened. I was... I just wanted us to be together. You, Dad, and the rest of us. Ironically, my decision not to say anything meant I would be alone. The thing I was trying to prevent still came back to haunt me. I should have just come clean and told you everything like Carlos wanted us to do. He did the right thing... and I just wanted to be normal. Anyway, I'm sorry for making you feel like I chose him over you. I loved you both and thought my silence was me not choosing... but now, I realized that he had made his choice when I saw him with that woman. I should have told you, Mama."

We both sat there in silence, neither of us saying a word. This was a special moment for us to reflect and enjoy our moment of mending our relationship. I felt this huge weight lift off of my chest, and I didn't even know what else further needed to be said.

After about ten minutes, Mama and I went back to the living room as it was time for Manny to profess his love and beg the woman of his dreams to take him in marriage. I could feel the tension in the room as everyone, but Sandi, realized what was about to go down.

I stood at the corner, watching Manny fumble in his pocket for the ring box. Sandi did not even notice, as she was being distracted by Jennifer, Carlos' girlfriend. Manny went down on one knee, and suddenly all talking ceased around the room. Sandi glanced about to see what was going on and followed everyone's gaze, turning around to see the man she loved with one knee on the floor. I could tell from the look in Manny's eyes that this was a man in love.

As I thought about me someday doing this exact thing with the woman of my dreams, Elaine's face flitted through my mind. I had been talking to her each night this week, and she was definitely doing some work to get to a happier place. She acknowledged starting therapy, and they even were going to try something new – a task her therapist had given her. He couldn't wait to see her again and had not felt this sappy about a woman in a long time. Sure, it wasn't possible they would be married tomorrow, but the possibility was there, and it made a secret smile escape his lips as he watched his brother pledge his love to his future wife.

"Oh my God," Sandi said, clasping her hand to her mouth after realizing what was happening. Everyone was dead silent as we all watched in anticipation and glee. Manny opened the box to show her the ring, and Sandi gasped, covering her mouth with her hands shaking with shock.

"Sandi, I love you, and you are the only person I want to spend the rest of my life with. You make me want to be a better man, to sing my love for you from the mountain tops, and I actually can't even fill a single sheet of paper with all the reasons I love you...I can't wait to start our journey together as man and wife. Will you marry me?" He looked so happy. True happiness; that is what I felt in that room from my younger brother.

"Yes!" Sandi said, already tearing up and nodding. Everyone roared in approval, happy at the outcome. I did not shout as much as they did, but I did smile and clap with them all. Even though we weren't particularly close, Manny was a passionate guy who deserved long-lasting happiness. He was my baby brother, and I was genuinely happy for him. Seeing him hold Sandi and kiss her... I couldn't help but let my mind wander to Elaine and how it would be to hold her close to me and kiss her. I knew she was still keeping some things from me, especially when it came to her parents, but I never asked because I had family issues of my own that were uncomfortable to share. Like my family, though, it was time to put in the effort to see if this attraction between them could grow to something more.

Now that I had started to build the bridge between Mama and me, I felt more comfortable moving forward with my life and opening up to her. Mama had told me that she wished I had never left the house which made me feel sad, but that was done, and we needed to focus on the present. Watching what happened to my parents made me insecure about things like relationships, but seeing how happy people close to me were made me more open to the idea. I wanted to feel complete because, in the end, everyone wants to love and be loved.

"It's a leap of faith," I murmured to myself. Taking out my phone, I texted Elaine, apologizing for not calling her and asking to meet tomorrow. She responded quickly and asked what we were going to do.

He let her know that it was a surprise.

She loved that idea if the emoticons she texted back were any indication, and he was smiling again as he put the phone back in his pocket. Though now he was on the hook to come up with an amazing date with little time to plan. Hopefully, Carlos would have an idea, or he might have to break down and ask Joey. At this point, he was willing to do anything needed to impress Elaine and enjoy just a little time in her company.

ELAINE

I ate my food calmly while my dad talked some gibberish about the fashion industry and how it related to California laws. I usually zoned out when either of my parents began talking about things like this. Right now, what was on my mind was one hunky dark-haired man. Rigo was supposed to call yesterday but didn't all day, as I checked my phone a hundred times. Then he sent a message asking me to go out with him today. I couldn't hold my excitement in, and it got even better as he told me he was planning a surprise outing. All these new emotions were a bit too much to handle. I barely got angry over anything, but yesterday, I was all over the place. I displaced my issues on everyone, and my mother even had to call me out on it.

"How are you feeling, dear?" I heard my mom's voice and looked up, the usual bored look on my face, a mask that I hoped would not reflect my current internal feelings. "From the looks of it, you seem your usual self."

Ugh, you've been seeing this kind of look on your daughter's face for years and cannot tell that something is wrong? Anyway, I was used to it by now.

"What happened?" my father asked, looking more amused than worried.

"I'm not sure. She was just very manic yesterday, which was unusual since our Elaine is always calm and collected," my mother explained to him as I sat right here in earshot.

"And this is different from her normal moods, how?" He asked, looking confused.

I was not really offended, to be honest. They had said worse to me over the years. Sometimes, I wondered if I was just a doll for them to look at and remember that they had created something together that needed to be properly groomed at all times. Neither of them knew a thing about me. All they did was send money to my account and consider it parenting.

"So why were you so antsy yesterday? Do you have a boyfriend?"

I almost choked on my food. How the hell did she know that? Rigo wasn't even my boyfriend, so what the hell? Wait. Did I want him to be my boyfriend or... ugh, my mind was so jumbled right now.

"That reaction was unexpected," Dad said as he gave her mother a tiny grin.

"I know, right? I was just joking, but it seems there is a boy you like."

I remained quiet and continued to eat my food. They did not even care about me enough to berate me for not answering them.

"Oh, well. I'm sure it's the Domer boy, Kevin."

That dumb loser could never hold a candle to Rigo. Of course, the fact that her mother still referred to men that she liked as boys were infuriating. She was twenty-five years old, and she needed a man, not a boy!

"Oooh, that'd be great!" Mom chimed in. "Sheila and I are

good friends. Imagine if her son and my daughter get married."

What are we in? Medieval times? Are they seriously talking about arranging a marriage for me?

"Craig is coming today with Sheila. Why don't I ask them to bring him along? That'd be great, r-"

"No!" I yelled, shocking them as I slapped both hands down on the table. Oh, shit. I'd yelled a bit too loud, I realized, as I sat back in the chair with a thud.

"Now, I see what you meant when you said she was acting unlike herself," Dad mused in her mother's direction once again.

I felt my phone vibrating and checked it to see that Rigo was calling. I jumped up and excused myself to take the call.

"Is that the Domer kid?" Dad asked, and I rolled my eyes. I was not even hungry, so it was not like I needed to eat. I just headed out of the room, knowing that I couldn't return after the call or risk being interrogated.

"Hello?" I said, walking out of the room.

"You're upset, I know. Let me make it up to you."

"Look, you can do what you want. It's not like I was waiting for your call or anything." *Liar, my brain shouted at me.*

"Is that so?" Rigo's deep baritone drolled over the phone line. "Are you ready to do out with me in a bit? We didn't decide on an exact time yesterday."

"Maybe," I said, trying to play hard to get. I wanted to secretly know how much he would try to win me over, though I would definitely give in by the end of the conversation.

Rigo laughed, and just that was enough to make me blush. I loved the fact that he was laughing because of me. I enjoyed talking to him. No other person in my life had ever been able to make me feel this way.

"How about we meet today at the place we first met," he

proposed, and I just had this feeling that this was going to be a big meeting.

"Sure. What time?"

"Two o'clock sound good to you?"

"Yeah." We talked some more before I hung up and went to my room to decide what to wear. Around 10 am, I heard some noise downstairs, and as I listened at the door, I realized we had some visitors. The maid had come to call me since my parents wanted me to welcome them. I went downstairs to see the Domers. Darn it; I forgot that Dad was talking about calling them. I could see that arrogant dumbo, Kevin, and his smug face.

"Come on down, honey, and say hello to our guests," Mom instructed. I was incredibly good at hiding what I felt inside, so I went down with an emotionless mask on my face. The Domers were used to it since they knew I was not an expressive person.

"Hello, Mr. Domer and Mrs. Domer," I said with a slight smile. Then I turned to Kevin. "Hey, Kevin."

"Hey." Even the way he spoke annoyed me.

"So, shall we crunch some numbers?" Dad said, leading Mr. and Mrs. Domer to the living room.

"You two have fun!" Mom said before joining them. The moment they were completely out of sight, I quickly turned to him before he could speak any further.

"I already made plans, but of course, my parents are so controlling and never listen, so I am sorry, but I have other things to do." He looked at me with confusion.

"The only reason I am here is that they said you were alone, and I should come to keep you company."

"Like I need your company. I know what you really want, and I am not interested in you." His eyes widened with a look of outrage. "I told you I have plans," I went on. "I am sure you can call one of your other lady friends." His face changed, and he looked even angrier.

Kevin tried putting his hands around my waist, but I immediately pushed him away. "I told you; I have somewhere to be."

Kevin frowned. He was always trying to make a pass at me, and I was constantly telling him that I was not interested. I went to my room and got dressed. By 11:30 am, I was out of the house. I had a strange feeling as I drove off that he was up to no good. I decided not to think too much about it. Usually, my driver took me wherever I wished to go, but I drove myself for obvious reasons this time.

I got to the place where Rigo and I first met, and his car was there. I had texted him that I was on my way, but he was ambiguous on whether he was there yet or not. Thankfully, I recognized his car. Parking mine and getting out, I knocked on his window, and he rolled it down.

"My lady," Rigo said to me, and I grinned from ear to ear.

"So now you remember me." He got out of the car and hugged me tightly. Ugh, his scent was so good. I wanted to be in his arms forever.

"I always remember you," he responded. "The family stuff I told you I had kept me occupied for much longer than I anticipated." I had held off for a while, so I decided to just ask as we began walking down the street.

"You know... you don't talk much about your family." I tried to say it as casually as I could, but it came off more like curious.

"Neither do you."

"Yeah, but... I don't know. I just wanted to know more about it." I probably should have, but I was not feeling weird for bringing it up.

He began to speak before I had to give in any information. "When I was young, I moved out and went to live with

235

my Tia Lola." That was a welcomed surprise. I listened attentively to what he had to say about his family. "Mama and I
just reconciled for the first time in around a decade, so
yeah... it was a pretty big deal me being there yesterday. This
entire thing has been an opportunity for me to get back to
my roots and grow closer to my siblings."

"I'm really happy for you," I said to him. It was great that
Rigo felt close enough to me to share that with me.

"My dad is a political figure, and my mom is a fashion
guru or whatever they call themselves. I spoke to them about
all of us seeking family therapy because of what I feel, and
they agreed. I am not proud of my parents, and so it's difficult to talk about, and I don't like talking about them," I
explained. "I am an only child and have always felt alone and
separate from this world. It had been weighing me down
because my parents had taught me never to express myself
overtly. I had finally had enough the other night, and I was
ready to die when I saw a car about to hit me... but then I
met you." He smiled and gazed at me. I felt like he could see
into me. His eyes suddenly looked above me, and he crum-
pled his brows, looking perplexed. I turned around and saw
Kevin with two other guys.

"So, this is who you're seeing instead of being with me,"
Kevin snarled as Rigo must have seen something in my face
because he stepped between Kevin and myself.

"This is going to be amazing to tell all your friends about
your slumming it," Kevin said as he closed in on me, and I
just tried to get my lungs to start working again. I needed to
figure out something and quick, or Rigo was definitely going
to cause a scene I would never be able to recover from.

RIGO

J had a hard time stopping my fist from connecting with the man's face. I didn't fully understand what was happening at this moment, but the arrogant, snide, and overly aggressive comments by this idiot were not sitting well with me. I saw that Elaine tried to step between us, but I was not risking him doing something to her and maintained my stance between them.

"Listen," I started trying to hold my temper in check. This was one of the attributes of my personality that I had worked hard on over the years. Still, when women, children, or others not in a position to defend themselves came under attack, I still seemed to bluster and step up to their defense. "I don't know who you are, and I'm guessing that friends are not a word that Elaine would use to describe you, which means I don't care who you are," he said, reaching down to take Elaine's hand. "So, we are going to be on our way.

Elaine just stared at me with big huge eyes that looked on the verge of crying at this moment. I was not having any of it and reached my big palm out to gently massage her cheek, not caring who was watching. "It's your choice – stay or go with me."

"You can't leave with that neanderthal," the man shouted like he honestly believed he had the power to control. He appeared like a young child on the verge of throwing a tantrum, and to be honest; I was just about to start laughing openly in his face, which I knew was a bad idea.

"Let's go," Elaine said gently, but I felt her hand grip mine for dear life. "I'm sorry, Kevin, but I don't want to date you no matter what our parents believe is best. And as for Rigo, he's a much better man than a boychild like you," she said as we started to walk away.

"Listen here," the guy said again, jumping in front of us. "You know that one word to your parents, and you will be grounded to the house for life. They will never allow you to throw away their reputation and everything they built for this," he said, running his eyes up and down me like I was some disgusting science specimen below his notice.

"I know," Elaine said weakly as we stepped around the man and kept walking. Luckily, this time he didn't follow, but I noticed Elaine sneak a peek over her shoulder.

"I think it is time for you to explain that," I said under my breath. "You are a grown adult; how in the world could your parents ground you from anything?"

"I still live with them," she said weakly, causing me to turn to her with huge eyes.

"Really?"

"Yeah. They have a big house, and," she stopped and swallowed hard, "security and everything is already on hand. They have kept me in this bubble for fear of me falling in with bad influences or doing anything that might soil their sterling reputations."

"Okay, I'm sorry, but who are these people?"

"Honestly, if you ask anyone from these parts, my dad is a pretty big hitter in political circles and mom in fashion. They are rich, and as you know, they and others think that means the world revolves around them. I just became caught in that cobweb of their lives by virtue of birth alone," she said with a sigh glancing up at me. "And that is Kevin, who is supposedly the man, or boy they want me to marry."

"Are you kidding?" I said, turning to her as if she had lost her ever-loving mind. "He is horrid."

"Tell me about it," Elaine said, drawing a quick breath. "I definitely will hear about that tonight, so this date of yours better be amazingly worth me being bad."

"Oh, I think it will be," I said, stopping right in front of my bike. I had this great ride to this winery planned but now standing here worried this might be a little too low brow for her.

"You want me to get on that," she said, pointing to my bike. The expression in her eye was not anger, though, but rather this curiosity spiked with eagerness.

"Yep," I said, staying brave as I handed her a helmet.

"Sounds like fun," she said, plopping the helmet on her head, as I chuckled and put on mine also. Then we managed with a few false starts to align on the seat, and soon we were pulling from the lot headed to the open road.

As the wind zipped into my face and Elaine's hands tightened around my waist, everything but the two of us faded from my mind. I was determined this would be one of those days that she would not forget, and I tried to push all thoughts of how different our worlds were from my mind.

When we finally arrived at the winery, she slid from the bike and, with a gasp, staring out over the valley. "This is breath taking," she said, staring with huge eyes.

"I thought we could mix a little high-class wine tasting

that is more your speed," I said with a grin, "with an after wine tour hike in the hills, which is more my speed. Best of both worlds and see where the day takes us from that point."

"I love that idea," Elaine said. "I do adore a good wine, though most the time, I end up at parties where the liquor is watered down and simply intended to get you hammered."

"I know that feeling," I said as we walked slowly toward the group gathering at the entrance of a building that said tours above the door. The lady who was corralling everyone did a double-take between Elaine and myself, with a tiny toss of her nose in the air. "I don't think she likes this pairing," I said, ducking to Elaine's ear to give the joke, which was a play on wine pairing verbiage.

"Well," Elaine said, stepping up on her tiptoes, "I think in that case," she said, suckling my earlobe, "we should really give her something to not like."

I turned toward her, fully turned on now and shocked by the words just as she planted a loud and wet kiss on my lips. I was not a man that could turn down an invitation like that and returned the affection in kind until someone cleared their throat.

Elaine looked into my eyes as she backed up and gave a laugh. "That should teach them."

"We are getting started," the snooty lady up front said as I straightened my back and tried to get into the ambiance of the wine information and tasting. Mostly though, my entire body was tuned in to the beautiful, spontaneous woman next to me.

I could not believe that someone that looked like her had the sense of humor and joy in life that she did. She honestly hadn't put up a single word of dissension about me planning this entire day. I don't think I have been with another woman that didn't try to control everything. This was refreshing and honestly made it that much sweeter when I realized from the rapt attention on her face how much she enjoyed the surprise I had prepared.

ELAINE

*A*s we headed back from the winery, I was flying in the clouds. I loved the feeling of being on the back of Rigo's motorcycle, but honestly, it was the three hours spent doing a winery tour with him and then exploring the hills we found on the way back that had made this day perfect. Before meeting this man, I would never have imagined this kind of outing, the stunning scenery, great exercise, and conversation that could be had with the right person.

Rigo could talk about a million subjects, and he was kind, funny, and self-deprecating. When he talked about his brothers and family, though, I fell a little more in love with him with each word. It was obvious that despite some family tension, they all showed up for each other all the time. Heck, he had just moved multiple states to be closer to them all despite misgivings to be closer.

I knew that I was in for a huge lecture when I got home this evening, and honestly, it would be worth it after this perfect day. My therapist would be proud of me, at least, I thought as I tightened my hands about Rigo's stomach. The man was wider than my arms could stretch, but I didn't care as I laid my head against his back and absorbed his heat. I might not understand what he found to appreciate about me, but the list I was starting of all that I adored about him grew with each moment.

As he crossed into my neighborhood and finally to the entry of my house, I wondered what was going through his mind. Sure, I was trying to get a little jab in at the parents, and this time was not going to hide where I lived. I quickly realized that Rigo might be profoundly important in my world, and any lies between us would eventually come out. Being straight-up honest from the start, I decided it was the only way to go.

Finally, he stopped short of the locked gate, and I slid from the bike. Removing my helmet, I saw him staring at the mansion with the strangest look on his face. It wasn't the wonder that many people had when they took in my home or even the greed. This was almost a sadness, as if realizing how different we were, yet that made no difference to me. I needed to ensure he knew that before he left.

"You really live here," he asked, looking completely uncomfortable all of a sudden.

"It is my parent's house, yes," I offered as I looked him dead in the eye. "This is not my choice, and maybe soon I will downsize to something more my speed."

"You know that I'm a pretty simple guy," he said, looking at me with confusion written on his face. "I think that maybe even too simple for someone like you."

"What do you mean someone like me?" I said, feeling my temper starting to flare.

I was not going to allow him to cast me aside because of my parent's wealth. I needed to be judged on me alone, and he was going to have to understand that. I was working through therapy to stand on my own, be taken seriously, and build a life with an identity totally apart from my parents.

Rigo was a big part of that work, and I needed him to understand.

"My parents have money, position, and the like. I haven't even fully figured out who or what I want to be because I live in their world. I had the best time I've had in a good long while with you today, and I need you to be with me for me or not at all," I reminded him sternly.

A smile slipped across his lips. "I'm with you," he said with a little head bob. "I do love it when you get bossy."

"Great. Then kiss me," I said, not caring that at any moment, my parents could gaze out from a window of the house and see us.

He planted his perfect lips on mine, and I felt myself melting. Holding tight to his neck, he slid his hands around my waist, bringing me up flush against his massive body. I felt so tiny and protected at this moment; I never wanted it to end. Finally, though, I had to back up.

"Tell your Mama I said hi," I said to him. "I hope to get to meet her soon."

"I would like that," he said, putting his helmet back on, and then with a revving of the engine, he was gone.

Inhaling, I walked toward the entrance, feeling like someone accused of a crime headed to their day in court. If my parents had heard from Kevin, spotted the motorcycle, or seen Rigo – a fight was sure to ensue. I couldn't stop their reaction, but I was ready for it as I turned the handle on the main door and stepped inside. The second I entered, they pounced.

"We need to talk," my father bit out, looking uncomfortable and mad at the same time. He directed me to the sitting room off the grand foyer, and mother was sitting with a tissue in hand just staring in my direction when I entered.

"Did you seriously tell Kevin you would never date him?" Her mother asked the second I was inside.

"Yes," I offered back without hesitation. Lying to them or trying any longer to be someone else was just not going to get us anywhere, so I went with the truth. "He is mean, entitled, and tries to boss me around like a child doing his bidding."

"I have never seen that side of him," my father said, walking to sit next to my mother and take her hand in his.

"That is because, like me, I think he tries to be when you and his parents want him to be when you are around. When he is out in the world on his own, it is another story completely," I said and watched them process that information.

"You do not believe you can be yourself with us?" My father said, and I was a bit surprised that he seemed to be open about discussing something like this.

"No, I don't. I know you have all these expectations of what you want me to do, where I should be seen, and who I should be with. That leaves little for me to decide on my own, and honestly, it also leaves me feeling worthless," I finished dropping into an upholstered chair opposite them.

"Is that why you are having with a biker like the one that brought you home? Do you think he can show you what you should be? You know they only want one thing from you and then will drop you," her father admonished.

"His name is Rigo. He has a great job, is a kind man, loves his big family, and drives a bike from time to time. Today, I felt more alive with him on that bike exploring than I have in an awfully long time," I finished with a huge sigh of relief as I realized for the first time, my parents were actually listening. "I don't sleep around, and I don't party in a manner that would disrespect either of you. I don't do drugs, be rude to others, or intentionally ever step out of bounds because I know you both have important reputations to maintain. That said, I do need to find my own life and start figuring out who I am, separate from the two of you."

"Okay, how do you propose to do that," my mother said, looking me dead in the eye.

"Seriously? Can we truly talk about this?" I asked, sitting forward in the chair excitedly.

My mom glanced at my dad, then back at me. "Yes, let's discuss."

"Awesome," I said, feeling on the verge of tears of happiness, as we started down the road of a real conversation for the first time in years.

RIGO

I am trying to get caught up on a ton of work. Learning a new role such as the one I took on while also keeping my head above water was a bit tough. Luckily, the entire staff here was amazing and pitched in to answer any of my questions. After nearly a month now, things were going amazingly well until we took on this big new project. I had agreed to go overseas as I felt I understood all the parameters.

As I finished with the timelines and some vendor emails, I double-checked all my files for a meeting on Friday. Then standing went to chat up the finance team about budget numbers as I still hadn't seen those come through. Just before I could make it to the door, my phone started vibrating back on my desk. I felt my heart flutter as I figured it was probably Elaine.

We had been in daily contact and out on a number of dates now. She was even volunteering at this interior design firm that she had approached through a friend. She hadn't really ever worked but was thinking she needed to have something that she could passionately throw herself into. As someone who had to work, I envy her not to consider money when trying out different roles. That said, the big smile she wore these days made me so much happier than that first night we met which still scared me when I thought back to seeing her there in the middle of the road.

For instance, last night we had done bowling. Seriously, I couldn't even recall how many times in this life I had been bowling, but she had never been. It was hilarious watching her try to acclimate to the ball's weight and learn little tricks from others in lanes around us. She was so sweet and chatting with everyone, even after almost maiming a guy when she accidentally lost control of the ball and nearly wiped him out.

Then they had walked a short distance to an ice cream shop he loved to frequent. Her indecision lent itself to them standing for nearly thirty minutes of her wavering before they finally ended up with six different scoops of ice cream that devoured outside in a nearby park just hanging out. He honestly forgot quite often how well off she was, as she just seemed to derive so much joy from the little things it made his heart swell.

Shaking my head out of my own thoughts, I lunged for the phone. Unfortunately, I immediately saw it was a message from Carlos asking me to call as soon as possible. That was not good, as he never interrupted my workday.

I picked up the device and connected the call to him immediately. "Hey," I said when he picked up. "What's up?"

"Mama's in the hospital," he said, sounding like he was actually crying. I felt the words register with my brain as my hands shook and fear spiralled throughout my entire body.

"Is she okay?" I asked hurriedly, as my heart was hammering so hard against my chest, it was stealing my breath.

"Rigo, I think you should come to see her," he said softly, and those words caused tears to well.

"I'm on my way," I said. "Text me the information, and I'm headed out in five as soon as I let people know where I'm going."

"Okay," he said and disconnected.

Spinning to sit in my big chair again, I sent off emails to HR and my boss. Then I also typed an email to finance asking for the information I needed, knowing I could check on all that later from home.

Closing down my system, I stowed it in the bag sitting at the base of my credenza and flung the straps over my head. Then grabbing my keys and coffee mug, I was headed for the door at a jog. As I got in the truck and headed toward the hospital, I called Elaine.

"Hey, sexy," her voice wafted out of my speakers. "Did you miss me?"

"Yeah," I said half-heartedly, as worry about my mother was taking over my entire body at the moment. I knew she was sick and in her final days. Having that moment actually upon you, well, that was another matter totally.

"My mom is in the hospital," I said, trying hard to keep my voice level and failing.

"Oh, I'm sorry," Elaine said gently. "Do you want me to come to see you? I don't know how much help I can be, but I could at least be a shoulder of support."

"I would love that," I said before I could even think through all the ramifications of having her meeting my family under such circumstances. "I can send the information, and even if you want to wait until you get off, that would be amazing."

"Of course," she said softly. "I hope your Mama is okay." She finished as I read out the information. "I will see you soon," she said when I finished.

"Thank you," I returned and then disconnected, feeling a modicum better.

I didn't know how bad this would be, but I wanted Mama to meet Elaine before the end. Knowing that all her sons were happy and settled was something she talked about a lot these days. He hadn't really gone not a huge amount of detail with everyone about Elaine, especially about her name. His brothers did realize he was dating, and he shared a few more tidbits with Carlos. It was probably not the right time to bring them together, but it might be the last for Mama, and her approval was important to me.

As I found a parking spot in the massive hospital lot, I could feel my hands going sweaty, shaking, and my entire body throbbing with worry. I did something I hadn't done in years, as I raised my eyes toward heaven for a quick prayer and then exited the vehicle. Jogging toward the building, I went in the entrance that Carlos had told me to, and he was standing directly inside.

He had obviously been crying, and all I could do was walk forward and wrap my arms around him. For the longest moment, we just stood like that before we backed up.

"How is she?" I finally asked, bracing for the worst.

"They say it won't be long now. Her organs are all shutting down," he said as all hope evaporated from my being.

"What happened? I saw her just last night, and she was tired, but everything seemed okay," I said, trying to apply reason to something this awful.

"She just woke this morning and could not even lift her head she was so weak," Carlos said, putting a hand on my shoulder. "I have a feeling she has been holding on with sheer willpower until we all made up."

My head hung, but I squared my shoulders, slapping my hand onto his back. "At least we are together and have each other during this time. We did make peace with her, and that is the best gift we could have given her in the end."

"Agreed," Carlos said with a bob of his head as we walked slowly toward the elevator to go see Mama.

ELAINE

I was so nervous that I turned around and thought about running more than once before entering the hospital's front door. For someone that lived my life in the public eye, meeting Rigo's family under these circumstances should have been a walk in the park. It most definitely was not!

I didn't really know the condition of his Mama but knew that in times of trial like this, people tended to get stressed out. I thought maybe it would be best if I didn't interrupt this day for all of them, and again I turned toward the exit. Stopping, I lifted my eyes toward the ceiling and sighed. Immediately, I remembered that first night that Rigo and I met and how I had been doing this same thing. At that point, it was because of the incessant chatter of my girlfriends. Today my hesitation was because I was facing something that scared the shit out of me. I was better than this and could do it.

I turned one final time and headed for the elevators. I could do this, for goodness sake. I hit the number of the floor indicated and commanded my feet to move forward. I thought about all the work me and my therapist had been doing on conquering things that scared me—talking to my parents about what I wanted. I had even talked with Donna and Leslie about how I felt and things we might be able to do to strengthen our friendship and not stress me out. Every day was a discovery for me of how strong I actually was, and this would be no different.

I had been at work, helping with a showcase for the interior design firm that I was interning at. The lead partner was someone that had done my parent's house, and they had put in a good word. I was determined now that I had a foot in the door to win their approval on my own merits, though. This event they entrusted to me was coming together amazingly well, and I felt pride each time I nailed another element of it. I loved throwing amazing parties and putting this important event together; I thought it might just be the first of many.

As I walked the hallway to the room, I swallowed down all my apprehension, and finally, it was right in front of me. There were a bunch of voices from inside, and I waited until I finally heard Rigo say something. Then with a final mental push, I walked in.

All eyes turned in my direction, and Rigo separated to come toward me.

"Thank you for coming," he said, putting his arm about me to draw me further into the room.

No one said a word, which was a little odd. Then I was standing at the foot of a frail-looking older woman, though her eyes did snap right to me.

"Rigo?" The lady said. "Who is this?"

"Mama, this is Elaine Corvier, my girlfriend," Rigo said as my eyes rested on the sweet face staring back at me.

"Oh," his Mama said with a slight groan, "come sit here," she said, patting the bed next to her as everyone made a path for me. "I want to hear all about you, dear."

"It's great to finally meet you," I said, turning the tables. "Rigo talks about you all the time."

"Well, he has kept you a big secret," his Mama said to her in a whisper. "So, let me tell you a few things that I have never told anyone about my boy."

"Mama," Rigo grimaced as several men that had to be his brothers all stood to give him crap. I turned my full attention on his sweet Mama as she struggled to speak. It seemed to give her so much joy, though, to talk about her boys, so I was going to absorb every moment.

I couldn't wait to spend time with Rigo's brothers, but this time with his mom was so special. I found myself humbled to be brought into such an amazing dynamic and not have anyone trying to get rid of me. I knew the family wanted this time, yet they all deferred to what this sweet lady needed. This was a family of enormous strength and courage and love for each other.

As I found Rigo's eyes, I couldn't help but smile teary-eyed at him as I realized just how lucky I truly was to have found him that evening I almost my life. I thought to myself God definitely worked in mysterious ways and that night I became a firm believer. I had always heard stories about how God had changed people lives but I didn't believe in any of that stuff until it actually happened to me. Now I am grateful and have a different outlook at life.

His mother's eyes drifted close only about ten minutes later as Joey surged forward. "There is a tiny waiting room right around the corner they have set up for us," he said. "Angela and then brought dinner," he said as everyone gave a slight nod and started the direction he had pointed.

"So, girlfriend?" Carlos said, turning to me the second we were out of earshot of the hospital room and walking into the waiting room. There were trays of food laid out on a table, but I figured this was going to turn into an inquisition of sorts as I looked again at Rigo.

"Yes, girlfriend," she said.

"I know who you are," Manny joined in.

"And I know you," I spat back. "You were a regular in a lot of the same clubs as my friends and me," I said, glancing to the girl next to him, "but apparently, someone finally tamed you."

"Sandi," the lady said with a huge smile in my direction, "I like you, and I think you will do well with this crowd."

"Thanks," I said as I moved to put my arm around Rigo, "I have already heard so much about all of you; I couldn't wait to meet you though I had hoped maybe under other circumstances."

The door suddenly flung wide open, and my parents actually stood outlined in the doorway. I stared at them like they had lost their minds. "What are you both doing here?' I asked, confused about this turn of events.

"The driver has been keeping us informed latterly of your whereabouts for your own safety," my father had the nerve to confess. "When he said you came to the hospital, well, we were worried. We thought maybe you were going to do something," he stared at everyone in the room. "Who are these people?" He said, turning his nose into the air.

"This is Rigo," I said, pulling him front and center. "My boyfriend."

"What?" My mother asked, and she glanced at the visible tattoos. "Is this some kind of phase you are going to get out of soon? Did you tell Dr. Nilton about him?"

"No, I adore Rigo, and his family is here because their mother is very sick," I said pointedly. "I'm here to support my boyfriend and all of them – so there is nothing for you to worry about."

"Well, that is nice, but we need to go now," my father said

as I stood my ground right where I was. "Now," he said, firmer holding out his arm as if expecting me to go along.

"No, you are being rude and unkind to my friends," I said. "I am going to remain here, and you can take the car with you. I will find my way home."

"Please do not do this," my father said. "These are not the kind of people you should be associating with," I stopped him with my hand in the air.

"You need to leave now, and don't say another word," I replied in a tone that left no room for argument. "You are elitist snobs, and I adore these people who make me feel welcome and have been nothing but kind. Please go, now."

My mother looked around, "it was nice to meet friends of our Elaine's," she said after a minute. Then she grabbed my father's hand and dragged him from the room.

I inhaled deeply and turned. "I'm sorry about that."

"No worries," Manny said. "We have an interesting family dynamic also, and you stuck up for us in the end. You are alright by me."

I chuckled as I glanced at Rigo, leaning in to lay my head on his chest. This was definitely a family I wanted to know more about and truly become a part of.

RIGO

I stood just blankly, looking out at northing, and running a hand alongside the inside of the collar of my shirt. I was not someone that enjoyed suits, ties, and the like for any reason. There were only two causes that would have me dressing this nicely, weddings and funerals.

"The turnout is amazing," Joey said, coming alongside me as we greeted guests coming from the funeral.

It had been the worst week of my life losing Mama, but her funeral was definitely a testament to how many loved her. The church had been jammed packed with people standing, and the priest even commented on it being one of the biggest funerals ever he had officiated over. That was something to be sure of. As he glanced about, he was grateful all his brothers were here, happy with wonderful women by their side. They had all provided Mama the best gift ever in knowing they were building happy futures in her final days – and doing it together again in the same town.

"I am shocked as they just keep coming," I responded to Joey as Manny and Carlos stepped away from the people they were chatting with to come toward us.

"Your girlfriend is amazing," Carlos offered to me as I looked across the room to see Elaine working feverishly with Sandi, Jennifer, and Angela to set out a spread fit for a king.

"Agreed, she has been a lifesaver in getting this all taken care of so we could focus on family," Manny replied.

"Thanks," I said. Elaine had really surprised me since the first moment she showed at the hospital.

Not a single moment of entitled, weird behavior out of her. Rather she had made everyone comfortable, answered all questions forthrightly, and just slipped right in with everyone amazingly well. Her parents, of course, I could not extend the same compliment. They were horrid even after finding out about Mama being a patient and demanding that Elaine leave them all immediately.

"Care if we join you all," Carmen, Estrella, and Juanita asked, coming alongside them all?

"Absolutely," I replied, not feeling the least bit of resentment. In this moment of grief, we were all family and together stronger than we would have been suffering separately.

It was amazing how we all had been able to band together and pull today from the ashes of our grief. We would all miss Mama's presence, and she was the glue that would hold us together in the years to come. Memories of the good and bad times with her a chapter of our lives no one present today would ever forget.

"I'm going to miss her so much," Estrella said into a handkerchief in her hand. "I was not prepared for her to be gone, no matter how long I had to get prepared."

"Agreed," I said. "I'm grateful I did move when I did and not wait until next year like they originally were thinking. Spending these last few weeks together with all of you and her was a gift I won't soon forget."

"Totally," Carmen said. "I think that in her passing, we all were given a gift. We could come to terms with our pasts, work on overcoming all those things unsaid and honestly allow her peace in Mama's passing."

"True," Joey said. "I always tried to mediate, and it felt unnatural sometimes how hard we all fought against each other. This, though, has warmed my heart, and I'm happy we can all be together."

"You definitely are a born mediator," Manny said without hesitation. "I guess we can start another family disagreement just to help keep those skills sharp if you need us to."

"I'm good," Joey said with a slight chuckle. "I would guess I will have kids someday that will make me practice that skill again."

"Verdad," Carlos finished. "I can't wait for all our kids to come along and fight love and tease each other just like we have done to each other."

"I would never tease you," I replied to Carlos, who immediately turned disbelieving eyes in my direction.

"What about the girl you sent to ask me out to junior prom?"

"Oh, pizza face Polly," Joey said with a huge chuckle. "That was amazing, and she was so sweet."

"Right?" Carlos grumbled. "she was so shy her face would turn the shade of a tomato, and it took her five minutes straight of stuttering to get a single question out."

"And it gook you just as long to answer," Manny finished. "It was so painful and sweet to watch."

"Right?" Carlos grumbled. "Nothing like you taking Rachel McGibbons apart with that tongue of yours in that debate in front of the school."

"Oh, I think Principal Madder had to go to therapy after trying to break that one up," I laughed aloud, remembering that fine day. Manny definitely, unlike Carlos, had a way with words that was not to be trifled with.

"I'm actually surprised Mama survived all of you as kids," Juanita added.

"True, and I would expect our kids to be even worse when they gang up together," Joey said.

"Oh, that is definitely going to be something to see," Carlos laughed as they all went silent once again.

It was a somber day for us all, but the memories we had of Mama would get us through. It would be those happy times that we would share with the next generation and always keep close to our hearts.

ELAINE

"The event was such a success," I said, jumping into Rigo's arms when I saw him waiting outside the massive building downtown. I had told him that since it was a Friday, we could go out and have some fun if he would wait for me. I hadn't been expecting things to go this later, though, and was pleasantly surprised to find him still patiently waiting when I got outside.

"I knew you would do it," he said, glancing down into my eyes as he moved upward to claim his ample mouth with my own. I did not normally enjoy public displays of affection, but with Rigo, I was breaking every rule I ever thought to make for myself.

"So, what amazing night do you have planned for me?" I asked, just slightly concerned, as it was already late into the evening, so the normal outdoor options we enjoyed were out. Also, I quit trying to figure out how Rigo's brain worked, as I always found out; in the end, he still could surprise me.

"I thought we would have you do something you are really good at tonight, but for an amazing cause," Rigo said, waggling his eyebrows at me.

They had last weekend done something he was good at, attending this strong man competition. He had not known when they arrived that he was going to be pulled into the competition, nor that Elaine had signed him up. It was so much fun as he did this log roll and managed to take third place before ending up in the water. The woman had actually thought ahead and packed his clothes, just in case of such an occurrence.

That turned out to be good because he went on to win the ax chipping contest, and this from a man that had only done that twice in his life. There were a fair amount of city boys that had ducked out at the sight of his massive arms and tattoos before they even saw him go at the massive tree trunk.

Then the ax-throwing contest, and finally this pie eating. In the end, he had done fairly well for himself and even gone home with a third prize standing. He had no idea where she had come up with the idea for her date but knew it must have taken some big planning. She had faithfully played the part of cheerleader every step of the day and bragged quite a lot about his prowess. He had made sure tonight was just as much thought on his part.

"Okay? I'm intrigued and just slightly on edge," I said as he opened the passenger door and I climbed up inside. He didn't offer any further explanation, and instead, we chatted about my event the entire drive. I knew he was trying to distract me, but honestly, it was so adorable his trying this hard I just couldn't help but play along.

Then we stopped in front of this older brick-style building. I glanced about but didn't see anything but a community center sign, which caused my brow to furl even more. Rigo still didn't give me a hint as he came around the truck and, offering me his hand, helped me from the truck.

He wrapped an arm around my waist and walked inside.

There I was met with a huge group of older people sitting about in nice clothing. They all had suits and dresses but didn't seem to have a particular reason for being in the room as they were sitting in chairs around the perimeter. I honestly didn't understand.

"Hey," Rigo said as one older lady that looked about seventy-five walked toward us. "How are you, Mrs. Garcia?" He asked, bending to kiss her cheek.

"Great. Is this the sweet young lady you were telling us about?" She asked, turning to Elaine.

"Elaine Corvier," I said, taking her hand in a brief shake. "I'm sorry Rigo didn't tell me what I am doing here."

"Oh," Mrs. Garcia slapped Rigo's arm playfully, 'he said you would be willing to do some dance classes for us. Our normal instructor broke her hip."

"Oh, he did," I said, looking up at Rigo, who was biting down on his lip, trying not to laugh.

"I have seen you dance, and you will be great," Rigo said down to her.

"You will pay for this," I mumbled at him as I followed Mrs. Garcia.

Soon we had all the old people on their feet, twirling, dancing, and having the time of their life. They were about the sweetest crowd I had ever hung out with, and I had the best time. For a group I thought would not have a ton of energy, they shocked me as we did dance after dance. Soon, I dragged Rigo out on the floor to also help show them some partner moves.

I don't think I have laughed so hard in my life. They all were telling stories and kissing, hugging, and loving on their partners. It was one of those moments I would never have thought to put myself in the middle of and yet would not have for the life of me.

Three hours later, sweating and totally tired, Rigo and I

headed out of the center. "How did you like that surprise?" He asked me.

"Honestly, I had so much fun. Those are some of the sweetest people I have ever met, and I totally underestimated how long they could keep up that pace," I said, shaking my head.

Suddenly, the door burst open, and Mrs. Garcia walked out, right up to me, and wrapped her arms around my shoulder. "You are the best. We would love to have you back anytime," she said as she then turned and walked back inside.

"I think you are a hit," Rigo said. "And," he pointed across the green space outside of the community center. "I made sure our favorite food truck was in the area tonight."

"Yes," I said, rubbing my stomach. "I'm so hungry I could eat a full steak dinner without a thought."

"You know I love you, right?" Rigo said quietly, causing me to turn to him in shock.

"What?"

"I do. I love you so much," Rigo said with this sad look on his face. "I didn't think I would fall this hard and fast, especially that first night we met. I love the fact that you will throw yourself into new things without balking, that you are taking the time to do therapy and solve some of your issues. You are open and communicative even about all the tough issues, and that also makes me want to be around you even more."

I felt the heaviest tugging on my heartstrings.

"I've never said those words to anyone except my parents, and even that has been years," I admitted. "I love you, though. You make me want to be a better person, and I love how supportive you are of reinventing myself. You talk about the good, bad, and little things with me like I matter. And most of all, I can't wait," I said, coming close to him to wrap my arms up and over his shoulders. "I love you, Rigo, and I cannot wait to see what amazing life we can build together. The adventures we can take on and the new memories we can make together."

He bent to kiss me so sweetly; tears rose in my eyes. I could not believe how full my heartfelt this morning, and this amazing man loving me was a gift I could never have expected.

"Now, I admit I would love to stay and make out," I said, "but I need food."

Rigo just laughed, "yes, ma'am," he said, tucking my hand into the crook of his arm as we headed in the direction of the food truck.

RIGO

I stared at the envelope on the passenger side of the car and thought about shredding it. I mean, nothing good could come of the information inside, could it? Months after I had turned in the kit, the results had come back. I had honestly been expecting it to disprove the gossip that had long haunted me, but in fact, the opposite happened. When I saw the results, I had just sat staring at the sheet for the longest time, unsure what in the world I was supposed to do with the information. I called my brothers together for an impromptu meeting. That was where I was headed now.

We were meeting at our favorite pub, which also featured outside seating. I had zero ideas how the three of them would react, but we didn't keep secrets. That was a vow we had all made after Mama died. It had been secrets that tore us apart for years, and none of us wanted to revisit those dark days. In sharing everything, we not only could help each other but also not bottle up emotions.

Today, I would imagine they would have a lot of feelings about this news. I inhaled and wished for just a moment that I had not given in to my curiosity and not filed that kit. It seemed a good idea late one night when I saw the advertisement on the television, but honestly, four months later, I regretted it horribly.

Finding a parking spot, I took the manila envelope in hand and exited the cab of my truck. Walking toward the pub, I realized that Joey and Carlos were already seated outside. I didn't even need to go through the main restaurant but rather lowered myself into a chair across from the two of them.

"How's life?" Carlos asked, giving me a direct gaze. "We haven't seen you for a week due to that project you are on, or are you avoiding us?"

I gave a slight chuckle, "no, definitely super busy. It is being launched next week, and then things should get slower again. Maybe we can all take a ride next weekend to celebrate?" Then I thought that maybe they wouldn't be talking to me by then because of what I had done. I felt the sadness seep in.

'I'm game," Carlos came right back.

"Definitely," Joey said.

"For what?" Manny's voice interjected as he came up behind me, slapping my back.

"A ride next weekend to celebrate Rigo finishing the big project he is one," Carlos told him.

"Excellent," Manny said, sitting down.

We all ordered drinks, as I tried to find the words silently to break my news to the entire group. The waitress finally had everything in her little tablet and turned from them. This was the moment of truth, as goosebumps broke along my skin, and that tingly tension climbed up my spine. I honestly hoped that they were going to take this, consider it and then see the positive side of my news.

"So, what's the big news that can't wait?" Joey said as all

three turned to me. He captured my gaze and wouldn't let me turn from him.

"Okay," I cleared my throat as I gripped the envelope in my lap under the table. "I did this thing a few months ago, long before I made the decision to come home. I honestly had forgotten about it with everything going on lately and Mama passing."

I realized I was rambling, but this didn't seem like the sort of thing that you just spit out. Maybe if they could see how much this messed me up, they would be more merciful with their responses in the end.

"Did you kill someone?" Manny asked, with a confused and worried look on his face.

"No," I said, turning to him, "what in the world? That is what you think of me? I could kill someone?"

"You have this face that looks like this is about to be the worst possible news," he said with a shrug, glancing at my other two brothers for support.

"No," I huffed. "I ordered one of those DNA tests from the television. I just had heard of all of dad's affairs a couple of times and thought maybe we had some other siblings out there. Now, please understand it was just curiosity, and I thought it would turn into nothing at all."

"Okay?" Joey said. "But?"

I took the envelope out and laid it on the table, but I didn't say anything for the longest time. I glanced from Joey to Carlos to Manny, but no one uttered a word.

"It came back with two matches."

Silence.

No one said a word, and for a moment, I honestly thought no one was breathing as quiet as it was. I waited for them all to process this, as I honestly had nothing else I could say to them to soften the blow. Like me, they would need to work through it, find their own questions.

Joey reached out and picked up the envelope. He turned it over and unsealed the little metal piece. Then he slipped the single sheet of paper out and appeared to read the information before handing it to Carlos. My heart, by this point, was pounding so hard against my rib cage that I was certain those around me must be able to hear it. I wanted to jump up and run, scream at them to say something, or just expire on the spot. The stress of not knowing what was going on in their heads was killing me.

Carlos finished and held the paper out to Manny, who took it. I sat with my head downturned, not wanting to meet anyone's gaze. I didn't want them to all be mad, not talk to me or allow this to drive a wedge between us.

"Wow, two new brothers on dad's side if I'm reading this, right?" Manny said aloud as my head whipped to my left side, as I realized his tone was not mad.

"Yep," I said. "I'm so sorry. Honestly, that is not what I was expecting – not that I guess I knew what to expect, but that was a shock," I found myself stumbling along and finally forced myself to quit speaking.

"Wow, I guess considering Mama had Carmen, Juanita, and Estrella from her second marriage, it isn't crazy he also had more kids," Carlos said. "You are right. I guess in all these years since we cut contact and refused to see him, I just hadn't given any thought to him having more kids."

"So, now what?" Manny asked as they all turned to me.

"You aren't mad at me?" I said, feeling my air rush from my lungs gratefully.

"Of course not," Manny said, slapping me on the back. "Extra siblings just means more family in the end. I would never have thought to do this, but I'm definitely not mad."

"Me neither," Carlos said with a definitive shake to his head.

"I think we should try to reach out to them," Joey offered

up. "I think we all can agree family is the most important thing to all of us. We can see if they are interested in meeting us at least; what say you all?"

"Agreed," Carlos offered, shaking his head profusely.

"Definitely," interjected Manny.

"I would definitely be up for that," I said.

"Excellent," Manny said, handing me the paper along with the envelope. "You started this crazy ride; you do the leg work and let us know what you need from us. I trust you; if you reach out and they seem creepy or off in any way, we agree not to meet them. If, on the other hand, you think it is worth a meeting, then as a family, we will consider the best way to make that happen."

"Will do," I said as the waitress put the beers, we ordered in front of us.

"To the family," Joey said, grabbing the glass and holding it into the middle of the table.

"Family," Manny said, raising his glass.

"Family," Carlos said.

"Family," I said as we call clinked glasses and then tipped back a cold one.

EPILOGUE

Rigo

S ix months later
     Me, Manny, Joey, and Carlos were all sitting side by side in the airport terminal. It had been a long and twisty road to get here, and today was one of those days in our lives where everything changed. We had all agreed together to meet our new half-brothers Ricas and Mario. These two would be younger obviously than all of us, by quite a bit. Still, they had agreed and been eager to learn more about us and vice versa – so here we sat.

Elaine and I were going strong these days, and honestly, it was amazing how far we had come. She was living with me full-time now, and I had been ring shopping for weeks trying to find the perfect piece of jewelry to show her how much I loved her. I no longer could imagine even a day going by without her in it and expected to make her a proposal by Christmas this year.

She was also working with a couple of people to set up her own party planning business. In the meantime, she did small gigs here and there for friends and was honing her skills, vendor relationships, and such with each passing day. I was so proud of her as she continued to work on herself and her family dynamic through therapy. If anyone had told me I could be this happy and settled down with a woman just a year ago, I would have told them they were nuts.

"Anyone else feel like throwing up?" Joey finally broke the silence. "I don't think I can remember the last time that I was this nervous."

"Agreed," Manny bit out. "I know I'm normally the one with some wicked comeback, but I have nothing for this situation."

"I'm simply curious if they will look like us or be more reserved. I don't know, having been raised by our own father after he abandoned us, what they have been told," Carlos spoke his thoughts aloud.

"Yeah, they seem pretty chill and open from the couple of short conversations we have had," I offered.

Basically, we all had been on four phone calls together with Ricas and Mario. They seemed tight like me and my brothers were, backing each other up each step of the way. They had been curious as to what family might be out there, which was why they did the DNA test all those months ago. I understood that feeling, as I also had been the one to do the DNA test to see about additional siblings we might have. Now that both Papa and Mama were gone, it was up to us to decide what kind of people and relationships we all wanted. I figured all my brothers and me together would make our decision once we could meet these two in person.

"I just hope they like cars and motorcycles," Carlos offered causing us all to give a little chuckle.

"And big, noisy and crazy family gatherings," Joey said. "I think with all our girlfriends and fiances; they have gotten even noisier in the last few months."

"Agreed," I offered. "And can we talk about the fact that Elaine is ridiculous about how over the top the ones are her plans?"

"Thank you," Joey said. "Angela actually said that she thought Elaine should do all of them after that last bash she threw. It was amazing."

All head bobs made me so happy. Elaine adored all my brothers, and it was amazing to watch how easily she assimilated into my family. If you did not know her background or the immense privilege to which she had been born, you wouldn't guess from her actions these days.

"I know Sandi has been tapping her for wedding planning also," Manny put forward. "I'm surprised at how perfectly she is hitting the nail on the head with everything Sandi wants and bringing it to life."

"I've told her that instead of doing it for fun, she should become a professional event planner," I said, watching the door to the aircraft hoping that it wasn't much longer.

"That is a great choice for her. Seriously she would do amazing business," Carlos replied.

I felt my heart was full to brimming over having these three by my side. I adored Elaine and the life we were building, and despite the sadness that still seeping in over losing Mama so quickly after my return – life was good. I could not have hoped for a better outcome when I uprooted to come back near family.

Then the announcement board let us know that the plane had arrived, and the first passengers filtered in. All four of us stood in quick succession as I wiped my hands down the front of my pants. My heart was beating out a heavy rhythm against my rib cage, and I felt flushed from head to two.

Then two men, younger than all of us but absolutely the same dark hair, big physiques, and lopsided grins, entered the main building. I felt my breath suspend movement, and their eyes turned to us.

"Holy moly," Joey whispered. "They definitely look like us.

On unsteady legs, I moved forward with my brothers to welcome two new ones to the mix.

"Hey, I'm Rigo," I said, extending my hand to the first one.

"Mario," he said but grabbed me suddenly by the shoulders and pulled me tight. "It's so good to finally meet you."

I slapped a hand on his back, "welcome to the family. It's great to meet you also."

"We have been waiting for this since we got the results of the DNA," Ricas said.

"Our family was not all that excited about us making the trip. Our cousins and mom have always told us the worst stories about your side of the family, in all honesty," Mario said though his brother punched him in the arm.

"Hey, let's air all the dirty laundry on the first meeting," Ricas said to his brother.

"No, it's all good," Manny said, moving toward them. "You can never go wrong being totally honest with us, and we will do the same. All we can do now is let the past go, and let's start learning about each other by spending time communicating in each other's company, and we will figure this all out as we go," he said. "Sound fair?"

"We have step-sisters from our mom's second marriage," I said. "They might be a good source of information on how we all navigate blending the families and some of that work we are still doing. They will love to meet you this trip if you are game."

"Absolutely," Ricas said.

"I agree," Mario said. "Just one request for the weekend?"

"Name it," Joey offered.

"We want to ride here in California. We have been dreaming of taking motorcycles out on some of the roadways you sent pictures of," Mario said with eager eyes toward them.

"We can definitely make that work," Manny said, as the five of them fell into line and headed out of the airport.

I knew it might be a fun weekend, but there would be tough moments also. We were family, though, so hopefully, in the end, we could all work together to find common ground and build a future together.

RICKY

RICKY

I could not get my body under control and think for sure nausea would get the better of me. I shouldn't be this surprised at the outcome of his search, but still, who in their right mind was ever prepared for something like this? I hoped that I would be able to deal with this latest bit of information maturely and decide what to do about it like a grown-up. As much as I wanted to, the facts in black and white on his screen triggered all kinds of memories and thoughts that were wreaking havoc with my mental and physical wellbeing at this moment. I had survived several terrible years, and each time I thought that a new beginning was right around the corner, some other majorly earth-shattering development occurred. I was done with it. *Why couldn't he just live a quiet, ordinary life without any more curveballs?*

Still, this could end up being good for him and his future. And maybe I needed to keep an open mind; I reminded myself. After all, while mom had claimed that she knew about dad's first wife and possibly some kids he had, it had been with venom in her voice. There had never been anything but contempt, animosity, and anger in everything I was told about my father's first family. Most of the horrible things were implied about his wife not doing right by him. The stories would make me ill to my stomach at the misdeeds done against my father until I got older and realized that there were two sides to every pancake. I don't know if everything was all dad's doing or what mom knew firsthand because, unfortunately, she had passed in the last year, leaving Mario and me with more questions than answers. We had a few cousins who still tried to interact with them, but they were so ugly about anything we would ask questions about that I left things to lie when they were around.

Still, reading this information and the truth of all the lies I had been told made me wish my father dead all over again. It should not have been a huge shock to find out that the scumbag married my mother, poisoned her against his first family, and then cheated on her when she got sick had another kid or possibly more. Of course, this had come to light a bit late to make a difference, but when the truth of my father cheating on every woman he had ever been with – well, it had changed me forever.

The DNA test referenced had just been for one man in the database, but in researching the man, it came to light, there were references in his bio about four brothers and three sisters. I am not sure if those were all fathered by my own DNA contributing parental unit as I now started to think of my father, but that was a lot of new family to wrap my head around. This was supposed to have been a way to learn more about my heritage and clear up some of the ambiguities that were fed me when I asked questions about my father's first family. I did not want to throw my life further into a tailspin by unveiling this level of discovery.

I've been so busy these days that I didn't take any time for myself or a love life of any kind. It was a big reason that I thought finding more family, a bigger support network, and just people to help me care for Clara would be great. I don't think in my wildest dreams I had imagined exactly what I would do finding this other family, though. So here I sat, reeling, having no idea what I should do next.

A knock at the door sounded, and I launched from the chair to head to the front door. I was expecting my brother Mario to show up, as I had texted him a while ago regarding needing to see him at his earliest convenience. Sure enough, Mario was standing at the door, looking perplexed as he came right inside the foyer.

"That text scared the shit out of me," he said to me. "What in the world could be that important?"

The truth was that I had been shaking and on the verge of a nervous breakdown when I sent it. We had a shorthand that we used only in the worst of situations, which I felt qualified. Now seeing the terror radiating from his gaze, I realized I might be overreacting. I guess the only thing to do was share the information and let him make his decision on the matter.

"Come in here," I replied, going back to the guest room where I had a desk set up as a semi-office space. This was the only space I could lock up safe from the prying hands of a toddler in the entire house.

"So, you know how crazy I was after everything that happened with Carla?" I said, turning to my brother, looking him dead in the eye to impress how important this was to me.

"Yeah. She really shocked the hell out of me. What did she do this time?" Mario asked me as his shoulders slumped and his face puckered into a sour expression that showed the disgust he had for my ex, the mother of my child, and hands down, the worst person I had ever met.

I had fallen for Carla hot and heavy right after high

school when Mario and I had first decided to go in on our bike modification and custom fabrication business. Carla loved fast bikes, me, and the dreams she fostered of the life we could have together.

Then when we had been together for three years, we found out she was pregnant. I was over the moon, ready to marry and begin our family that I always dreamed of. Though she stalled every step of the way, making things more permanent between us, which probably should have been a red flag for me. I was just so excited to become a father and try to do everything different for my child than my father had done for me. When my beautiful daughter Clara was born, we even named her after Carla by simply rearranging some of the letters.

Then weeks after the birth, Clara's father died, and things were tough for Carla as we navigated that loss. At first, it was pain meds to numb her pain, and I didn't know because I was always working. When it became evident, she had a major problem, I told her she needed to go to rehab. The day I took off work to drive her to a facility, she told me she was not going to go and that she wasn't sure about them being together anymore.

So, he had his doubts and wanted to confirm Clara was his. Even if she hadn't been his at that point, he was willing to fight for her and get full custody. Luckily, he didn't have to because she was his daughter.

Everything for me had changed in the moment of Clara's birth, and I was now a parent which was a dream come true and I would try and do the best for my child. That night after the doorbell rang Carla had thrust her baby girl into my arms and told me she was headed to Europe, she confessed she had been dating some creep for a while and she was going for a whirlwind band tour with him. That evening Clara left with her loverboy and they didn't see her after that.

Parenting and taking care of his baby girl was difficult but with his brother's help he managed to get through this. He was determined to be the best father for his daughter and would do his best to create the best life for his baby girl.

That was the last we had heard from her, not for lack of trying on my part as I felt some contact would be better than none for my daughter. Since the phone number I had was disconnected, I still would send pictures, and updates to her email. I just never wanted to have Clara think I was the one that didn't make an effort to foster a relationship with her mother. Clara was now two years old and the center of my world. She never asked for momma anymore, and time just continued forward. Though the heartache I felt was getting better, I still couldn't find it in me to give love a second chance.

"I'm not obsessing about finding true love," I said, swallowing hard as I pulled myself out of my wandering thoughts. "This was about dad."

Mario turned to him with an odd expression. "What about him?"

"You know we found out about the cheating right before mom passed. I know that she always fed us all that information about dad's evil first wife and how miserable he was. I just wondered if that were true based on how much we came to find out he lied about," I said with a sigh. "After Carla, I got to thinking about him having done this to someone else. I was up late one night watching tv, and one of those commercials for the ancestry kits came on, and in a weak moment, I called and ordered one. I ran the DNA through this ancestry site online and registered for notifications should it ever match to someone."

"And?" Mario said impatiently for the punchline.

"Nothing popped," I said. "That was a while ago, but tonight I got this alert," I retorted, glancing down at the notice from the site. "It hit on a guy that ran the results for himself, but it does say he has three brothers and three sisters also."

"Whoa," Mario said, falling into the chair behind me and just staring. "I kind of always thought there would be someone out there. I mean, dad was a player, as we, unfortunately, found out, but that many brothers and sisters. That would probably make them older, right?"

"I would guess, considering dad's health and age," I said. "I'm just not sure if I should pursue it. With both dad and mom gone, I just thought," I bit down on my lip to turn toward Mario. "It might be nice for the girls and us to have some additional family besides the few cousins that barely seem to tolerate us anymore. We got each other's backs and are doing okay, but what do you think," I asked with a shrug as he sat waiting for Mario's response?

We have a great custom bike business that kept both of us afloat financially, along with the freedom for me to take care of anything Clara needed. That was great, but the business growth was fast, outgrowing our location. With a larger space came the responsibility of more staff and longer hours for a time. Mario had twin girls, nearly five, and I had Clara to care for in addition to their jobs. These days, neither of us had a social life and no help except what we paid for during daylight hours when at work. It was a grind being single parents and each other's only source of support, but many people had so much less, so we counted our blessings and not the trials.

"I think we should respond," Mario said, shocking him to his core. "We would only fret about them being out there and not knowing. If we chat and they seem odd or condescending, we stop all communication and feel like we know everything we need to. Agreed?"

"Agreed," I replied gently in return. "Also, we both have full access to any communication, and we are a team, right?"

"Always," Mario said. "There is no question about that."

"Okay, so how in the freaking world do we start this email?" I asked my brother, who only inhaled deeply and stared straight ahead for the longest time.

"I guess we go with him and take it from there," Mario said with a chuckle as I took the keyboard in hand to formulate an introduction email to our half-brother or brothers. I had no idea what we would find but felt that old spark of curiosity firing, honestly the most surprising part of the evening.

DANIELLA

I turned around, gearing up for a fight. I am convinced Dr. Dan Wheeton was being a douchebag again and purposely rubbing up against my backside. The man's ego was bigger than the stories I have heard about his conquests of the nursing staff here at the hospital. I am not now, nor will I ever be interested in adding my name to his list of past trysts, though he did not seem to be getting the message no matter how cold or distant I made myself.

Sure, the nursing station on the pediatrics floor was crowded, but he was the only one that failed to maintain personal space when I was around. It was not blatant enough for me to report him, but honestly, I am going to break a finger of his if he didn't stop it. He would reach for a file, nearly aligning his entire body to mine, in what I'm sure he thought was a smooth move. It just made me want to vomit or possibly throat punch him.

"Can you take these labs for me?" Ellen asked, giving me a knowing smile as she held out a small tray of samples. The woman was my direct boss and seriously the most kind-hearted person I knew.

"Thank you," I mouthed and immediately took the packages and fled the space without another word.

"Daniella," Dr. Weeton shouted out as he raced to catch up with me before I made a full getaway into the elevator to the basement where our lab was located. I had everything I could do not to scowl at the man as I brought my features into a mask. Unfortunately, he was one of the best pediatric surgeons in the country and a bright shining star of the hospital. The success of our department hinged on how many private clients came to see him for their delicate operations, and by virtue, that meant he helped keep me employed. Thus, being rude could cause undue consequences that I was unwilling to pay, so I would have to play nice.

"Yes," I asked; turning to him, I plastered the brightest smile I could muster on my lips? Hopefully, this really was work-related, and he wouldn't try asking me out – again! That had been happening in roundabout ways for a couple of weeks now. I honestly just prayed he would be enthralled by new prey shortly as there were a lot of pretty nurses around the hospital and leave me in peace.

"You know there is the cocktail this Friday evening, honoring me for that award I won," he said as his chest puffed a bit, and he looked haughtier than ever. Was it too much to ask that tall, dark, and handsome could maybe not be such an egomaniac? Without his annoying personal habit of believing himself god's gift to womankind, he wasn't half bad.

"I had heard," I respond, and I know where this was going. I decided to head it off before he could get a word in edgewise. "Congrats on the award that is great for the hospital and your resume. I wish I could be there that night, but I had promised my sister to watch my nephews that evening. You all have the best time, though," I said and turned

287

to briskly walk away, hoping that would deter any more advances.

"Well," he said, catching up to her and moving to stand in her direct path. "Maybe you could join me for a celebratory drink on Saturday?"

Damn! The man was persistent.

"I'm sorry, Dr. Wheeton," I said, deciding to bite the bullet and put the man down gently. "I do not date men I work with, and besides, you are one of my bosses."

"I can keep a secret if you can," he said, giving her a smarmy look that made me want to rebuff him harder.

I knew darn well that was a lie, and he would keep no secrets. The man's entire repertoire of conquests was well known about the hospital, and I had caught him talking to doctors and orderlies alike about some of them. I just was not about to be caught up by his good looks, charm, and paycheck. No matter how many good attributes the man had, monogamy and love did not seem to be something he was capable of at this time in his life.

"I'm sorry," I said. "I am not interested in you for that kind of relationship."

"Whoa!" He said emphatically, holding up his hands to stop anything else I might say, "I said nothing about a relationship," he looked horrified by the word, causing me just a tiny smile.

"Oh, I thought," I stopped as I fluttered my lashes suggestively at him and bit on her lip provocatively. "I'm sorry, I guess I misunderstood. No worries, but I really need to get these to the lab," I said, holding up the samples as I pivoted and rushed on down the hall before he could utter another word.

I didn't want to meet just a great guy but rather the right guy. I had in my teens been one of those wild teenagers that gave my parents grey hairs with my partying, dating, and barely passing school. That said, I have quieted down, gone to college to get a nursing degree, and had a fabulous job. I also had two amazing nephews, the best family even if they did sometimes meddle a bit more than I would have liked, but we got along wonderfully. My parents, having been happily married forty years now, were the ideal I hoped to one day find for myself, and Dr. Wheeton definitely could not match that kind of loyalty in a relationship. Few men could, and besides, I find dating tedious, so I didn't do it often.

Someday I kept telling myself it would happen for me. Until then, I was not going to settle for some secondary affair that might impede my career that I adore here at the hospital for a roll in the sack. No matter how good I might have heard that Dr. Wheeton was in that area.

As I made it to the lab, I gave myself a silent pat on the back for again managing to dodge the man and his no longer subtle stalking of my person. I knew the only reason he was interested was that I continued to say no. He was like a hunter who loved the hunt, but once the prey was bagged quickly lost interest and moved to new adventures. That was not going to be me – no if and or buts about it!

RICKY

I was sitting on the plane separated from Mario, as I had been upgraded automatically based on the large volume of miles I had accumulated. He had to sit in economy, and I was pretty certain I was going to hear about this when we landed. I hadn't even made eye contact with him when I was notified about the upgrade, as I knew it was sort of mean. I knew that the first-class accommodations meant that I could make this nerve-wracking flight in general comfort, not sandwiched between strangers.

As I sat there with my head against the pane of glass, looking outside the plane waiting for us to get underway, I was stupefied about how this had happened and what we would find on the other end of this flight. Rigo, Manny, Joey, and Carlos were all going to be meeting us at the airport. After months of chatting back and forth, we had hired a babysitter we trusted for the weekend and jetted off for an in-person meeting. I hadn't been this nervous in forever. I had four brothers in addition to Mario. If I had been searching for a little more support group, I had found it.

The brothers all were engaged, and thus they would be

spending the weekend with all of them as a group. It sounded like a lot of what they would be doing. Actually, more like just getting to know each other from years spent not even knowing the others existed. Well, the truth was there had been whispers, innuendos, and outright lies it seemed by his father that his mother had perpetrated about that side of the family. I can't ask my mother what the truth was as she sadly had passed on, and the mother to the other boys had just recently passed. We will need to spend time blending and finding our truth.

It was hard as Mario, and I were so tight, and from what I heard, the other four brothers were also, so I don't know what the dynamic might be like once we try to act as a group.

A stewardess pulled me from my thoughts, asking me if I would like anything to drink. I loved this service as I ordered a soda and light snack, which definitely would be more than Mario got – not that I would rub it in that much, I thought with a little chuckle to myself. I enjoyed traveling when able, and to date that had not been something Mario did not do enough to accumulate the same benefits as I had.

The flight amenities included drinks, snacks, and some decadent chocolates, which put me in a great mood as we finished the long trip. When the Captain came over the speaker to announce the seat belt sign was going on and prepare for landing, the nerves once again grabbed hold of my stomach and twisted. I was sorry that I had eaten so much as the nerves started in earnest, thinking about how I would be meeting my brothers after we deplaned. Inhaling, I tried to calm my insides and just hoped for the best.

I waited as everyone filed out so that I could cut in next to Mario; he gave me the oddest look as we walked out into the airport.

"How are you doing?" Mario asked me quietly.

291

"I feel like I want to throw up, to be honest," I reply. "How was your flight?"

He grimaced at me, "you know how you just hate it when you see that person seated next to you and realize they are going to talk your ear off the entire flight?"

"Yeah," I said, trying to hold my smile in check, as he pointed to an older, oversized woman that was sitting in one of the chairs that we had just passed.

"She literally could write my biography based on how many questions she asked during that flight. Oh, and I know about her four kids, dead husband, six grandkids, and three dogs," Mario said with crazy eyes.

"Sorry," I said, biting hard on my lip. "But not really."

He punched me for that comment, which I definitely deserved.

"Truly though, are you getting anxious about meeting everyone?" He asked in a hushed tone for my ears alone as we continued walking toward the exit and the fated meeting with their new family members.

"I just don't have any idea what this is going to look like. It has been easy back and forth in email and the few phone calls. Now for a whole weekend, though, what if things go super bad and we hate each other?"

"That's what we have each other for," Mario said. "I think we need to have a secret sign. If we give this sign, we clear out without any questions on either side."

"Sounds good," I said to him. "What sign?"

"How about we pull on our right ear?" Mario offered and then demonstrated. "Like that."

"Got it," I said.

"Seriously, they sound like good guys, and we all have the bike thing in common. Carlos even owned a garage and was telling us about that new space he thought we might like,"

Mario said. "It is worth looking at if you don't see any red flags."

"Would you uproot your entire life and move out here?" I asked. "I mean, I would be willing to do so if I believe it the right move for Clara and would add value to her life having cousins and family around. I would do anything for her."

I had thought a lot about this very thing. I wanted my daughter to have a big, raucous family, and if that meant a move, she was still young enough to make that work. He would absolutely never consider it thought without Mario by his side. These new brothers would be a unit, and he needed his brother to navigate these comings days, weeks, and months.

"The girls start school in just a few weeks," Mario said. "If you think this is a positive after this weekend, then we have to make a move. We don't want to ever have the kind of regrets that mom had – do we?"

"No, definitely not," I said as I inhaled and waited for the flight to land. I didn't speak a word as I readied to exit the plane and then walked tall beside Mario as we wove our way out to the area where guests could wait.

We saw four guys that looked just like us with the same dark hair, big physiques, and ease grins come into view. I felt my breath suspend movement, and their eyes turned to us.

I moved forward with my brother to great the four new siblings I had recently found out about on unsteady legs.

"Hey, I'm Rigo," the first said, extending his hand to me.

"Ricky," I said but found myself grabbing Rigo by the shoulders and pulling him in tight. "It's so good to meet you."

Rigo slapped a hand on my back, "welcome to the family. It's great to finally meet you also."

"We have been waiting for this since we got the results of the DNA," I said.

"Our family was not all that excited about us making the

trip. Our cousins and mom had always told us the worst stories about your side of the family, in all honesty," Mario said though his brother punched him in the arm.

"Hey, let's air all the dirty laundry on the first meeting," I said to my brother.

"No, it's all good," Manny said, moving toward us. "You can never go wrong being totally honest with us, and we will do the same. All we can do now is let the past go, and let's start learning about each other by spending time communicating in each other's company, and we will figure this all out as we go," he said. "Sound fair?"

"We have step-sisters from our mom's second marriage," Rigo said. "They might be a good source of information on how we all navigate blending the families and some of that work we are still doing. They will love to meet you this trip if you are game."

"Absolutely," I said.

"I agree," Mario said. "Just one request for the weekend?"

"Name it," Joey offered.

"We want to ride here in California. We have been dreaming of taking motorcycles out on some of the roadways you sent pictures of," Mario said with eager eyes toward them.

"We can definitely make that work," Manny said, as the five of them fell into line and headed out of the airport.

I knew it might be a fun weekend, but there would be tough moments also. We were family, though, so hopefully, in the end, we could all work together to find common ground and build a future together.

DANIELLA

J was ready for a drink and some food after a long shift. We had a number of emergencies with some long-term patients today, and those were the hardest. Some of the kids were chronic cases, and you grew close to them, felt for their families, and were sad when they took a turn for the worse. That was the hardest part of my job. The most rewarding was one of those patients finally was cured and went home for good. Today it had just been rough situation after rough, and I was grateful to finally be done.

"So, how was work?" Trish asked as I hopped up on a stool at the high-top table, where we had agreed to meet up.

Trish loved this place as they did live music, comedy, and other entertainment while you ate, which I could have done without. Peace, quiet, and light conversation were all I needed at the end of my day, though I didn't tell her this. The food was okay if you like hamburgers and comfort food. I liked cleaner eating myself though that meant I took a lot of ribbing about eating similar to a rabbit from everyone from Trish to my sister. I could get down with a cold beer and a burger, though, with the best of them. Besides, to keep things fair, we switched off who picked the spot, and tonight was Trish's pick, so I supported it just as she would when the tables turned.

"How was work?" She asked me again as my brain sailed in a myriad of directions, and I realized I hadn't given her a verbal answer to her question when I sat down.

"You know, saving lives and kicking butt," I said as the waitress who knew us well slid my favorite chilled bottle of brew across the table.

"Yeah, same here. The ER has been a tad bit busy this week, but I did hear about the conjoined twins you had," Trish said, sounding more excited about the toddlers joined at the chest wall than her role.

She was a trauma nurse, and the pace of her role made mine look like a walk in the park. She was truly gifted under fire and married to her career like me. It was one of the things we commiserated about a lot when either of us had a tough day. We also worked in the same hospital though you wouldn't know it during working hours as our paths rarely crossed. That didn't mean we liked to focus on our work outside of the job; rather, a quick catch-up and onto other topics was normally the pace of these frequent dinners.

"So, guess who I finally asked out?" Trish said as she gave a light drum roll on the table.

"Please tell me you didn't ask out that Paramedic Pete," I said to her rolling my eyes in her direction. The guy was a bodybuilder who literally asked everyone to feel his muscles every chance he got. Once, he had done that when wheeling a man into the OR directly from his rig due to rebar in the guy's chest. Apparently, Pete had a show coming up that week as he did that as a side hustle and was extremely keen on female validation. It had taken everything I had not to turn my nose up at him. He was a total tool, and what Trish saw in him, I would never understand.

"You know I have been waiting patiently for him to notice me," Trish said with the most excited look on her face. "I did have to ask him, though, so I'm not sure if that is a good sign or a bad."

"Bad," I said, trying not to sugarcoat my response.

Unfortunately, Trish had an insatiable need to date losers, and her list grew with each new name she added. She was a prolific dater that didn't seem to last more than a couple of weeks in any given relationship. Of course, she had a tough childhood, and some of that spilled over into this pattern. Also, she got bored easily, so even the one or two men she had gone out with quickly shed and moved to the next hot body. It was a routine almost as old as our friendship and played out like a train wreck I wished I didn't have to see time and again.

"You need to finally say yes to Dr. Dreamy," Trish said to me, making me cringe. "Then we could all double date."

"Not if you paid me a million dollars," I said, looking I'm sure as if I might be physically sick at the suggestion. "Trish, I don't want to be the laughingstock of the entire hospital, and seriously, Dr. Wheeton shares all the details of his dates with everyone. He is about as discreet as a billboard on the side of the highway."

"Okay, but you have to date again," Trish said, sounding more like a petulant child than a grown adult. "I know you love your nephews and want an amazing marriage like your parents. That said, you have to date to get to the marriage point. You do realize this, correct?"

"I do," I reassured her. "I promise I will know the right guy when he walks in. I just don't have the time or energy to put into the wrong guys," I said and immediately reached out to put a hand over hers. "I didn't mean that the way it sounded."

"No worry," Trish said. "I'm willing to kiss a thousand

toads to find my prince. If you think magically the right one is going to wander into your life, more power to you."

"Thanks," I said as we took a break in the conversation to order. When the waitress started to walk away, I began a new line of thought, "what about the fundraiser for the family house. Are we going to have a meeting with that group this week to review and assign our next tasks?"

"Yep," Trish said, picking up her phone. "I will make a note to get an email out bright and early tomorrow. Oh, and you did tell me when Max's birthday party was. I know his actual birthday is Tuesday before my vacation but is the party after I get back?" She said, wrinkling her nose at me. "I know I'm the worst aunty ever."

"No, it's the Saturday before you leave," I said to her with a slight condescending shake of my head. "What would you do without me to remind you of things?"

"I don't know," she said, looking horrified, "and let's never find out."

"Deal," I said as we continued to enjoy the evening and dinner, just shooting the breeze as per normal.

RICKY

*I*t was the week of our first trip with the girls to California, and we were going to be accessing everything for a possible move. I know it seemed pretty fast after just the first meeting with our family out there, but Carlos and I had an opportunity to join forces and take on a new facility for his automotive repair and our fabrication business. Separately Carlos's business and ours in that space made no sense with the size of the parking lot and square footage. Together for both businesses, though, we could expand and have a great roadside showroom to boot that was sure to draw more business than we could hope from in our current spot. Of course, in the interest of protecting everyone, we did have an attorney making sure that all the business paperwork was in order. At the same time, we were working toward a great family dynamic that would, of course, take time. Business though was business, and Mario and I had been waiting for the right time to do this for years. This just seemed right.

Clara had wanted to sit by the window when they got on the plane, as she loved to watch out the window. Having her cooped up in the space was tough as she wanted to play I, Spy, then asked about a million questions as we winged through the air. Why was everything so small? Could she walk out on the wings? Was a plane faster than a bird? And it went on and on until he was grateful when they finally touched down, and she would be able to get out and stretch her legs. He loved her little curious soul, but honestly, it could be exhausted from time to time also.

I worked to gather Clara and all the toys, her blanket, and such as we got ready to exit. I was feeling super worried once again about this trip which was odd because so far, with Rigo, Carlos, Joey, and Manny, everything was better than I could imagine. We talked regularly, texted daily about business along with personal, and it all felt like we had been part of each other's lives for much longer than we had.

We waited patiently to exit the plane, Clara holding tight to me the entire time. I inhaled as we finally started forward and hoped this was the trip that finally cemented everything.

I did notice Mario up ahead with Livia and Marina, and they looked just as subdued as Clara. This was the first trip we had managed with all of them in tow. Despite their young ages, it was important to see how they would gel with the family and if there were any red flags of any kind before a final decision was made.

"Daddy," Clara said, gazing at me from her vantage point closer to the ground. "I don't feel good," she offered up as we just barely came into view of Rigo and Manny. Mario and his girls beat us there, and we were within earshot ourselves.

"Oh, honey," I got worried as this was her first time on the plane. "What hurts?" I asked as I lifted her to my arms. She did feel warmer than when we boarded but not sickly enough to raise major concerns in my mind.

"My ears," she said as her little lip protruded out a bit. "It hurted a lot."

Clara was not a kid who complained a lot, so I took notice when she did. I had been super fortunate that she was healthy and rarely struggled with even the cold. If she was stating that she was unwell, something was up. A light bulb suddenly went off as I realized that she might not understand how to clear her ears and make them pop since she had flown before.

"I bet it does hurt," I said, digging in my pocket for the chewy candy I had kept on hand just in case. I held one out to her, "if you chew on that, it might help your ears pop."

She happily put it in her mouth and started going to town chewing it. One emergency averted, I focused ahead on meeting up with everyone.

"Is she not the cutest thing," Manny said coming up to us to get a good look at Clara. "I'm going to have to ask that you try to rough her up or something," he said, looking at me. "Sandi is going to want a kid immediately when she gets a load of your three," he said, gazing over at Livia and Marina hooked by a hand to Mario off to my right.

"Can you say hi to your uncle Manny?" I asked Clara as I rubbed her back gently as she now had her face buried in my shoulder. "She can sometimes play shy until she gets to know you," I explained, as Manny gave a knowing nod.

"I totally understand," he said. "I bet Clara decides I'm the coolest Uncle ever soon enough."

"Hey now," Mario grumbled as Manny just chuckled.

"Well, everyone is back at the house and excited to welcome you all," Rigo said as they all turned to start the long walk out of the airport. I had gotten into a habit of traveling light with Clara so we didn't have to wait for luggage so we could head straight out to the vehicle. Luckily, Mario and his girls were light travelers also, it would appear as he indicated they didn't need to wait for luggage either.

"So, Carmen, Estrella, and Juanita planned a welcome

picnic for you all today," Rigo said. "I would like to apologize now as I believe they have every member of the extended family coming out to see you. I hope you have a good memory because you are going to need it to remember everyone."

"Is that going to be weird?" Mario asked, catching my attention as I turned to see what he was thinking. "I mean, I know that by blood, they aren't related, so how does that side of the family feel regarding dad?"

That was a good question, as I immediately felt my skin prickle even at the mention of our father. This was quite a pickle he left us to navigate due to him not being able to be faithful. I hoped that no one would be overly mean as that would not fly with me having Clara there if someone got disrespectful.

"Honestly, about the same as I imagine you do," Rigo offered after a second. "I will be honest, that it was hard, especially with Carlos and I, who felt like we betrayed Mama when we had to tell her about dad. She had a great second marriage, though, and in the end, she didn't hold on to resentment. She wanted her family – all of her family to love, support, and have each other when she was gone. I don't know about all of you, but you are family no matter the tenuous blood relation to the sisters or not," Rigo said, turning slightly to capture my gaze. "How do you feel about that?"

"I just want my daughter to have people around that love her, support her, and foster her as she grows. I don't care if blood, honorary aunts and uncles, or the like. If you are kind, supportive, and non-judgemental, we can make this work," I replied, glancing at Mario to see his feedback on this subject.

"I was so angry at dad by the time mom divulged the truth of his affairs. It was her death bed confession because I think she knew that something like this might happen, and possibly she had said things she shouldn't have over the years," Mario offered. "I think we don't focus on history but what kind of family and support system we can build for the future. We have kiddos, and you all will too soon," he said, glancing between the children sandwiched into car seats between them. "That needs to be the focus and not things that happened we can't control."

"Well said," Manny offered in return.

"Great, then let's get this weekend off to a great start and see about talking you definitely into this move," Rigo said. "I know Carlos, who is the quietest of us by far, is over the moon about this expansion plan."

"Good because we won't be able to back out once the ink dries on the paperwork," I said, feeling the tremors of excitement and worry spread like wildfire in my system. Everything was moving so fast, yet no red flags were telling me to slow it down. In fact, with each passing day, I got more excited to see what the next chapter would look like for Clara and me.

DANIELLA

$\mathcal{M}$y phone would not stop buzzing in the pocket of my scrubs. Normally I didn't try to pick up personal calls during my shift unless on a break as it was against the rules unless an emergency. Glancing down, I noticed it was Trish again, though, and thought that maybe there was something up as this was not normal behavior for her. She had never called me in the hospital, that I could recall, so I just felt this warranted a pick-up to make sure there was nothing urgent needed.

"What?" I connected the call and harshly spoke into the device. "I'm working, and you know the rules. This better be a massive emergency."

"I know," Trish said calmly in a tone I couldn't quite figure out right off the bat. "I have a pediatric patient down here that you need to come see," Trish said.

That was super odd as she could just call the nursing station, and whoever was available would be dispatched. The normal process was a doctor, as most nurses could handle anything in their department. Something was super hinky about this call, but I couldn't figure it out quite yet.

"Why not call for a consult?" I asked, feeling her brows knit together in confusion even without seeing her in person – that was just a Trish thing to do. There was a standard operating procedure for getting someone from her department down to the ER – calling them on a personal phone, was not it. It should go through the nurse station and then be assigned out to whoever was available. Normally, a doctor, to be honest, would go if needing specialty services, and then a nurse by extension had to be invited by said doctor. So many weird thoughts were spiraling in her head, trying to understand Trish's need to call her directly. Her senses told her something else was at play.

"Get down here now!" Trish disconnected the call leaving me staring at the phone beyond confused.

"What's wrong?" Ellen turned to look at me. The head nurse was such a mothering creature, making this the perfect department for her kind of empathy. Luckily, that extended to the staff, which would help me today as I made this odd request.

"That was Trish asking me to come down to the ER," I said, still staring at the phone like it was a foreign object. "That was just weird."

"Sweetie, I hate to break this to you, but Trish is weird," Ellen said, which immediately caused me to chuckle.

"I guess," I said, slipping the phone back into my pocket. Trish took her job just as seriously as I did and was a senior staff member in her area. She wouldn't risk that on a whim, I decided, inhaling deeply.

I should probably see what this was all about.

"We are slow up here," Ellen said gently, prodding me further. "You go on down and see what the woman wants. I would hate for it to be an actual emergency and our team not respond."

"True," I replied, still feeling like there was more to that call. "I will just do a quick check and be right back."

"No worries," Ellen said as I fast walked to the elevator.

The trip down three floors was quick; as I entered the ER, I glanced about to see if I could find Trish's distinctive head of hair. Instead, my eyes latched on to a very tall, dark, tattooed, and stunningly beautiful specimen of the male variety. I could feel his gaze to the pit of my stomach, and then it slid down to the moist juncture at my legs. The reaction was so out of the norm for me during my work shift, where I was in the thick of handling patient issues and normally so diligent in maintaining a totally professional demeanor.

To further cause me alarm, Trish was standing next to him with her back in my direction. She appeared to be working on someone sitting on one of the hospital beds. I surged forward, trying to keep my gaze from going back to the huge man and that face – good golly, no one should be that handsome.

"You called me down," I said to Trish, keeping my gaze trained on her, and when she stepped back, I felt my heart flipflop in my chest. There was a tiny version of the man in a little bitty girl with the same big chocolate eyes, ringlets of black hair, and holding to his hand for dear life.

"This is Ricky," Trish said, extending a hand toward the man, "and his daughter Clara."

"Hi, I'm nurse Daniella Roman," I said to Ricky, who gave a slight head bob, and then I moved to the little girl. "What seems to be the problem?" I asked the question of anyone in the room that might shed light on why these two were in the ER today.

"She has been complaining of pretty severe tummy aches all day," Ricky said as I began to wonder why this was my problem.

"I need a nurse to do an ultrasound," Dr. Nelson, who worked the ER, said coming into the space.

"And you could help?" I turned to whisper to Trish under my breath.

"No, I thought you could help as you have a gentler hand with these things," Trish replied, giving me a knowing smile.

Suddenly everything fell into place in my head, and I nearly growled aloud at her. She had seriously called me down here to meet Ricky, not Clara. The ailing child was not my idea of a good segway to meeting her father, and I would have to speak with Trish when this was over. Right now, though, I had to get to work on fixing this sweet baby.

"Okay," I said, glancing back at Clara would immediately turn to her father when Trish wheeled in the mobile ultrasound.

"It really won't hurt," I said, "I'm going to have your daddy help, okay?" I said to Clara as I turned to Ricky. "If I can have you sit on the bed next to her, maybe she will sit still for me," I said, hoping he saw my silent pleading.

"Okay," he said, looking a tiny bit white around the mouth. "You don't think it is anything too serious? Do you?"

"I'm not sure, but if there is someone else you brought with that might help calm her down," I said though I was a bit worried about dad's mental state also at this moment.

"My brothers," he said, looking sheepish. "But you can't get one of them to help, or I will never hear the end of it," he said in a whisper as if they might actually hear the conversation from the waiting from a good distance away.

"Tell you what," I said, trying to hold my smile in check. "I will work. Okay?"

"Kay," he said, doing as I told him. They were seriously the sweetest little duo, and I had to wonder where this angel's Mama was as I would want to be here if it was my child. Surely, a man that looked like him was not single, but I checked his certain ring finger to confirm and found nothing! That was crazy but not what I should be concentrating on right this minute; I reminded myself.

It took about thirty minutes to finish up the ultrasound, and by then, the x-ray they had done earlier was finished. The doctor came back into the room with a chuckle.

"Well, good news," Dr. Nelson said, "it's just a case of bad gas we have," he said, moving to scrunch Clara's feet to her chest as a long fart ripped out of her body. "With all the travel and changes in diet, sometimes these things can happen."

"All of this for gas?" As I lowered my gaze, I heard Ricky say under his breath, drawing a teasing smile from me.

"It actually happens a lot with kids, and you always are better off safe than sorry," I reassured him.

A short time later, all the paperwork was done, and Ricky and Clara were on their way out.

"Hey," I said as they headed toward the exit. "Do you live close to here?"

"Yeah, we are moving into a house just a few blocks away," Ricky said with a questioning glance in my direction as I held up a finger for him to wait a second.

I moved to the nursing station, grabbed a piece of paper, and wrote some information down. Extending it to him, I gave a bright smile.

"My sister runs Sunshine Academy right around the corner on fifth. She is reasonably priced and has an amazing program that I'm sure Clara would do well with," I told him by way of explanation.

"I agree. When I was researching this area, that place had the best reviews of any I found. I checked there, though, and they said they were full," he replied with a grimace.

"Take that and ask for Trina directly," I said, knowing that my sister would help me out if there were any possible opening she could make.

"Will do," he said, taking the paper. "Thanks."

Trish actually pushed me in the ribcage as I watched them walk out. Clara stared at me until the door closed on them, shielding them from view.

"Why in the world did you not get that man's number and make plans to catch up later?" Trish barked at me, looking as if I had just committed a cardinal sin.

"Did you call me down here for the man or the injured child?" I asked, turning to her with indignation on my face, placing both hands on my hips, hoping to stop any further inquisition on her part.

"Both," she said with a shrug and a cheeky grin. "Tell me that was not the finest looking man you had seen in a long time, and that kid was adorbs – if you like kids. Which you do!"

"Right, but ten bucks says he has a wife or girlfriend," I retorted, turning to head back to my floor.

Trish just chuckled at my backside, "that wasn't a no from you. All I hear is excuses," she said as I just continued walking toward the elevator.

She wasn't wrong. That was the type of man that could end my celibacy streak with a single kiss, as I would be weak to withhold anything from him at that point. I wasn't in the habit of asking men out, especially in front of their kids, though. I had a bad feeling for him I would break a lot of my longstanding rules. The only one I never would bend on was sleeping with married men, which was something I should have found out while I had him here. I just shook my head as I didn't figure our paths would cross again and tried to put the incident in my mind. I had a job to do, and I needed to get back to it, or I wouldn't be able to help the next father-daughter duo that walked into the hospital.

RICKY

I could not get the adorable nurse out of my mind for some inexplicable reason. I normally wasn't into the blonde all-American-looking types preferring dark, curvy, and shorter than Daniella had been. That said, the minute our eyes connected, I had felt it like she ran a finger over my sensitive skin, and she had still been halfway across the room. The woman had the sweetest voice as she worked with Clara to fix the little injury on her chin, and she had those blue eyes that I found himself drowning in each time they turned in my direction.

Now, here I stood like a big lug at the front desk of the Sunshine Academy, waiting to talk to this Trina person about getting Clara in here. I hoped that Daniella wasn't messing with me, and her name alone would be enough to warrant an opening for my little girl. This had been one of my first choices when I was calling around as they had all five-star reviews online, a great academic rating also for a preschool, and it was the brightest, most cheerful building I had ever seen up close.

I had not even gotten past the initial call last time, as the receptionist had immediately told me the place was full. For that reason, I didn't figure I had a chance in hell of getting Clara in, but I was a father willing to make himself a bit uncomfortable and grovel should it come to that for Clara to be safe and happy.

"Can I help you?" A woman walked out of the main office area and came around the large main counter that ran the length of the open welcome center. She was Daniella's sister for sure, from her lithe frame, same flawless face, and those eyes were definitely something the sisters shared.

"I know this is a bit unorthodox," I said, suddenly feeling all nervous inside. "My daughter had a small accident yesterday because I had her at work with me," I rambled on like this was relevant. "Anyway, I was at the hospital, and this nurse helped us. Then I told her about the daycare situation, and she gave me this," I said, handing the paper to her.

She looked down at it, and a weird smile crossed her face. "My sister told you to come here?" She glanced up at me and then examined me like some sort of specimen she was trying to figure out. I honestly was fidgeting under the scrutiny of her gaze but tried to maintain my calm.

"Yes, ma'am," I said as I felt the tendrils of fear climb my spine. I hoped this wasn't a joke or something I was being set up for. It wasn't every day that a stranger helped you find a daycare spot for your child with another family member, of course, but it had all seemed up and up until Trina started laughing slightly.

"First, don't call me ma'am," she said, extending her hand. "Call me Trina, and you are?"

"Ricky," I said as my shoulders slumped, and it seemed like she was going to help me. I was so stunned that I wanted to hug the sweet lady.

"You have a child that is how old?" She asked.

"Clara is two," I said proudly. "She is super smart, obviously potty trained, and just a joy."

"I see," Trina said. "Well, Daniella never asks me for a favor, and when I never say – I mean never in this life has this happened. Do you have siblings?"

"Brothers – five of them," I said, finding how easily that slid off my lips. While these changes were happening fast in my life, I truly felt the connection with Carlos, Rigo, Manny, and Joey happening more each day.

"And as you know, if they ask for favors, you can't say no," she said with a grin. "I would have to put Clara in the three-year-old class and see if that works for now. Would that be acceptable?"

"Yes," I said, super relieved. "I just want her close to me as I open a new shop here and get settled in. It is just me parenting her, so should you need anything, I will be sure and provide," I said with a rush of satisfaction that I found her a good place to hopefully settle and make friends.

"What type of shop do you run?" She asked, looking interested, which he knew she didn't need to be. It was the same way that Daniella had engaged with Clara throughout the trying process of getting her chin fixed. They both had empathetic souls that showed.

"Custom fabrication and motorcycle rebuilds," I said proudly. "My brother does repairs of all kinds. I believe we are taking that massive old showroom for carpets on the corner up on fifth and Broadway and turning it into what we hope becomes a staple in the community here for everyone. We had a shop in Texas for years, but this is a leap of faith, to be sure."

"So, you just moved here on a whim?"

"Nah, my father was from this area, and he, along with my mother, moved to Texas well – I guess for a fresh start before I was born. My older brothers all live out here still, so this is a sort of homecoming," I explained.

"Super cool. Glad to have you back. So, we will need someone beside you to pick up Clara in case of an emergency. The mother is not in the picture at all?"

"No, not even sure where she is at this point. She definitely could not take Clara, and I did get court documents establishing that back in Texas just in case she ever did try anything."

"Excellent. We have a great check-in and check-out process that should help mitigate any concerns," Trina said. "Let me show you around, and then we can get some paperwork done. How does that sound?"

"Amazing. Thank you," I said with a huge sigh of relief.

"No, you need to thank my sister," Trina said. "Maybe take her out to dinner or a movie sometime."

I stopped as if not understanding this sudden change of direction. "I'm sorry you want me to take Daniella out on a date?"

"Please," Trina said, making a sign of praying. "I have tried setting her up, my parents have, and nothing has worked. The woman is a saint, loves my sons, her nephews, works like a dog at the hospital, and I just want to see her happy. That said, she is also seriously the pickiest human I know when it comes to men she will date. So, the fact that she gave you a personal recommendation to my daycare means a lot. She is absolutely into you, and I think you should maybe surprise her at the hospital with her favorite Italian food, which is gnocchi, and her all-time favorite dessert is Tiramisu. I should tell you that amazing food is the key to her heart."

"I don't know that I can show up at work with a fancy dinner without her knowing I'm coming. I just don't know if it is a good idea to get involved with anyone, as I've been single for years since my daughter was born," I said, though, for the first time in years, I had to admit it was appealing.

"She did you a favor; I promise she would say yes," Trina said, making a prayer motion with her hands. "Please? And of course, it would need to be your idea and not mine as she can never know that I had a hand in this."

"I will see what I can do," I said as fresh beads of sweat broke out along my back. For a man who normally played things safe, I was way outside my comfort zone and doing some crazy things these days. "I will say having her favorite food in hand will give it away that someone close to her had a hand in the planning."

"True, but what if you are the perfect match," Trina said, "I'm willing to risk it."

"Alright then," I said with a laugh. "I will think about it seriously."

The idea of asking Daniella out had me smiling the entire time I walked behind Trina. What was the worst that could happen? A single date that either led somewhere or didn't – at least I would be back up on that horse after taking a bad fall with Clara.

DANIELLA

I was bent over the desk in the nursing station, trying hard to finish up the charts from the morning, when Ellen punched me in the side. She was sitting right next to me, and when I glanced in her direction, she inclined her head to the other side of the desk. I looked up and found myself gazing at Ricky as my entire body flushed from head to toe, and I felt unable to speak for a moment.

"Hi," he said with a grin as I glanced at him to see if Clara was with him.

She wasn't, which was odd as I didn't know why he would be here without her. Of course, my overactive imagination was going haywire, and a lot of things that I would love to do with him, void of Clara, played through my errant brain. It was crazy that this man with a single look could cause me to totally go mentally blank or to dirty scenarios of us naked. I was certain I had to be losing my mind, and I tried harder to focus on what was happening.

"Hello?" I said slowly, with a heavy question in my tone. Seriously? Hello was the best my stupid sluggish brain could get out of my mouth. Nothing pithy or funny – just hello!

And now I was having an internal argument with myself rather than continuing conversation.

"Can I help you?" I managed to blurt out.

"I was wondering if you ate lunch yet?" He asked with a smile that definitely must make women's panties melt everywhere he went. The man could not be here asking me to lunch, was he? I was not the type that normally garnered this type of attention, so I wanted to ensure that I did not misunderstand the intent.

"No, she hasn't," Ellen finally volunteered for me as I gazed at her giving her crazy eyes for the overstep. *What was happening in my world today?* "There is this amazing café out on the roof upstairs, that she loves the sandwiches from there," Ellen continued to help. "Besides, you can space out from other diners for a little private conversation," she said, giving Ricky a knowing smile.

"Perfect, but I sort of brought lunch for her," he said, glancing back in my direction. "You game to see how I did selecting foods that will make you fall for me?"

I nodded as I gave Ellen an expression, I hoped got the point across that she was in trouble when I got back. Then I absently followed Ricky to the elevator. I was dumbfounded that he was hereafter dreaming about the man for three days straight. I figured I would manage to say or do something to reinforce that he shouldn't have made this effort, but the silence I was exhibiting didn't give me a chance. My brain could not form a sentence when this man was around, and I needed to snap out of it!

"Did you get Clara enrolled in daycare?": I finally managed to ask. I had forgotten to call and tell Trina about sending him to her center and hoped there was no issue. I needed to remember to call Trina later today and talk to her about this situation. In all, since she had started the daycare, Ricky and Clara were the first recommendations I had personally sent Trina's direction. Knowing my sister, she was going to have some questions, and I was going to get an earful. That was okay if it meant that I got to see more of Ricky.

"Yes. I was feeling so grateful over the last couple of days I thought the least I could do was lunch," he said with a grin in my direction, gripping a nondescript paper bag which gave me no clues as to what he would have brought. I truly hope that it was something that I would eat, considering that I'm a tad bit picky. "I hope that is okay. You seem a little shell-shocked, so I hope I didn't overstep."

"You didn't overstep, but I am surprised. How is Clara?"

"Well, you know, after her five-thousand-dollar emergency room visit for gas, doing great," he said with a touch of sarcasm in his voice as he chuckled.

"I know medical expenses with kids can add up."

"Yeah, but nothing is too much for my baby girl," he said with a slight head bob. "I was fortunate it was something simple, but I wouldn't want expenses to stand in the way of medical care and find it was something critical."

"You sound like a great dad," I said, feeling my heart melt a bit, "I will say, though, this is a first where I had a parent of a patient come back to bring me lunch," I said, hoping that at least sounded sincere and would explain my earlier mutism.

"Really? You are beautiful. I figured men would find excuses to come back and visit you once you patched them up," he said and honestly didn't seem to be kidding in the least.

"Nope," I returned as we stepped out on the patio. "Oh, my goodness, it is the perfect weather for sure. I'm really glad you did come by today as I rarely get out for lunch."

"Awesome," he said, glancing at the sky. "That is the perfect amount of sun and shade to enjoy lunch. Is there a particular spot you would like to sit?"

As we walked to a spot that was in a tiny alcove totally protected from the elements, I found myself groaning when Dr. Wheeton turned to greet me.

"Is this your boyfriend?" He asked in a snarky tone that made my teeth chatter. The man seriously thought that he was a gift to all womenkind and none of us would dare step out with someone else.

"I am," Ricky said, shocking me to the core before I could utter a word. "Ricky Mendoza and you are?"

"Dr. Wheeton, I'm sure Daniella has mentioned me before," he said in that tone again that made me want to slap his stupid face.

"I'm sorry she hasn't," Ricky said, weaving an arm around her waist. "Though we don't do a lot of talking, if you know what I mean." He said, glancing so lovingly down to me, I nearly fainted under the intensity of his look.

Dr. Wheeton sputtered and then hurried off.

"I'm sorry," Ricky said, bending to my ear. "I thought that would help, as you should see the look on your face when he turned to us."

I gazed up at him, "I think I might kiss you for that," I replied before I could filter the statement properly.

"Maybe we wait for date number two for that," he replied, giving me a full toothy grin that made me go gooey inside.

"Is this a date?" I asked more for my clarification and avoided any future misunderstandings.

"It's as close as I've been in years," he said with a shrug. "Besides, if I call it a date, my brother Mario will give me a pass for a while even if this doesn't work out."

"Excellent, same here with my sister Trina. She is always trying to set me up," I retorted. "I wouldn't be surprised if she made you come to do this lunch in exchange for taking Carla in."

I watched his face, and the truth was evident. The man

was not a good liar or someone that hid his emotions well.

"She did tell you to ask me out in exchange for taking Carla," I replied.

"In all fairness, I wanted to but wouldn't have done it without a little push," Ricky admitted.

"Well, I have to give you credit for stepping outside your comfort zone to make sure Carla is in a good place," I replied. "I'm good with lunch and just conversation if you are?"

"Totally," he said as we sat down, and he put the bag with food in the middle of the table.

Something about Ricky made me want to know more, and I had this tiny doubt in my head that one lunch was going to be enough. It was a good place to start, though, and figure out if there was enough to maybe truly build on for a second date.

He unraveled the bag and pulled a container out that he put in front of me. I leaned down to sniff and then opened it as my eyes went wide.

"Is that gnocchi?" I said, totally in shock. "Trina did give you pointers, didn't she?"

"She loves you and said you don't date at all," he said. "I felt pretty special that she thought to give me the pointers to make this first date perfect. I'm pretty sure with this," he said, putting the second container in front of her. "I have a second date sealed."

I peeked inside before I looked up at Ricky with a head shake. "Tiramasu. Really?"

"So, now I just have to nail this conversation thing, huh?"

"This is quite literally my favorite meal ever," I said to him. "You would have to suck at talking to not get a second date. This might be my favorite lunch in years," I said with a goofy grin on my face that I could not wipe off.

I was excited to see where this lunch could take us for the first time in ages.

RICKY

J could not literally stop the warm gurgly feelings welling up after that amazing lunch with Daniella. We talked for an hour and a half without a break. She was so passionate about her job, loved kids, and had wonderful ideas of things he needed to do in his new city. Seriously, when it was time to leave, it was with leaden feet that I made my feet leave her.

"Where were you?" Carlos asked as I walked back into the shop. "Sorry, that sounded accusatory. We have the inspector coming by at two, and I was worried you wouldn't make it back. I'm a total nut job today worried about this."

Carlos, who was normally the most constant, quiet, and even-tempered of his brothers, was pacing the floor. He looked totally out of sorts which was so unnerving, as I thought we had this well in hand.

"We have it together for this inspection, and whatever they bring up, we will handle," I said, putting my hands on both of his shoulders to stymie the pacing. "I had lunch with Daniella again today as I didn't realize we had anything else needing done for this inspection."

"Isn't that number three in a row," Carlos asked with a huge knowing grin in his direction. "Any chance you might ask her out on a real date? Or better yet, invite her to the get-together this weekend."

"Yeah, that should scare her off good," Mario said, walking into the space. "I am scared about this get-together after hearing all of you talking about what goes down at these things."

"Hey, I resent that comment. I love our family, and I think we throw some amazing parties. I have faith that Daniella will do great," Carlos said quietly, though he didn't look upset in the least. "You guys never had big get-togethers like that?" Carlos asked, turning to me and then toward Mario again.

"No," Mario interjected. "We had mom's family, which consisted of the one sister and two cousins that were close to where we lived. She didn't like making that move to Texas but always told us it was necessary. She would talk about how many friends in the neighborhood she had back here in Cali and many of them she thought of as better family than the ones we had."

"Was dad the reason they took off after I outed them," Carlos said softly?

I just looked at him, and the look on his face held so much pain that I wanted to make it better. Carlos was the quieter of all the brothers, and he seemed to carry the burden of the past with his mom and brothers heavier than any of them. Also, the very recent passing of their Mama seemed to still be something all of this side of the family were still coming to grips with.

"Carlos, I think the one thing we can all agree on was our father was not a good man. He couldn't keep it in his pants and be faithful to a single woman at any point in his life. Our mother also confessed, knowing that while she was the reason that he left your Mama, he had other affairs on her," I let him know feeling like he needed this truth to assuage whatever was bothering him.

It seemed so wrong that after everything my father did to all of his children, burdening them with a legacy of lies and hurt, we had to live with it. All we could do was try to put it to rest, be better fathers than he ever was, and love each other enough to fill the gaps he left.

"I appreciate you telling me that," Carlos said with a small shake of his head. "I adore Jennifer with all my heart, and the thought of ever doing to her what that man did to my mother breaks my heart. I want to be a great father, good partner, amazing brother and get past it. I feel like I have given him too much of my time worrying about the fact that I was the one that broke up my family."

"What do you mean?" Mario said.

"I found out about your mom being with my father and told mine," Carlos admitted. "I'm sorry, but I think that after the divorce, him taking you all to Texas was because of that. I believe honestly he would have happily carried on with two lives forever if possible."

"That doesn't make it right, and definitely not something you should be ashamed of," I responded. "I hated him for everything he did, but I'm finding out that takes a lot more energy than I want to give. I think we all bond together as a family, grow this business and raise our children to be happy, well-adjusted members of society. That will prove that he didn't destroy any of us."

"True," Carlos said. "Have I told you how excited I am to be able to grow this business with both of you? I had been dreaming about doing this forever, but I just didn't think I had the ability to do it myself. I'm a bit of a control freak, but you all have such great experience it is helping me to share this load."

"Same with us," I responded. "Mario and I have considered leaving the small town we lived in and expanding the business for at least three years. Only when I met you and saw this place did I see the dream take shape."

"Now, we just need to talk an inspector into giving us an occupancy certificate, and we can see where this goes," Mario said excitedly.

"Oh, and I should tell you that for the first time last night, Jennifer brought up having kids," Carlos said with a shake of his head. "While I love this business idea, both of you having adorable little ones around could be a problem."

"Come on," I teased. "A little Carlos or Jennifer to keep my Clara company would be amazing."

"And my girls will love babying new cousins," Mario added.

"Well, at this rate, I would expect a new crop of Mendoza's to hit with Jennifer, Angela, Sandi, and Elaine all married, planning a marriage or the like inside this year. I think we are going to have to all hold on tight as this is going to be a crazy ride," Carlos added.

"Bring it on," I said, turning when I saw the truck with the city logo on the side. My insides twisted as I mentally reviewed the checklist we had been working on to get this place open in record time. Now I just had to hope this guy was reasonable, and we got the go-ahead for this next opportunity.

DANIELLA

"**A**re you sure about this?" Trina asked me as we exited the car. The music was spilling out into the street, and there appeared to be a lot of people already filling the house and backyard as the party was obviously in full swing.

I inhaled deeply and tried to steady my nerves as I looked up at the house. This was the worst idea ever to make one of the first times I see Ricky outside of the hospital be here with his friends, family, and apparently half the neighborhood from the sounds of things.

"He said that it was just going to be family and friends," I said, staring wide-eyed and the ginormous gathering of people.

I glanced back at Trina and her nephews. They, along with my parents, were all of my family on this planet that I spent any time with. On top of this, I could count on the people I considered friends. This gathering was so far outside the normal situation that I was fascinated and worried that I might not fit in.

"I want to go," Max said, piling out of the car, as Martin,

Trina's husband, came around the side carrying two-year-old Leo. The younger one was a bit bashful and, like Clara in the ER a few weeks ago, would take a little bit to warm up.

"Daniella," Ricky himself came around the side of the house with arms wide to greet me. He had to have been watching, which of course, made her immediately go mushy. I immediately started toward him and allowed him to fold me in his big arms.

We have had three lunch dates now and talked about everything from the weather to our jobs. He was proud of getting the certificate to open the shop after the inspection, and today was a celebration of that next big step for him and his brothers. I thought even the fact that after knowing each other for such a short time, all of those men were coming together to form such a strong community with half-siblings and others was a testament to how amazing Ricky and his family were.

When he had invited me out to meet everyone, my first response was to immediately turn him down. That seemed premature before ever having an official date outside of the hospital, but I just couldn't tell the man no. I was curious to meet all the important people and take this next step. It might not be traditional, but that didn't make it wrong – did it?

"Hi," I said, going up on tiptoes to kiss him lightly on the cheek. Then turning said, "you know Trina, of course."

"Trina, glad you could come," Ricky said, leaning down to give my sister a quick side hug.

"And this must be Leo," he said, pointing to the little guy in Martin's arm. "My Clara is always talking about how much she loves playing with Leo at daycare. She says they love to dress up and play My Little Pony."

"Yeah," Leo said, finally piping up in his dad's arm to look at him with a smile.

"And you," he bent to the other boy, "have to be Max."

Of course, I adored my nephews and had a tendency to gush about them, so Ricky had heard a lot about these two little guys. I adored that he loves children, but honestly, I had never found someone this devoted to his family. It was a big plus in my mind, to be sure.

Max enthusiastically shook his head. "Can I play with the kids?"

"Absolutely," Ricky said as he turned to Martin. "Ricky Mendoza, welcome."

"Martin Holmes," he said, taking Rica's hand in a firm shake while balancing Leo in his other arm. "Thanks for having us all."

"Sure, come on in," he said as they all trucked to the fence opening that led to the backyard.

"You have to be Daniella," a man that was a brother to Ricky from the coloring and size of him came up to us immediately. "I'm Mario."

"Great to meet you," I said, extending my hand. Then a cluster of other men and women all filed through introducing themselves. I already knew the names – Manny, Carlos, Joey, Rigo, Carmen, Juanita, and Estrella- that was just the beginning.

"I hope there is not a final exam later," I said to Ricky quietly as the number of people again nearly overwhelmed me. There were cousins next, neighbors, and people from a host of other associations with the family.

The backyard looked like a New Year's Eve party or something of that size and breadth. There were lanterns up in the trees, some sparkly lights, bright tablecloths, and tables of food that were certain to ensure no one would be leaving here hungry today. A couple of grills were going, and it was a whirlwind of activity that I struggled to keep straight, so I just stayed anchored to Ricky to ensure I didn't get lost in the masses.

"No, we should have had everyone wear name tags," he said, turning to my ear. "I forget some of them outside of my brothers and their fiancés and wives."

"That makes me feel better," I said as I turned to Angela. "Can I help with anything?"

"Nope, food is on the table right inside the patio," she said, taking the salad I brought. "And the cold drinks in those coolers," she pointed.

"Awesome, I appreciate it," I said as Trina, Martin, and I headed in that direction. People stopped, chatted, and generally welcomed us in like we were old friends.

"This is the friendliest group I have ever met," Trina said as we took a drink and joined a table that had a couple of openings.

"So, you are Rica's girlfriend?" One of the women asked.

"We have been getting to know each other," I said, trying to downplay how serious the relationship was, though I was meeting all of his family, so that might come off a bit strange.

"I'm actually a half-sister of his half-brothers," the woman said, looking confused. "Heck, just call me Carmen," she finished with a grin. "I know he introduced all of us, but you looked confused back there when you first came in."

"Carmen, so nice to meet you, and I agree I'm a bit overwhelmed by everything going on. This is super amazing to get all these people to come together. So, whose house is this one again?"

"Rigo just bought this, so we decided to inaugurate it and celebrate the new shop opening," she said with a huge smile. "You live in the area?'

"Yes, my sister runs the Sunshine Academy, and I work at the hospital as a pediatrics nurse," I offered back, not knowing exactly how much Ricky had shared.

"Amazing," Carmen offered. "I heard you had to walk both Ricky and Clara through a little emergency room visit recently?"

"Yep, and it didn't even hurt," a tiny voice said next to me.

"Hi, Clara," I said with a huge grin. "I'm glad it didn't hurt; how is that belly feeling?"

She bounced her head back to show me. "It is all better, but then I hurted my finger," she said, holding up her index finger that had a bandage, "and the kids tried to take my band-aid off on Fwiday."

"Oh, I'm sorry, but I see your daddy must have gotten you some cool Frozen ones," I responded, seeing the Frozen-themed one covering the injury.

"I love Elsa," she said as if that explained away the new dressing.

"I have never seen the movie, but I have a lot of patients that adore it," I said to her as she looked horrified.

"You have to see it," another little girl said, coming up to her. "It's the best ever, and we have seen it a billion times."

"A billion?" Mario said, coming up behind the little girl, "Daniella, this is one of my girls, Livia, and that one," he pointed off in the distance, is, "Marina."

"Nice to meet you, Livia," I said again, hoping that I wouldn't forget any important names.

"We are twins," Livia said, explaining her sibling tie to Marina.

"I bet that is super cool," I said, wondering at which of the women gathered was their mom.

"Not always," Livia admitted. "Are you dating Uncle Ricky? He and my dad said they were never going to date again because they were sad when Carla left, and my mom died."

I had no idea how to respond to that and not say anything

wrong. I took a deep breath and tried to formulate a proper response.

"Sorry about your mom," I said softly.

"It's okay. It was when I was born, so I didn't even know her. Uncle Ricky has helped raise us," she said as if just having another conversation.

"That is wonderful," I said, realizing we hadn't gone into a lot of details about Mario and his girls as they just got to know each other. I am certain there is more to that story, but I learned dealing with kids is never leading them, letting them tell the stories in their hearts, and just being a good listener.

"Are you liking the move to California?"

"I was scared at first, but I love all the new people here," she said excitedly as Marina called out to her.

"Gotta go," she said with a wave of her hand before running off.

"Wow, you have your hands full," I said to Mario, who just smiled as he watched his daughters out playing.

"Definitely, but it wouldn't change a moment of it," he said nostalgically.

"They are going to convince my brothers to start having babies, I think," Carmen said with a grin in my direction. "More nieces and nephews to spoil. I can't wait."

"I know some people can get overwhelmed with so many people and noise going on," Angela said, coming to sit in the one open chair at the table, "I for one love the chaos."

"I work at a hospital, so chaos is calming for me. When things are super calm, we all are on edge just waiting for the next big issue," I replied with a smile. "The noise, happy giggling, and chatting all somehow are balms to my soul," I said, realizing I hadn't stopped smiling since I arrived.

"I know," Trina offered. "She will come over when I'm trying to just get a few minutes of rest from the boys after a long day at work and take them outside for me. Daniella is out there throwing balls, chasing them around, and playing tag until they are exhausted. She definitely has more stamina for it than I sometimes do."

"Come on, you are a full-time daycare owner and a mom," I defended. "I just do what I can to take some of that burden from you."

"Sounds like she will fit in well with this family," Angela said, grinning at me.

Oddly enough, that kind of statement would have scared me with previous men I dated; it simply made me feel welcome and included here. I glanced out to where Ricky was playing with his brothers and some of the kids. Our gaze collided, and I could feel it as if he were touching me physically – he was just the best guy ever. I wanted to know everything about him, his big family, and what exactly this thing was that we had started.

I sat there watching everything going on. No one wasn't talking to someone, working on the food, or playing games out further on the lawn. Obviously, this group often came together as easygoing as everyone came and went into the house. It was such an amazing feeling, and I realized that I was not off put or uneasy at all. I glanced out to the kids all playing together and knew that it was what I wanted for my own children someday.

They were all raised together, and that was so cool for them. They had built-in playmates, confidantes, and siblings,even if not by blood. It was a balm to my soul as I could see myself part of this group in the future, and as my gaze found Ricky, I felt my heart shift. The man really could be the one that I have been waiting for, and this amazing family of his would just be a bonus. I found myself hoping this would work out, and nothing bad happened to drive us apart before we could see just how far this could go.

I was surprised to see another group of people start up the walkway to the yard despite us having been there for quite some time. I found myself grinning as Ricky came to join me, sitting and watching people.

"Does everyone just come and go at all hours?" I asked, not sure of the dynamic of this party.

"Definitely, there is always a ton of people, but they show up late, some we won't see even though they said they would be, and it will be rowdy until midnight. Dancing will go on until no one can stand back there," he said, thumbing his hand toward the backyard. "I know the sisters try like most do to get RSVPs, but it is a useless endeavor. We will not even have any idea probably who actually was here, but everyone will have a great time," he said, talking loud over the blasting music.

"Will you get in trouble for the noise?"

"Nah, everyone does it on this block," he said, leaning back as I laced my fingers with his, just smiling. It was a far cry from my family gatherings, and I loved it!

RICKY

"**K**eep your eyes closed," I said as I held onto Daniella's hand, leading her to the location of my surprise. Mario, Manny, Carlos, and Rigo had all helped plan this as I wanted it to be over the top and special. My brothers were surprisingly all super romantic and liked big gestures for the woman they loved, so it had been a fun bonding experience for them to work on together. He just had to hope this resonated with Daniella in a way he hoped.

Daniella had been amazingly patient in the first two weeks of being open at the new shop and was great about not pressing me for more time when I was stretched with conflicting responsibilities. I went to have lunch as often as possible, and she attended the family celebration that one weekend, to which all my family had the best reviews of her, so that had buoyed him also. That was all I could manage with the inventory arriving from Texas and new tasks to get done before we opened. Then came the deluge of orders, customers, and staff that needed to be hired. It was a good problem to have, but I had not allowed any extra time to spend with Daniella – something I wanted desperately to do. So, I carved out this night for just the two of us.

"Are we there yet?" Daniella asked as she held tight to my hand, continuing to follow my lead. It was dusky outside, so I struggled just a little to see the terrain under our feet. I was concentrating so hard that I was not keeping her as up to date as possible.

"Okay," I said, allowing her to take off the blindfold.

She glanced about at the little picnic table I had covered with a cloth, the cool candle-like lights I found, and the amazing dinner that Sandi and Angela had actually prepared for me to bring out there. They even had come to set the place up and wait until we showed just a few moments ago before driving off to give us privacy.

The view was a little area on a hillside overlooking the city, and the twinkling lights down below were romantic and breathtaking. I personally had never been out in a place like this for a date, and this was by far one of the nicest places I had been with a woman either. I would have to give my brothers and their significant others big kudos when I see them later.

"This is amazing," Daniella said as she took it all in. "This is a lot of work you did just for me."

I led her to the table where we sat on the same side. "Well, I had a lot of help from my family in preparing the spot and food," I said. "I admit I have been distracted with the grand opening and everything it has taken to relocate out here. I did not want you for a second to think you were not important to me, though."

"I appreciate that," she said, leaning in to kiss the corner of my mouth. I took advantage to press the kiss deeper and soon realized I needed to step back, or we might end up in the bed of my truck, taking this date in a very different direction.

"So, you really haven't dated after Carla? Not even once?" Daniella asked as I started opening the little serving trays of food that had been laid out on the table.

"No, honestly, I couldn't figure out how to have my daughter, a business, and try again with a woman. I also knew that Mario and I were talking about leaving that small town for quite some time. I knew everyone there, and no one captured my attention enough to risk getting stuck there and never having a chance to explore other things."

"Really? So did I capture your attention?" Daniella asked me with a glint in her eye that mesmerized me.

"The moment you walked into that emergency room, I totally forgot everything looking into those blue eyes," I said just as I found myself doing now. I could gaze into those blue depths for hours and never get bored.

"Yeah, the eyes are from dad's side," she said with a smile. "My mom always said that was the first thing that reeled her in also."

"Your parents are still married today, right?" I said, trying to recall the conversation where we had discussed them. The details were few that I could remember.

"Yes, they are truly the example I hope to have in my life of a love I attain someday. They still only have eyes for each other and are the best team you could ever imagine meeting," she said with a shrug of her shoulder. "I just find that most people have such a transitory thought process about relationships today. If the marriage doesn't work, divorce, or don't get married, just hop from relationship to relationship. That has always been a huge turn-off. I believe that I will find what my parents had, and I am not going to settle for less."

"That is great," I said, realizing it was the complete opposite of my experience. "My father was one of those that thought monogamy in marriage was a suggestion he didn't need to follow. I also want that steady, loving, loyal relationship, but for a long time, I worried that because of what he did, maybe I was predisposed to cheat on someone also. It turned out it was Carla that did that to me and not me that stepped out."

"She cheated on you," I said, not sure what woman in her right mind would do such a thing. Ricky was guarded to date on how much he would say about his ex, but I was curious to know whatever he wanted to volunteer. Knowing that information was a good indicator of any red flags he might exhibit that he wasn't over her or made us a bad fit.

"She did, but I didn't even know that until the end," he said with a shake of his head. "Her father died when we had been dating a short time, and the relationship got super toxic after that. She started doing drugs to fix her pain, I think, and it went from pot to meth in no time."

"Why did you stay with her?" Daniella asked.

"I was young, dumb, and thought I could fix her," Ricky answered honestly, as the pain of that time in his life was evident on his face. "Then she got pregnant, and I thought for sure she meant it when she said that she would stay clean. Considering Clara was drug-free at birth, that took effort. I was so happy and saw hope that we would finally be the family I craved," he sighed. "Until the minute she told me there was another guy and had been forever. I had to paternity test for Clara to confirm she was mine. Still, I tried my hardest to try and make a co-parenting relationship work. I was worried she would take my daughter and not let me see her," he said with a chuckle. "Until the day she was the one that dropped her and never looked back."

"Man, that had to be hard, but it is a testament to your loyalty and devotion that you tried for that long," Daniella said, reaching out to cover my hand with hers and give it a soft squeeze. "You are an amazing man and dad. Clara is lucky to have you."

"I try, but you can see why opening myself up in that way again was not appealing for a long time," Ricky said as the pain was still etched in every square inch of his face. "I don't want myself or Clara to ever get hurt that badly again. Clara getting close to someone at this age now that just turned their back on her would be devastating, and I don't want to put her through that."

"I think as long as you go into your relationships knowing that you are going to do everything possible to make it work and you are willing to put in the effort, you can overcome your past," I returned, hoping to see a lightening of the burden of his past that weighed heavily on him.

"I am glad you believe that because I want to be the father, husband, and brother that all my family members deserve. I want to use my father's history just as a cautionary tale of everything I intend to avoid in my own life."

"I think you are doing fabulous," Daniella said. "Though I do have a question for you. I was wondering about when you told me you are working on Saturday. You can say no but thought I would ask."

"Sure, what's up?" I ask, making sure to home in on her words carefully.

"I thought I would take Clara with Trina myself and the boys to the little carnival out at the fairgrounds while you work," she said, biting on the corner of her lip nervously. "Would that be okay for her to spend time with me separately? It would solve the problem of finding someone to watch her."

"I would love that," I said, bending to kiss her. "You know she is a package deal with me, so making sure you all get along is critical to us getting along long-term."

"Oh, I'm hoping we get along," Daniella whispered huskily, "for a good long time."

"Excellent," I said, bending to kiss her again hungrily.

"Seriously," she said, finally pulling back. "We better eat before this all gets cold, or we will have to answer to your family."

"Yeah, and then we can try for dessert," I said, waggling my eyebrows at her as she playfully punched me in the belly.

DANIELLA

"How about this one?" I asked, walking up to a little ride that had teacups and looked not as scary as some of them we had seen. I looked down at Clara, who seemed like this might be the one I could talk her into. She had given an emphatic shake of her head at the big ride with loops the boys had wanted to try, so this was an improvement.

"I'm not allowing the boys on that with you," Trina said as I turned to her, worried.

The look of pure terror on my sister's face halted me in my tracks. I was ignorant to the workings of a fair, having not been to one in a million years, it seemed. The determination in her voice literally had me worried that maybe there was something wrong with the ride.

"Is it dangerous?" I asked, totally confused but wanting to understand. I didn't have children; I hadn't brought any out to this event before though my sister had apparently been out here in the past.

"It spins," she said, which still didn't tell me why I

shouldn't take Clara on the ride. Trina's eyes were the size of half dollars, though.

"Is she going to be scared?" I asked quietly, trying not to worry the little girl. Clara wasn't saying much, but her eyes spoke volumes about her internal thoughts. The sweet girl had this way of watching my nephews in wonder, awe, and slight worry about what they might do next. Several times when they got loud, Clara would slip behind my legs bashfully.

"Only if you take mischievous boys with you," Trina said. "Max spun it so hard last time I lost my lunch in a trash can as soon as I could get away from the ride."

"Oh," I said, staring at Max and Leo, who seemed innocent enough, but Max was looking at the teacups with glee in his eyes.

"I want to try again," he said to his mom. "That was so much fun."

"Yep, exactly why I didn't eat anything today," Trina said as I giggled at her.

"Good luck, but I think Clara and I are going in one all by ourselves, right?" I asked the quiet tyke holding tight to my hand.

Clara shook her head up and down enthusiastically.

"So, are you having fun?" I asked Clara as she gave me a tentative smile.

"Yeah, but those clowns I didn't like," she said, referencing the little game area they had just passed through.

"I don't like clowns either," I said to her. "You want to take a picture for your daddy though we can send him, so he knows you are okay?"

She nodded happily this time as I lined things up for a selfie. I texted him *alive in one piece and having fun* with the attached picture.

Looking good, he texted back with made a goofy grin

spread across my face. The man seriously had done a job on my heart already, and if that wasn't bad enough, his cute little girl, Clara, sealed the deal. So far, I could quite literally find nothing wrong with the man, which was a first in my life.

"Your dad said you are looking good," I told Clara as the ride started moving.

Clara slid closer to me and didn't say too much for the entire ride. Though when it was over, she looked up at me with a huge grin, "that was fun."

I'm glad, I thought, as I would hate for her to go home to Ricky, a traumatized kiddo that had hated everything. Max and Leo met us at the entrance to the ride and wanted to go to the petting zoo, which Clara did wholeheartedly endorse and followed close behind them. I fell in line with Trina.

"So, she looks to be having fun," Trina said, but she had that tone in her voice that told me right away she had something on her mind.

"Say it," I blurted out, not wanting to even guess what she might need to get off her chest.

"You haven't dated in years and then a single dad with a little girl? Are you sure about this?" She asked, leaning into my shoulder. "You know I love you and will have your back no matter what, but I want to ensure you know what you are getting into."

"I know that was not the order of things in my dreams," I said softly, thinking about the case. "Ricky was honestly the biggest shock I've had in a long time, and I honestly do keep expecting something bad to happen. He is so easy to be with, a genuinely nice guy, ambitious, a great dad, and so far, I can't find anything wrong with him. You know me, I am trying hard to find his flaws. I just can't tell you how easy it is being with Clara and him," I sighed. "I'm so happy that I am at a loss to explain it myself."

"I'm glad," Trina said. "I have to say his family was

amazing and so welcoming. I am with you seems like the real deal, but here is the true test – you up to introduce him to mom and dad yet?"

That one did stop me in my tracks. I had never introduced a single boyfriend after high school to my parents. That seemed like sacred ground to me and reserved for the one I felt really could be my husband. The odd thing was that while that had always been an off-limits thing in my previous relationships, I thought that it was something that probably should be sooner rather than later with Ricky. I was falling for the man, and if mom or dad didn't approve, that would prove a death knell to any future together.

"I think I'm going to have to," I said out loud, causing Trina to gasp. "I mean if they hate him, wouldn't I want to know that now versus a year from now."

"I guess," Trina said. "Wow, I knew it would happen for you someday, but I have to say I didn't see it being with someone like Ricky or this quickly."

"You and me both," I said as we continued to the petting area.

That night as I finished dropping off Clara and settling in bed, I decided to broach the subject with Ricky about meeting the parents. I waited until he was getting ready to walk me outside and then mustered the courage.

"I would love to introduce you to my parents," I said, being sure to keep my eyes trained on his face. The man wore all his emotions on his sleeve, making it super easy to know what was going on in that head of his by his eyes. "What would you think to say dinner one of these nights?"

"You said that isn't something that you normally do," he immediately returned, as I mentally slapped myself, recalling that conversation that he was referencing.

"That is true," I said as I inhaled and tried to formulate a defense. "I have met your entire family, though, and most extended friends after that one amazing party. Additionally, Clara and I had an amazing time, and I think this is headed in a serious direction – don't you?"

He immediately nodded as he thoughtfully seemed to contemplate that. "I do, but I would hate to -" he stopped with a heavy sigh.

"I want them to meet you," I reassured him, wrapping my arms up and over his neck. "Say yes."

"Fine, how can I say no to you," Ricky said, bending to take a long, sweet draw on my lips.

"You know I think I'm falling in love with you," I admitted to him as I stood on the porch, not caring who might over-hear us. I wanted to shout it from the rooftops that this was the man I had waited all my life to find.

"That is good because I am falling for you," he replied as I leaned in to give him a long, hearty kiss. "You better go before I convince you to stay overnight."

"Not yet, we agreed with Clara and Rigo home that could not happen here," I said as I blushed hotly. "Soon though, I'm going to be able to keep you with me day and night."

"Definitely," he said with one final draw on my lips.

"Ricky!" A woman's voice screamed, causing us both to jump apart. "What the hell are you doing?" The woman continued as she ran towards us, face flushed, looking a tad bit crazy.

I turned as if in slow motion to the hot, curvy brunette staring daggers at me and then back at Ricky, trying to figure out what exactly was going on. Ricky looked like a man that was stunned, speechless, as his mouth hung open, but no words came out.

"Who are you?" I demanded, wishing the ground to open wide and swallow me whole. I never had in a million years expected Ricky to have another woman coming to his house at this time of night. Honestly, though, the obvious shock is radiating from him was doing bad things to my insides as rage started to climb.

"His baby mama, Carla, and who exactly are you?" She said loudly as I inhaled and just started walking past her.

I had thought Ricky didn't have anything to do with Carla for the last two years, so how had she found him without him being the one to divulge his new location? Honestly, I didn't want to know or any drama, so I got in my car as he came rushing down the sidewalk toward me and just drove away.

"Daniella," he shouted a second before I closed the door and slammed my key in the ignition. I could not deal with this right now; I told myself as I squealed my tires, getting away from him.

A few blocks away, I felt the prickles of anger start to take hold, but I continued to breathe until I got home and could collapse into bed and cry it all out. The drastic turn that the day had taken wreaked me, and I just could not process it as I fell into a deep sleep, hoping I would wake to find it all a dream tomorrow.

RICKY

I had everything I could do not to scream at Carla for showing up at such an inopportune moment after all this time without a single word from her. Heck, I didn't even know until this very minute if she was even alive. I knew that screaming obscenities at her would solve nothing, so I tried to get a hold of my emotions to figure out my next move. All I kept seeing was Daniella's face in my mind, though.

Daniella was so hurt that I worried about what she was going through, but I couldn't very well chase her and leave Carla standing on Rigo's property. Besides, she had taken off like a bat out of hell to where I had no idea. Additionally, Clara was asleep upstairs, and I would not allow Carla unfettered access to her until I knew the purpose of her visit. She would cause an even bigger scene for sure if I didn't start talking to her, and I had zero ideas what it was I was supposed to say.

"What in the world are you doing here?" I finally asked, trying to figure out what ulterior motives she must have for this visit. "Also, baby mama, was that the best you could come up with?" I couldn't believe that was how she would describe herself and was certain it was intended to harm Daniella and his relationship. She might want to shack up with other men, but Carla definitely didn't like him having outside interests despite her being gone for years now.

"I mean, I show up and expect you to be looking after our daughter's well-being. Only I find you are sucking face with some blonde woman right out here on the street for all the world to see," Carla said, looking unapologetic in the least. In fact, she looked like someone up on a moral high horse, which he thought was funny considering all the crap she had put him through.

"It has been nearly two years since I have seen you. Did you stay celibate during that time? Oh no, that's right, you cheated on me first, did every drug you could get your hands on, and took off on your daughter without a backward glance," I spit out. I was so mad and just wanted her to understand the emotional toll her leaving had elicited on us. I had a daughter that had no idea who her mother was, and that same person was standing there trying to make me into the bad guy—not happening!

"That is all water under the bridge," Carla said super calmly, though I was suspicious of that more than I would have been having she started hurling insults back at me. Normally, she only came around when she needed something, and I was beginning to suspect this visit was going to be more of the same.

Even when we were dating, it was all about her. As a man lovesick, I couldn't see it during the time spent together, but hindsight had a way of making things so much clearer. She was a narcissist and a user. That was not something he could afford to allow back near Clara until he fully understood her motivations.

"I had to work to find you, as you weren't giving me your

address or anything on those emailed updates. I found your details out through social media posts about the business and your move. It took me stalking you for a bit and others around your business to find out you relocated here," Carla said. "I was shocked to find out that you came out here to California, bought in on a bigger shop, and seem to be doing great for yourself. I also loved seeing pictures of my little girl, who looks to be getting so big."

"We are doing amazing here in California and have found a new family that is providing support for Clara also. Thank you for acknowledging what I have done for her, but what does that have to do with you?"

"I want us to try and be a family again," Carla said as she sidled up to my body and laid a hand on his chest. "You remember how good things were between us," she purred, running a long fingernail inside my button-down shirt. "I know for a fact that I can get you turned on quicker than that skinny woman could."

I just looked down at her and wondered how I had found this act of hers attractive. She was catty, a cheater, and thought I was dumb enough to let it all be water under the bridge and welcome her back with open arms? Was she taking something, or did she just need something from him? He would guess it was the latter.

"Why are you here? Where is the boy-toy – the musician?"

It was not that I wanted to know, as her presence here without him spoke volumes. The problem I had was that if she didn't have a man supporting her, it was her standard practice to return to him begging for another chance. That was exactly what this looked like, though I found it totally ridiculous that she thought that might work based on how long it had been since she had left. My head was spinning, and being honest, I sort of hoped that the boyfriend was just at a hotel, and she wouldn't truly be here for him personally. If she just wanted to see Clara, they could work with it.

"Turns out he had a few other fans out on the road," she said, clucking her tongue. "I'm not putting up with anyone stepping out on me. I thought I could come back, and we could work on raising Clara and enjoying this newfound success of yours. Is this the house you bought?" She asked, and I could see the greed gleaming in the depths of her eyes.

Carla had been raised in apartments pretty low income, but that hadn't stopped her from having caviar dreams. I knew that was a lot of the pull of the musician she had followed onto the road when his band was touring. She had sunk her claws in, hoping to follow the guy to better things than him and their little girl. I could not allow her to drift in and hurt that little girl when she got bored and left again. Visiting her daughter was something I would allow, but it would be on my terms. There was no us in that future, except for co-parenting Clara.

"Listen, this is Rigo's house, my brother and –" I stopped when she held up her hand.

"I'm sorry, your what?" Carla said, holding her hand up to cease me from talking until I explained things to her.

"I found out about my father having four additional sons after a DNA test, and that is a big reason that Mario and I moved out here. We are working on building some relationships with a huge group of the family we never were given a chance to meet. While here, Mario is staying with Carlos, and I'm staying with Rigo until we find places of our own."

"Wow, four more brothers," Carla said, looking dumbfounded by that information. "That is something as you always wanted a big family. It must be like a dream come true for you and Clara to have all the support and love of a huge family," she said, and I saw the little storm cloud forming in her eyes. She had wanted that also, but instead, she had ended up bouncing around to relatives who weren't interested in anything but the check from the state to help care for her.

Carla's past was one of the hard knocks and tough breaks that was part of why I had tried for so long to help her. It had also made her tough to the point of almost being unable to make true human connections, and while he didn't want to contribute to her unhappiness as she was the mother of his child. He could not allow her to stomp all over him again.

"Listen, if you get a hotel close," Ricky said, trying to be as reasonable as possible. "We can get together and let you see Clara. Maybe ease into you visiting from time to time again."

"What about you and me?" She asked, looking confused. "I know you always wanted your children to have two parents to love them. I think we can work on putting our family back together again and maybe even adding another baby or two."

I inhaled, realizing there was not a cell in my body that wanted this woman any longer. I couldn't forget her cheating, and while I would work to co-parent with her – that was it.

"We are never going to be together again," I said gently.

"What that blonde woman got her grip on you that tight? It won't last, you know?"

"Carla, go get a hotel, and we can work on you seeing Clara," I said again softly. I didn't want to fight or aggravate her, but I was over this argument. There was nothing between us any longer, and I was not going to let her get under my skin or any reaction. I loved Daniella, and that, along with Clara, was all I was focused on.

"Ricky, I will take that little girl with me if I go," she said, causing my heart to palpate harder. "If you aren't going to be able to find it in your heart to forgive and start over, then I have to do what I feel is right."

I honestly worried that I might reach out and strike her for even suggesting she would take Clara from me. Considering her behavior these last few years, she definitely wouldn't have a leg to stand on, but even attempting a court case would hard Clara and put her in the middle. I had always wanted to avoid this, and Carla knew what she was doing playing that card. I was better than that, but not going to leave any doubt about where that threat would lead.

"Are you completely clean?"

"Hey, now," Carla said, and I definitely had my doubts on that front also. "We aren't married or anything, so you can't ask me those questions."

"But a judge will. You have to be clean and prove it before a judge is going to even allow visitation," I said gently but firmly.

"We don't need to get all that fancy with judges and stuff," she said.

"Yes, we will, as the only way I can trust you to have Clara's best interest at heart is to follow a fair custody arrangement administered by the courts. So, be sure you are ready to put in the work and stay clean, as you won't even get visitation rights if still addicted to drugs. You definitely won't get full custody of her after abandoning her and being gone this long," I said, keeping the temper out of my voice. "Clara deserves to know you as her mother and us to get along for her sake. I will do whatever is needed to make that happen except getting back to you. You broke a sacred trust, and after what my father put my mother through, that is just nothing I can forgive," I said. "You have my number call in the morning, and we can arrange for you to see Clara."

I turned, intending to go back into the house. I needed to try and get a hold of Daniella and explain what had happened. I could not lose her over Carla deciding to pay an unscheduled visit and try to blackmail me over Clara. I just remembered the look on Daniella's face was pure and utter heartbreak, and I worried about where we might stand as the dust settled.

"Ricky!" Carla screamed at that point, but I walked inside, turned off the light, and went into the kitchen.

Rigo was sitting there looking at me with empathy in his eyes. "I'm sorry about that. Seems like she is going to be a bit unreasonable," he said as he pushed a cold beer across the country to me.

"I want to do right by Clara, and I can't block her mother from her," I said, taking a long swing. "I didn't think she would ever come back into our lives like this, but I want that for my daughter. I don't want her growing to have questions like I did and having to find her answers in a DNA register because no one was honest with her."

"I get that, and I think that makes you an amazing dad," Rigo offered. "I know that what dad did was hard but losing him and never really knowing that last half of his life definitely left a mark on me. I applaud you for doing the right thing and trying to be the better man for Clara," he said softly.

"Yeah, but I'm just hoping she didn't kill my relationship with Daniella," I said, shaking my head.

"I don't think she has yet, but I have to say – not sure if Carla sounds ready to let things lie. She could still cause a good amount of drama yet," Rigo offered back to me.

"Yeah, I figured as much," I said, rolling my shoulders, wishing things could be easy but knowing that was probably a pipe dream and I needed to gear up for a fight.

DANIELLA

I was simply going through the motions five days later, trying to avoid all contact with Ricky despite the numerous texts and calls daily. Luckily, he hadn't shown at the hospital as I had requested some time to process things, and he had respected that, though a tiny voice in my head had hoped he would do the opposite as I missed him so much. I felt like I was underwater drowning in my sorrow and just didn't want to be saved at the moment.

Ricky had told me he wanted to explain things, but I just didn't want to listen. I had opened myself up, met his family, and for a moment could see the future laid out in front of me with him, Clara, and maybe even another child or two. Then SHE showed up, and it all evaporated in a single heartbeat.

"Did you do the last of your rounds?" Ellen asked as I wandered back into the nursing station.

"Yep," I said and handed over the charts.

"Any chance you are going to snap out of this mood soon?" She asked me, causing me to pause and look at her dead in the eye.

"I will try," I promised and then turned to go.

"Stop," she said as I turned back to find her patting a chair she had pulled out for me.

I fell into the chair and just stared at her.

"You know that man made you happier than I had seen you in the five years you have worked for me," she started. "I don't know what exactly the trouble is, but the fact that you are this morose tells me this was not a mutual decision to part ways."

"His baby mama showed up at his house after our last date – her words to describe herself, not mine," I said, feeling like a zombie as no expression came forward on my face. I was numb and didn't want to feel anything.

"Okay, and what happened?"

I just looked at her confused, "what do you mean?"

"I mean, you knew he had a kid, right? And you knew it didn't pick her in a cabbage patch. She had to have a mother someplace?"

"I did, but he claimed no contact. She was standing on the porch where he lives now out of the clear blue and shooting daggers at me," I responded, trying to explain my stance to Ellen, who didn't seem to be getting what the problem here was.

Suddenly, my cellphone vibrated in my pocket. I pulled it out to ensure it wasn't any kind of emergency and saw it was Trina.

"I have to take this," I said to Ellen. "What's up, Trina?"

I listened to her babble about Carla coming to try and get Clara from daycare and how I was on the list but not her mom. Then she had tried to get Ricky at work, but he wasn't picking up his phone. She needed someone to come to help ease the situation with Carla.

"I'm on my way," I said, hanging up and glancing at Ellen. "Apparently, baby mama just showed at the school and tried to take Clara."

"Daniella," Ellen said gently. "Please hear the man out, and don't jump to conclusions. You deserve to be happy, but you have to realize that Clara has another mom that will be part of the picture. You need to have the grace to help him balance that out if you truly want to be in his life. If you can't do that, then tell him, and move on."

I stared at her until a grin broke through on my face. "Thank you for that slap back to reality," I said. "I needed it."

"Any time," she said, turning back to her computer as I took off running toward the door. Luckily, I quickly navigated the school and walked inside to find Carla at the front desk.

"What are you doing here? I just came to get my daughter and found out that they are refusing me," she blurted out angrily.

Something was bothering me about how she even knew where Clara was and if Ricky had told her or not. As I was blocking Ricky from giving me information, I figured she was the next best source. Besides, there was just something underhanded about her that made me grit my teeth.

"How did you know she was here?"

"Ricky and I were having, you know, catch-up time," she said with a grin on her face that told me she was trying to get a rise out of me, "and he let me know."

"Huh, so he told you she was here but didn't get you added to the list to pick her up? That is odd?"

"Are you calling me a liar?" Carla said, moving into my personal space, which just made me grin. The woman was lying and just clinging to the last vestiges of hope that she could drive me away. I would not allow that and knew I had made a huge mistake not letting Ricky tell me his side of the story.

"No, but I am," Rica's voice boomed through the small space. "I told you that I would arrange for you to see Clara at a time that worked for everyone. I did not tell you she went here, so how did you find out."

"I was worried about her safety and followed you this morning," Carla admitted as I gasped at the audacity. The woman was unhinged, and the brazenness of her actions ridiculous.

"I have full custody because you did not show to the last hearing," Ricky said, holding out a piece of paper to her. "You can be arrested if you take Clara from someplace that I am not aware of."

"You can't do that; I'm her mother," she argued. "That woman," she said, pointing to me, "is not the mother."

"Daniella has nothing to do with this," Ricky said. "You need to leave and now, or we will be forced to call the police."

"I need to see Clara now," she demanded angrily, causing all of us to gap at each other.

"You can see her this weekend," Rica's bit back, not budging.

Her shoulders slumped, "I won't be here as my flight heads back to Texas tonight. I need Clara to go with me and already have the flight booked with her on it."

"No," Ricky said, furrowing his brow. "What possessed you to think that I would allow you to take my daughter without a care in the world."

"You can have more, but if I don't bring her home with me, I can't stay with my family," she whispered. "I don't have a dime, and they miss her and want her with me."

"No, you want the benefits you can claim because of her," Ricky said. "You don't love her, and the next guy that comes along, you will leave her again. It would help if you went now or again. I will be forced to call the police."

"Ricky," she said with a pleading tone.

"Now," he said, firm but not loud enough to disrupt anyone.

"You haven't heard the end of this," she said as she slumped to the door.

"I'm sorry," he said, turning to Trina and me. "I had no idea what her game was," he said as he gazed at me. "I need to talk to you, but I want to go get Clara and take her home. Say you will have dinner with us?"

I glanced at Trina, who only raised an eyebrow in my direction with a grin.

"I would, but I truly have to get back to work," I said, remembering that I had volunteered to pick up a shift for another nurse. I knew it was bad timing because, more than anything, I did want to talk through things with Ricky.

"I promised to work another shift tonight," I said to him. "I promise we can talk tomorrow if you can make time."

"Works for me," he said. "I'm going to call, and you will answer this time, right?"

"Yes," I agreed with a bob of my head. I will answer."

"Good," he said, bending to kiss my cheek as he went to get Clara.

"Are you working?" Trina asked me, giving me that sister look that said she could tell when I was lying.

"I forgot about tonight, but unfortunately, I am," I admitted as I had literally blacked it out earlier. "I will talk to him though and make it right – I promise."

"Good," Trina said with a little sigh, "I was getting sick of grumpy Daniella."

"Funny," I said, heading back to the hospital.

When Ellen saw me, she just shook her head.

"You took another double, didn't you?"

"Yes, but I did talk to him, and things are going to be okay," I said to her as I slid behind the desk.

"Girl, you were not gone long enough to truly make it up to that man," she said, giving me a knowing look that was filled with all sorts of innuendos.

"You behave," I told her with a grin, starting on rounds.

My life had been such a whirlwind since Ricky came into it, and it made me feel big emotions. Even the fact that I was so mad as to block him out when I thought that he might have invited Carla here was disconcerting to me. I knew I was head over heels for the man, and I needed to start acting like an adult and work through our issues. It was evident that even if Carla was around, her interactions with Ricky were limited, as he had clearly not added her to Clara's school pick-up list nor wanted her there today.

I made my way through two hours of work that felt like six, wanting to see Ricky. I figured on break; I would text him and solidify plans to see him first thing in the morning. I didn't care if I didn't even sleep tonight if it meant I could see him before he headed to the office.

As I slouched out to the nursing station had made it through all my rooms again, I stopped in my tracks. There standing with the biggest bouquet I had ever seen was Ricky.

"What'cha doing?" I asked, sauntering up to him as a smile split my face. "Did you bring flowers for a sick patient?"

"Nope, actually, these are for my broken heart since I haven't gotten to see you," he said as I reached him. "I'm hoping that you will let me visit and explain myself," he said as I jumped up into his arms and kissed him firmly on the lips.

"I would love that, but I don't have a break for it," I checked my watch.

"Oh, I got this," Mary, the lead that took Ellen's job on evenings, said to me. "You go take that break now," she whispered with a big wink in my direction.

"Excellent," Ricky said, "thank you,' he said to Mary as I took his hand and started down the hallway.

When we were near the elevator, I remembered the

supply closet and, grabbing his hand, dragged him inside. I rocked him back against the door, my hands on his chest, and kissed him as my life depended on it.

"I thought we were getting dinner," he said as he slanted his head, deepening the kiss as I was nearly out of breath, hot and needy. This man was able to bring me to my knees without barely trying, though it turned out flowers were a big, huge plus.

"I was thinking dessert," I said, putting my hands under his shirt and drawing it up.

"Whatever the lady wants, the lady gets," he said, kissing me hard in return as we made up for the misunderstandings and days apart in the most energetic way possible.

I no longer cared if I got written up or fired – it would be so worth it!

RICKY

I finished the checks that needed to be done for this inaugural ride and waited for Daniella to arrive. This was the first Saturday both of us were off and did not need to be home at any particular time. I was looking forward to an amazing time showing her my favorite pastime.

As she pulled to the curb, I waved as my heart took flight. She was so beautiful, always smiling, and the woman I honestly hadn't known existed. Every moment was better than the last with her, and the future was laid out in front of us full of possibilities.

We have now been dating for a few months without any other problems like Carla popping up at the worst times possible. It turned out that my ex-girlfriend had come just to get Clara for the government assistance. Unfortunately, that was a generational issue with her family that didn't seem like she was going to break. Honestly, Carla was smart as a whip, and if she applied herself could find a great job to support herself. There was something wrong with her thinking, though, and until she grew up and got things

358

together, it was most likely that she wasn't going to see much of Clara.

"So, are you game?" I asked Daniella when she got out of her car. I held my arms out like a game show host toward the new bike as her eyes went wide.

"You want me to ride that with you?" Daniella asked me, looking at the new custom bike I had just finished after working on it bit by bit for years. I had even paid for it to come out from Texas in pieces and just now managed to get it to put together at the new shop.

"Scared?" Manny asked as he came alongside them with Sandi right behind him.

I thought it was amazing that all the significant others rode with my brothers. Heck, I thought it was something that we all had the same passion in life. Each of them had a bike that was as unique as they were, and together, we would make a formidable pack out on the road today – I couldn't wait. The only thing standing in the way of us hitting the open highway was a final answer from Daniella.

"You just hold on tight and will get the hang of it," Sandi sang out to encourage Daniella.

"Okay, why not," she said, catching me off guard. I figured it would take a little more work. Though, to be honest, Daniella was up for anything from teacups with toddlers at the local fair to his crazy family gatherings – this should be a walk in the park for her.

"Are you sure that Carmen is okay watching all three girls for the day?" Mario asked as he came out of the house toward his own bike. He seemed a little bit worried though I figured it was not the fact of Carmen as much as leaving the girls.

Because we were limited on family and friends, we had done everything together with the girls on the weekend. Babysitters were so expensive that only the most critical of outings did we do without one or the other of us staying with the children. This was so much better and gave us both the chance to recharge while all their little ones could be with cousins and other family.

"Juanita and Estrella are all here to help," Rigo interjected. "Trust me; they will sugar them up and run them ragged for you. They adore kids, though, and it will be amazing fun for them."

"I think they are waiting for us all to add to the fold," Carlos said as he joined in the conversation. "Mama might not be here to spoil the grandkids, but the sister definitely will."

"Amen," Joey said with a huge grin. "I have to say Ricky and Mario; you are amazing examples for all of us of the kind of fathers we want to be. I know that I worried after all that dad had done to us that I wouldn't make good husband or dad material. Watching how you are doing despite all the bumps, trials, and roadblocks makes me excited to take on the same."

"Agree," Carlos said. "Besides what we have, and dad didn't is each other. I can't even tell you how often I tell Jennifer how blessed we are that you two came out here. You completed our family, and I'm grateful we all found each other. I can't wait to see how our family blossoms and grows from here."

I felt my heart melt as Daniella laced her fingers into mine. "This is all I ever wished for when I was younger. A huge, happy, and cohesive family. I know we have minor disagreements and have undergone a lot of change this year that will take time to smooth out," I said with tears threatening my eyes, "this is the culmination though of years of dreams on my part."

"Agreed," Mario said, slapping me on the back. "Now, let's ride."

There was a resounding round of agreement as the bikes revved in the street, and he noticed many curious eyes turned in their direction. My other brothers started to pull away from the curb one by one. I handed Daniella a helmet that I had brought specially for her from the shop.

"You got this," I said, bending to kiss her sweetly before she put her helmet on. "You know I love you."

"And I adore and love you," she said, pulling the head protection into place. She looked a bit shaky trying to mount the bike the first time, but we managed with some gentle instructions.

Once we were situated, I looked into the street for a clearing and took off. When the wind hit my face, I felt the freedom of the road ahead, and yet there on the horizon were the bikes of my brothers, my pack, and my family. I could not begin to express how that truly humbled me and made me feel. I tried to envision what the future was going to hold for us, but I was excited to get started on the journey with this group.

As Daniella's arms tightened about me, I felt my heart fill to the brim. She was the answer to another prayer for unconditional love, acceptance, and someone to walk through life with me no matter the consequences. I couldn't wait to see what that future could look like for us and even what my next kiddo would look like when Clara got a sibling. Maybe blonde like her with those eyes that were so expressive.

I put my hand over hers as she clung to me and felt a pulling at my heart as I raced into the future with my entire family by my side.

EPILOGUE

One year later

My phone would not stop buzzing in the pocket of my scrubs. Normally I didn't pick up personal calls during my shift unless they were the daycare or Ricky. Glancing down, I noticed it was Trish again, though, and thought that maybe there was something up as this was not normal behavior for her. Though the last time she pulled this kind of thing, I ended up walking into an ER and meeting the love of my life.

"What?" I connected the call and harshly spoke into the device. "I'm working here," I tried to sound tough, but I ended up smiling into the device. This gave me major déjà vu vibes from the first time I saw Ricky in the emergency room with Clara. Trish still liked to take credit for introducing us, and I had to give it to her – she had done really well on that front.

"I know I have a pediatric patient down here that you need to come see," Trish said, sounding truly urgent.

"What are you up to?" I asked immediately. My senses

went to high alert, certain that she was trying to pull a fast one of some kind on me.

"Get down here now!" Trish said and disconnected.

"What's wrong?" Ellen turned to look at me.

"That was Trish asking me to come down to emergency," I said, still staring at the phone like it was a foreign object. "That was just weird as you know she doesn't do that often, though we all know it has happened before."

"You are her favorite pediatric nurse, so no surprise she tries to circumvent procedure to get you to do her bidding," Ellen said, giving me a stout head shake. "You had better go. We have everything up here covered."

"I guess," I said, slipping the phone back into her pocket. "I will make it quick though, if someone else can handle it, I will be right back."

"No worries," Ellen said as I quickly made a beeline to the elevator.

The trip down three floors was quick; as I entered the ER, I glanced about to see if I could find Trish's distinctive head of hair. Instead, my eyes latched on to a very tall, dark, tattoos and stunningly beautiful specimen of the man variety.

"Ricky," I said as our eyes connected. He was wearing a suit today, which was odd, as I scoured my memory banks to remember if he had told me about any kind of meeting or something that would explain that attire. Nothing came to mind as I walked briskly to their location. As soon as I was within a couple of feet, he fell to a knee.

My breath was suspended, goosebumps broke along my skin, and I could not form a thought. I just stood there dumbfounded in the middle of the ER, not sure what I should do. I had long dreamt of this moment, but to be honest, this hospital setting was not the backdrop that I had imagined. Though now that the moment was here, I could not imagine anything more spectacularly perfect.

"Daniella," Ricky said as I noticed that Trish was holding her hand over her mouth to his right side. "You know I love you more than life, and we have the best adventures together. Clara adores you, and my family has welcomed you with open arms, as has yours done for me. I want to wake every day beside you and call you my wife for the rest of my days on this earth – marry me," he said, extending the ring.

I just stood there in shock.

"This is where you say yes," Trish bit out in a harsh whisper.

"Yes," I mumbled as applause exploded all around me.

Ricky rushed forward, and I ran to him as he gathered me close. "I love you," he whispered into my ear.

"I love you," I mumbled, shaking and so happy I didn't think anything could ever top this moment.

"You know that I'm going to want to be the maid of honor, right?" Trish said to me with a loud cackle.

"Of course, I would expect nothing else," I said as I wrapped my arms around her.

Ricky glanced down at me, "you might want to hold that thought," he said with a grimace as I felt my insides tremble. That look on his face had me a tad bit worried, to be honest, as he took my hand and led me outside.

"She said yes," he shouted ad Manny, Rigo, Mario, Trina, and literally a huge crowd of additional people all came running out from many directions.

There we were, jumping up and down like crazy people on the sidewalk outside of the hospital. Everyone wanted to see the ring, give me hugs and ask questions about the wedding. I had been engaged for less than five minutes, and they were asking me so many questions about my big day that my head was swimming.

Ricky leaned down to my ear, "I figured I would give you one last chance to remember what you have agreed to," he said as I turned to look him directly in the eyes. Putting my hands on either side of his handsome face, I could only lean in and kiss him solidly on the lips.

"You are the biggest surprise of my life," I whispered to him, "and I can't wait to spend the rest of my life with you and all your crazy, wonderful, and very involved family. I think our kids will never want company, support, or fodder for writing a great book when they get older."

"Kids? How many exactly did you have in mind?" Ricky asked, causing my face to flush.

"Boy and girl at least," I said, "close in age, and Clara will be the best big sister in the world."

"Agreed," he said. "Though I was thinking four to six would be good," he said, glancing about at his own siblings.

I inhaled deeply as the chatting, talking, cackling, and craziness went on all around me. While I would never regret joining this amazing family, four to six kiddos seemed like a lot. I was still mulling over a response when Ricky laughed loudly and grabbed me about the waist, and brought me firmly up against his massive body.

"I'm teasing," he said. "I will be happy with any kids we are blessed with, but most of all, I just can't wait to start my life with you."

"Agreed," I said, kissing him, as the entire group of family members faded into the background as my body only registered this amazing, fabulous man.

MARIO

MARIO

$\mathcal{M}$ARIO was ripped from his sleep by the two bombarding bodies of his twin girls on top of him. They were jumping up and down, announcing that they couldn't find the clothes that he knew darn well he had laid out for them the night before.

"They are on the handles to your closet door," he mumbled, hoping for another moment or two of sleep.

"Not these, we want the purple ones with the pink flowers," Livia said as if he was the biggest dumbbell that ever lived. He was trying his hardest to get his sluggish brain to start working again and help him figure out what outfits they could be referencing.

"What outfits are you talking about?" He asked, sitting upright on the bed, trying to wake up and rubbed his eyes as he tried to focus and stretched his arms into the air.

"The flower ones, remember the ones we got at Target," Marina said with an air about her that she didn't know why I was acting so confused. Unfortunately, it was always two of them against me, so I would be outmaneuvered at each step. I was long used to the dynamic but normally had more sleep

369

with which to tackle them. Last night with the custom order at the bike shop, I was working and getting everything ready for their first day of school, the day had slipped away from me, and I managed only a couple of hours of sleep. Not a good situation in the least when dealing with five year old twins.

Mario stood and shuffled to the girl's room, searching for the outfits in need, and groaned a few moments later as he recognized them at the bottom of the laundry hamper. He held up several other options, which were all turned down. He then was faced with the tough task of wrangling Livia and Marina for the first day at a new school into an outfit they didn't want.

After another ten minutes past he sat defeated on the floor, as all he was managing so far were tears, screaming, and two well-placed kicks that barely missed critical body parts on him. He was grateful to have the support of Ricky downstairs helping start breakfast and even Clara as a sweet cheerleader for the girls. If he could get them to agree to go to the kitchen, they might all enjoy breakfast together before their first big day.

Clara was a definite morning person like her dad, Ricky. Mario was not a chipper person in the mornings, and his girls had taken his lead in this regard. To top it off, they were in a new place, meeting hosts of additional people, and the last few months had been a bit of an upheaval for everyone. He didn't fault them for their terrible morning moods, but that didn't make it any less critical that he somehow managed to get them to school reasonably dressed and ready for the school year.

He knew this move to California to meet his half-siblings and extended family was the right thing for them all long-term. That simple twist of fate now had him and Ricky in business with Carlos, one of his newly acquired brothers.

They were also expanding and doing even more work than he could imagine, along with spending time with all the new family that this move had brought them. Then Ricky met his girlfriend Daniella, and his ex-Carla was finally starting to be a distant memory as he found happiness again. Even for the positive, change for children this age was hard, so he needed to be patient and just keep reinforcing a schedule and routine. Growing up with cousins and a huge support system that came with all of this would definitely make it easier for everyone.

Helena, his wife or rather his now deceased life partner, had a magic touch when it had come to his girls, but now it was miserable for him to manage alone in these tough days. He sat on the floor for a moment to just give himself a tiny break before going in for round two. The little respite made his mind travel back in time to his sweet wife.

They had been high school sweethearts that were about as opposite as any two lovers could be. She was the school nerd, debate team member, and school newspaper editor. On the other hand, he played football and barely made it through school, mostly because Helena tutored him to keep his grades where they needed to be. She had been amazing and then even headed off to be a teacher while he started his brother's fabrication and bike business. Things looked ideal for them, and they found out about the girls. To say Helena had been over the moon was an understatement, as being a mother was a long-term goal. The timing might not have been ideal as they both were still getting started in their careers, but they made it work.

He had asked her to marry, and they made it a quick courthouse affair that Ricky stood as his witness for and a friend of Helena as the only ones present besides the love-birds. They had a quiet dinner and then started life out as newlyweds. Honestly, he had been so fortunate those first

371

few years he had to pinch himself often for a kid that never thought to have a family, Helena and the girls had made his life a dream. Until the night just prior to the girl's third birthday when Helena was rushing home from the cake shop with a princess-themed confection and a man not paying attention had ran the light. In a moment, his life had turned on a dime, and everything since had been different.

He quickly learned how to parent independently, with Ricky and him tag-teaming their three girls as best they could. He no longer had a social life or anything revolving around the girls and work. He was good with that, but occasionally he would think about how nice it would be to have a partner to depend on once again for just a second set of hands or an encouraging word at the end of a day. No woman, though, wanted a ready-made family with obstinate twin girls and the complicated family ties that he now boasted. He thought maybe as they aged, he would again be granted time to consider dating, until then, though he just needed to keep putting one foot in front of the other, doing the best he could.

He launched from the floor with renewed energy and, grabbing both the girls under the armpits, headed for the stairs. Maybe some breakfast and Clara time would put them in better moods to dress for the day. If not, he would have to beg Ricky to be the second set of hands dressing them as he would not allow them to be late on their first day of kindergarten. Even at their tender ages, he was a firm believer that a good first opinion could set the tone for the future, and he intended his girls to love and be adored at this new school.

VALENTINA

"*M*ama, I do not need you are fixing me breakfast like a small child nearly every day," she said with a light chuckle as she shook her head.

Unfortunately, her father had passed a year ago, and now Valentina was the last thing her mother had to worry about, which meant a lot of attention focused her direction. She had bought the house next to her parents three years ago when her father got sick, so she could easily be on hand when they needed anything. Now in hindsight, that was not the best decision though she had spent his final days making him so happy; it was these next twenty to sixty years she hadn't thought out.

"I am hoping to keep you healthy, fed, and hopefully with some spare time to go find a nice man," her mother started the same argument they always had about this time.

Her mother was old school in her beliefs in how the family was intended to work. Women married kept the house and tended the children. Her greatest disappointment in life had been the emergency right after Valentina's birth that rendered her unable to have other children. Valentina would have loved to have additional siblings, but that just wasn't the plan.

Her parents, though, had done everything in their power to give her an amazing childhood, and she had a lot of nieces and nephews that, unfortunately, over the years, had mostly moved out of California for family, work, or other reasons. Now only once a year at best would she get time to visit family, normally in the summer when her teaching was on hiatus. The fact she had attended college and now taught was another oddity that drove her mother mad. She was chomping at the bit for grandbabies, and Valentina working as much as she did was not a good thing in her mom's eyes either.

In addition to her teaching day, she tutored kids in desperate need at the shelter down the street at night. She also ran a literacy class for English as a second language adult at the community center. Overall, she felt totally fulfilled and gave back to the city she adored, even if she was still single. That was not acceptable in her mother's eyes. Despite her admiration for all she accomplished until she was married or provided grandkids, she would continue to have a mother cooking, cleaning, and setting her up on blind dates.

Valentina pulled the plates out of the cabinet to set the table for their breakfast together. As much as she would love to say she despised these efforts of her mothers and felt them a bit dated – she also loved how much she adored her and was glad to have one parent still so close.

"So, did you get all the information about that cruise we talked about," she asked her mom, who immediately bristled and stood a bit taller. She didn't turn to make eye contact, but Valentina knew that she didn't want to consider such a thing.

Her mom had this weird thing about maintaining the

routines that she had before her husband died. Going out, having fun, and moving forward with her life somehow seemed unkind to him in her eyes though Valentina knew her father would want her mom not to continue mourning him. He had asked her in his final days to press her mom into finding happiness and staying busy as best as she could. So, while her mom brought up grandkids, she continued to throw new activities in her direction.

"I will agree to go with my friends if you go on a date," her mother said, looking her dead in the eyes. "It has been a year now since that horrible man you dated, and you need to move on now."

"Mama, Steven did not injure me that much," she said through the sound of the man's name made her clench her fists.

She had met him through one of her friends at the school who set them up. Apparently, what her friend didn't know was that he was still sleeping with his ex-wife and another parent at the school. It was a tad bit awkward after their second date when he showed up to her classroom when they were doing the monthly birthday party for kids celebrating that month. Several parents were volunteering in the joint classroom event, and the woman was there with her son. The second Valentina had seen the horror on both their faces, she had known. Her mother had relented in any blind dates since.

She was missing dating, though, so it might not be the worst idea in the world to find a date if it would get her mother on that cruise. It was a trip that her dad had intended for them to take, but his crazy hours at his job and Valentina had made that nearly impossible – and then it was too late. Now all her mama's friends had been trying to talk her into a single lady's cruise for a while, and she had the ammunition to make that happen. How hard could it be to find an unsuspecting man to ask out on a single date? A guy that would make it at least possibly fun would be nice, but she wasn't going to hold her breath. She could write a bestseller on the bad dates she had experienced to date, and the truth was not one had ever stuck. She seriously thought that maybe her standards were impossible to meet for the contemporary male.

She just wanted loyal, family loving, no cheating, hot as sin, and great dad material. Someone employed and kind to her mother would pretty much guarantee him Prince Charming status. The elusive man had not surfaced yet, but good enough for a single night out she should be able to manage.

"Okay," she said, holding her hand out to her mother. "I will even agree to bring him home to meet you," she said, waggling her eyebrows. "You better get booking that cruise."

Her mother raised her coffee cup to her lips, gazing at Valentina over the cup as she took a long draw on the liquid.

"Agreed," she finally said, sealing her fate by placing her hand in her daughter's and giving a firm shake.

Now she just had to find a living, breathing man she could tolerate for at least one evening. It would be worth it to see her mom take at least one step into a new adventure.

MARIO

ario walked into the kindergarten class and stopped short when he saw all the heads perfectly bent to do the assignments in front of them. It was simple tracing projects from what he could make it, but it also told him irrevocably he was late – and his girls for the first day of class. He grimaced as he glanced up to find the teacher starting his direction. He had messed up, obviously, but I was not sure yet how, considering he double-checked the start time twice on the sheet the school sent him.

"Good morning," a beautiful Hispanic lady with big expressive eyes, curvy hips that swayed in perfect rhythm as she walked, and a smile that lit up the room greeted him and his girls. "You must be Livia and Marina Mendoza? I'm Ms. Valentina," she said, turning to gaze at Mario. "I prefer my first name for the kids, and you must be Mario," she said, holding out a hand to shake his.

Each of the twins held his hand like a lifeline they refused to give up. They had attended a daycare back home, but this new introverted, slightly bashful approach was definitely a new thing for both of them. He glanced down at the girls and dislodged Livia so he could shake the new teacher's hand. There was electricity crackling along with the connection, and he quickly pulled back, appalled that such a thing could happen right in a kindergarten class with his girls in attendance.

"I thought we would be on time this morning," he grumbled, glancing about teetering between confused and angry at himself.

"Normally, the principal gives the parents extra time the first day of class," she said with a bright smile. The woman seriously was smoking hot to be a kindergarten teacher, and he was an ass for letting his hormones continue to interject themselves in this conversation.

He gave himself a slight shake to focus on getting his children moving toward their first day in this new classroom. He had no idea why this had to be the day his long-dormant hormone kicked in, but they needed to stop. He was already on edge, which was causing him internal turmoil that was unneeded.

"Oh, sorry, I thought I had read through everything carefully, but it's been a rough few weeks," he stammered as the girls started tugging at the hands, he was holding them with.

"Why don't you let them go to their tables," Valentina said, and you and I can chat in my office for a few moments. She indicated with a flick of her wrist a door off to the right of the classroom. He thought all teachers made an office in the classroom directly, but this was tucked back behind her desk for privacy.

Before responding, two helpers moved forward, welcomed the girls, and shepherded them off. He gave a weak goodbye, but neither of them were listening as his shoulders slumped forward.

"Follow me," Valentina said.

That turned out to be a horrible idea, as his errant eyes

could not stop staring at her swaying backside. She wore a colorful loose-fitting skirt and top that perfectly complimented her dark skin. Her hair was longer than he first thought as he noticed it falling in dark waves down her back. She was the prettiest teacher he had ever met, and that included several he had crushed back in his school days.

She opened the door into a bright little office space, mostly made that way by the students' artwork. There were no windows in the space, but it was big enough they wouldn't be sitting on top of each other. Something that he wouldn't haven't minded trying but figured this was neither the time nor the place.

"So, you moved here recently, correct?" Valentina said, lowering herself to a chair behind a compact desk.

"Yes, we wanted to be closer to my brothers and extended family," he replied, not wishing to get into that complicated history.

"You have a lot of siblings?"

"Five brothers and three sisters by the association of sorts," he replied. His family dynamic was messy, but he had come up with a concise way of trying to explain even the three women he considered the sisters he never had.

"Wow! I always wanted siblings, but that was not in the cards. The get-togethers, you must have are sure to be loud and amazing with all those people," she observed with a huge grin.

"You have no idea. I think that when they start dating a new woman, and bring the girlfriends around, and if the girlfriends survive one family outing – well then it's pretty much a done deal for marriage."

"Oh, my mother would love you guys," she said. "She has been constantly trying to marry me off. I think that she just wants family around again after my father passed, but I wish she would find a social life separate from me," she grumbled.

Mario was stunned to find her single. How could a woman like her still be single, he just couldn't compute that in his brain.

"Were you married? Or are you divorced?"

"No," she chuckled. "Honestly, I'm a bit picky and don't like drama. Dating is always drama, in my opinion, and I have a lot of things that I can be doing with my time that I find more beneficial. Plus, I haven't met my prince charming yet."

"I get that," he said. "I was married to the love of my life, and we had dated since high school. It was easy and just flowed, so I haven't had to get in on the dating drama. I have heard stories though through my brothers and others."

"Your wife passed?"

"Yes, two years ago," he sighed.

"I'm sorry for your loss," she said. "Is there anything I should be aware of regarding the girls? Do they remember her? Have traumas, likes, dislikes, or anything else you think would help me be the best support to them?"

He just stared at her for a moment, caught off guard by the empathy she was showing.

"They have faith memories of their mother but are okay talking about them. They have been uprooted, so they seem to be a tad quieter and reserved. I have worked with both to know letters, basic words, numbers, colors, and such. I think they should be good students."

"Excellent," she said, making notes as she gazed at Mario to the extent, he just got the strangest feeling she was sizing him up. Maybe she didn't like single fathers or something, but the silence got unnerving after a long minute.

"Did I say or do something you didn't like?' He finally asked.

'No," she said, putting out a hand. "I'm sorry I made this

stupid bet with my mother this morning, and I need to find a victim – I mean date to help me out fast."

He laughed. "And you are considering me for the victim? I don't date, and wouldn't that be a conflict of interest or something?"

"Probably. I don't date either but to get my mom to go on this cruise she really needs to do, I promised to go out on a date. I was not truly sizing you up for such a thing, but wondering if you had a single brother maybe," she said, looking so cute he just could not handle it.

"I do not have a single brother, but why is this so important to get your mom to take this cruise?" He asked, now totally into this.

"So, I can have just ten days of peace," she blurted out and then covered her mouth, looking shocked at herself. "Seriously, I can normally filter better, but I'm just at my wit's end. I live next to my parents and without my father to baby and look after – guess who the next choice has become twenty-four seven? I just need a break."

"So, you really don't think this date will lead anywhere? Cuz I was thinking I am single."

"Nah, I've been down this road, and I think there might be something wrong with me."

"Do you know any fun things in this area to do?"

She just stared at him as this funny smile burst forward from her lips. "If the guy would allow me to plan the date, I know exactly what I would do? But I think I would want to surprise him."

Mario stared at her, shocked at the words nearly tripped off his lip. He could not go out with his girls teacher, could he? It was one fun night away; what could go wrong?

"When and where?' He asked as she looked stunned as she gazed back at him.

"Friday night, at six. If you write your address," she

pushed the paper across to him. "I can swing by and pick you up."

"Sounds like an adventure," he said, "but don't you have my address in the file."

"True," she said, flushing as she glanced at the file in her hand. "I will be there and on time. Now about Livia and Marina, I have a feeling they are going to have a wonderful year in my class."

"I think so too," Mario said, feeling more the schoolboy himself than his daughters.

He had zero ideas how he would explain this weird turn of events to all his brothers, but he was certain he would get a lot of teasing for it. But it would all be worth it.

VALENTINA

"*S*eriously, I think I might have had a stroke or something," Valentina said lightly, smacking her head to her hands that were resting on the table in front of her. "I asked him out when he was just there trying to enroll his twins in my class. What in the world? My mother had me so rattled I think my sanity is fleeing."

Serena laughed at her friend as she shook her head and giggled. They had been through a lot together, having known each other since college, and she was the only one Valentina was about to tell the truth about her lapse in judgment.

"I will say that might not have been the smoothest date request I've ever heard," she snickered. "But goodness, I'm pretty impressed he said yes."

"Well, I did tell him it really wasn't a date and that my mother made me do it," Valentina said, glancing at Serena, "maybe that made the difference?"

"Well," Serena looked at her biting down on her lip hard, "I'm going to say no. Honestly, I have no idea based on what you said that a man would take you up on that offer. Other than you are beautiful, caring, sexy and not always crazy."

"Thanks," she grumbled.

"So, we need to go out and do bus duty today," Serena said. "You ready?"

"Today's not my day," Valentina looked at her best friend and fellow teacher, confused.

"Right, but I swapped with Rachel and Gwen because I need to get an eye full of this new man of yours. You know I need to approve before you go out with a complete stranger!"

"Ugh," Valentina said.

She really didn't care about doing duty helping all the kiddos get on buses as she enjoyed seeing them off to their parents and the like. She did worry about seeing Mario again up close and personal. The man had seriously walked into her classroom and stolen all common sense from her in one look. It was baffling.

Sure, he was six feet tall, dark, tattooed, and handsome as sin, but that did not explain away her lapse in judgment. He also had those adorable girls, and she did happen to be a sucker for children. That also couldn't explain her asking him out, despite desperately hoping to get her mother on that cruise. The truth was she adored her mom and just wanted what was best for her. Maybe it just had been too long since her last date, or maybe Mario did have some magical power over her. She wasn't certain which but going outside and having to see him again was not something she had bargained for this close to her mind-boggling overstepping this morning.

"Come on, we need to go face the music," Serena said, tugging playfully at her arm.

"You are really enjoying this, aren't you," she mumbled at Serena as they walked toward the front of the school, where soon hordes of children would run out in masses.

"Do you remember when I first started dating Hank? The weekend we went to that carnival?"

"The Hershey kiss on the seat of that ferris wheel?" Valentina snickered. "You tried to wipe it off your butt with that ice material that looked white, and it turned that horrid yellow color."

"Yep, and as I recall, instead of being a good friend and telling Hank the truth about what happened, you tried to tell him about a bowel disorder I had. He was horrified, and I'm shocked we made it to the second date," Serena said.

"You had it coming," Valentina replied. "You made me come out on that date with you because you didn't think you would have anything to talk about. Your mother basically pleaded with me to be the third wheel."

"I still think my mom likes you more than me," Serena admitted with a slight scowl on her face.

"I don't think so; besides, you gave her a grandbaby, my beautiful goddaughter," Valentina said as they stood outside at the first checkpoint waiting for the kids.

"And your mom would be just as over the moon – " Serena stopped talking, and her eyes went wide as she turned to stare at something behind Valentina. "Please tell me that is not him?"

"What?" Valentina said, turning to see Mario and someone that had to be his brother due to how alike they looked, right by his side.

"Right side, that is him," she whispered.

"Oh, I think I know what overcame you this morning," Serena said, actually fanning her face. "That man is smoking hot, and that has to be a brother? I definitely approve one hundred percent!" She whimpered.

"Hey," Mario said, drawing close to them, and Valentina silently chastised herself to behave. "This is my brother Ricky," he said with a hand flourish to the guy next to him.

"And you have to be the kindergarten teacher that pulled

off a miracle today?" Ricky teased, reaching out to give her hand a hearty shake.

"I'm sorry," she returned to him, so confused again.

"Mario tells me you asked him out, and he accepted?" Ricky gazed up at his brother with a huge teasing grin.

"Yeah," she said, clearing her throat nervously.

"I've been working on getting him to go out on a date," Ricky said. "So, thanks for managing that one for me. I am hoping to be seeing you around; the family is going to love you; I have a good feeling and that doesn't happen often."

She turned to Mario and realized that while he might have shared the asking out part, he might not have shared the fact it was a one-time deal. He held her gaze firm, and she decided to just let it go. Things would work out the way they were meant to, and lucky for her, at that very moment, the bell rang, and kids poured out the door. When she finished sorting everyone out and looked again, Mario and Ricky were nowhere in sight. That was okay; she already knew the next time she would be seeing him for sure and found herself looking forward to it a lot more than she had thought she would at first.

"I am in awe," Serena said when they crossed back into the school. "That man is fine, and so far, his family seems cool also. Still think you had a stroke and didn't do the right thing asking him out?"

"I guess time will tell," she responded, but secretly she was excited to see where this might go.

MARIO

*M*ario tried his best to focus on the bike in front of him. He would be seeing Valentina later tonight and was finding it nearly impossible to stay focused on anything these days as her beautiful face continued to pop up in his mind's eye. The truth was he was also still walking the girls to school in the morning in an effort to see her, but so far, no luck. He didn't want to appear stalkerish, so he hadn't gone inside but now here they were on the morning of their first date.

"How is it working out with the girls going to aftercare where Clara goes," Ricky asked, coming alongside him?

"Great. They are opening up, and the difference five days has made is already remarkable," he said. "I'm glad that Daniella's sister was able to make that work for us all. They even pick them up, so I don't have to run out in the middle of the afternoon."

"So," Ricky said, bobbing from foot to foot nervously, "I have something that I need to tell you."

"Okay," Mario rose, wiping his hand on an old rag he held for just that purpose.

When working on these bikes, the oils and other materials were all over the place, but he didn't like messing up the metal on them if it wasn't absolutely necessary. Ricky always told him he was the most meticulously clean fabricator he had ever met, and he took pride in that.

"So, I think we should sell the old house," he started to say, "back home."

"Okay," Mario responded.

They had been keeping it in case of this business with finding all their family, the expansion or something else didn't work out. Now that Ricky had Daniella, it seemed reasonable that he would no longer look at that as a fallback plan. Mario still had a few reservations, though seeing the girls setting as well as they were, even those were fading.

"Do we need to discuss in more detail?" Ricky asked, gazing at him directly. "I thought you would be more reluctant about cutting that last safety net."

"I don't know," Mario said, really thinking about it. "I just feel like at this point, even though I'm still not a hundred percent here, you are. Even if I never talked to Carlos, Manny, Joey, and Rigo again, I would want to be where you are to see Clara and you. With Daniella now in the picture, I realize that has to be here. Besides, leaving the house situation back there not fully resolved feels a bit. I don't know like not committing to this."

"I agree," Ricky said. "You like the house we have here, right?"

"I do, but it is still a rental, and even though someone I know," he leveled his brother with a direct gaze, "doesn't spend a lot of time there since hooking up with a nurse. I figure you will make it official shortly, and in time, I will find a home for the girls and me."

"Who knows," Ricky said. "Maybe you end up with a teacher of your own and get your second chance at love."

"Hey, let's get through the first date first," he said. "I am nervous to begin dating, and then I allow her to set everything up. What if she decides to make me go dancing, or worse?" He scowled at his brother as all his worries again flooded his brain.

"I mean, Valentina seems pretty responsible and sweet," Ricky offered. "I have a hard time believing she is going to force you to do anything that you don't want to do."

"I guess," Mario said as he glanced back at the bike. "Do you need anything from me to put the house on the market?"

"Not for now, but obviously, if it sells, I will need you to go with for paperwork," he replied, glancing about. "How are you truly doing with all the changes? I know that we hardly have any time anymore when someone from the extended family isn't around, and I've been meaning to check in."

"Good," Mario said with a head bob. "I think that if we had been raised with everyone up in our business, the noise, and the chaos, it would be easier. It will just take time, but honestly, I'm so glad to have the family," he sighed. "I just wish we could all find some peace about dad."

"What do you mean?" Ricky asked, furrowing his brow at Mario.

"I know that they all have tough feelings about mom," he started in. "I get that they hated dad for what he did, and even Carlos has issues with him especially, but it is related to catching him with mom. They despise her, which is not how I feel, as you know, so sometimes there are things said that are hard," he finished with a slight sigh.

"I get that," Ricky said. "I also know that sometimes I am a lot more stoic and sometimes make it seem like I don't care. That is never the case, and I'm sorry that you feel like this. I should be there for you more."

"That is not your job other than to hear me out when I have a tough day," Mario said. "You have literally been the best brother even when we don't see things eye to eye. I could never imagine anyone else."

The sound of someone clearing their throat had Mario turn to see Carlos hanging his head in the doorway. He felt flush from head to toe and felt bad for what he had just said.

"Carlos," he sighed, not sure what to say. "I'm sorry I didn't think you would overhear."

"No," Carlos said, walking in gently to the work bay where Mario was working. "I am glad I overheard. I did have a ton of guilt when I told my mother about my father's cheating and only in her final days did, we finally clear the air about all of that. I honestly hadn't thought about how hard it might be to hear us talk about it knowing that was your mom."

"Yeah, but you all have been super amazing, and I believe we all have a lot of trauma from what our father did to all of us," Mario countered. "Not one of you has said anything to us personally, and it is hard to be in this place as I understand why our mother would be someone that you all dislike. I just," he sighed as he let the sentence hang. "I don't want to cause any issues with us or our relationships which is why I haven't said anything when in group settings."

Carlos sighed, "I can't even imagine and honestly appreciate you bringing it up even if I did kind of eavesdrop," he said as his face turned a bright cherry red. "I think we are all doing our best healing from the past we all had in some regard when kids. On a bright note, we are half-siblings by blood, and you accept Carmen, Estrella, and Juanita, who are removed from you by blood in total. I think that by just being honest and understanding each other that our parents choices were not our decisions we can continue to navigate and build this new family dynamic."

"Agree," Ricky said, slapping Mario on the back.

"I agree also," Mario said. "Yes, I think it will sometimes

be hard, but we can do this. For my girls, I know that being raised with all the cousins, aunts, and uncles they have here will hopefully give them a much broader worldview. I hope they grow up with less of the hurts than we all have."

"I hope so too," Carlos offered. "When Jennifer and I have kids down the road, I know yours are going to be great cousins and role models to them. I think this is the best outcome I could have imagined not that long ago when my mother passed."

"Thanks," Mario said. "It makes me feel better having this conversation, and I will try to be more open in the future."

"Sounds good," Carlos said. "Now about that bike for Roman, which is what I came in here for. He called for an update."

"Sure, let me show you where I am but also one little concern that I have," Mario said as Carlos came closer, and he gave Ricky a tiny nod overhead.

He did have a great life here in California, and he hoped that it only got better from here.

VALENTINA

*V*alentina checked her reflection in the mirror for the final time, giving herself a little grin. She was looking forward to tonight and had sent Mario instructions on what she needed him to wear for the unique evening. She was honestly looking forward to tonight, despite not knowing what to expect from something this strange for a first date. On the other hand, she sure hoped that Mario was one of those guys that didn't mind getting dirty and was down for odd and strange fun.

She gave a slight shake of her head, grabbed up her bag, and headed for her Jeep. She was needing to move, or she would be late, which was something that caused her unneeded stress. She hated ever being late for anything and was more the ten-minute early kind.

She quickly found Mario's house, and when she pulled to the curve, he came through the door nearly a second later. She felt her throat go dry as he started walking toward her. He was dressed super casual in a t-shirt and cargo pants, exactly as she had expressed. Unfortunately, she hadn't realized how the t-shirt would hug those biceps of his, nor that he would be sporting a five o'clock shadow that only enhanced his handsome face.

"Hey," he said, hopping into the passenger seat. "Right on time, though I am intrigued about what you have planned for the evening as this is the most casual, I have ever thought to dress for a first date. My brothers were telling me I wouldn't make it to a second like this."

Valentina felt her heart stutter. "I thought we agreed this was a one-time thing," she muttered.

"And I thought we should keep things open for now," he said, staring her in the eye.

For a moment, neither of them said a word as she drowned in his chocolate eyes. The man was seriously hot, and she could feel the heat of him reaching out like a warm hug across the space of the interior of her Jeep. She cleared her throat and put the vehicle in drive.

"So, no other clues into what we are doing this evening?"

He asked, but she was enjoying being the one in charge. Besides, she was looking forward to this so much she sort of worried that if given notice of where they were headed, he might have declined. She didn't know Mario well enough, but some men might think this was not their cup of tea.

"It's a two-part event," she said with a chuckle. "When I first read about it, I thought it had to be a mistake, but I confirmed that two other people I know did both of these events before. Oh, and I promise you will never have a first date like this, and we will have décor for the house if we like."

"I would bet my house and yours look very different inside," he returned, not missing a beat.

"Why do you say that?"

"Crayon drawings, Barbie dolls, toys, and a lot of pink throughout mine – how about yours?"

She laughed, "country chic and clutter-free. I guess we know who runs your house, as they are starting to my classroom."

"Are the girls a problem in class?" Mario asked, leaning forward in his seat to turn and stare at her face.

"No, but they definitely have minds of their own. They are super smart and making friends," she laughed. "I just made a mistake the other day of asking them their favorite pets, and Livia gave me a ten-minute lecture on how some pets can't be kept in the house."

"That would be my fault," he laughed heartily at that one. "I keep forgetting how kids absorb everything. They wanted a chick and a rabbit at Easter this past year, and I gave them a lecture on what I didn't consider house pets. Mostly, it was a lot of made-up crap as I don't think anything furry outside a dog should live indoors. That said, I could not manage a dog either with those two hellions running my house these days."

"I understand," Valentina replied. "Honestly, they are warming up great, and this first week has already seen them coming out of their shells nicely. They will do wonderfully. They do keep mentioning a Clara – do you have another daughter?"

Valentina had never dated a man with kids, much less two. The idea of three would probably be a dealbreaker for her as that was a lot to take on, in her opinion.

"No. Clara is my niece, and after my wife passed, we moved in with my brother Ricky who you met. He had a daughter named Clara with his fiancé at the time and ended up raising her alone, so really the girls have pretty much always lived together and are tight as sisters."

"So, you live with your brother – the one that came to school to pick up the girls the first day?"

"I do legally still live with him, but he now has a fiancé Daniella that he stays with most of the time. They are planning a fall wedding this year, so I'm going to be all on my own," he sighed. "For the first time, I'm finding out what it is like not to have a second set of hands around all the time to help. I'm grateful they are able to dress themselves most of the time, or I would be drowning right now."

"I can imagine," Valentina said, seeing the turn ahead where she needed to go. As she pulled into the big warehouse, Mario made a weird noise that had her turning to him. "Scared yet?"

"Not yet, but this is not what I was expecting," he said, squinting at her. "I can take care of myself, though," he said with a slight head bob, "so not too worried."

"Yeah, you definitely are ripped," she said and then instantly wished she could slap herself. "I mean, you look like you stay in shape. Do you work out regularly at a gym or something else?"

"First, I have some great genetics, as you saw Ricky, and all the rest of my brothers look the same. We work in bike shops lifting heavy stuff all the time, but we do have a small gym we always keep on hand in the garage to get in quick workouts when the girls are down. I just feel better if I go to bed de-stressed and tired."

"Makes sense," she said. "So, do you ride bikes or just build them."

"We all ride for sure. We can definitely make that happen if you ever have an interest."

"Can I get back to you," Valentina said with a worried glint in her eyes? "I'm not sure about motorcycles."

"I promise with the right safety and driver you are as safe as in a car," he muttered, eyeing the building.

"Let's see how this first outing goes, and then we can discuss," she finished.

"Can you tell me know what we are going to be doing?"

"Nope, you have to see it first," she said, jumping down

from the Jeep as he did the same, falling in line with her. "You won't need that workout tonight to de-stress," she said as he whipped his head to her, looking even more confused.

She could only shake her head and laugh as she pulled open the door and walked in.

MARIO

"*O*kay, that was crazy," Mario enthused as they left the devastation behind them in the small work area. The person leading them led them now to a huge open bay area and gave Valentina some instructions, while he just grinned from ear to ear.

The first activity of the night was called smash therapy and had included them being able to select an instrument to smash televisions, pottery, and the like with. Then apparently, some of the resident artists in this building that had small studios used the pieces for mosaics, artwork, and other things. It was so much fun, and Valentina had laughed like a kid the entire time with him.

"So, we are going to create this size," Valentina said, waving a hand at the painting. "I called in the perfect size for the canvas that would go in my house, which I hope it's okay."

"Wait, we are literally creating art for your house?" Mario said with a chuckle glancing at the glaring white canvas laid out on the floor. "What if we mess this up bad?"

"It's abstract art," Valentina said, glancing at him like he had lost his mind. "We wing it and then have amazing conversations during future gatherings about the extensional things we see in the abstractness."

He laughed at her as he couldn't help but note how stunning she was. The flushed skin, minimal make-up, and glow of happiness looked great on her. He was beginning to think that he couldn't top this evening, and he definitely didn't want this to be a one-and-done kind of thing.

"Okay, please tell me that you at least put in for colors that would work with your décor," he asked, biting down on his bottom lip worriedly.

"I even brought paint swatches," she giggled. "I can't wait to see how this works out, and I promise no matter what, I will love it. I decorate with kids' artwork, so it can't be that much worse."

"I guess," he said, glancing at the buckets, paintbrushes, and other tools laying around. "Where would you like me to start?'

She pointed at the paintbrushes. "If you just start spattering, I think the bucket drip process he was telling us about would be great to try after that."

"You are an adventurous soul," he said, picking up a brush and standing at the edge of the canvas. "I have never painted so much as a small piece of art since elementary school, and you think committing to putting this in your house is a good idea?"

"Sure, why not," she said.

"What is your mother going to think of that?" Mario asked and saw her face pale suddenly as she cocked her head in thought.

"I hadn't thought that far ahead," she said. "Not that she would be worried about the painting as I sincerely love abstract works. I'm more concerned about having to tell her about tonight and this outing – mostly you."

"Why me? Can't you just tell her that you bought it some-place and not divulge it was on a date?" He asked, turning to fully cue into her as he saw confusion, worry, and then some anxiety appear to cross her features.

"I can't lie," she said.

He just looked at her like he didn't understand. Sure, people might not lie as a general rule, but everyone lied by omission or little white lies once in a while.

"My mother is like a human lie detector," Valentina said. "I could tell her anything, and she would know this is a date."

"And you don't think she would approve of me? Is it the tattoos, the job, or the kids?"

"What?" She turned to look at him with her face squished up in the most adorable way. "None of that. She would love you and would spoil your girls like crazy should she ever find out who they are."

"I'm really confused then. Why wouldn't you tell her about this date?"

"It's a one-time thing, and I don't want to date someone that will just break my heart down the road," she muttered angrily as she violently tossed paint from a brush on the canvas breaking the stark whiteness up.

"I'm sorry I know I have to be missing something, but what makes you believe I would hurt you? And break your heart?"

"Men always do," she stuttered out, flinging more paint at the canvas. "And I really like you, so I can only imagine how much that would suck. Why do you suppose I had to ask you of all people out? You do know that was a first for me," she said, turning to him with crazy eyes.

"You do know you are going a tad bit nutzo on me, right?" Mario laughed. "I don't know why you invited me out that first day in your class, but I presume it was to get you, mom, out on a cruise."

"Nope, you short-wired my brain, and I thought you were the hottest thing I ever saw enter my classroom," she admitted as Mario seriously thought he might fall for the woman right then and there.

"Are you always this blatantly honest with everyone?"

"No!" She said, sounding alarmed. "I don't understand when you are around, it seems any filtering ability my brain has goes away, and I just want to tell you everything."

"That could end up being a good thing," he said.

"You think I'm crazy," she whispered. "I promise I'm not. I'm a great teacher, a good daughter, and a nice person."

"I know," Mario said, dipping his brush in some light blue paint and throwing it at the canvas. "I have a feeling we are going to be getting to know each other a lot better in the near future. You will find I'm a good guy, don't play games, and love my family enough not to bring anyone around that wouldn't fit right in with them. So, you keep telling me exactly where I stand and how you feel. I, in turn, will promise to do the same – deal?"

She stared at him for the longest time. "Deal. I really am not crazy."

He just laughed and pointed at the canvas. "Let's get this canvas painted. I have a stomach that needs food and a curfew of midnight."

She turned with the biggest smile to do just that. He couldn't help but fall for the woman right then and there. She was so cooky, kind, funny, beautiful, and he suddenly realized that had Helena been here, she would have adored Valentina on the spot. That was enough for him to give her the benefit of a second date, and maybe this thing turned out to be more than either of them ever could have reckoned.

VALENTINA

"*A*re you sure about this?" Valentina found herself asking Mario the following weekend as they were getting ready to ride with his brothers. He had come over to get her from the house on his bike, and she was trying to work up the gumption to get on the back. He just patiently sat holding out a helmet.

Since the first date, they had talked every night, and every conversation got better. This weekend Carmen had agreed to be the babysitter for Ricky and Mario to allow for a long ride up the coast. They were actually going to do a group wine tasting with all their significant others at a winery about two hours north of her. She was truly looking forward to everything but the ride as she still had this fear of motorcycles that didn't have a basis in her experience as she had never been on one.

"Hello," she heard a voice sounding behind her as her stomach hit the pavement. Her mother normally did a senior's exercise class this Saturday, and she had assumed she wouldn't be home when Mario came by.

This was not going to be good.

"Valentina," her mother said in a tone that already told her she was in trouble. "What is the meaning of this?" She waved a hand at the bike as her eyes traveled Mario aggressively from head to toe.

"Mario Mendoza, this is my mother, Alma Parillo," Valentina said, introducing the two. Her mother did not extend her hand but rather turned to her daughter with slanted eyes and her hands tightly crossed around her breasts.

"It's nice to meet you, Alma. Your daughter is an amazing woman," he said as Valentina wished her mother would say something, but the other side of her brain warned that she might not like what came out of that mouth at this exact moment.

"That is wonderful, and how long have you known my daughter?"

"About two weeks now. We had our first date last weekend, and today she is riding with me, my brothers, and their fiancés and girlfriends," he offered as Valentina wanted to hit her hand to her head.

She was no longer breathing as she realized how to hurt her mother was from the look she was giving off. Valentina had not told her about Mario because the truth was, she hadn't expected much after that first date. Additionally, she did feel a bit guilty that he was the parent of a child in her class and knew her mother would not like that.

"How many brothers?" Her mother barked rather than say anything untoward.

"Four," he returned. "I also have three sisters."

"Children?" Her mom started the interrogation in earnest.

"Five-year-old twins," he said, not hiding from the truth, which would be good Valentina, though, until she heard the harumph her mother elicited. "My wife died two years ago in an accident, and the girls are in Valentina's kindergarten class."

"I'm sorry for your loss," her mother said, softening a little. "Why do you suppose that my daughter has not told me about you yet?' She asked, directing her stare at Mario like a hardened interrogator that she was in this moment.

Valentina was sweating but knew that interrupting would just make it worse. She wouldn't blame Mario if he decided to pack things up and head out on the bike alone at this stage.

"I think that she doesn't want to get your hopes up that we might be a good match. She has a lot of respect for you and wants to be certain of a man's intention before introducing them to you," he returned as her mother sat there stunned.

"You are good," she said, softening completely. "Does your family do dinner together on Sundays?"

"No, though we do have regular get-togethers," he said, not certain where this was going from the confusion on his face.

"Good, you come to dinner on Sunday at five," she dictated. "And bring the children."

"Mother," Valentina barked out at her mom. "Maybe you should ask him first, and me."

"Why? You obviously like him as you are willing to risk your life holding him tight on the back of his bike. I want to meet the children and get to know him," she said, staring directly into Valentina's eyes, daring her to deny her that one little thing.

"Mario, would that work for you?" She turned in a slightly softer tone.

"I can make it work," he said as he blew out a soft breath. "Can I bring a dish of any kind?" He turned to her mother, extending the offer.

"Nope, I enjoy cooking and will see you then," she said, pivoting fully and returning the direction of her front door.

"Wow," Mario said when she was out of earshot. "I don't know if I passed the first interview or not?"

"You definitely did," Valentina said. "I guess this is not going to stay a casual and one-time thing, huh? What about bringing the girls to dinner? That would be odd with me being their teacher."

"Yep, maybe we cross that bridge and decide what to tell them when not standing this close to your mother's home," he said pointedly, handing her the helmet. "You ready?"

"Man, I forgot the drinks," he said, holding up his finger as he walked toward the house. "Give me a second."

She inhaled and turned to find Ricky staring at her, which worried her with his expression on his face.

"Did I do something wrong?" She asked him.

"No, but," he stared past her as if checking that Mario was still out of earshot. "Please be careful with him. He's such a nice caring guy with a big heart that sometimes I wonder how we are even brothers. He's been through a lot, and I don't want to see him hurt or heartbroken."

"I understand that," Valentina said. "You were there when Helena passed?"

Ricky nodded. "It nearly broke him, and without Livia and Marina, I don't know if he would have gotten out of bed most days there for the first few months. You are the first foray back to dating for him, and I'm just worried. He's the best brother to me, and my job is to watch out for him."

"I understand and promise I will do everything in my power to be honest, upfront, and kind to him," she reassured him.

"Thanks," he said. "What about your mom?"

She laughed, "she's a mom that can be a mama bear with

me, but she means well. I have faith he will win her over," Valentina confessed.

"Good," he said, glancing up behind her as Mario's footsteps came closer.

Valentina was surprised at the interaction but respected his brother for being so blunt and caring in such a manner for his brother. She realized how important that sibling bond was and what she had been missing and totally appreciated Ricky's opinion.

"We good?" Mario asked.

"Absolutely, let's do this," she said, slamming the helmet over her head and swinging her leg up.

She would not back down from this light challenge when her mother was probably learning. This relationship had just gone from a one-week-old getting to know each other – to serious in the span of an inquisition by her mother. She hoped that Mario was as unmoved as he seemed, but at this stage, getting on the bike seemed less scary than that exchange.

As he put her arms around Mario and he pulled from the curve, the wind hit her face with a breathless rush. She felt free, and the warmth of him holding her tight allowed her safety at the same time. Yep, it was completely possible that when she had least expected the man of her dreams had walked into her classroom, and she was beginning to realize nothing would ever be the same.

MARIO

"How did it go?" Ricky climbed the steps to fall into the chair next to Mario late on Sunday. It was nearing midnight, but he felt awake still, though the beer he was nursing should hopefully do the trick in putting him to bed soon.

"It was good. I think," Mario said. "You remember how dad was just mean sometimes and such a jerk."

"Yeah, he had a mean backhand and a nasty attitude to boot," Ricky sighed, "what made you think of him?"

"I was thinking how mom with her direct questions, gazes that could see your soul and the way she would look at me actually scared me more than him," Mario offered in return.

Ricky laughed heartily. "I would agree. When I brought my first girlfriend home, I think I was in eighth grade, and she was pretty sweet. Sandy Mader was her name. She walked in, and mom started shooting off questions like she had committed a murder. It was not good," he sighed, glancing out into the darkness beyond the patio.

"Wasn't she the one whose brother beat you up the next day for disrespecting her and not standing up to mom for her?" Mario asked as Ricky snickered.

"Yep. I think my test of all women was if they could make it through an interrogation with mom. I knew her intentions were good, but in hindsight, she was fierce to the point of chasing everyone away."

"Yeah. Well, I don't think Valentina's mom is that bad," Mario started. "She seemed nice, made a great meal, and truly was kind to the girls. I did get the feeling that maybe I wasn't her first choice of a man for her precious daughter. Though I will say by the end of the night, I felt like we had reached a bit of an impasse of sorts," he said. "Got me thinking of Helena and how we didn't really have much of this when we were dating. She had been raised by her grandparents and tossed around so much she didn't have any relationships that meant anything to her until me."

"Yeah, you two were each other's entire world. When dad and then mom passed, she was there every step of the way, but you are right – she didn't bring hardly any family around, except for that one aunt, even when they were alive. Valentina living next to her mother seems like they are tight," Ricky said. "Are you reconsidering moving forward with her?"

"No. I have the absolute best time when I'm with her," Mario said. "I know that her being the girl's teacher is not ideal, but everything else is wonderful. How did you think she got on with everyone during the wine tour and ride?"

"Amazing. She is great, funny, smart, and I didn't hear one bad word about her. Daniella raved that she thought they could be great friends," he returned.

"That's what I thought. I just don't know as fast as this seems to be moving if I'm doing the girls a disservice. What if we move super fast and it fizzles, then they are caught in the middle? They have so many other changes they are working through. What if this causes them to need therapy?"

Ricky laughed, "whoa, take a breath. Tell me what you have found wrong with her so far."

Mario really had to think about that question. He had not met anyone since his wife that he jived with so well. She laughed a lot, was smart, kind, and just the nicest soul. He tried to find a negative about her and just couldn't come up with one.

"I don't think I have one yet," he grimaced. "That is why I'm worried. What if these are those rose-colored glasses mom always worried us about?"

"Well, even if you had them on all of us meeting her and her mother meeting you – someone would tell you something if they felt there was anything that needed to be addressed. As for the girls, they are young and will adjust. As long as you give them the ability to talk to you about anything that could be bothering them and not a revolving door of different women, I have to believe they will adjust. How do they like Valentina?"

"They adore her," Mario said. "They giggle and have stories since they are in class with her during the day. They ask her questions she patiently responds to, and they seek her out for help even on little things."

"That is great," Ricky said. "I know that Clara was one of my biggest hurdles to get over with Daniella. In the end, I didn't need to worry, as she treats my daughter as if she is her own. Even tonight, she was asleep in her bed when I left, and Daniella was the one that shoved me out the door to check on you while she watched Clara. You know it might just be that after a number of rotten years, our luck is changing for the better," he replied.

"Maybe," Mario said. "You know I've always been the cup half empty kind. I like to be prepared for anything, so I look for all that could go wrong in any situation."

"Yes, I know," Ricky retorted sarcastically. "I just try to believe all will work out, and so far, these days, that is holding. So, when do you see Valentina next?"

"I was thinking of an elegant dinner and movie on Thursday as I know I promised to watch Clara for Daniella and your date night next Friday."

"Sounds good," Ricky said. "Who knows, maybe we should plan to make our nuptials a double wedding this fall."

"Whoa!" Mario said as his heart started thudding painfully against his ribcage. "Let's get through a month of dating at the least before you start planning the rest of my future, please."

"Fine," Ricky said. "I was just trying to be helpful."

"Right?"

"Oh, and we did get a full offer on the house back home. I have to find a lawyer tomorrow to handle the paperwork from here so that we shouldn't have to travel back," he said, looking directly at Mario. "You are still good with cutting the last of the ties with home?"

"Yeah. This is home now. No matter what happens with Valentina, I'm all in here," he said, taking a long swig of the beer. "Let me know when and where for the paperwork."

"Will do," Ricky said as they sat, finishing their drinks side by side.

It was a gorgeous night, and he couldn't wait to see what the next weeks, months, and years would bring for his family. He hoped that Valentina was going to be part of that journey long into the future, but right now, he was only able to take one day at a time. He was never getting too far ahead of himself. IF there was one thing that losing Helena had taught him was life was short, and so he needed to take it all in as he could and never rush things. He would savor every moment and let the future bring what it would.

VALENTINA

*T*hey walked away from the movie hand in hand. The action flick was not her normal cup of tea but spending time with Mario was worth it. She had made a deal anyway that the next movie would be her choice. This give and take was so easy with them, and she loved about Mario. He was pretty laid back, but she had to believe that having been married once before had learned some of these attributes from that relationship. It didn't bother her that he had been married and widowed; in fact, she and Serena had a long conversation about that.

Never had she dated anyone in a similar situation, and that had been a big point of hesitation at first. She always believed that someone who lost a spouse might not move on without closure to a new relationship. Serena had been a great source of confirmation that was not always the case, and she had even asked some great questions that Valentina broached with Mario. He felt after the length of time his first wife was gone that loving someone knew was possible, though as the mother of his children, Helena would always hold a special spot in his heart. Valentina loved the honesty and, with time, knew that he was feeling for her the same as she did for him and had no further reservations about forwarding this relationship.

"I know you said you weren't an action flick lover," Mario said as they strolled the starlight streets, "but was that horrible?"

"No," she replied, trying to hold her face in check, but his quick laughter told her she failed. "Did Helena like action flicks?" She wanted to ask Mario questions about his wife, Livia, and Marina's mother. This seemed as good a time as ever to broach the topic.

He turned to her with a wry grin, "You really want to discuss my dead wife on our date?"

"I would love to learn more about her," she admitted. "You mentioned she helped you become more relax as a person and not be as high strung. It's nice to hear stories about her because it helps to understand what a lovely person she was as a mother and wife. Plus, I can see the way you light up when you talk about her and it allows the girls to have that special bond and feel connected to their mom."

He stared at her for a long time, and she worried that she might have just blown their entire evening asking such invasion questions.

"You're not wrong," Mario said with a slight sigh. "You should know about Helena because she did inform so much of my life. I also work hard to keep her alive for the girls, and any future partner needs to be open to continuing. So, in response to your question – she hated action flicks."

"Man, I knew I would like her. Was she a rom-com woman also?"

"Definitely," he said, rolling his eyes. "In fact, she couldn't watch the action flicks, as she said it made her nervous through the whole thing. She was seriously this sweet, white girl, the class nerd back in high school when I first met her. Absolutely, not my type, and the first time I talked to her, she walked me off the ledge from hitting a bully out by the buses before we were headed home one night," he laughed.

"Wait, how did she stop you?" Valentina asked, not having seen that coming.

"She literally stepped between us, put her finger in my face, and said there were little kids on the bus. We needed to act like role models and not bullies," he laughed. "I don't know what it was, but I think I fell in love with her right then and there. She just had this way of immediately being able to quell my anger when it would flare up," he sighed. "And I had a lot of it from my father to hormones; I was a hot mess for years. Helena never saw that in me, though – always just the good. She loved me in my tough years more than I deserved," he said.

"I would have loved to have met her," Valentina offered back. "Whenever you want to share stories about her, let me know. I want to understand that history and even your love for her. And I will continue to try and disguise how much I hate action flicks as long as we can trade-off for rom-com once in a while."

"I promise to do just as good a job disguising how I feel when you make me sit through a rom-com," he returned with an arched brow in her direction. "And I love that you are good with me sharing about Helena. Thank you," he said, pulling her close.

She relished this openness between them but was ready to get this date back on a current footing between them. She didn't mind sharing memories, but this was her time to build some of her own with Mario.

"Maybe you end up liking the movies we watch," she said, "what then are you still going to give me attitude?"

"Definitely. I don't need you ever gaining the upper hand on me," he said, holding his face taunt as if trying not to laugh.

"I think I might already have the upper hand," she said, leaning in to huskily whisper in his ear, causing him to stop in his tracks.

"You, Ms. Parillo, are playing with fire," he grumbled in a tone that told her he was feeling this connection between them as he circled her waist.

She put her hands up and over his shoulders as he bent to her. An inch above his lips, just as she felt every nerve ending hone in hoping for a mind-bending kiss – he stopped short. She wanted to scream and drag him to her. She decided to let him take the lead even if it killed her, though.

"You know I'm going to kiss you," he said.

"I would hope so," she responded, looking at him quizzically.

'I just want to be sure we are in agreement on that at least," he chuckled as she playfully hit his arm, and he crashed those amazing lips into hers.

The man could make her moist, dizzy, and needy, all with a swipe of that mouth across hers. The need for this man was growing with each interaction but not once yet had it led back to a bedroom, and she prayed that would happen soon enough.

"Wow," he moved back from her. "I have to say that is my favorite part of the evening each time we go out now. I just feel like everything keeps getting better and better and can't wait until the next time I can be with you."

"I agree," Valentina said, standing up on tiptoes to kiss him again. "I've never felt this with anyone, and I would love to say it scares me, but it has been so easy that all I feel is this overwhelming need to be with you every chance I can."

"What about your mother? I would bet she gave you an

earful after the dinner last weekend," he said as she realized that the elephant in the room she had been avoiding all week was about to come out.

She turned, laced her fingers with his, and continued walking. She rehashed all the conversation from after Mario and the girls left that evening. Her mother was torn as she had been over the fact that he had been married, had children, and wasn't the exact version of what she expected for her daughter. On the other hand, as for Mario himself, she had nothing but glowing things to say.

"She liked you personally and said the girls were smart, well-behaved, and amazing," she started with the good news. "Of course, she would prefer you have not been married, have children as she doesn't think you will want more after two and that you were a tad less tattooed."

"Is that all?" Mario said with a light hoarsening of his voice. He sighed as they walked a moment longer before either of them spoke. "Would you want more kids even with the two girls that I have?"

"Of course, at least one, especially since I didn't have any siblings having a child would be the ultimate for me" she replied, not hesitating in the least, as he glanced over at her. "Wouldn't you?"

"I guess I hadn't really thought about it before," he answered truthfully. "I would expect if I married again, though, that my wife would want at least one child of our own. I see no issue with that. Do you think your mother, for instance, would love that child and not be able to accept Livia and Marina?"

"No, I think she would end up spoiling all of them," Valentina admitted. "I have always wanted to have a child, though, and go through that process of pregnancy and feeling the baby kick inside and just being a mom. I would definitely not want to give that up unless there was a true medical reason or something catastrophic."

"I understand and I can totally see the girls being big sisters and helping out. I can't, however, minimize the tattoos," he returned.

"I wouldn't ask you to, as I think they are hot – at least the ones I have seen thus far," she said as she flushed brightly, thinking about all of them she still had to unveil.

"Okay, then I think that settles it; your mom will just need to come to love me in time," he chuckled as they closed in on her house.

She glanced up to gauge the last of the distance they had to go before she was home. She wished he would come in with her tonight but figured he had the girls. She wasn't one to sleep around by any means, but she wanted Mario on so many levels that it was this soft strumming need that pulsed inside her all the time these days.

They walked silently up the stairs to the patio area, and she turned to him.

"I had a great time," she said, warning herself silently not to say anything she would regret. He might think her too forward if she was the one to suggest anything further this evening.

"I did too," he said, pulling her in for a kiss. "I will call you tomorrow to set up something for this weekend."

"You better," she said, watching him turn to go.

Swallowing hard, she called out before she could stop herself.

"Do you need to be home right away?"

He turned slowly to her, glancing at his watch. "I'm good until the start of business tomorrow," he replied, walking back in her direction. "What about your mom next door?"

"We'll set the alarm for super early, and you can sneak out," she said like a teenager with a boy in her room.

"Sounds perfect," he said with a heavy sigh as she turned to open the door, and they both slid inside.

The second the door shut, he backed her up against the wall and kissed her silently as she started undressing him with a strength, she didn't even know she possessed.

MARIO

*M*ario was whistling as he worked a custom piece of metal the following day. The radio was going, and he was in the best mood, despite the extreme attention he had to pay to the current project. He was making these little wing-styled items on the back wheel piece, and it had to be perfect. He was so inside his own brain he didn't notice at first that Carlos and Ricky were both standing in the doorway.

He glanced up to check the time and inside collided with Ricky's gaze. His heart thundered hard in his chest at the look on his brother's face. When he moved to Carlos, who looked as if he might be about to vomit, he felt goosebumps climb along every inch of skin. Something was horribly wrong.

He turned off the radio and, standing facing them, took a deep breath and waited. For the span of a minute or so, not a word was forthcoming from either of them. He started running through scenarios for what could have happened to have them looking this distraught. Did a customer write a bad review? Someone get hurt, or worse? Was it one of the sisters or his brothers? Finally, he realized that he was starting to lose it and just needed to force the words out of them.

"What is wrong? You both look like someone died," he said as Ricky glanced at Carlos waiting. When Rigo, with Manny right behind him, came running into the shop full tilt, he realized that this was bigger than he thought. It looked like someone died from the newcomer's face, which did nothing to lessen the worry ricocheting around his gut.

"Did you hear?" Carlos finally asked as spiders of worry pierced Mario's scalp.

"What!" He screamed, unable to handle the tension mounting in the room a second longer. "I've been working in here all morning and have no idea what you are all going on about. You have me totally scared to death, and I need you to just spit it out already."

"Mario, there is a situation at the elementary school where Livia and Marina attend," Ricky finally whispered as his voice broke.

"What are you talking about?" He asked, grabbing up his phone to see if there was any news from the school. They would have contacted him first, not his brothers.

There was a text message that caused his knees to buckle, and he grabbed at the cabinet to hold himself up. The message simply said:

All students are sheltering in place, and we will notify parents as more information becomes known. At this time, reports of shots fired have not been confirmed.

He started running for the door as fast as she could manage due to the fact that the shock was wreaking havoc on his body. He glanced about the parking lot, not sure where his truck was or what he should do next.

NINA DALLAS

"My truck," Ricky screamed, coming up right behind him. "You are in no condition to drive right this second."

Mario swerved and went over to the vehicle in question, piling into the front passenger seat without a thought. The other three all jumped into different doors. His brain was sluggish and unable to understand what he had read. No one was talking, and all eyes seemed to be on him in the driver's back area of the extended truck cab.

"What happened?" He muttered as she glanced from Rigo to Manny, capturing Ricky's gaze in the rearview mirror.

Nobody would meet his eyes, and he, for the first time in his life, worried that his girls could be in grave danger. This was not the kind of thing he had ever prepared himself for, and the scenarios his brain was manufacturing were not good at all. He needed someone to tell him the facts so he could start figuring out what he was supposed to do.

"There were just reports on the news of some kind of disturbance at the school," Manny was the first to say something, but he was absolutely selecting his words carefully, and the look on his face was evasive.

He felt like a small child who nobody wanted to tell anything to, and it was pissing him off.

"I need you to be more specific," he bit out. "My girls are in there, and I need to know what we are dealing with. The text says gunshots were reported," he said, holding out his phone to them absently, despite the note saying that was unconfirmed that did not as a father of students inside make him feel better.

"There are reports of that," Rigo volunteered. "I'm sure that the girls are okay and safe as the reports said no reports of injuries were known when I saw the news report."

Mario's brain went totally blank, as he couldn't even formulate a response. Parents were never supposed to face the possibility of their children leaving this earth before

420

them. Honestly, of all the obstacles he had faced as a single dad, not ever before had the thought of losing the girls crossed his mind. The panic was holding his entire mind and body hostage.

"I don't understand. This is an elementary school. Why in the world would someone do that," his brain suddenly reminded him of something else that, for some reason, he had blanked out – Valentina.

"Valentina is a teacher there and is probably inside also. They all must be scared to death."

"I would imagine that the teachers are trained in this day and age for just this kind of thing," Ricky said, glancing back at him. "I'm sure they are going to be okay."

Mario stared out the window as the elementary school came into sight. The lights of many ambulances, police cars, and even a huge SWAT van were up ahead. For the first time since his wife died, he offered a prayer heavenward for safety and then glanced back at his phone. He wanted to search the internet for what was known about the situation.

"Don't," Rigo said, putting his hand over the phone. "That will just make it worse. We are nearly there and can get the information that is available first hand."

Mario looked at him with blank eyes; he couldn't draw a breath; his chest hurt so bad. "The girls have to be okay," he mumbled, not certain how he would ever forgive himself if something happened to them.

Of all the emergencies he had ever thought to come to pass in his lifetime, not once had this made the list. Him in an accident on the bike or doing something at the shop had been on his mind before. The girls are getting hurt riding a bike or around the house horsing around – maybe. Them being in true danger at school happened to someone else, not his family. Until today it would seem.

As the truck slowed and Ricky found a spot to park, he

launched from the vehicle before fully stopping. Moving toward the barrier that the police had up, he tried to find someone that could answer a question. All he could see, though, was the stream of SWAT officers starting to inch toward the school, which of course, was straight from a movie and not his life.

"I can't believe this is happening," he muttered to himself. He glanced about at all the parents holding each other, milling in an area where police were directing them.

That morning when he dropped Livia and Marina at school, he would have remembered to say he loved them if he had any indication this would happen. He didn't think he had said it that morning, and he hoped that they knew that. He hoped they knew he would be right here waiting for them when they got out of this – because they would walk out of that school unharmed. He had to believe that was true, or he might actually go mad.

"Mario," a female voice called out as he turned to see Alma, Valentina's mom staring back at him. "This is just a false report, right?" She said as tears glistened in her eyes.

"I don't think so," he said, opening his arms as she just walked into them in a daze. He turned to stare at his brothers as the activity moved around him, nothing making a lick of sense. He tried to give Alma what comfort he could until she finally pulled back slightly from him.

"What do you know?" She asked as unshed tears gleamed in her eyes. "Are they telling us anything or just making us stand here and wait," she bit out. It was obvious that the emotional toll of the situation was hitting her pretty hard at this moment, also.

His heart was hurting for her, his girls, and all the families out here waiting nervously. They had been confined behind a line of policemen as some specialized police team was now entering the building. He didn't have the answers and couldn't do anything to assuage Alma's feelings, considering he was underwater with his own turmoil.

"They have told us to wait here," he gently replied. "I tried texting her, but no answer."

"I don't think I've ever been this scared," Alma whispered to him, glancing at her hands which were shaking so bad she wouldn't have been able to hold anything steady. "Mario, I can't lose her – she is all I have left. I don't know what my life would look like if she didn't come back to me," she stuttered as a sob escaped her throat.

He looked at his brothers, but they also seemed at a loss. What could he possibly say to make this better, as her daughter, like his own, were stuck inside there? The waiting out here might be bad, but he could only imagine what all those people locked down inside must be going through.

"Alma," he said, "Valentina has been trained for this, and I have to believe she will have gotten her class to safety. We just need to be patient and let the police do their job. I'm with you in the crazy worried department as both my girls are in there with Valentina."

"I'm sorry," she said, swiping a hand under her eyes to clear the tears. "I know you have to be just as worried," she said, grabbing his hand. "We have to believe they will be okay."

"Agreed," he said, standing to face the school; he glanced heavenward for a small prayer. Not something he would normally do but seriously, today, he was taking every last bit of help he could get.

The wait went on for what seemed hours, but in reality, it ended up only being another hour and a half. He knew that years from now, this moment would be etched in his mind forever, and time would still stand thinking about these moments when he had no idea if his girls were coming back to him. Or, for that matter, the very new relationship with

Valentina would be cut short by violence and nothing of his own doing. So many thoughts all competing for dominance in his brain was giving him a headache – and yet he stood stoic watching the front door of the school, waiting for a sign.

VALENTINA

*V*alentina kept her ears trained toward the door for any sign of a noise she couldn't recognize. Her adrenalin was spiking, and she felt as if she might actually pass out. That was not an option as the twenty pairs of eyes huddled into this space, some on top of others, needed her to stay calm. The other two helpers had stepped out during reading circle for just a moment when the alarm sounded, leaving her now in charge of the entire class. These kids were rockstars, though, and had been listening when they did the drills.

The windows were covered, the floor locked in place, and all of them holding their friends moved into this office space at the back of the classroom like tiny sardines. She was grateful that she worked at one of the newer schools that had separated the teacher's office area in such away. Under normal circumstances, it was said to provide more privacy, but the truth was it was locked, had no windows, and as a precaution for terrorists, weather, or other forms of harm that could befall the school.

"Is my daddy coming?" Livia asked her, tugging lightly on her leg.

She turned to stare at the small girl as her brain conjured up a picture of Mario. She couldn't fathom what he must be going through with his entire world in this small, confined space with her, and him having no idea what the outcome would be. Valentina shook her head as she had more than enough to worry about with all these kids. She couldn't allow worry or thoughts of Mario to take hold.

"I'm sure he is waiting outside," she said, crouching low to Livia with a finger to her lips. "Remember, we all need to stay super quiet."

"So, the bad guy doesn't find us with guns," one of the boys said, which of course, set off a course of whimpering through the children.

"Raymond," Valentina said softly, trying to get all of them through his process meant not terrorizing their little minds more than necessary. Sure, it was the alarm for someone armed being in the building, but these little minds didn't need that to ruminate on when stuffed in this space like they were. They had to believe they would be okay and stay quiet for their safety. "Remember, we need to only talk, when necessary, right now," she whispered, trying to provide an example of the volume that should be at when needed.

Raymond gave a dutiful nod as Valentina tried to dislodge Livia, Marina, and three other girls holding her tight. She knew they needed the strength of a calm adult right now, but she also needed to stay trained on the door. She moved slightly to lay her ear there and could hear nothing beyond which, of course, she thought was a good sign.

She again found herself imagining for a moment the condition Mario must be in on the outside. All these children had parents and guardians that must be close to the brink of losing it as they waited for word. She couldn't even imagine what she would do, finding her children locked down in such a way and not able to get to them. She had been through so many training sessions, but none had fully prepared her for the feeling that would be rioting inside her at this moment.

The silence of the kids around her all staring at her was causing her dread to climb with each passing moment. She picked up the phone on the desk and saw that Mario had texted but right now, she couldn't read that as it was the instructions to only check for information from authorities or school administration. She also didn't want to take her eyes from this massive group of kids. If they had been any other age, this many couldn't have fit in this small space, but she still worried about them not breathing well, being suffocated, or panicking should something start to occur.

She put the phone away though her mind kept traveling back to the text from Mario. She didn't want to get in trouble, but the rules were not to contact anyone outside the situation. This was done partly in case they were monitored and partly because, in recent years, leaks to news organizations had become a real issue to manage during such a crisis. She understood that reasoning, but the truth was talking to anyone outside this room would be preferable to not knowing what was happening beyond the door. Shaking her head, she focused on a new crisis as one of the kids started to cry loudly.

"Ms. Valentina, Anthony peed his pants," one of the kids said again louder than she would like. After all, these were kindergarteners, and silence was not a mode they were good at even under these circumstances.

"It is okay," she said, grabbing paper towels from the closet and then moving through the sea of kids as gently as possible as there was no spare room in the space.

"Anthony," she said, bending low as she wiped up the accident. She should have gloves on, she reminded herself

427

but at the moment, just preventing liquids on the floor was the most critical thing she could do. "It's okay, and I understand how scared everyone is. Are you doing okay?" Valentina whispered.

He shook his head, jaw clenched, looking petrified.

"Ms. Valentina," Livia said to her as she was now two children away from her position, "do you think our daddy is waiting for us outside?"

Valentina glanced from Livia to Marina, "I know he is, and soon you will be able to go see him."

She turned to see about anything else she could do for Anthony when she heard another little girl whimper.

"It's okay," she heard Livia say.

"Ms. Valentina won't let no bad guys get us," Marina reassured the classmate. She was standing tall next to her twin, and Valentina felt a smile spread on her lips despite the worry gnawing at her gut. Those two were something indeed. Kids could be so resilient; she just hoped they truly made it out of here with no one hurt.

"Do you think she will let a bad man in that door?" Marina whispered.

"No," Livia said. "Ms. Valentina is big and strong. She won't let anyone get to us. Promise."

Valentina was grateful someone thought that of her because she was feeling pretty helpless at this very moment. As she turned to access the other students, she couldn't help but notice all their sweet faces turned in her direction. They all did think she had all the answers – which was terrifying and reassuring as they weren't panicking at least.

BANG! BANG! BANG!

At that moment, a huge noise filled the space as kids screamed and moved back against the door. She saw her phone bouncing on the desk out of arm's reach as the kids held her in place. It sounded like someone going in through a window, but she was not about to call out or say anything until she knew if it was friend or foe.

Several kids grabbed her hands as she felt frozen in place. She recalled from training who was out there couldn't get through the second door, but they might be able to shoot it.

"Everyone down," she whispered, setting an example, and pulling all that were within arm's length down with her.

Not a word was said as noise sounded outside the room. Her skin was alive with goosebumps, tingles raced all over her skin, and her breath suspended in her lungs.

"SWAT – Ms. Parillo please open," a man's authoritative voice shouted out as a child near her screamed, but for her, she surged forward, knowing that this was finally over.

Valentina was sitting in the little area, dazed, and confused, as the police continued to ask questions. Then the administrators came to ask her a bunch of new questions. All she cared about at this moment was her kids all being safe. When she looked up and saw her mother running toward her, she came undone, falling forward into her hands and sobbing hysterically.

"Are you okay?" Serena's voice sounded just as her mom wrapped her arms about her snuggly.

"I thought for sure something bad was going to happen to you," Alma said, putting her palms on either side of Valentina's face and tilting it upward. "I'm grateful you are okay."

"Me too, mama," she said as she hugged her mom tightly, glancing at Serena. Her friend did not look nearly as spun out as she was feeling, and she needed to know if maybe it was her. "Mom, could you go get me a water," she asked, directing to a man handing them out a little ways away.

"I'll be right back," her mom said and left.

"Why do you look like nothing happened?" Valentina turned on Serena, and the tone of voice shocked even her.

Serena's eyes went wide.

"I am in shock," she said. "I was in the lounge, though, and didn't have kids in my care. That had to be a lot to handle on your own. I was going to try and come to you," she said, crouching down to look at Valentina.

"The rules about sheltering in place, though, would not allow that," Valentina returned. "I kept it together but all those kids. I can't even explain all the horrid scenarios that went through my head, but they don't prepare you for the silence."

"What?" Serena asked, gazing at her questioningly.

"The kids were silent, snug as sardines in that room just looking to me for all the answers," she whispered. "What if I had failed them, and this had turned out worse," she said as she began to shake uncontrollably.

"But the silence is what they teach all of us," Serena said. "These kids listened and executed. You did your job, and everyone goes home tonight," she said, hugging her best friend. "Look around; the kids will be okay."

Valentina did just that, glancing up to see Anthony first, wet a little on his bottom but happily chatting with his mom. Then her eyes collided with Mario, and her stomach seized painfully. He had both his girls tethered to him, but still, he took time to seek her eyes.

"Thank you," he mouthed to her.

She felt the weight of guilt building again as she gave a slight nod and then reached for the water her mom was holding. When she turned back in his direction, he walked in the opposite direction. He would never have forgiven her if something had happened to those girls. She was their teacher, this was her job, but still, they would have been over if something happened. There was no doubt in her mind.

She glanced at Serena; she couldn't date someone in her classroom. What if this happened again? She couldn't put herself or him in that situation. What had she been thinking? She realized her mind was spinning out now, but the stress was not allowing her any leeway.

"You can go home, miss," the police officer finally said.

"I will call you tomorrow," Serena offered as she started walking with her mom.

She hoped that tomorrow would feel better than she did today, but she had a bad feeling it would not be okay again for a good long while.

MARIO

The second he walked in the door, he was assailed by a wall of people that had shown up at the house to check on him and the girls. He wasn't certain how to process everything himself, but his daughters immediately took his hands in firm grips. While it would be nice to care for family, he wanted to be super vigilant about ensuring they had what they needed first and foremost.

"Sorry," Carmen said as she grabbed him close before bending to check on the girls. "We needed to be sure you were all good."

He was shocked, overwhelmed, and humbled at her sentiments. It was still odd that the sisters, while truly not related by blood, were seriously close as family to him. They adored his girls and cared for him so much he could not ask for anything more in some bonus siblings.

"We didn't get hurted," Livia said proudly, though Mario did notice the two girls were still holding tight to each other.

He noticed Ricky giving him a strange look as he held tight to Clara. He would imagine that everyone with a small child tonight in their city would be holding them a bit tighter and grateful to wrap their arms around their kiddos.

"How are you holding up?" Carlos walked up to him next, with Jennifer in tow.

"Doing as good as can be expected," he offered in return, though he did have a moment of gratitude to see the turn out for him and the girls.

"Great. If you need anything," Jennifer said, "I'm always a call away."

"Thanks," he said as another pair of arms enveloped him.

"I was so scared," Juanita groused at him.

"I'm sorry, wasn't much I could do to prevent that," he replied.

"I'm just glad you are okay," she said. "We brought food."

He had to chuckle. "Of course, you did," he said as Ricky came alongside him, clapping him on the shoulder.

"This is amazing and everything we missed as kids," he said softly for his ears alone. "Family that shows up in the good and bad. Your girls," he said as they both glanced to where Livia and Marina were being fawned over, "are so lucky to have all these people in their corner."

"I'm lucky to have always had you," he said with a look at his brother. "Everyone else is just icing on the cake. Father might have been an ass and treated a lot of people badly, but at least our moms still managed to instill in us the love of familia."

"I couldn't agree more," Ricky returned as Daniella moved to his side to offer her words of comfort also.

Much later that evening, after everyone cleared out, the girls continued to go between happy, crying, and scared in turn. He knew they were struggling to process what had happened. Luckily, there had been counselors on hand with information about talking to children at this age about what happened. He wasn't supposed to ask questions or lead them to tell the story. Rather it was his job to soothe, respond and just keep the emotional rollercoaster to a minimum as best as possible.

With a lot of perseverance, dinner or what little he could get them to eat was over. It was amazing that everyone had pitched in to make a great meal and give some company to keep the girls occupied for so long. Now, he had to work to get them down to bed, which was difficult. After everyone was gone, he moved to tubs, adding some of the lavender scents that Jennifer had dropped by telling him it would help with a sense of calm and help with sleeping. He was honestly grateful for his family and any insights, as this was new territory for him to be navigating.

Finally, more than an hour and a half after their normal bedtimes, he was wrangling them into bed with promises of stories. Each of them settled in and got pretty quiet suddenly, causing him to need to check-in and see how they were doing.

"How are you, Livia?" He asked, brushing his daughter's hair back lightly.

"I miss mommy," she said, causing his heart to stutter painfully in his chest. "She read the best stories and would help us play dress up."

Mario didn't even know how to respond to that. Considering how young they were when their mother passed, he always assumed that the impression she left was not impactful. Like this, the tougher moments of life have a way of teaching him that erroneous way of his thoughts. When things were overly difficult, traumas were fresh, of course; they would want a mommy to comfort them. A daddy playing both parents' roles was tough to reconcile, and he himself knew that he would sometimes be out of his league.

"Mommy did the build-a-bear so we could have him with us always," Marina said, jumping from the bed to go grab both of the little princess-dressed bears. She passed one to Livia as he sat there, still not fully understanding the words he could elicit to help his children.

They were the loves of his life and the people for whom he would give his own to protect. Words, though, were hard to come by, and he had zero ideas what it was that was expected of him in a moment like this. Raising his eyes heavenward, he wished himself that Helena could give deliver him a message on how to best help her babies at a time like this.

"Mommy always said we should pray for what we want," Livia said, wiser than her years if you were to ask Mario.

"Good idea," Marina said as both girls sank to the floor as a mute Mario could only sit in wonder.

"Dear God," Marina said.

"We love you, and thank you for all the food, toys, and daddy," Livia intervened.

"We ask you for a new mommy here on earth to take us to build-a-bear so we can find new outfits for princess Beary and princess Jazzy," Marina added to the prayer.

"And we ask for a mommy to take us to the park, read us cool stories in the good voices and never leave us," Livia said.

"Thank you for Ms. Valentina, who is pretty, nice, and helped us today – even when Anthony peed on the floor," Marina added.

"That was gross," Livia said, looking up at Mario, who could only nod. He hadn't heard that part of the story of the incident at the school today. This was not the moment to ask probing questions, though.

"Bless us, bless everyone, good night," Livia finished as both girls uncrossed their fingers and jumped into bed.

"You can read now, daddy," Marina said as if it were any other night.

Mario though couldn't talk over the lump in his throat as

he tried to focus on the book in front of him. The unshed tears in his eyes were definitely posing a few problems with his reading ability. Seriously though, he realized again and not for the first time just how out of his depth he was raising these two girls on his own.

~

Three days after the incident at the school, Mario finished putting the girls to bed and stood for the longest time gazing at them. Perspective was a funny thing in how a single moment in time could change yours forever. He had never been so scared as that hour spent waiting outside the school for news of his children, and now he didn't want to spend a moment away from them. They would be going back tomorrow and, after speaking with them, seemed okay with that, which was surprising to him how resilient children could be even in these circumstances.

Finally, he turned down the hall to the main living area hoping that he might be able to catch Valentina tonight. She had not taken a call from him except right after getting everyone sorted out after the incident.

It turned out that a dad and mom were locked in a terrible custody case. The dad had unfortunately thought it a good idea to force the administration to give him the child he had lost rights to, and a gun in his waistband lent credence to the fact he wasn't leaving without an issue. In the end, it was all bluster, luckily, and he had been subdued after holding the front office hostage with no one hurt.

"How are they?" Ricky asked as he walked from Clara's room. They had spent the weekend with them just as a precaution and to be on hand, Ricky said, but Mario knew the family in total was shaken by what had happened. They had all brought meals and gathered at his house throughout the weekend.

"They seem okay, but I think tomorrow being back in class will be the test," he offered back.

"And you – how are you doing?" Ricky asked.

"I don't know. I haven't slept more than two hours in a row the last three nights and find myself rising to go check on them at the oddest hours," he responded with a heavy sigh. "I haven't heard from Valentina and worry that she is truly traumatized, and even her mother won't answer my calls. Overall, I would say I'm bad to fair only at this moment."

"I can totally understand," Ricky said. "Though I will say that this weekend had reminded me how lucky we are. We have amazing kids and the family – they really showed up for you and the girls. Together we seem to huddle down, and I love that about this new reality of ours," he said. "Honestly, though, in your shoes, I don't know what I would do."

His cellphone vibrated at just that moment. Bending to pick it up, he noticed it was a text from Valentina.

Sorry to do this. After a lot of consideration, I think we should take a break. I'm not in a place where I wish to discuss this right now, but maybe someday we can have a coffee and rehash. Valentina

"What's wrong?" Ricky said, standing from the couch where he was seated and walking to Mario. "You look like you have seen a ghost or are about to lose your shit. I'm not sure which right this second."

"She broke up with me," he said absently as if in a dream. "I would think that this is a tough time, and no one should be making major life decisions," he bit out, reciting the advice the crisis counselor had given them as they were picking up the girls the other day.

"Are you sure?" Ricky said, squinting his gaze at Mario.

He held out the phone for his brother to read the message. "Not sure, I could misinterpret that. Should I try her back?"

Ricky just looked perplexed for a long time. "No, she won't answer just as she hasn't been. You will drive yourself mad with this right now on top of everything you need to do to ensure the girls are okay," Ricky offered. "Give it a little time. You of all people know that everyone processes trauma in different ways."

"I guess, but breaking up," he just continued to stare at the phone. "I guess that it was new and probably better now than later. After seeing how her mom was that afternoon, I would expect she also is struggling."

"Agreed. Her mom was a mess," Ricky said.

Alma had clung to Mario right up until the moment they started releasing people from the school. She sobbed and cried, saying things like she couldn't go on without her daughter also. Mario's heart broke for her, and despite Valentina being an adult, he could understand how she felt as that was amplified for him with two girls that had been in there with Valentina. From all accounts, through their teacher had been calm, kind, and never hollered as the girls told him.

"I think I need to go to bed," he said with a heavying sigh to Ricky.

"Mario don't let this add to your mood right now. I know this is hard, but I'm certain this is just a result of what happened, and you have to give her time to heal."

"I know," he said, clapping his brother on the shoulder, "see you in the morning. Thank you for staying with us through this."

"Always, we are brothers," he said as Mario passed him, shuffling to bed.

He was certain he wouldn't get any sleep tonight either,

but his mind and body were running on empty. Hope was gone at the moment, worry his only companion. He just needed a few hours of shut eye, and hopefully, he would at least be in a place to start processing all of this.

Three weeks later, he was still going through the motions when he decided to take action. The girls had made a card for Valentina that he was holding onto as she wouldn't talk to him, so he decided to try another route. He finished at the shop early and made sure that Ricky could pick up the girls if he weren't back in time.

He got in the truck and made a beeline for his destination. When he got there, he gathered everything from the front seat and headed for the door knowing this was probably the most reckless and ambitious thing he had attempted in a long time.

Ringing the bell, he noticed his hand shaking like a leaf. He ran the sweaty palm down his leg as he waited, and then the door creaked open.

"Mario?" Alma greeted him with a confused look on her face. "You know Valentina is at school, and she lives next door."

"I came to see you," he said, holding up the conchas and flowers he had in his left hand.

She gave him a curious look but opened the door to let him inside.

Mario drives over to Alma's house during school hours after a few weeks after the shooting to express his feelings towards Valentina and how much the girls love and adore her.

"How did you know that I love pan dulce?" Alma asked,

glancing at the pan, and taking a long deep breath into her nose.

"It was my mother's favorite, and when she needed a little pick me up, this was my go-to for her," he said with a light shrug as they walked into her kitchen. "I thought I would take my chances and see if you also enjoyed it."

"Well, so far, you are doing well," she grinned, taking the flowers, and walked across the room. Bending, she took a vase from one of the cabinets and arranged the flowers without another word. Finally, after what seemed an eternity, she turned back to him. "So, what brings you out to see me when you knew my daughter would not be next door?"

"I miss her. My girls miss her," he said, pulling the envelope from his back pocket and laying it reverently on the countertop. "They made her a card of their own will the other night, thanking her for keeping them safe during that scary incident at the school. When they finished, they decided amongst themselves to make one for you also," he said, laying the second one out for her to get. "They said you agreed that maybe you could be their Abuelita."

Alma looked uncomfortable for a moment before she gave a long sigh.

"We talked that night I watched them for a couple of hours so you and Valentina could check out that art show she wanted to go to," she said. "They told me how they didn't have an abuelita as your mom died before they were born, and I guess your wife didn't know her family. They actually shocked me by saying maybe I could fill that role," she said, walking toward Mario.

He honestly wondered what the woman thought of him. She was not cold, but their first meetings had definitely not been overly fun for anyone. Now, she seemed to tolerate him and like his children. Was she rooting for him and Valentina, though – he would bet not?

"You don't like me. Do you?" He asked the question that had been bugging him for a good long while.

"I didn't like you when we first met. Immediately without even knowing a thing about you, I will admit, I thought my daughter could do better," Alma admitted.

Mario had to respect the honesty and the balls it took to tell him that to his face. Though there was a softening a few moments later, telling him that maybe that stance had changed.

"I just heard single father and thought the worst. Also, I honestly imagined Valentina with someone more educated. She had made such a big fuss about the school her entire life and then college. She is a teacher, and I don't know. I figured that would translate to someone more buttoned-up like that."

"You know, despite the tattoos and no college, I've done pretty well for myself. I own my business with my brothers, care for my girls alone, and I did well in school," he said, wrinkling his nose, "I just didn't like it a whole lot."

"You and me both," Alma said with a chuckle. "By the time Valentina was in math in eighth grade, I could no longer help her. I get that you aren't exactly as I imagined the first time we met. I will admit that sometimes people – well, me for sure – can be judgemental at my age. I took one look at you and decided who you were without getting to know the real you," she admitted with flushing of her skin as her head bobbed forward in shame.

"I get that a lot, to be honest," Mario said. "Unlike most people, you at least tried to give me a shot."

"And I have found you that you are a good man, father, brother, and I would imagine a good husband. I'm sure that losing her young wife had to be hard, but you stepped up for your girls, which is to be commended. Additionally, as much as she might not want to admit it right now – my Valentina is in love with you," she said, moving toward him. "I would like to apologize for anything I might have said or done early in our knowing each other that was rude or unfair," she extended a hand to him.

"No worries," he said, shaking her hand. "So, Valentina really loves me huh," he asked with a glint in his eyes.

"Yeah, but that shooting changed things for sure. I know that everything before seems so small as I think about how Valentina could have been gone in the blink of an eye," she replied, shaking her head. "You have to grab life each day and tell those people you care about that every day. You, of all people, know better than most that life can be short and unfair. So, what are you going to do about winning my daughter back?"

"I'm working on that," Mario admitted. "I probably should move quicker, as I have two little girls already determined you are going to be their Abuelita."

"Yeah, scared me to death when they just came out with that," Alma nodded, turning to grab a couple of plates from the cabinet. "I didn't know what to say. Kids can say the darnedest things sometimes."

"Tell me about it. They stump me at least once a day," Mario admitted as Alma started doling out the pan dulce. "The stories I can tell you."

"I know how big a handful Valentina was," Alma admitted. "You are going to be a saint raising two of them."

Mario chuckled as they sat, swapping stories for the next hour. He was feeling a lot better, and the truth was he enjoyed having someone like a mother to chat with again. They had so much wisdom to give, and Alma managed to convince him he needed to find a way to talk to Valentina and set things right. He just didn't know exactly how he would manage that yet.

VALENTINA

"Mom, I do not need you fixing me breakfast like a small child nearly every day," she said with a light chuckle as she shook her head. She felt the fear return when her mom turned weary eyes in her direction.

"You've had a tough couple of weeks, and I'm leaving on my cruise in days," her mother said. "I wanted to give you one last breakfast. Well, actually one last breakfast every day until then," she laughed.

"Are you excited about getting away from everything for a little while," she asked her mom, feigning a smile.

It had been a month exactly today since the incident in the school. She still woke sometimes at night, had students with behavioral issues arising at the oddest time, but for the most part, things had started to go back to normal. For the first week, her mother hadn't left her side at all, and that married with everything she was having to file and do at school – she was burnt out. More than once, she had nearly called Mario to go out for a cup of coffee to talk but realized with two girls that also had been there; he had his hands full.

She knew that breaking up with him had been the right

thing to do, even if the timing sucked. She didn't want him, or her being pulled apart as they navigated those tough moments. He had a lot of family by his side, and the girls from all impressions at school were doing amazing now. She had regretted the rash emotional decision within seventy-two hours of sending that text. It was the most spineless way to break up with anyone, but even then, she knew hearing his voice would have broken her.

"Earth to Valentina," her mother said, snapping fingers in front of her eyes. "Have you called him yet?"

"No, and I don't intend to," she complained at her. "Have you packed yet?"

"Actually, I finally did last night," her mother replied, putting a plate with bacon, eggs, and wheat toast in front of her. "And you need to eat also. I know you have lost weight in the last month, and I don't approve."

"Mom, I'm eating," she said though that was as close a lie as she ever told her mom. Food didn't taste right, and she felt like someone going through all the motions and feeling nothing in these last weeks. She would not give in and tell her mom, though, as she didn't want to impinge on the coming vacation that had taken so much to talk her into. "I didn't think that you even liked Mario when you first met him. Are you truly now thinking that he could be the one for me?"

"I didn't like the man," her mother admitted turning to face her head with a heavy sigh. "I honestly imagined you with someone more educated like you. College, learning new things, and all of that was so important to you that is what I thought you would gravitate towards."

"I think Mario is smart, just not maybe book smart. He does run his own business and does well for himself," she found herself defending him.

"I know. Your father and I never attended college, and we

had a wonderful life. It just was different with you, but no judgment as I agree that Mario makes a great living for himself and his children. I think the bigger issue for me was the children if we are talking frankly," she continued. "I thought that when you fell in love, married that you would then have your own children. I never expected you to fall for someone that already had them."

"I would agree with you," Valentina replied. "Sometimes what we envision for ourselves is just not the reality of what happens out here in life. You can't judge a book by the cover. I know Mario looks rough, didn't go to college, and married with children. He loved Helena, his first wife to her death, and does everything for those girls."

"I get that now as I've grown a bit closer to him," Alma admitted. "I think it has been a great lesson for me on honestly not judging people before I get to know their heart. Mario has an amazing heart, and I know that this situation with the school has been hard on everyone. I hope that you both get a chance to sort it out and see if this love I saw flickering between you can still be saved."

"Maybe," Valentina. "You know I will always love you no matter what. I hope you have the best time on this cruise, and who knows what will happen by the time you get back."

"I will eagerly wait to see," Alma said with a grin.

"You know I love you, and I'm the luckiest woman ever to have you by my side," she said with a huge smile walking to where her mother stood and wrapping her arms firmly around her. "I can't wait to make you a grandma soon, and I truly wish dad could be here to see us now."

"Mijita," her mother said, hugging her tight, before she pulled back to look in her eyes, "He is always with us. He would be so proud of you and that heart and head of yours that helps you make amazing decisions for the future. It was that smart brain that brought all those kids through a crisis, and he would love that about you. He would also be happy that you found true love, and I have a feeling he would have approved Mario right away."

"You think?" Valentina said, feeling a slight swelling in her heart. That was all the endorsement of Mario she would ever need.

"I know so," her mother said, pushing her hair back from her face and kissing her cheek. "You were the joy of his life and the only woman that ever gave me a run for the money in his heart. You need to be happy. That is all he would have ever wanted for you."

"I'm trying, mama," she whispered. "I'm really trying," she said, putting a hand over her heart and raising her eyes toward heaven as she hoped, like her mom, that her father was looking down happy with her every day.

They made small talk, and finally, she pulled all her materials together and headed for the door. She made the short drive on autopilot and headed into the teacher's lounge. She no longer cringed when entering the school, and life for her looked pretty normal again - or at least that is what she told herself.

"Have you called him yet?' Serena asked, coming up to her on the left.

Valentina laughed and turned to her best friend. "No, and you are the second person already today to ask me that," she replied with a grin. "You do know that Mario and I only dated a few weeks, and my current mood doesn't have anything to do with him."

"You don't lie well," Serena said. "I've told you before that within your second date, I knew you were meant to be. I don't blame you for a single second breaking up or at least asking time after what happened here. We all needed to focus on ourselves and process what happened. I just have seen you handle all this super well, but you still won't work bus duty which tells me it might be to avoid a certain tall, dark and handsome bike-riding dad."

"Even my mother is now asking if I had called him," Valentina admitted. "And I have bus duty this morning, so there," she said, sticking her tongue out at Serena.

"Oh, I'm in for this," Serena said, suddenly piping up. "Let's do this," she said as Valentina growled.

"Have you seen Mario at the bus pick up since this started?"

"I have," Serena said. "Come on, let's go do this, and you can prove that you are all over him."

Valentina swallowed hard and followed her out the door. She tried to calm her breathing and hoped that maybe Mario would just miss the pick-up for today. I had practiced what I would say the first time I saw him again but didn't know if I was up for that this morning. Honestly, I just needed a single day or maybe a week without all the emotional turmoil.

Valentina settled into a routine to get the first kids off the bus, trying to forget Mario. Three buses in, and then she turned to the lane where parents drop kids off, and as she walked back from the second car, she saw him. Livia and Marina hugged him, and a brunette stood next to him. The woman was bubbly, hugging them, and looked so comfortable with the group. She felt the anger, the disappointment, and the bemusement at him replacing her so quickly.

"What the hell?" Serena said, following her line of sight. "You want me to go give him a piece of my mind?"

"No, it's all good," she said, turning to go to the next car.

She turned as the child walked into the school and her eyes collided with Mario. She scowled at him allowing her gaze to slide to the woman standing next to him and then arching a brow in question.

"Valentina," Mario called out, but she continued to the next car.

447

"Valentina," he shouted again, this time sounding closer.

"Don't you start," she said under her breath as he came within a few feet. "I don't want to get into this with you and," she turned to see the woman headed toward us. "I am at work. Please leave," she said, turning and putting him in her rearview mirror – it was well and truly over, she realized, but that didn't stop the tears from trying to fall. She swiped her eyes angrily as she headed toward the classroom to get the day started. Today was definitely not going to be a good one; at least she could try again tomorrow.

MARIO

$\mathcal{M}$ ario just stared into space, not sure what had happened that morning. He was so excited when he saw Valentina for the first time since the incident. Despite taking the girls to school every day, she hadn't been on pick up or drop off duty since that afternoon when the school was held hostage by a madman. It seemed a good sign that she was out this morning, and then she had left him in her wake like a dirty rag without giving him the time of day.

He had been thinking through it all day and still didn't know what in the world to do about things between them. They would have to be in the same room for parent-teacher conferences even if she never wanted to consider a relationship again. She could not run away as she had today. It was time to figure things out, but he didn't know how to go about it as she wouldn't answer phone calls; talking to her at school was rude as that was her place of work. That left one option in his mind.

Mario went downstairs, where Ricky was watching television. Daniella was on duty at the hospital tonight, so he stayed here, keeping him company as he did a lot these days.

"I need to go out for a bit," Mario said with the firmest voice he could muster. "Can you watch the girls?"

"No worries," Ricky said, turning to look him in the eyes. "Tell me you are going to set things straight with Valentina finally."

"I think I have to follow what happened this morning. I understand if dating me is that abhorrent to her, but we have to be able to be in the same space at some time down the road and not have her fleeing from me like I have the plague."

"Agreed," Ricky said. "Go get'r tiger."

Mario walked out the door before he could lose his nerve and got in his truck. He tried to prepare a speech, but his brain appeared to be sluggish and not sure what he should say to win the woman he loved back. He didn't fully understand her current state of mind, and it seemed a bad idea to lay at her feet all the anger and resentment he had.

On the other hand, he did need to get through to her and have an adult conversation. What had happened at the school was bad, but they needed to discuss a way forward and not just ignore each other – it made no sense to him to act in such a childish manner.

Pulling up to the house, he glanced in the mirror to ensure he was at least presentable. Except for the big black bags under his eyes, he was as good as possible with what he was working with. He inhaled to center himself and got out of the car.

Walking toward Valentina's house, his feet felt like they were heavy like cement as he slogged toward the door. He was trying to silently find the words he needed to say to her to convince her she was the only woman for him. He needed her in his life, and no matter what life threw at them, together they were stronger.

He rose a hand to ring the bell, and the door flung wide in his face. He honestly couldn't recall a single word that he had practiced saying to her in his head for the longest time. She was so beautiful and so angry he was afraid he was already out of options before he uttered a word.

"You have some audacity showing up here?' Valentina barked at him, totally taking him aback. She was fuming, and her nostrils flared as she spoke. It was not a pretty sight and had him completely second-guessing this visit.

He knew that she needed space and had tried to be respectful of that. Anger, though, he had not been expecting in the least. He didn't know what could have led her to this place, but there was only one way to find out.

"Are you mad at me?" He questioned as his forehead squished into deep caverns of concern.

"You brought a new girlfriend to school with you today," she barked back at him, looking on the verge of slamming the door. "I missed you so much, and you just moved on like I was nothing."

"Wait," he said, putting a hand to the door before she could completely close him out. "That was Juanita," he said with a shake of his head, realizing that he should have known how that would look. "I'm so sorry," he whispered, as she remembered that Juanita had been out of town for a conference when Valentina met the rest of the family. She hadn't been able to meet her, so of course, that would come off wrong at the school him just showing up with a woman like that that she did not know.

"Juanita?" She said as her shoulders slumped heavily. She stared at him for the longest time, not muttering a word, "you are right; I didn't meet her yet. I can't believe that I thought you would do something like that to me."

"Yep, my sister. She hadn't been to the school yet and wanted to surprise Livia and Marina by helping pick them up," he said, moving forward. "I missed you too," he whispered, coming nearly fully aligned with her body. "And now

I'm going to kiss you unless you stop me," he let her know, gazing deep into her eyes.

"What's wrong?" She asked.

"I need to be sure before we go any further that you fully understand how heartbroken I was by you breaking up with me and how you did it. I can't go through that again. No matter how tough things get between us, we have to be able to talk about them."

"I see," she said, bobbing her head as she understood that it had been the wrong way to handle things.

"I am not willing to put my daughters through more pain and have to explain to them that my pain or breakup has nothing to do with them. It simply is not something I wish to make them understand or go through again. As a child, when we see our parents struggle, kids tend to think it's their fault or that they did something wrong. That is what happened when they found out about us breaking up. They thought that maybe it was something they did at the school that day or said to you could've caused this," he let her know.

"No, I had no idea. Of course, I was just struggling as a teacher, feeling like I hadn't done enough that day, and you're your kids, along with others, could have been hurt. You are right. I put my feelings ahead of everything, and not being a mother myself, I honestly didn't think about Livia and Marina," she said, taking his hand in hers. "It will never happen again. I have a lot to learn, but I understand and admire how you put your children first all the time, even over your own feelings. I promise I will work hard to earn all your trust back and put the girl's needs in the forefront of my mind."

"Thank you," he said. "I truly want us to make this work and appreciate you hearing me out. And now I'm going to kiss you unless you stop me," he let her know, gazing deep into her eyes.

. . .

"I really missed you, Mario, and appreciate you are giving me this time," Valentina whispered, running her hands up the back of his neck to draw him closer. "But I think I'm going a bit crazy without you, so I need you to kiss me and not stop."

"Your wish is my command," he said as he kicked the door shut and claimed her lips in a make-up kiss that neither of them would soon forget.

～

The next morning, Alma met him at his door as Valentina and he decided to sneak in a trip out of town before she left on her cruise. She agreed to watch the girls, and Mario was going to skip out on work; Valentina called in to her job for some personal time. Their plan was just to ride to Yosemite and spend the day reconnecting. It was not how either of them normally operated – calling out to work and leaving on short notice. With everything that had gone on, it was a little something they could do just to truly connect and take a breath in the midst of the tidal wave of emotions that had plagued them of late.

"Are you two ready for school?" Alma asked as Livia and Marina ran toward her to wrap their arms around her legs.

"Abuelita," they shouted in unison, and something in Mario shifted as his eyes collided with Alma's.

"Thank you," he said, leaning in to give her a hug. "You are the best thing that could have happened to them."

"You go make my girl happy. I got your two," she said, simply hugging him back before moving to the kitchen. "What about breakfast before school?" He heard her ask as he grabbed his overnight bag and took off for the door.

When he walked outside, there was Valentina already leaning against the bike. She looked so beautiful she stole his breath, and he couldn't believe she was truly his. After all the heartbreak, misunderstandings, and bad days in the past, the future was looking bright.

"Your mother is trying to feed them breakfast," he said, thumbing a finger toward the house.

"Not surprised," Valentina said. "She sneaks into my house to fatten me up nearly every day. Don't worry; I think food is her love language, which I heard this morning might be yours also," she gave him a sidelong glance.

"She told you about the pan dolce that I brought when trying to figure out a way to win you back," he said, walking up to her and wrapping his arm around her waist to pull her in for a long, slow kiss.

"She loves it," Valentina said.

"So, am I going to have to sweet talk you onto the bike this time?" Mario asked, remembering how hesitant she was the last time they rode.

"Nope, I'm ready. After this last month, riding with you is the least scary thing I can think of doing," she said, grabbing the helmet he extended to her.

They rode, stopped to eat, used restrooms, and just drove a little more. It was cathartic to be out in nature, with the wind in her face, arms wrapped tight around Mario with nothing to worry about for forty-eight hours. They finally stopped quite late in the evening at a trailhead.

"You ready for an evening hike," Mario asked as they got off the bike.

"It might take the entire hike for my legs to stop feeling like jello," Valentina replied, "but I'm game."

Honestly, she would go anywhere this man asked her to and never wanted to be away from him again. She had realized last night after he left her house that she just made things tougher when she didn't accept his help. After the incident, not talking to him, assuming he hooked up with someone else without any questions and other errant emotions could have been avoided. That realization made her know that he was truly the one she was supposed to be with. He was the man that she needed to walk through this life with, plan a future with, and have children with. She was going to do everything in her power to make this relationship the best possible.

After changing out of the leather they wore on the bike and getting snacks and water into their backpack, they headed out. Mario seemed to have a plan, and she was game to go with it.

They hiked until she was certain she was going to sleep well tonight.

"Just up there," Mario said after what seemed like a super long time. She glanced up, and the spot didn't look like anything special, but he seemed excited, which was all the motivation she needed to keep climbing.

"Look at that," Mario said, looking out over the landscape below.

"Wow," Valentina said though not sure if it was because she was out of breath from the climb or that view.

"This is Half Dome which is the highest peak out in these parts," Mario returned to her. "You know, this reminds me that we have been through a lot of scary things of late. The thought of you or the girls getting hurt by that madman at the school. You never want to talk to me again."

"I'm sorry for that, Mario," Valentina whispered. "I know that life is full of surprises, and sometimes I don't handle them exactly as I should."

"I understand; we both have been through a lot. We have lost loved ones, suffered tragedies, and pondered life with so much uncertainty. I think we both need to agree to embrace faith and give love a second chance. Hang on with both hands no matter the obstacle and work through it together," he gushed.

"I couldn't have said it better," she said, coming alongside him to wrap her hands around his waist. "I love you, Mario, and honestly, I can't spend another day without you."

"And I love you, Valentina. I'm with you. Through thick and thin – we are a team," he said, lowering his mouth to hers.

"Now, are you ready for something amazing?" Mario said, pulling back from her.

"I think you are going to have a tough time topping that," Valentina said, looking out over the breathtaking sight.

"I'm going to try," he said, grabbing her hand and tugging her to follow him.

Life was a journey with many amazing things to discover; he couldn't wait to see where the path led.

EPILOGUE

ive years later

"Sweet goodness," Mario said, glancing about at the chaos ensuing in all directions with kids, parents hollering for them to behave, and a million other noises. Valentina and he were hosting the family gathering, and as a group, they thought it would be amazing to get a Christmas card with all the kiddos and extended family. The poor photographer was going to earn her fat tip today, he thought, looking at the girl that must be about twenty-five trying to wrangle Carlos and Jennifer's one-year-old little girl. There were over thirty of them now to fit in the frame and enough small children with minds of their own that were having none of it.

"I think we should have worn them all out and taken a shot of them sleeping," Joey said, walking toward the group holding two toddlers in check by the hands. She looked like most of them did, happy, bemused, and slightly worn out.

It was crazy that all the brothers had children nearly the same age, and nobody in the family had probably slept more than a couple of hours in years. They were also happy, always

NINA DALLAS

lending a hand and the family Mario had only dreamed of as a kid. Despite all the noise, he would never trade a single moment of it to leave these groups behind. They rarely even vacationed apart as much as they loved spending time together.

"Do you think we could have even managed to get all of them sleeping at once," Elaine laughed as she also had a little girl in her arms that was kicking up a storm as she held her outward from her body to avoid bruising.

At this point, all the brothers Carlos, Joey, Manny, Rigo, Ricky, and Mario, were each holding at least one child, with each of the wives holding another. In a lot of the cases, they didn't even have the little ones that belonged to them. They were a true representation of it takes a village as they had so many kids between them in the last five years it was total chaos.

The cousins looked after each other, fought with, and loved like siblings. The brothers all rode together as the wives gave them a solid weekend a month off to take care of that itch, and in turn, they took diaper and child duty one weekend a month for nails and spa day.

Mario glanced around and realized that he could never have imagined a more noisy, loud, boisterous, and amazing existence when he was growing up. He would bet that some of this generation might wish they had been single children, but few of them would not benefit from this amazing family.

He just laughed as he stood his ground for the pictures, as Valentina came alongside them with their little girl Arial. She was the joy of both their lives and Livia, and Marina spoiled her senseless. They were always dressing her up and showing her off to friends. It was an amazing life, and he couldn't want anything.

"You have that sappy look on your face," Valentina whispered as she laid her head on his shoulder.

458

He just gazed at his wife and honestly thought back to that moment years ago when they discovered their brothers through a DNA test. The shock and confusion that both Ricky and he had wrestled with as they considered coming out to California to visit for the first time. He could never have known boarding that plane exactly how things were going to work out. Though this massive family gathering defied any dreams, he had and left him wanting nothing from life. He had a wife, sister, nieces, nephews, brothers, and so much more these days – he was a truly lucky man.

"Did you ever think this would be your life?" He asked as he turned to lay a kiss on her forehead.

"You mean sleepless, noisy, and never needing a gym for chasing this many toddlers?" She glanced up at him, just as her happy mother started their way with Daniella and Ricky's newest addition cradled in her arms.

"Exactly," he replied.

"My mother found heaven in this family," Valentina said. "Though she did recently tell me that her request for grandkids did not include this big of a family. Though she was grinning from ear to ear when she said it."

He glanced to where Alma was rocking the baby, and other kids all ran about her. She was a tireless babysitter, cheerleader for all his family, and sometimes a therapist. Where they had lost two biological mamas along the way, Alma filled the role to perfection and seemed as if she always belonged in the family.

"I think with us missing our moms, yours just got elected as the adopted Mama for all of us," Mario said, glancing down at her. "You know I love you."

"And I will love you, until my dying breath," she said with a smile up to him.

"Say cheese!" The photographer called out as everyone turned in mass toward her and the rapid clicking started.

"Cheese!"

"Cheese!"

"I don't want to!"

"You can't make me!"

"This is dumb!"

"Mom, he is pushing me."

"Make her stop."

The shouts and mumbles went on and on, but the photographer continued to distract and snap away.

The woman looked plum worn out as she finally glanced down to her camera, and a smile spread across her lips. The photographer glanced up and gave a big thumbs up with hopefully was a good sign that their family photo was a done DEAL.